He's a desert sh...
modern...

An Ordinary Girl
and a Sheikh

Three exciting, dramatic romances from three
favourite Mills & Boon authors!

An Ordinary Girl and a Sheikh

LIZ FIELDING

BARBARA MCMAHON

NICOLA MARSH

First published in Great Britain 2011
by Mills & Boon, an imprint of Harlequin (UK) Limited,
Eton House, 18-24 Paradise Road, Richmond, Surrey TW9 1SR

AN ORDINARY GIRL AND A SHEIKH
© by Harlequin Enterprises II B.V./S.à.r.l 2011

The Sheikh's Unsuitable Bride, Rescued by the Sheikh and *The Desert
Prince's Proposal* were first published in Great Britain by Harlequin Mills
& Boon Limited.

The Sheikh's Unsuitable Bride © Liz Fielding 2007
Rescued by the Sheikh © Barbara McMahon 2007
The Desert Prince's Proposal © Nicola Marsh 2008

ISBN: 978 0 263 88446 3

05-1011

Printed and bound in Spain
by Blackprint CPI, Barcelona

THE SHEIKH'S
UNSUITABLE BRIDE

BY
LIZ FIELDING

Dear Reader,

My first book, *An Image of You*, was published many years ago, and I still remember the rush of excitement, the thrill of receiving a phone call to say that this publisher, who had been part of my reading life for so long, wanted to publish my book. This year I will be writing my fiftieth Mills & Boon® romance, and the thrill remains.

Love truly is the most powerful human emotion, and there is nothing more rewarding than writing—and reading—a story that reveals the strength, tenderness, the unique capacity for sacrifice of the human heart.

In *The Sheikh's Unsuitable Bride*, Diana Metcalfe lives in a small terraced house in London, while jet-setting Sheikh Zahir al-Khatib lives in luxury in an exotic and beautiful palace. Yet it is not the vast social gulf that divides them, but the demands of family and duty that seem destined to keep them apart. Only love can find a way…

With warmest wishes,

Liz

Liz Fielding started writing at the age of twelve, when she won a writing competition at school. After that early success there was quite a gap—during which she was busy working in Africa and the Middle East, getting married and having children—before her first book was published in 1992. Now readers worldwide fall in love with her irresistible heroes, adore her independent-minded heroines. Visit Liz's website for news and extracts of upcoming books at www.lizfielding.com.

CHAPTER ONE

'LEAVE that, Di.'

Diana Metcalfe backed out of the rear door of the minibus she was cleaning and, stuffing a handful of chocolate wrappers into her overall pocket, turned to face her boss. The woman, unusually, looked as if she was just about at the end of her tether.

'What's up, Sadie?'

'Jack Lumley has gone home sick. He's the third today.'

'The café's meat pie strikes again?'

'So it would appear, although that's the Environmental Health Officer's problem. Mine is that I've got three drivers with their heads down the toilet and a VIP with a packed schedule arriving at London City Airport in a little over an hour.' Despite her worries, she managed a wry smile. 'Please tell me you don't have a hot date tonight.'

'Not even a lukewarm one.' Who had the time? 'You want me to work this evening?'

'If you can.'

'It shouldn't be a problem. I'll have to give Dad a call, let him know he'll have to give Freddy his tea.'

'How is your gorgeous little boy?'

'Growing like a weed.'

'Daisy keeps asking me when he can come over for another

play-date.' Then, 'I'll fix up something when I call your father. You don't have time, not if you're going to meet that flight.'

Diana blinked. Meet the flight…? 'Excuse me? Are you saying that I get the VIP?'

'You get the VIP.'

'But I can't! You can't…'

Sadie frowned. 'You've been checked out on the car haven't you?'

'Um, yes…' Company rules. Everyone could, in theory, drive any car, in the Capitol fleet. In theory. But this was the newest, most luxurious, most *expensive* saloon car in the garage—pride and joy of Jack Lumley, the company's number one driver. While she'd anticipated a shuffle round to take up the slack, an extra job or two, never, in her wildest dreams, had she imagined she'd ever be entrusted behind its leather-covered steering wheel.

Or entrusted with one of their top drawer clients.

'Thank goodness for that,' Sadie said with feeling.

Apparently, she could!

Diana slapped a hand over her mouth, but not quickly enough to catch the word that slipped out.

Sadie sighed. 'Please tell me you don't use that kind of language when you're on the school run, Diana.'

'Me? Oh, please! Where on earth do you think I learned a word like that?'

'Are the kids really that bad? My father took it on as a public service, something for the local community, but I won't have—'

'The kids are okay,' she said quickly. 'Really. They're just at that age where shocking the grown-ups is a sport. The trick is not to react.'

'The trick, Di, is not to join in.'

'I don't…' Realising that she just had, she let it go. 'Right.'

Sadie looked thoughtful. 'I've half a mind to put Jack on

the job for a week or two when he's fit. Teach them to think twice about their language. Teach him to think twice about eating dodgy meat pies on my time.'

The senior driver of Capitol Cars reduced to driving a minibus full of lippy primary school kids?

Having swiftly recovered from her shock, Diana grinned. 'Now that's something I'd pay good money to see.'

They exchanged a glance. Two single mothers—one at the bottom, the other at the top of a male-dominated business—who between them had heard every chauvinist put-down, every woman driver joke in the book. Sadie, with obvious regret, shook her head. 'Unfortunately he'd resign rather than do that.'

'Totally beneath his dignity,' Diana agreed. 'I'm sure learning that I've been driving his precious car will be punishment enough.'

Sadie just about managed to stop herself from grinning back and snapping back into 'boss' mode she said, 'Yes, well, just remember that at this end of the business the clients prefer their chauffeurs politely invisible.'

'No singing, then?'

'Singing?'

'I find it keeps the passengers from using bad language…'

'I'm serious!'

'Yes, ma'am.'

'Right. Well, come on. I'll brief you on Sheikh Zahir's itinerary while you change. This is a full dress uniform job. And yes, before you ask, that includes the hat.'

'Sh…Sh-Sheikh?'

Diana thought she'd managed to cover her near slip pretty well, but Sadie's quick glance suggested that she was not fooled.

'Sheikh Zahir al-Khatib is the nephew of the Emir of Ramal Hamrah, cousin of his country's ambassador to

London and a billionaire businessman who is single-handedly turning his country into the next *über*-fashionable get-away-from-it-all tourist destination.'

Diana instantly lost any inclination to sing. 'He's a genuine A-list VIP, then.'

'You've got it. The Mercedes is at his disposal full-time while he's in London. The hours will, inevitably, be unpredictable but if you can hold the fort for me today, I'll have someone else lined up to take over tomorrow.'

'You don't have to do that,' Diana said a touch fiercely, hoping to counteract the initial impression of irresponsibility. She might not be Jack Lumley, but her passengers were never short-changed. 'I can handle it. At least until Jack has recovered.'

This was the chance she'd been waiting for, an opportunity to prove herself capable of taking on the big jobs, to move up from the no-frills end of the market—the school bus, the airport runs—to driving one of Capitol's limousines and big money; she wasn't about to meekly surrender the Mercedes to the first man to recover control of his stomach.

'Give me a chance, Sadie. I won't let you down.'

Sadie touched her shoulder, a gesture that said she understood. 'Let's see how it goes today, shall we?'

Okay. She got the message. This was her opportunity to show what she could do; it was up to her to make the most of it.

Diana responded to the challenge by peeling off the latex gloves she used for cleaning out the minibus with a decisive snap. Then she stepped out of her garage overalls and replaced them with well-pressed trousers, a fresh white shirt and, instead of her usual Capitol Cars sweatshirt, her rarely worn burgundy uniform jacket.

Sadie, consulting a sheet on the clipboard she was holding, said, 'Sheikh Zahir is flying into the City Airport in his private jet, ETA seventeen-fifteen hours. Wait in the short-term parking area. The VIP hostess has the number of the car phone and she'll give you a call when his plane touches down so that you can be at the kerb, waiting for him.'

'Got it.'

'His first stop will be his country's embassy in Belgravia. He'll be there for an hour, then you're to take him to his hotel in Park Lane before leaving at nineteen-forty-five hours for a reception at the Riverside Gallery on the South Bank, followed by dinner in Mayfair. All the addresses are on the worksheet.'

'Belgravia, Mayfair...' Diana, unable to help herself, grinned as she buttoned up her jacket. 'Be still my beating heart. Is this a dream? Should I pinch myself?'

'Don't go all starry-eyed on me, Di. And keep in touch, okay? Any problems, I want to hear about them from you, not the client.'

Sheikh Zahir bin Ali al-Khatib was still working as the jet touched down and taxied to the terminal.

'We've arrived, Zahir.' James Pierce removed the laptop, passed it on to a secretary to deal with, and replaced it with a gift-wrapped package.

Zahir frowned, trying to recall what it was. Then, remembering, he looked up. 'You managed to find exactly what she wanted?' he demanded.

'One of my staff located it via the Internet. Antique. Venetian. Very pretty. I'm sure the princess will be delighted.' Then, 'Your usual driver will be waiting at Arrivals but we've a very tight schedule this evening. You'll need to leave the embassy no later than eighteen-forty-five hours if you're going to make the reception on time.'

Diana pulled up at Arrivals, squashed the stupid little forage hat firmly into place, tugged down her uniform jacket, smoothed the fine leather gloves over the backs of her hands. Then, her head full of snowy robes, the whole Lawrence of

Arabia thing, she stood by the rear door of the limousine, ready to leap into action the minute her passenger appeared.

There were no robes. No romantic headdress caught by the wind.

Sheikh Zahir al-Khatib had, it seemed, taken on board the dressing-for-comfort-when-travelling message. Not that she'd have had any trouble recognising him, even without his VIP escort.

The grey sweatshirt, soft jeans and deck shoes worn on bare feet might be casual but they were expensive. The man, tall and rangy, with dark hair that curled around his neck, might look more like a sports star than a tycoon, but his clothes, his head turning looks, did absolutely nothing to diminish an aura of careless arrogance, the aristocratic assurance of a man whose every wish had been someone else's instant command from the day he had first drawn breath.

The very pink, thoroughly beribboned gift-wrapped package he was carrying provided no more than a counter-point that underlined his authority—the kind of presence that raised the hairs on the back of her neck.

Sheikh Zahir al-Khatib, it had to be admitted, was danger-ously, slay-'em-in-the aisles, gorgeous.

He paused briefly in the doorway to thank his escort, giving Diana a moment to haul her chin off the ground—drooling was such a bad look—before affixing a polite smile to lips that she firmly compressed to contain the usual, 'Did you have a good flight?' chat as she opened the rear door of the car.

No chat.

This wasn't a family party returning from a trip to Disney, eager to share their good time as they piled into the minibus, she reminded herself.

All that was required was a quiet, Good afternoon, sir...

It wasn't easy. There were two things she was good at: driving and talking. They both came as naturally to her as breathing: one—just about—paid the bills, the other she did for free. Sort of like a hobby. A fact that had featured prominently in her end of year school reports.

Talking in class. Talking in Assembly. Talking herself into trouble.

Since she mostly got the kids and the hen parties—jobs where a bit of lip came in handy if things got rowdy—it wasn't usually a problem, but she understood why Sadie would only give her a job like this if she were really desperate.

Why she'd reserved judgement on anything more than a fill-in role.

Well she would show Sadie. She would show them all, she promised herself—her parents, that older generation of neighbours who gave her that no-better-than-she-should-be *look*—and she began tidily enough.

Her smile was regulation polite as she opened the door smartly so that nothing would impede his progress.

'Good afternoon—'

She didn't get as far as the 'sir'.

A small boy, skidding through the terminal doors in her passenger's wake, dived through the closing gap between the car door and Sheikh Zahir, to hurl himself at the woman who'd just pulled up behind them. Before Diana could utter a warning or move, he went flying over her highly polished shoes and cannoned headlong into Sheikh Zahir, sending the fancy package flying.

The Sheikh's reactions were lightning-fast and he caught the child by the back of his jacket before he hit the ground.

Diana, no slouch herself, leapt for the ribbons.

The package was arcing away from her, but those ribbons had their uses and she managed to grab one, bringing it to a halt.

'Yes!' she exclaimed triumphantly.

Too soon.

'No-o-o-o!'

She held the ribbon, but the parcel kept travelling as the bow unravelled in a long pink stream until the gift hit the concrete with what sounded horribly like breaking glass.

At which point she let slip the word she'd promised Sadie that she would never, ever use in front of a client.

Maybe—please—Sheikh Zahir's English wouldn't be good enough to grasp her meaning.

'Hey! Where's the fire?' he asked the boy, hauling him upright and setting him on his feet, holding him steady while he regained his balance, his breath, and completely dashing her hopes on the language front.

Only the slightest accent suggested that the Sheikh's first language wasn't English.

'I am so-o-o-o sorry...' The boy's grandmother, the focus of his sprint, was overcome with embarrassment. 'Please let me pay for any damage.'

'It is nothing,' Sheikh Zahir replied, dismissing her concern with a graceful gesture, the slightest of bows. The desert prince to his fingertips, even without the trappings.

He was, Diana had to admit, as she picked up the remains of whatever was in the parcel, a class act.

Then, as she stood up, he turned to her and everything went rapidly downhill as she got the full close-up impact of his olive-skinned, dark-eyed masculinity. The kind that could lay you out with a smile.

Except that Sheikh Zahir wasn't smiling, but looking down at her with dark, shaded, unreadable eyes.

It was only when she tried to speak that she realised she'd been holding her breath.

'I'm sorry,' she finally managed, her words escaping in a breathy rush.

'Sorry?'

For her language lapse. For not making a better job of fielding the package.

Deciding that the latter would be safer, she offered it to him.

'I'm afraid it's broken.' Then, as he took it from her and shook it, she added, 'In fact it, um, appears to be leaking.'

He glanced down, presumably to confirm this, then, holding it at arm's length to avoid the drips, he looked around, presumably hoping for a litter bin in which to discard it. Giving her a moment to deal with the breathing problem.

So he was a sheikh. So his features had a raw, dangerous, bad boy edge to them. So he was *gorgeous*.

So what?

She didn't do that!

Besides which, he wasn't going to look at her twice even if she wanted him to. Which she didn't.

Really.

One dangerous-looking man in a lifetime was more than enough trouble.

Definitely time to haul her tongue back into line and act like the professional she'd promised Sadie she was...

There wasn't a bin and the Sheikh dealt with the problem by returning the sorry mess of damp paper and ribbons to her. That at least was totally masculine behaviour—leaving someone else to deal with the mess...

'You're not my usual driver,' he said.

'No, sir,' she said. He had twenty-twenty vision, she thought as she retrieved a waterproof sick bag from the glove box and stowed the package inside it where it could do no harm. 'I wonder what gave me away?' she muttered under her breath.

'The beard?' he offered, as she turned to face him.

And his hearing was...A1.

Oh, double...sheikh!

'It can't be that, sir,' she said, hoping that the instruction to her brain for a polite smile had reached her face; the one saying, Shut up! had apparently got lost *en route*. 'I don't have a beard.' Then, prompted by some inner demon, she added, 'I could wear a false one.'

Sometimes, when you'd talked your way into trouble, the only way out was to keep talking. She hadn't entirely wasted her time at school. She knew that if she could make him laugh, she might just get away with it.

Smile, damn you, smile…

'If it's essential,' she added, heart sinking. Because he didn't. Or comment on what was, or was not, essential.

'What is your name?' he asked.

'Oh, you needn't worry about that,' she assured him, affecting an airy carelessness. 'The office will know who I am.'

When he made his complaint.

She wasn't even going to last out the day. Sadie would kill her. Sadie had every right…

'Your office might,' he said, 'but I don't.'

Busted. This was a man who left nothing to chance.

'Metcalfe, sir.'

'Metcalfe.' He looked as if he might have something to say about that, but must have thought better of it because he let it go. 'Well, Metcalfe, shall we make a move? Time is short and now we're going to have to make a detour unless the birthday girl is to be disappointed.'

'Birthday girl?'

Didn't he know that it was seriously unPC to refer to a woman as a 'girl' these days?

'Princess Ameerah, my cousin's daughter, is ten years old today. Her heart's desire, apparently, is for a glass snow globe. I promised her she would have one.'

'Oh.' A *little* girl… Then, forgetting that she was supposed to only speak when she was spoken to, 'They are lovely. I've still got one that I was given when I was…'

She stopped. Why on earth would he care?

'When you were?'

'Um, six.'

'I see.' He looked at her as if trying to imagine her as a child. Apparently failing, he said, 'This one was old too. An antique, in fact. Venetian glass.'

'For a ten-year-old?' The words were out before she could stop them. On the point of stepping into the car, he paused and frowned. 'I mean, *glass*. Was that wise?' She had the feeling that no one had ever questioned his judgement before and, trying to salvage something, she said, 'Mine is made from some sort of polymer resin.' It had come from a stall at the local market. 'Not precious…' except to her '…but it would have, um, bounced.'

Shut up now!

Her shoulders lifted in the smallest of shrugs, disassociating the rest of her from her mouth.

'Since it's for a child, maybe something less, um, *fragile* might be more sensible. Glass is a bit, well…'

Her mouth finally got the message and stopped moving.

'Fragile?' Sheikh Zahir, still not smiling, finished the sentence for her.

'I'm sure the one you bought was very beautiful,' she said quickly, not wanting him to think she was criticising. She was in enough trouble already. 'But I'm guessing you don't have children of your own.'

'Or I'd know better?'

'Mmm,' she said through closed lips. 'I mean, it would have to be kept out of reach, wouldn't it?' She attempted a smile to soften the message. 'It is…was…a treasure, rather than a toy.'

'I see.'

He might be dressed in the most casual clothes, but there was nothing casual about his expression. He was still frowning, although not in a bad way, more as if he was catching up with reality.

Face aching with the effort of maintaining the smile, Diana ploughed desperately on. 'No doubt princesses are less clumsy than ordinary little girls.'

'Not,' he said, taking her breath away for the second time as he finally responded to her smile with a wry contraction of the lines fanning out from his charcoal eyes, 'in my experience.' Nowhere near a slay-'em-in-the-aisles smile, but a heart-stopper none-the-less. At least if her heart was anything to go by. 'You're not just a pretty face, are you, Metcalfe?'

'Um…'

'So, how much would it take to part you from this hard-wearing toy?'

She swallowed. 'I'm sorry, but I don't have it now.'

His brows rose slightly.

'It didn't break,' she assured him. 'I gave it to…'

Tell him.

Tell him you gave it to your five-year-old son.

It was what people did—talk incessantly about their kids. Their cute ways. The clever things they did.

Everyone except Miss Motormouth herself; how ironic was that?

She'd talk about anything except Freddy. Because when she talked about her little boy she knew, just knew, that all the listener really wanted to know was the one thing she'd never told a living soul.

Sheikh Zahir was waiting. 'I gave it to a little boy who fell in love with it.'

'Don't look so tragic, Metcalfe, I wasn't serious,' he said, his smile deepening as he mistook her reluctance to speak for an apology. 'Let's go shopping.'

'Y-yes, sir.' Then, with a glance towards the terminal building, 'Don't you want to wait for your luggage?'

She'd assumed that some minion, left to unload it, would appear at any moment with a laden trolley but, without looking back as he finally stepped into the car, Sheikh Zahir said, 'It will be dealt with.'

Sadie was right, she thought. This was another world. She closed the door, stowed the remains of the precious glass object out of harm's way and took a deep breath before she slid behind the wheel and started the engine.

Shopping. With a sheikh.

Unbelievable.

Unbelievable.

All James's careful planning—every second accounted for—brought to naught in an instant of distraction.

But what a distraction…

Zahir had walked through the arrivals hall expecting the efficient and monosyllabic Jack Lumley to be waiting for him. Instead he'd got 'Metcalfe'. A woman whose curves were only emphasized by the severe cut of her jacket. A woman with a long slender neck, against which soft tendrils of chestnut hair were, even now, gradually unfurling.

And a mouth made for trouble.

The kind of distraction he didn't have time for on this trip.

No complaints. He loved the excitement, the buzz of making things happen, didn't begrudge a single one of the long hours it had taken to turn a small, going-nowhere company running tours into the desert into a billion dollar business.

He'd single-handedly taken tourism in Ramal Hamrah out of the stopover business—little more than a place for long-haul passengers to break their journey to shop for gold in the souk, take a sand dune safari—into a real industry. His country was now regularly featured in travel magazines, weekend newspaper supplements—a destination in its own right. Not just for the desert, but the mountains, the history.

He'd created a luxurious tented resort in the desert. The marina complex was nearing completion. And now he was on the point of launching an airline that would bear his country's name.

He'd had to work hard to make that happen.

Until he'd got a grip on it, tourism had been considered little more than a sideshow alongside the oil industry. Only a few people had had the vision to see what it could become, which meant that neighbouring countries were already light years ahead of them.

Perhaps it was as well; unable to challenge the dominance of states quicker off the starting blocks, he'd been forced to think laterally, take a different path. Instead of high-rise apartments and hotels, he'd gone for low impact development using local materials and the traditional styles of building to create an air of luxury—something entirely different to tempt the jaded traveller.

Using the desert as an environmental spectacle, travelling on horseback and camel train, rather than as a rip-'em-up playground for sand-surfers and dune-racers. Re-opening long-ignored archaeological sites to attract a different kind of visitor fascinated by the rich history of the area.

And a change of attitude to international tourism in the last year or so had given him an edge in the market; suddenly he was the visionary, out in front.

Out in front and on his own.

'...*you don't have children of your own...*'

Well, when you were building an empire, something had to give. A situation that his mother was doing her best to change. Even as he sat in the back of this limousine, watching Metcalfe's glossy chestnut hair unravel, she was sifting through the likely applicants for the vacant post of Mother-Of-His-Sons, eager to negotiate a marriage settlement with the lucky girl's family.

Make his father happy with the gift of a grandson who would bear his name.

It was the way it had been done for a thousand years. In his culture there was no concept of romantic love as there was in the West; marriage was a contract, something to be arranged for the mutual benefit of two families. His wife would be a woman he could respect. She would run his home, bear his children—sons who would bring him honour, daughters who would bring him joy.

His gaze was drawn back to the young woman sitting in front of him, the soft curve of her cheek glimpsed in the reflection of the driving mirror. The suggestion of a dimple.

She had the kind of face that would always be on the point of a smile, he suspected, smiling himself as he reran the range of her expressions—everything from horror as she'd let slip a word that was definitely not in the Polite Chauffeur's Handbook, through blushing confusion, in-your-face take-it-or-leave-it cheek and finally, touchingly, concern.

Glass. For a child. What on earth had he been thinking? What had James been thinking?

That was the point. They hadn't been. He'd just ordered the most expensive, the most desirable version of the child's wish and James had, as always, delivered.

A wife wouldn't have made that mistake.

Metcalfe wouldn't have made that mistake.

Nor would she settle for a relationship based on respect, he suspected. Not with that smile. But then she came from a different world. Lived a life unknown to the young virgins from among whom his mother would look for a suitable bride.

Very different from the sophisticated high-achieving career women who he met in the line of business, who lived their lives more like men than women, although what she lacked in gloss, sophistication, she more than made up for in entertainment value.

He dragged his fingers through his hair, as if to erase the unsettling thoughts. He didn't have time for 'entertainment'. And, with marriage very much on the agenda, he shouldn't even be thinking about it.

As it was, he had to snatch this hour to celebrate a little girl's birthday out of a crammed schedule when he should, instead, be concentrating on the reception for travel journalists and dinner with the men who had the financial power to make his airline a reality.

'Are you a permanent fixture, Metcalfe?' he asked. 'Or will Jack Lumley be back on duty tomorrow?'

'I couldn't say, sir,' she said, glancing up to look in the rearview mirror, briefly meeting his gaze, before returning her attention to the road. 'He was taken ill earlier today.' Then, 'I'm sure the company could find you someone else in the meantime, if you insisted.'

'Someone with a beard?'

'Yes, sir.'

Her dimple had disappeared. She wasn't smiling now. Not even close. She thought he objected to a female chauffeur?

'And if I did?' something made him persist. 'What would you be doing tomorrow?'

Her eyes flickered back to him. They were green, like the smudge of new leaves in an English hedgerow in April.

'If I'm lucky I'll be back at the wheel of a minibus, doing the school run.'

'And if you're unlucky?'

'Back at the wheel of a minibus, doing the school run,' she repeated, letting loose another of those smiles, albeit a somewhat wry one, as she pulled into the forecourt of a massive toy store. She slid from behind the wheel but he was out of the car before she could open the door for him and looking up at the façade of the store she'd chosen.

It hadn't occurred to him to dictate their destination. Jack

Lumley would have taken him to Harrods or Hamleys, having called ahead to check which of them had what he was looking for, ensuring that it would be gift-wrapped and waiting for him, charged to his account.

No waiting.

No effort.

Like an arranged marriage.

A gust of wind whipped across the vast forecourt of the store and Diana grabbed for her hat, clutching it to her head.

Sheikh Zahir had made no move to enter, but was staring up at the storefront and, heart sinking, she realised that she'd got it wrong.

Sadie was right. She wasn't equipped for this...

'I'm sorry,' she said. 'This isn't what you expected.'

He glanced back at her. 'I left the decision to you.'

True. And she'd made her best judgement...

'I thought it would be quicker,' she explained. 'It's certainly easier to park.' Then, 'And, to be honest, you don't quite meet the Knightsbridge dress code.'

'There's a dress code?' He turned to look at her. 'For *shopping?*'

'No bare feet. No sports shoes. No jeans. No backpacks.' She faltered, realising just how foolish she must sound. As if anyone would turn *him* away for being inappropriately dressed. 'Not that you're carrying a backpack.'

'But I tick all the rest of your boxes.'

'I expect it's different for royalty.'

'Just as well not to risk it,' Sheikh Zahir said gently. If he was laughing at her, he was being kind enough not to do it out loud.

On the point of congratulating herself that she wasn't such a juggins after all, he said, 'Okay. Let's do this.'

Let's. As in 'let us'. We.

'You want me to come in with you?'

'Surely you were told that royalty never carries its own bags?'

Now she was quite sure he was laughing.

'The rumour is that they don't carry money either and you should know that I can't help you there.' Then, 'Besides, I really shouldn't leave the car.'

'Are you refusing to come with me?' he enquired, a faint edge beneath the chocolate silk of his unbelievably sexy accent. A reminder that she was there at his bidding. 'The school run is that appealing?'

Maybe she'd been too quick to leap to judgement on the 'kind', she decided, locking the door and following him without another word.

Inside a store of aircraft hangar proportions, aisle upon aisle of shelves were stocked with everything a child—and quite a few grown-ups—could possibly desire.

Diana found herself staring at the shopping trolleys, the serve-yourself warehouse-style shelving, not through her own eyes, but through the eyes of a man for whom 'self-service' was undoubtedly an unexplored concept.

It was most definitely another one of those 'oh, sheikh' moments.

'So much for this being quicker,' he said, looking around. 'How on earth do you find what you're looking for?'

'With difficulty,' she admitted, realising that at one of those Top People's stores, someone would have found exactly what he was looking for in an instant. 'The, um, idea is to get you to pass as many shelves as possible. That way you're more likely to impulse buy.' Then, 'How many people, do you suppose, leave with the one item they came in to buy?'

He turned to look at her. 'That sounds like the voice of experience.'

'Isn't that what I'm here for? My experience? You're the one who bought something made of glass for a little girl.'

'Actually…' He stopped, shook his head. 'I take your point,

although I'm now beginning to think I'd be better advised to buy Ameerah shares in the company.'

'Shares in a toy shop?' she said, clutching her hands to her heart. 'Now why didn't my parents think of that?'

'Because they're not so much fun to play with, I imagine,' he said seriously. 'Not what a little girl imagines for her birthday surprise.'

'True, but just think what I could do with them now.' His brows rose slightly, inviting an explanation. 'Instead of the five-minute gratification of a plastic car for my favourite doll, I could now afford to buy my own taxi. Be my own boss.' Then, because his eyebrows lifted another millimetre, 'I'd go for the fun version in sparkly pink, obviously…'

CHAPTER TWO

ZAHIR watched as Metcalfe swiftly turned and walked across to the enquiry desk, jolted out of his preconceived notion of who she was, what she was.

Not just an attractive young woman at the wheel of a car, but an attractive young woman with aspirations, dreams.

Not so long ago, he'd been there.

People assumed that because he had been born the grandson of the Emir of Ramal Hamrah life had fallen into his lap. Maybe they had a point. He'd been indulged, he knew that, with every benefit that life could bestow, including a privileged education in England, the freedom of post-graduate studies in America. But there was a price to pay.

Duty to his country, obedience to the family.

He'd spent two years in the desert, with his own life on hold, as companion to his grieving cousin. His reward had come when Hanif, seeing that his heart lay not with the slow-grinding wheels of government, but in the fast-moving world of big business, had given him his first chance. Had given his own precious time to convince his father that he should be allowed to tread his own path.

Had taken time to explain that what he was doing was as important for his country as playing the diplomat, the courtier, particularly when he would be such a reluctant one.

Even so, he'd had to go to the market for the money he'd needed to build his empire from the ground up, but, while his name could not guarantee success, he knew it had opened doors for him. People had been polite, inclined to listen, because of who he was, whereas even now he could see that his chauffeur was getting the most grudging attention from the assistant at the desk.

'Do they have what we're looking for?' he asked, joining her.

'Who knows?'

As she went to ask for help from an assistant, Diana was desperately wishing she'd gone for the obvious shopping destination instead of trying to be clever. In Knightsbridge she would have had to stay with the car to fend off the traffic warden while he 'shopped' all by himself.

'If they have any they'll be with the novelty items.' Her imitation of the assistant's couldn't-be-bothered gesture, made without looking up from whatever she was finding so gripping in the magazine she was reading, was meant to be ironic. 'Over there, apparently.'

Maybe Sheikh Zahir didn't 'get' irony because he turned to the woman behind the desk and said, 'We don't have a great deal of time…' he paused to check out her name tag '…Liza. Would you be kind enough to show us exactly where we can find what we're looking for?'

She turned a page and said, 'Sorry. I can't leave my desk.'

Big mistake that, Diana thought, warmed by his 'we'.

'I can't', as she'd already discovered for herself, did not impress him one bit.

'The sign above your desk says "Customer Service",' he pointed out and then, as she sighed and finally looked up, he smiled at her.

Diana watched, torn between outrage and amusement as, without another word, the assistant leapt to her feet and scurried round the desk.

'This way,' she said, switching on a smile of her own. One of the hundred watt variety.

'We seem to have beaten the system, Metcalfe,' Sheikh Zahir said as, with a gesture, he invited her to follow the woman.

'Nice work,' she said, 'but somehow I don't think that technique would work for me.'

That earned her a smile of her own. Rather less than he had used on the assistant, but at the same time more, she thought.

Less teeth. More eyes.

'You use what you have,' he said with a shrug.

Fortunately, before she was called upon to reply, they arrived at a shelf lined with a colourful selection of snow globes.

'Cinderella. Snow White. The Princess and the Frog.' The assistant, her attention now fully engaged by Sheikh Zahir, indicated the range on display. She couldn't have been more enthusiastic if she'd made each one personally. By hand.

'Thank you,' Sheikh Zahir said as he picked up the Princess and the Frog.

'If there's anything else…?' she offered, lingering, transformed by his smile into a candidate for Customer Services Assistant of the Year award.

'I'll be sure to come and find you.'

It was polite, but there was no doubt about it. She'd been dismissed. Diana almost felt sorry for her as she backed away, dragging her tongue after her. Almost.

'The Princess and the Frog, Metcalfe?' he asked, holding out the globe for an explanation.

He had beautiful hands. Not pampered or soft. There was an old scar running across his knuckles and, although his fingers were long, thin even, it was the slenderness of tensile steel.

'I am not familiar with this fairy tale,' he said.

'I'm surprised you know any of them,' she said, forcing herself to focus on the globe. It contained a scene in which a girl, wearing a small crown, and a frog were sitting on the edge of a well.

'Disney has reached Ramal Hamrah.'

'Has it?' Of course it had. 'Oh, right. Well, I suppose this must be one he decided to give a miss.' She thought about it. 'Actually, he was probably right. I'd stick with one of the others,' she advised.

'But this girl is a princess. Ameerah will like that.'

Just like the assistant, who'd faded away with no more than an envious glance in her direction, Diana recognised the imperative. He didn't need words to issue an order. He could do it with a look from those dark eyes.

'It's not good,' she warned him. 'Cinderella is, admittedly, a bit wet, but at least she's kind. And while Snow White is not exactly a female role model…'

'I don't have all day,' he warned.

'No, sir.' She took the globe and gave it a little shake to start the snowstorm. 'Okay, this is how it goes. Spoilt princess drops her precious golden ball in the well. The frog offers her a deal. If she takes him home with her, lets him eat from her plate, sleep on her pillow, kisses him goodnight…' She hesitated as, distracted by the sensuous curve of his lower lip, she lost the thread of the story.

'He's a talking frog?'

She shrugged. 'It's a fairy tale. If you want reality you're in the wrong place.'

He acknowledged the point with the slightest movement of his head. Then, 'Kisses him goodnight,' he prompted.

'Mmm. If she promises all that,' she said, 'he'll fetch her golden ball from the bottom of the well.'

'A gentleman frog would have done it without strings attached.'

'A girl with any gumption would have got it herself.'

'You would have climbed down the well, Metcalfe?'

'I wouldn't have kissed the damn frog!'

'You disapprove?'

'There's no such thing as a free golden ball,' she said.

'No, indeed.' He did something with his eyes and, without warning, beneath the dark red uniform Diana suddenly felt very warm.

'Anyway,' she said quickly, running a finger under her collar to let in some cool air. 'She, um, agrees. Actually, she'd have promised him the moon—she loved that ball—and the ungentlemanly frog dives into the well, gets the ball and hands it over, at which point the princess shows her gratitude by legging it.'

'Legging it?'

'Has it away on her toes. Scarpers. Runs back to the palace without him.'

He laid one of those beautiful hands against his heart. 'I'm shocked.'

She'd been quite wrong about the irony. He 'got' it all right. He might not be laughing on the outside, but his eyes gleamed with amusement.

'I imagine the frog doesn't take that lying down?'

'As you said. The frog is no gentleman. He hops all the way to the palace, rats on the princess to the King, who tells her that a princess must always keep her word.'

'A princess shouldn't have to be told.'

'It might surprise you to know that holds good for common folk too.' Then, 'She isn't happy about it but she doesn't have much choice, so she lets him eat off her plate, but then she flounces off to bed without him.'

'She learns her lesson hard, this princess. Does the frog quit?'

'What do you think?'

'I think she's going to be sharing her pillow with the frog.'

'Right. It takes him hours to hop all the way up the stairs, find her room, but he gets there in the end and once more reminds her of her promise. Finally, accepting that she's beaten, the princess puts him on her pillow and even forces herself to kiss him goodnight.'

'I can relate to this frog, but can this story have a happy ending?'

'That rather depends on your point of view. When the princess wakes up next morning the frog has turned into a handsome prince.'

His brows rose a fraction.

'That might take a bit of explaining.'

Diana, whose view of the scene had been fixed in childhood by a picture book image of said handsome prince, fully clothed in princely trappings, standing beside the princess's bed as she woke, suddenly saw a very different reality and, quite stupidly, blushed.

'Yes, well,' she said quickly, 'it's that whole wicked-witch-cursing-the-handsome-prince thing. The princess had to have her arm twisted to breaking-point, but she did what was needed to break the spell. Da-da-de-da,' she sang the wedding march. 'And they all lived happily ever after.'

'You mean that now he's not a warty frog, but her equal, she marries him?'

'I did warn you. The girl is as shallow as an August puddle. It's why the prince married her that beats me.'

'Maybe the King didn't buy the "spell" story and produced a shotgun?' he offered.

'It's a nice theory, but the fact is that in fairy stories the girl always gets the prince. It's that love-at-first-sight, happy-ever-after thing.'

Zahir, hearing the scepticism in her voice, regarded her thoughtfully. 'You appear to be unconvinced,' he said.

'Do I?'

Metcalfe widened her eyes as if thinking about it. They weren't just green, he realised, but flecked with bronze.

'Maybe I am. You soon learn that it takes more than a handsome prince to provide a happy ending…'

He saw exactly the moment when it occurred to her that she might be heading for a foot-in-mouth moment. A reprise of the faint blush that had seared her cheek's a moment or two before. The nervous movement of her throat, as if trying to swallow down the words.

It was a refreshing change for someone to utterly forget who he was—say the first thing that came into her head without thinking it through.

'You'll get no argument from me,' he said, taking the globe from her, staring at her ringless fingers for a moment. No handsome prince, no happy ending for her. Although something warned him that it had been a lesson hard learned. 'In my country we do not pander to the sentimental Western view of marriage. Families arrange such things.'

'I can see how that would cut out an awful lot of emotional angst,' she said seriously. Then the dimple put in an appearance. 'Tough on frogs, though.'

'Indeed.' Turning swiftly to the display before the conversation became seriously out of hand, he said, 'So which of these heroines, in your opinion, is likely to provide the best role model for a modern princess? The "wet" one who stays at home and waits for a fairy godmother to wave a magic wand? The one who cleans up after a bunch of men who can't believe their luck? Or the princess who takes one look at the frog and takes to her heels?'

'Actually, I'm with you on this one. Forget the princess. That frog goes for what he wants and never gives up,' she said. 'He's a worthy role model for any child…'

He waited, certain that there was more.

'Any adult,' she added briskly.

'The frog it is. Shall we go and find that eager-to-please

assistant? I have a feeling that she's panting to get busy with the gift-wrap and pink ribbons.'

Diana resisted the temptation to make a quick dash home while Sheikh Zahir delivered the birthday gift to Princess Ameerah.

All things being equal, there should have been time to make it there and back, and all that talk of happy-ever-after had left her in desperate need of a hug from Freddy before his grandma put him to bed.

But the last hour or so had been a bit of a roller-coaster ride— rather more down than up if she was brutally honest. Which was why, since 'equal' and London traffic had absolutely nothing in common, she didn't dare risk it, gladly accepting the footman's invitation to park in the mews behind the embassy and wait for the Sheikh in the comfort of the staff sitting room.

Fingers crossed, she'd managed to deliver the Sheikh to the embassy on an up; the schedule had allowed plenty of time for traffic hold-ups and, despite the delay for shopping and story-telling, her knowledge of the short cuts had meant that they'd only lost ten minutes.

But, despite his relaxed attitude, his inclination to dally over fairy tales, once he'd made a decision and headed for the cash desk, he'd appeared to forget she was there, saving all his charm for the assistant who'd gone to town with the ribbons, making it abundantly clear that he could have her gift-wrapped too. All he had to do was say the word.

No doubt it was an everyday occurrence for him since he had not, apparently, been tempted by the offer—a warning, not that she'd needed one, that it would be a mistake to take him, or his dangerous charm, seriously.

After they'd left the store he'd only spoken to her to confirm that he would be leaving the embassy at a quarter to seven. Exactly what she'd expect, in fact.

Stupid to take it personally.

This was a job, nothing more, and, left alone with a pot of tea, a sandwich and a choice of cake, she concentrated on her own life and used her cellphone to call home.

'Mummy!' Freddy's voice was full of excitement. 'I got a "good work" sticker for reading today!'

'Wow! I am *so* impressed.'

'I wanted to show you. Will you be home soon?'

Diana swallowed. It was so hard not to be there when he came out of school, to have him sharing these special moments with her parents instead of her. Not always being there to read him a story at bedtime.

But that was reality for all working mothers, not just the single ones. Sadie might have a nanny, but in every other way their situation was much the same—not enough hours in the day.

Even so, she knew she was luckier than most... Her parents might have been tight-lipped and angry when she'd got pregnant but they had supported her. And they loved Freddy.

'Will you?' he demanded.

'I've got to work this evening,' she said.

'O-o-h...' Then, 'Will you be home before I go to bed, Mummy?'

'I'll be there when you wake up,' she promised. 'Be good for Grandma and Grandpa, won't you?'

'Okay.'

'Big hug.'

'Oh, *Mum!*'

Make that dumb Mum, she thought as she drank the tea, bit into one of the sandwiches that had been brought for her— who knew when she'd get another chance?—going through every idiot thing she'd said and done since she'd collected Sheikh Zahir from the airport.

So much for 'politely invisible'.

What had she been *thinking?*

Huh! No prizes for getting that one right.

She hadn't been thinking at all. The only thing that had been working from the moment Sheikh Zahir had stepped through the arrivals hall door had been her mouth.

Okay, so he'd made it easy for her, had encouraged her even, but that didn't mean she had to dive in and make a total fool of herself.

Would she ever learn to think first? Speak…sparingly?

Not in this life, apparently…

At this rate she'd be bumping along on the bottom of the food-chain for ever instead of doing the job she was born for. Not driving a limousine, lovely though it was, but following in her dad's footsteps, driving a London Black Cab, where chat was all part of the job. Except that hers, as she'd so confidingly told Sheikh Zahir al Khatib, would not be boringly black, but pink.

She groaned.

That would be the same colour as her cheeks.

The discreet burble of her cellphone might have been a welcome distraction, except that the caller ID warned her that it was Sadie.

So much for talking herself out of trouble.

His Sheikhness had, presumably, called the office—or, more likely, got someone else to do it for him—to demand a driver with a proper peaked cap and a set of male chromosomes the minute she'd dropped him at the front door of the embassy. Someone who knew his place, understood the shopping requirements of the VIP and, more importantly, didn't talk the hind leg off a donkey given the slightest encouragement.

And he *had* encouraged her.

'Di?'

'Mmm… Yes. Sorry. I'm grabbing a sandwich…' She began to choke as she tried to swallow and talk at the same time. She'd let the boss down, had let herself down…

She'd promised to be good. Had promised that Sadie would

hear about any problems from her. Who was she to criticize a princess who had run out on a frog?

'Okay, just listen. Apparently there's a broken water main in Grosvenor Place,' Sadie said, not waiting for her to gather herself, confess all. 'You'll need to cut down to Sloane Street to avoid it.'

What?

Sadie was calling to give her a traffic update? Not to demand an explanation for a priceless gift smashed beyond repair. Non-stop backchat. The shopping fiasco.

'Right,' she said, forcing down the egg and cress along with the lump in her throat. 'Thanks for letting me know.'

'I *was* expecting you to call me. I did ask you to keep in touch.'

'Every time I stop?' she asked, surprised. 'Does Jack have to check in every time he parks up?'

'You're not Jack.'

That was true. 'There's an up side to everything.'

'What's the down side?' Sadie said, instantly on to any suggestion of a problem.

'Nothing,' she said quickly. Then, 'Absolutely nothing.' And she allowed herself a small smile. The Sheikh hadn't split on her… 'We're running a bit late, that's all. Sheikh Zahir needed to shop.'

'Really?' Sadie instantly morphed from boss to woman at the "S" word. 'Where did you go? Aspreys? Garrard?'

'The Toy Warehouse.'

She didn't add that it had been her choice—probably just as well because there was a long pause before Sadie said, 'O-kaaay,' the last syllable stretched to breaking point. 'Well, I suppose that even a sheikh has ankle-biters to keep happy.'

'Not his,' she said quickly. Although, actually he hadn't confirmed or denied whether he had any children of his own. 'He wanted something for the Ambassador's daughter. It's her birthday.'

'As long as you kept him happy.'

'You'll have to ask him that.'

'I'm sure I'll hear soon enough if he's not.' Then, 'I called your father, by the way. He said he had it covered.'

On the point of reassuring Sadie that she'd already called home, she realised that she might not appreciate her priorities and left it at, 'Thank you.'

'You seem distracted, Zahir.' Hanif had drawn him to one side, away from the excitement of Ameerah as she showed her five-year-old brother and her little sister her new toy. Metcalfe had been right about the glass. It would not have done at all. 'Are there problems with the Nadira Creek project? Or the airline you're so keen to get off the ground?'

Zahir smiled. 'Business is never a problem, Han. Lucy's charities will not suffer.'

'Then it must be family. How is your father?'

'Pushing his pacemaker to the limits. He's in the Sudan this week, doing his best to broker peace…' He lifted his hand in a helpless gesture. 'I cannot help but feel guilty. It should be me.'

'No, Zahir. Your talents lie elsewhere.'

'Maybe.'

'There's something else?'

Zahir looked across the room to where the five-year-old Jamal was watching Ameerah, entranced by the snowstorm. Then, turning back to Hanif, he said, 'He's impatient for a grandson to bear his name. Impatient with me for denying him that joy. I'm afraid I've been a disappointment to him in every aspect of my life.' He managed a smile. 'But not for much longer, it would seem. My mother has taken it upon herself to find me a bride.'

He'd anticipated wry amusement, but Hanif was not smiling. 'Marriage is a lifelong commitment, Zahir. Not something to be entered into lightly, even to gratify your father. And the timing could be better.'

'A point I made quite forcibly. My mother's response was that if I waited until I had time, it would never happen.' He shrugged. 'Along with a lot of other stuff about being wilful, selfish…'

'She's anxious to see you settled, Zahir. You may be wilful, but you're not selfish and she knows it. You surrendered more than two precious years to watch over me. You did that for the family.'

'I did it for you, Han. For you I would surrender my life.'

That finally brought a smile to his cousin's face. 'Surrendering your life is easy, Zahir. Take it from one who's been there. It's the living of it that takes effort.'

'No one could accuse me of neglecting that duty.' He worked hard, played hard, lived hard. 'But it's time to do something to show my feelings for him. Respect his wishes.'

'If it's written, *insh'Allah,* whether it is your mother's wish or your own, it will happen and I wish you happy of your bride.'

'You believe in fate?'

Hanif sounded so certain, but then he'd seen for himself how fate had tossed the lovely Lucy Forrester into his cousin's arms. Who could have foreseen that in his future?

Or that the deliciously curvy and delightfully offbeat Metcalfe would be at the wheel of his car today.

'Can I borrow Ameerah for a moment? My driver found her the snowstorm when my original gift was broken. I'd like her to know that it was appreciated.'

'Her?' Hanif's brow scarcely moved. But it moved.

Diana checked her watch. It was time to go and bring the car round to the front but, as she stood up, the sitting room door burst open and a lanky, olive-skinned, dark-haired girl launched herself through it.

'Thank you!' she exclaimed dramatically. 'Thank you so much for finding me the snowstorm. I absolutely love it!'

Diana, taken aback by such an over-the-top performance, looked up, seeking a responsible adult.

What she got was Sheikh Zahir, leaning on the door frame.

Oh. Right. This was his doing…

'I'm very glad you like it, Princess Ameerah. Are you having a lovely party?'

'Oh, we're not having a party today. I had school and Mummy has to go out tonight. We're going to take all my class out on Saturday. We're going on a canal boat trip to the zoo and having a picnic. I begged Zahir to come but he said that it's up to you.'

'Me?'

'You're his *driver!*'

'Oh, I see.'

Diana glanced up at the man leaning casually against the door frame. His expression was giving nothing away and yet she had the strongest impression that he was making a point. Reassuring her that she wouldn't be reduced to the minibus, perhaps?

'I promise,' she said, turning back to the child, 'that, whoever is driving Sheikh Zahir, he'll have absolutely no excuse not to be at your party.'

'You see!' Princess Ameerah, triumphant, swung round to face him. 'I told you it would be all right.'

'So you did.' He ruffled her curls. 'I'll see you on Saturday, Trouble.'

She ran off, but Zahir remained. '*Whoever* is driving?' he repeated.

'Jack Lumley will be back at work long before Saturday.'

'But do I want him when you're so much more entertaining?'

Entertaining!

'Please,' she begged, 'whatever you do, don't use that word if you speak to Sadie Redford. This is my big chance and I'm doing my best to be totally efficient, one hundred per cent VIP chauffeur material. As I'm sure you've noticed, I'm not a "natural" and if you suggest that I'm "entertaining" I'll be finished.'

'I won't say a word, Metcalfe, but it's not true, you know. Natural is exactly what you are.'

She made a valiant effort to keep the groan silent. She wasn't entirely successful.

'I know what I am. Not the first driver you'd think of if you were looking for someone to take the wheel of the newest limousine in Capitol's fleet.'

'You're doing just fine.' Then, before she was overcome with gratitude, 'Just promise that you won't abandon me to the dull and efficient Jack Lumley and I won't breathe a word about just how "natural" you can get to Sadie Redford.'

She swallowed. 'You wouldn't…'

'Shall we go?'

Oh…sheikh…

'I'm just going to bring the car round,' she said and, aiming for Miss Efficiency, checked her watch—anything to avoid those dark, amused eyes that were inviting her to be 'entertaining'. 'Five minutes?'

'Why don't I just come out the back way with you?' he replied, standing back and inviting her to lead the way. 'It'll save you having to drive round the block, wasting precious natural resources.'

Was there the slightest stress on the 'natural', or was she becoming paranoid?

Buttoning her lip, she fought down all and every quip that sprang to her mind and neither of them said another word until she pulled up at the entrance to his hotel, where a top hatted commissionaire opened the door.

'Seven forty-five, Metcalfe,' Sheikh Zahir said as he stepped out.

'Yes, sir.'

Top Hat waved her into the parking bay reserved for the privileged few. 'You can wait there.'

Her brain was saying, *Me? Really?*

Maybe it was shock, or maybe her lip was so firmly buttoned up that the words couldn't escape. Instead, having managed a polite nod, she pulled over as if she'd expected nothing less.

It wasn't, after all, *personal*, she reminded herself. The honour was being bestowed on her passenger. On the car, even. On her Capitol uniform. It had absolutely nothing to do with her.

She called Sadie to reassure her that everything was still going according to plan and updated her on the traffic situation. Then she climbed out, walked around the car, duster in hand, checking for the slightest smear on the immaculate dark red paintwork, the gleaming chrome.

A couple of other chauffeurs nodded, passed the time of day, admiring her car, querying its handling, apparently accepting that, despite the missing chromosome, if someone had entrusted her with such a beast, she was one of them.

Maybe, she thought, she was the only one who was stopping that from being a fact. Living down to her image— single mother, relying on her parents for a roof over her head, help with childcare—rather than living up to her aspirations.

Maybe she'd become so used to hearing what she couldn't do, how limited her options were, that she'd begun to believe it.

Even the dream of owning her own taxi—where, as a teenager, she'd dreamed of owning a fleet of them, all pink, all with women drivers—had been reduced to little more than a family joke.

Next year you'll be driving your own taxi, Di...

Ho, ho, ho.

CHAPTER THREE

SUMMONED by the commissionaire, Diana was waiting at the kerb as Sheikh Zahir emerged from the hotel. This time he was not alone, but accompanied by a chisel-featured younger man blessed with the kind of cheekbones that could slice cheese.

Since he was the one carrying the laptop, he was, presumably, like her, a member of the 'bag-carrying' classes. Although, by the cut of his suit—and his hair—he outranked her by a considerable distance.

There was no mishap this time, probably because Top Hat was on hand to do the honours with the door and no one—not even a small boy—would have dared get in the way of his impressive figure.

The minute her passengers were settled she eased smoothly into the traffic, heading for the South Bank, managing, for once in her life, to remain 'politely anonymous'.

She had barely finished congratulating herself on this rare accomplishment when Sheikh Zahir said, 'Metcalfe, this is James Pierce. He's the man who makes everything work for me. You may, on occasion, be required to ferry him to appointments.'

'Sir,' she said, taking his tone from him. She was doing really well until, waiting for the lights to change, she made the mistake of glancing in the mirror and looking straight into his eyes. They did not match his voice. And his expression suggested that he wasn't fooled for a minute by her lapse into formality and her traitorous mouth let her down and smiled at him.

A mistake.

James Pierce, alerted by her response to the fact that she was not Jack Lumley, said, 'This is outrageous.' And he was looking at her when he said it.

Actually it couldn't just be the voice.

She didn't have one of those cut-glass BBC accents, but her mother had been a stickler for good diction and, apart from the occasional lapse, her speech could not, by any stretch of the imagination, be described as 'outrageous'.

It had to be the dimple, something she should have grown out of, along with the puppy fat. It was an embarrassment for anyone who expected to be taken seriously. Treated as a grown-up. Old enough to have a driving licence, let alone be behind the wheel of a limousine.

'When I made the booking with Capitol Cars I specifically requested…'

'Jack Lumley is sick,' Sheikh Zahir said, cutting him short. 'I'll call Sadie. She must have someone else available.'

Diana couldn't see James Pierce in the mirror, but from the moment he'd opened his mouth she did not like him and he wasn't doing one thing to change her mind.

His superior suit went with his attitude. She might be dumb enough to believe that they were on the same side, but he wasn't buying it. But then a man 'who makes everything work' for a billionaire sheikh probably wasn't.

'Why would we need someone else?' Sheikh Zahir intervened. 'Metcalfe is a—'

Please, please not 'natural' she begged silently, as the lights began to change and she had no choice but to check the mirror. He was still looking at her. Only his eyes changed, the rest of his face remained grave; the smile, she realised, was for her alone.

'—thoroughly competent driver.'

He knew, she thought. He knew exactly what she was thinking and he was teasing her, making her complicit in an intimate conspiracy against the stuffed shirt.

Without warning a warmth, starting somewhere around her abdomen, seeped through every cell of her body until she felt her cheeks begin to flush.

Fortunately, Sheikh Zahir had turned away.

'Don't tell me you're one of those dinosaurs who feel emasculated when driven by a woman, James,' he said, teasing him a little too.

'No…' His reply was unconvincing. 'No, of course not.'

'I'm very glad to hear that. As a lawyer, even if your field is corporate law, I know you wouldn't want to give Metcalfe an excuse to sue the pants off you for sexual discrimination.'

'I just thought—'

'I know what you thought, James, but as you are well aware, it's not a problem.'

He didn't wait for an answer, but immediately turned his attention to business, launching into some complex legal question regarding a lease.

It was an example she'd be wise to follow, she decided. Flirting through the rear-view mirror with a passenger was definitely not the action of a 'thoroughly, competent driver'. Quite the contrary.

Someone who was entertaining now…

Oh, stop it!

At the entrance to the Riverside Gallery, she climbed out and opened the door, keeping her eyes front and centre.

James Pierce stepped out of the car and walked past her without a word or a look. The word 'miffed' crossed her mind—one of her mother's favourite words to describe someone who'd had their nose put out of joint.

Sheikh Zahir paused and, realising that she was grinning, she swiftly straightened her face.

'What will you do until you pick us up, Metcalfe?'

'I've got a book,' she said quickly. Her message—*competent* chauffeurs were used to waiting around. They were ready for it.

Not actually true—the kind of jobs she was usually assigned didn't leave a lot of spare time to catch up on her reading—but he was just being polite and she'd make sure she had one with her tomorrow. Always assuming there was a tomorrow.

Maybe it was time to start brushing up on her Blue Book— the taxi drivers' bible that listed the shortest runs from a given point to any destination, the 'Knowledge' which had to be passed before a "cabbie" could get a licence.

Still he lingered. 'There's no reason why you shouldn't come into the gallery. Have something to eat. You could look at the pictures if the presentation bores you.'

Jolted out of her firm resolve not to make eye contact, she looked up. Swallowed. His smile had progressed to his mouth, tugging at one corner, lifting it a fraction, and something in the region below her ribcage flickered in response, taking her by surprise.

She covered the little gasp with a breathy, 'Th-thank you.' Then, firmly resisting the temptation to be led astray for the second time that day—he had chisel-cheeks to carry his bags, after all—she said, 'I really should…'

'Stay with the car?' he finished for her, saving her from wavering.

'It's advisable.' She gave an apologetic little shrug, then nodded in the direction of the gallery, cleared her throat and said, 'Mr Pierce is waiting for you, sir.'

'Zahir.'

'Sir?'

'Everyone who works for me calls me Zahir. It's the modern way, I'm told. It's not a mile away from "sir", so maybe, if you tried very hard, you might manage it.'

'Yes, sir.'

The smile fading, he nodded, 'Enjoy your book, Metcalfe.'

She watched him walk away. Still no flowing robes, just the standard male uniform of a dark suit, silk tie, although on Sheikh Zahir, she had to admit, it looked anything but standard.

Zahir.

She'd had the name in her head ever since Sadie had hauled her out of the minibus. Alone, she tried it on her tongue, her lips.

'Zahir…'

Exotic.

Different.

Dangerous…

She shivered a little as the breeze came off the river, sweeping over the acres of concrete paving.

Snatches of jazz reached her from a party on boat cruising down the river and, despite the chill, she tugged off her gloves and hat and tossed them on to her seat. Then, having locked the car, she walked across to the railing that ran alongside the river, leaning her elbows on it, looking across at the familiar skyline, dominated by the dome of St Paul's.

Focus, Diana, she told herself. *Keep on your toes. This is not the time for playing dangerous games. No first name nonsense with the handsome prince. Fairy tales are for children.*

This could be an opportunity to take a step up, earn enough to make your own dream into reality. Don't mess it up just because the prince has a pair of dark eyes that look at you as if…

Forget *if!*

She'd done dark and dangerous and wasn't making the same mistake again.

Freddy, her little boy, was her entire world. His future was in her hands, her duty was to him before anyone.

And, if that didn't concentrate her mind, then all she'd have to do was remember the way the bank manager had looked at her when she'd done what their seductive advertisements on the television had encouraged her to do and had applied for a loan to buy a cab, start her own business. His four point response:

1 Single mother.
2 No bricks and mortar, not even ones mortgaged to the hilt as collateral.
3 No assets of any kind.
4 No thanks.

He might as well have patted her on the head and told her to run along. At the time she'd been so angry. Had promised herself she'd be back…

Two years later and she was still no closer to impressing him. And if she was idiot enough to lose her head over a sexy smile twice, then she'd only prove that he'd been right.

Zahir finished his brief presentation to the gathering of tour operators and travel journalists and was immediately button-holed by the CEO of a top-of-the-range tour company, who was examining the display of photographs and the architect's model of the Nadira Resort.

'This is an interesting concept, Zahir. Different. Exactly the sort of thing our more discerning travellers are looking for. I imagine it's going to be expensive?'

'Reassuringly so,' he said, knowing it was what the man wanted to hear. 'Why don't you talk to James? He's organising a site visit and we'd love to show you what we're offering.'

Zahir moved on, shaking hands, answering questions,

issuing personal invitations to the hand-picked group of travel journalists and tour operators as he went.

Then the woman he was talking to moved to one side to let a waitress pass and he found himself looking straight out of one of the gallery's tall, narrow windows. The car was still there, but Metcalfe was nowhere to be seen.

No doubt she was curled up on the back seat with her book. Maybe he could catch her out, watch as, blushing with confusion, she scrambled to straighten that ridiculous hat.

He'd enjoy that.

But she wouldn't.

Metcalfe.

He'd offered his name, hoping for hers in return. She'd known it too and, wisely, had taken a step back from his implicit invitation to become something more than his driver. Well aware that, whatever 'more' he was offering, it wasn't going to be something she would be interested in. And how could he tell her that she was wrong when he didn't know himself what that was?

Or maybe he was fooling himself. They both knew. Had both responded to that instant, unfathomable chemistry…

Maybe James was right after all. Lumley might be dull but he wasn't distracting. He wouldn't have given a moment's thought about how he'd spend his time in the gaps between engagements. He certainly wouldn't have asked him to come into the gallery, been eager to show him what he was doing. Talk about his plans…

'Is your neutral energy target realistic, Sheikh Zahir?' the woman prompted. 'Really?'

'We're fortunate that solar energy is a year-round resource in Ramal Hamrah, Laura,' he said, forcing himself to concentrate on the job in hand. He'd taken the time and trouble to memorize the names and faces of the people he was to meet. 'I do hope you'll come and see for yourself.'

'Well, that's the other problem, isn't it? How can you justify expanding your tourist industry at a time when air travel is being cited as a major cause of carbon emission?'

'By developing a new kind of airline?' he offered with a smile. Then, remembering Metcalfe's wry comment when he'd done the same thing in the toy store, regretted it. With a glance, he summoned James to his side. 'James, Laura Sommerville is the Science Correspondent for *The Courier*…'

'Laura…' James smoothly gathered her up, enabling Zahir to excuse himself.

He tried not to look at his watch.

He was tiring of this kind of public relations exercise. His dreams were bigger these days. He was happier in the background, planning for the future. He had to find someone else to be the public face of this part of the business so that he could take a step back. Someone capable of fuelling the buzz of interest that would give his pet project wings.

Or maybe his desire to be somewhere else had less to do with ennui, more to do with wanting to be with someone else, he thought, doing his best not to snatch another glance out of the window. And failing.

Maybe it had everything to do with his unexpected, his unusual, his very lovely young chauffeur.

Distracted by a movement near the river, he saw that, far from being curled up with a book, Metcalfe was standing at the riverside railing, watching the lights come on across the river as dusk gathered. Hatless, her hair had been whipped loose by the breeze and, arms raised, she was attempting to twist it back into a knot…

A waitress paused in front of him with a tray, cutting off his view, and he moved to one side so that he did not lose sight of her as her jacket lifted, her shirt parted company with her waistband and she bared an inch of skin.

'Canapé, sir?'

'Sorry?'

Then, registering what the waitress had said, he looked at her. Looked at the tray.

'Thank you,' he said and, having taken the tray, he headed for the door.

'Some watchdog you are, Metcalfe. Anyone could have driven off with your precious car.'

Diana, who, despite all her best efforts, had been thinking about this extraordinarily beautiful man who'd invaded her thoughts, her life, jumped at the unexpected sound of his voice.

'They could try,' she said. 'Of course, if they got past the locks and the alarm, there is still the global positioning gizmo.'

'Those gizmos will get you every time,' he said, joining her at the rail. Then, 'So why didn't you come into the gallery?'

'Mr Pierce would not have approved,' she said, keeping her eyes fixed firmly on the north bank of the Thames. 'Besides, this view is more interesting than a load of old paintings.'

'"…all that mighty heart…"' he prompted.

'Wordsworth had it nailed, didn't he?' Unable to help herself, she glanced at him. 'How many Englishmen could quote an Arabic poet, I wonder?' Then, before he could embarrass them both by answering, 'Did the party end prematurely?'

'No, it's in full swing.'

'Oh.' He'd come out to see her. She looked at the tray. He'd brought her food? 'Does Mr Pierce know you've escaped?'

'Escaped?'

'You *are* the star attraction?'

'On the contrary, the Nadira Resort is the star of the show. Besides, I distracted James with a serious young journalist who doubts my probity.'

'Why?'

He offered her the tray. 'I thought you might be hungry.'

She stared at it for a moment, then, with a little shake of her head, said, 'No, why does she doubt your probity? Whatever that is.'

'Maybe integrity is a better word.' Then, 'You know journalists. Natural cynics.'

'That's one word for it.' Then, 'Why would she believe James Pierce and not you?'

'She won't. His job is to persuade her to come to Nadira and see the resort for herself.'

A smile from him would have been enough, she thought. One of his smiles could get him anything he wanted…

'Cynicism pays, then. Nice work…' she said, pushing the thought away. Not *anything*. Not her snow globe. Not *her*. 'If you'd said you were handing out free holidays, even I might have been…'

Tempted.

She left the word unspoken, but they both knew what she had been going to say. Embarrassed, she focused on the selection of canapés laid out on the tray—all the temptation she was prepared to indulge in.

'These look good enough to eat,' she said.

'Help yourself.'

The words sounded…loaded. An invitation to do more than take one of the exquisite little savouries. She forced herself to take the words literally. She wasn't hungry, but filling her mouth with food would at least prevent her from saying anything she'd regret.

Saying anything.

The small pastry she took exploded in her mouth, leaving a soft, warm centre of cheese. She wasn't totally acting when she groaned with pleasure.

'Have you tried one of those?'

'Should I?' Zahir asked seriously.

'Yes… No! Definitely not. You should leave them all for me and go back to your party.'

He took one, tried it for himself. 'I see what you mean,' he said, sucking a dribble of cheese from the pad of his thumb, leaving a crumb clinging to his lower lip, drawing quite unnecessary attention to it.

It was all she could do to stop herself from reaching up and wiping it away with her fingers.

Nothing in the world could prevent her from imagining doing it.

'Why don't we take this over to that bench?' he suggested. 'If we're going to do this justice we need to sit down.' Then, 'I should have brought us something to drink.'

'Us? Excuse me, but won't you be missed?'

'You want all this for yourself, is that it?' The words were serious, his expression anything but, and she laughed. It was so easy to laugh when he looked at her like that.

'You've got me bang to rights, guv,' she said.

'Help yourself. I've still got dinner to get through.'

He didn't sound particularly excited by the prospect of dining at one of London's most exclusive restaurants.

'I wouldn't have thought that was exactly a strain.'

'Fine food ruined by high finance. A recipe for indigestion.'

'That's what you get for mixing business with pleasure.'

'How wise you are, Metcalfe. What a pity the money men aren't as sensible.'

'I guess they take the view that time is money, so doing two things at once is earning them twice as much.'

'Especially if they're not paying for dinner.'

'Good point.'

He set the tray down, waited for her to sit and, having apparently debated with himself for a moment, sat on the far side of it so that it was between them. She couldn't decide if she was relieved or disappointed…

'I love this view, don't you?' Zahir said, saving her from having to admit to disappointment. 'So much history packed into every square metre.'

'You've spent a lot of time in London?'

'Too much,' he admitted cheerfully as he leaned back and stretched out his long legs. 'I was at school just up the river.'

'Really? Me, too.' Then, catching on to exactly which school 'up the river' he was talking about, she said, 'Obviously, in my case, it wasn't Eton, but the local comprehensive. In Putney.'

'Is that where you live now?'

'Mmm.' She stuffed in another taste sensation—this time something involving smoked salmon and sour cream—and shrugged. 'Twenty-three years old and still living at home,' she said, brushing the crumbs from her fingers. 'How sad can you get?'

'Sad?'

'Pathetic. Dull.'

'On the contrary. It is the way it should be. Women in my country live under the protection of their families until they're married.'

Not if they had a five-year-old son and no husband they didn't, Diana thought as, for a moment, they just looked at one another, confronting the gulf between them.

Zahir knew he should move. Stop this—whatever *this* was. While he was sitting here flirting with his chauffeur, wanting to do much more, his mother, his sisters, were sifting through the Ramal Hamrah equivalent of the 'girls in pearls' to choose his perfect bride…

Even as he urged himself to move, a gust of wind tugged at Metcalfe's hair, whipping a strand across her face and, acting purely on instinct, he reached out to capture it.

Silk, he thought, as it tangled in his fingers, brushed against his wrist. Chestnut-coloured silk, a perfect counter to the bronze-flecked green of eyes that widened, darkened as he looked down at her, and the temptation to wrap it round his fist and draw her closer almost overwhelmed him.

Almost. He was not so lost…

Slowly, taking care not to touch her cheek, he gathered it, then was left with no alternative but to tuck it behind her ear. Her ear, the smooth, fine skin of her neck, undid all his best intentions. The warmth drew him in, held him captive, and he spread his hand to cradle her head.

Until the last second she watched him, eyes wide as a fawn, but the second before his lips met hers she slammed them shut, caught her breath and, for the longest moment in his life, she was rigid, unmoving. Then she melted and kissed him back.

It was the crash of the tray that brought them both to their senses.

Metcalfe jerked away with a little gasp, looking at him for a moment, eyes wide, mouth full and dark, cheeks flushed, everything she was feeling on display. As if she knew, she looked away, glancing down at the tray.

'Pigeon heaven,' she said, breaking the silence, as the birds began to snatch at the scattered food.

He wanted to say something, but what? He couldn't even say her name. Metcalfe wouldn't do…

'I have to get back to the gallery,' he said, getting to his feet.

She nodded. 'I'll bring back the tray.' Then, when he still didn't make a move, she looked up at him and said, 'Diana. My name is Diana Metcalfe.'

'Like the princess?'

'I'm afraid so. My mother was a fan.'

'Diana was also a goddess.'

'I know. It's really rather more of a name than one very ordinary girl could ever hope to live up to.' She swallowed. 'Most people just call me Di.'

'There's no such thing as an ordinary girl, Diana. Each person is unique, individual.' Then, with a touch of anger, 'The world is full of people ready to keep you in what they perceive to be your place. Don't give them a head start by doing it to yourself.'

Diana stared at him for a moment, but he hadn't waited for her answer. With something that was more than a nod, less than a bow, he turned and walked quickly away.

Was he angry with her?

He needn't bother. Give her a moment to gather her wits, forget a touch that had stirred her to the core, waking feelings, desires she had thought stone dead, and she'd be angry enough for both of them.

As for that stuff about her 'place'. Easy to say, when your own place in the world was so far above ordinary that you probably needed an oxygen mask.

What did he know about her life?

Single mother at eighteen. And then, just as she might have turned her life around, her father had been disabled by a stroke, leaving her and her mother having to work full-time, run as fast as they could just to keep in the same place. All dreams on hold for the duration.

Tomorrow she'd bring sandwiches and a flask of tea as well as her standard bottle of water—the full 'chauffeur' kit—she promised herself, picking up the tray and tossing the remainder of the canapés to the pigeons.

Always assuming Zahir hadn't given James Pierce the nod to do what he'd wanted from the moment he'd set eyes on her and organise another driver. For both their sakes.

'Great start, Diana,' she said to herself. 'Professional, eh? Well, that's a joke.' Cheek and chat were one thing, but kissing the client? 'Failed on every count.'

Even if he didn't pull the plug, she knew she should phone Sadie right now and do it for him. But she didn't. Instead she walked across to the gallery on legs that felt as if they were walking on feathers. Handed the tray over to a waitress, taking care to look neither to left nor right as she headed for the ladies' to wash her hands.

But when, a few minutes later, she emerged, the first person she saw, through a gap in the crowd, was Zahir. She could have just put her head down and scurried out, but there was not a chance in the world that he would notice her, flirt with her. His attention was totally engaged by a tall, elegant blonde, her long cream-coloured hair twisted up in a simple stylish twist. Not some foolish girl, but a beautiful woman. Not wearing a hideous uniform, but an exquisitely embroidered *shalwar kameez*, the kind that cost telephone numbers.

As Diana stood there, temporarily mesmerised, the woman smiled and touched his arm in a gesture of casual intimacy. There was a relaxed easiness between them and she didn't doubt that they knew each other well.

It was as if she'd been slapped on the side of the head, given a reality check.

Sheikh Zahir was a man who would draw beautiful women to him like a magnet. Beautiful women in beautiful clothes, stunningly high-heeled designer shoes.

He'd kissed her because she was there. Because he could. It was what men did. They took what was on offer without a thought, nothing engaged but their hormones.

For heaven's sake, she only had to *look* at him to see how it was. Remember the drooling reaction of the assistant in the toy store.

As for her, well, she was undoubtedly giving out all the same signals and he'd responded to them the same way he breathed. Instinctively.

It had happened to her once before and she knew it didn't mean a thing. Not a thing, she thought, turning away and finding herself face to face with James Pierce.

He glanced across at his boss, then back at her, and, as if

he'd known exactly what she was thinking, he gave her a pitying smile and said, 'She's lovely, isn't she?'

'Lovely,' she managed. Then, unable to help herself, 'Who is she?'

'His partner.' Then, while her brain was processing that piece of information, 'You'd better get back to the car. Sheikh Zahir will be leaving in five minutes.'

She needed no encouragement to leave, escaping into the fresh air where she dragged in steadying breaths as she replaced her hat, her gloves, donning them as if they were armour.

She'd expected the blonde to be with him, but when, a few moments later, Zahir emerged, he was alone but for James Pierce.

'I'll leave you to mop up the stragglers, James. I want every one of these people to visit Nadira, experience it firsthand.'

'I've got all but a couple of broadsheet journalists who want to be coaxed but the princess will have them eating out of her hands before they know it.'

The blonde was a princess?

Why was she surprised?

'No doubt. In my absence, will you see Lucy safely to her car?'

'It will be my pleasure.' Then, 'I'll be on call should Lord…' James Pierce glanced at her, leaving the name unsaid, making it crystal clear that he doubted her discretion.

'Thank you, James. I think I can handle any query Lord Radcliffe is likely to raise,' Zahir replied, demonstrating that he had no such qualms.

Well, he'd kissed her. She was, presumably, at now his beck and call.

'Berkeley Square, Diana?' he prompted, as he stepped into the car.

'Sir,' she said.

'Come back and collect me as soon as you've dropped off Sheikh Zahir, Metcalfe,' James Pierce said sharply.

Sheikh Zahir held out a hand, stopping her from closing the door. 'Take a taxi, James.'

'It's no trouble,' Diana said quickly, not wanting to give the stuffed shirt any reason to complain to Sadie, determined to show him that nothing had changed. 'I'll only be sitting around, waiting.' She summoned a smile, the polite variety, for James Pierce. 'I'll be as quick as I can, Mr Pierce.'

She climbed behind the wheel, started the car and, using her wing mirrors, taxi-driver style, she made her way through London managing to avoid any possibility of eye-contact with her passenger.

And, since she was working strictly to the 'don't speak until spoken to' rule, it was a silent journey since Sheikh Zahir said nothing.

He was probably angry because she'd had the temerity to intervene over his suggestion that James Pierce take a taxi. He probably wasn't used to anyone arguing with him, although anyone with any sense could see that it had to be more sensible to be doing something, even transporting chisel-cheeks, than just hanging around waiting for him to talk his way through dinner. Or maybe, once kissed, she had joined his personal harem and was now his alone.

'Tosh, Diana,' she muttered under her breath. 'One kiss and you're losing it…'

And yet he didn't move to get out of the car by himself when she'd eased around Berkeley Square and pulled up in front of the restaurant.

Was that his way of making the point that it had changed nothing? Or everything?

Apparently neither. He was so far lost in his thoughts as she opened the door that it was obvious he hadn't even noticed that they'd stopped.

'What time would you like me to pick you up, sir?' she asked, taking no chances.

Zahir had spent the journey from the Riverside Gallery gathering his thoughts for the coming meeting. Trying to block out the image, the taste, the scent of the woman sitting in front of him. All it took was a word, a solemn enquiry, to undo all that effort.

'If you're not sure, maybe you could call me?' She took a card from her jacket pocket and offered it to him. 'When you've got to the coffee stage of the evening?'

It was a standard Capitol card. 'Call you?'

'That's the car phone number printed on the front,' she said. 'I've printed my cellphone number on the back.'

He took the card, still warm from her body, and, to disguise the sudden shake of his fingers, he turned it over and looked at the neatly printed numbers. It was, had always been, his intention to walk back to his hotel. He knew he'd need a little time to clear his head, no matter what the outcome of his meeting. On the point of telling her that she could go home, that she could have gone now if she hadn't insisted on picking up James, he stopped himself. Sending her home early might make him feel good, but he'd be doing her no favours. On the contrary, he'd be robbing her of three hours' work at the highest evening rate.

'Eleven-thirty should do it,' he said. 'If there's a change of plan, I'll give you a call.'

'Yes, sir.'

The 'sir' jabbed at him. But it wasn't just the 'sir'. For the first time since she'd handed him the broken toy outside the airport, she wasn't quite looking at him. She had her gaze firmly fixed on something just over his right shoulder and it occurred to him that Diana, with considerable grace, was telling him that she understood that his kiss had meant nothing. Giving him—giving them both—the chance to step back. Go back to the beginning. To the moment before an excited child had altered everything.

He could do no less. Acknowledging her tact with the slightest of bows, he said, 'Thank you, Metcalfe.'

CHAPTER FOUR

FOR the briefest moment Diana met his gaze. For the briefest moment he saw something in her eyes that made him forget the powerful men who were waiting for him, forget his precious airline. All he felt was a rush of longing, an overwhelming need to stop Diana from driving away, climb back into the car beside her and take her somewhere quiet, intimate, where their separate worlds, his and hers, did not exist.

But to what purpose?

For her smile? To watch it appear, despite every attempt she made to control it?

To listen to her, enjoy conversation that had no ulterior purpose. No agenda.

She might laugh, blush, even share a kiss, but with that swift return to 'sir' she had recognised the gulf between them even if he, in a moment of madness, had chosen to ignore it. She knew—they both knew—that in the end all they could ever share was a brief intimacy that had no future. Kind enough to take a step back, pretend that it had never happened, when a more calculating woman would have seen a world of possibilities.

Selling a kiss-and-tell sheikh-and-the-chauffeur story to one of the tabloids would have paid for her dream twice over. That sparkly pink taxi for weekdays and something really fancy for Sunday. And he knew all about dreams…

If she could do that for him, why was he finding it such a problem to do it for himself?

It wasn't as if he was in the habit of losing his head, or his heart, over a sweet smile.

He might have a streak of recklessness when it came to business, even now be prepared to risk everything he'd achieved. But he'd been far more circumspect in his personal life, taking care to keep relationships on a superficial level, with women who played by the same rules he did—have fun, move on—who understood that his future was written, that there was no possibility of anything deeper, anything permanent between them. Who would not get hurt by a light-hearted flirtation.

Diana Metcalfe was not one of those women.

And he did not feel light-hearted.

Yet, even when he recognised the need for duty before pleasure, he still wanted to hear his name on her lips, wanted to carry her smile with him. Couldn't rid himself of the scent of her skin, the sweet taste of her that lingered on his lips, a smile than went deeper the more he looked, a smile that faded to a touch of sadness.

He'd need all his wits about him this evening if he was going to pull off the biggest deal of his career to date and all he could think about was what had made the light go out of her eyes. *Who* had made the light go out of her eyes…

And, on an impulse, he lifted the card he was still holding, caught a trace of her scent. Nothing that came from a bottle, but something warm and womanly that was wholly Diana Metcalfe.

He stuffed it into his pocket, out of sight, dragged both hands through his hair, repeating his earlier attempt to erase the tormenting thoughts. He should call James right now and tell him to contact the hire company and ask them to provide another driver for tomorrow. Maybe, if she was out of sight, he could put her out of his mind.

But even that escape was denied him.

His first mistake, and it had been entirely his, was not to have kissed her, not even to have allowed himself to be distracted by her; he'd have to have been made of wood not to have been distracted by her. His first mistake had been to talk to her. Really talk to her.

He'd talked to Jack Lumley, for heaven's sake, but he'd known no more about the man after a week in his company than he had on day one.

Diana didn't do that kind of polite, empty conversation.

He'd said she was a 'natural', but she was more than that. Her kind of natural didn't require quotation marks. Diana Metcalfe was utterly unaffected in her manner. Spoke first, thought second. There was no fawning to please. None of the schooled politeness that the Jack Lumleys of this world had down to a fine art.

He wouldn't, couldn't, ruin her big chance, send her back to the 'school run' when she'd done nothing wrong.

He was the one breaking all the rules and he was the one who'd have to suffer.

Maybe an evening brokering the kind of financial package required to launch an airline would have much the same effect as a cold shower, he thought as he watched the tail lights of the car disappear.

Or maybe he just needed to get a grip.

'Excellency.' The *maître d'* greeted him warmly as he led the way to a private dining room, booked for this very discreet dinner. 'It's good to see you again.'

'And you, Georges.'

But as he followed him up the wide staircase he deliberately distanced himself from this international, cosmopolitan world. Reminded himself with every step of his own culture, his own future. Demonstrated it by enquiring after the man's family, his wife, not as he'd learned to do in the west, but in the Arab manner, where to mention a man's wife, his daughters, would be an insult.

'How are your sons?' he asked, just as his father, his grandfather would have done.

Diana drove back to the yard, filled in her log, wrapped the shattered remains of the snow globe in a load of newspaper before disposing of it. Vacuum cleaned the inside of the car.

Even managed a bite of the sandwich she'd picked up at the local eight-'til-late.

But keeping her hands busy did nothing to occupy her brain. That was away with the fairies and would keep reliving that moment when he'd kissed her and, for just a moment, she'd felt like a princess.

Zahir had wanted to send Diana away, had planned to call at eleven and tell her to go home, but somehow the moment had passed and when, leaving the restaurant, he saw her waiting for him, he knew that his subconscious had sabotaged his good intentions. And could not be anything but glad.

It wasn't solitude he needed at this moment, but the company of someone with whom he could share his excitement. Someone who had a smile that reached deep inside him and heated him to the heart.

'You've had a long day, Metcalfe. Can you spare another five minutes?'

'Yes… Yes, of course. Where do you want to go?'

'Nowhere. Will you walk around the square with me?'

Maybe he'd got the formula right this time, or maybe she caught something of the excitement he'd had to suppress in the presence of the financiers, but which was now fizzing off him. Whatever it was, she clicked the key fob to secure the car and fell in beside him.

'There are no stars,' he said, looking up. 'The light pollution in London robs you of the sky. If we were in the desert the night would be black, the stars close enough to touch.'

'It sounds awesome.' Then, as he glanced at her, 'I meant…'

'I know what you meant,' he said. She wasn't using teenage slang, but using the word as it was meant to be used. 'And you're right. It's empty. Cold. Clean. Silent but for the wind. It fills a man with awe. Reminds him how small he is. How insignificant.'

'Did your meeting not go well?' she asked anxiously.

'Better than I could ever have imagined.' A rare take-it-or-leave-it arrogance had carried him through dinner tonight. He'd cut through the waffle and, refusing to play the games of bluff and counter-bluff, had gone straight to the bottom line, had told them what he wanted, what he was prepared to offer. Maybe his passion had convinced them. 'Beyond the four of us at dinner tonight, you are the first to know what the world will hear two days from now. That Ramal Hamrah is about to have its own airline.'

'Oh.' Then, 'That is big.'

'Every deal is big, only the numbers change.' Then, looking down at her, 'When you buy your pink taxi it will be huge.'

'It'll be a miracle,' she said with feeling, 'but, if it ever happens, I promise you that I'll look up at the stars and remind myself not to get too big for my boots.'

He took her arm as they crossed the road and, when they reached the safety of the footpath, he tucked it safely beneath his before once more looking up at the reddish haze of the sky and said, 'Not in London, Metcalfe.' For a moment she'd frozen, but maybe his use of her surname reassured her and, as she relaxed, he moved on. 'I suppose you could go to the Planetarium.'

'Not necessary. In London you don't look up to see the stars. You look down.' He frowned and she laughed. 'Didn't you know that the streets of London aren't paved with gold, they're paved with stars.'

'They are?'

He looked down and then sideways, at her. 'Obviously I'm missing something.'

'We're in Berkeley Square?' she prompted.

'And?'

'You've never heard the song?' She shook her head. 'Why would you? It's ancient.'

Berkeley Square… Something snagged in his memory, a scratchy old record his grandfather used to play. 'I thought it was about a nightingale.'

'You do know it!'

'I remember the tune.' He hummed a snatch of it and she smiled.

'Almost,' she said, laughing. 'But it's not just the nightingale. There's a line in there about stars too.' She lifted her shoulders in an awkward little shrug. 'My dad used to sing it to my mum,' she said, as if she felt she had to explain how she knew. 'They used to dance around the kitchen…'

'Really?' He found the idea enchanting. 'Like this?' And as he turned his arm went naturally to her waist. 'Well, what are you waiting for? Sing…' he commanded.

Diana could not believe this was happening. There were still people about—Zahir's kind of people, men in dinner jackets, women in evening clothes—heading towards the fashionable nightclubs in the area to celebrate some special occasion. Laughing, joking, posing as someone took photographs with a camera phone.

Maybe if she'd been dressed in a glamorous gown she wouldn't have felt so foolish. But in her uniform…

'Don't!' she begged, but Zahir caught her hand and, humming, began to spin her along the footpath. 'Zahir…' Then, 'For heaven's sake, that's not even the right tune!'

'No? How does it go?'

Maybe his excitement, his joy, were infectious, but

somehow, before she knew it, she was singing it to him, filling gaps in the words with 'da-da-de-dum's and he was humming and they were dancing around Berkeley Square to a song that was old when her parents had first danced to it. A song in which the magic of falling in love made the impossible happen. Made London a place where angels dined, where nightingales sang and where the streets were paved with stars.

Dancing as if they were alone in the universe and the streets truly were paved with stars.

It was only when she came to the end of the song that she realised they had stopped dancing, that they were standing by the car. That Zahir was simply holding her.

That what she wanted more than anything in the world was for him to kiss her again.

And as if reading her thoughts, he raised her hand to his lips, before tilting his head as if listening to something very faint.

'Can you hear it?' he murmured. 'The nightingale.'

It was a question that asked more than whether she could, impossibly, hear a shy woodland bird singing in a London square.

It took every atom of common sense to ignore the soft touch of his breath against her cheek, his fingers still wrapped about hers, his hand warm against her waist. To ignore the magic of the nightingale's sweet song filling her heart.

It took Freddy's voice saying, 'Will you be home before I go to bed, Mummy?' The memory of her promise, 'I'll be there when you wake up.'

'No, sir,' she managed, her voice not quite her own. 'I think you'll find that's a sparrow.'

And with that she shattered the fragile beauty of the moment and the danger passed. He took a step back and said, with the gravest of smiles, 'I forgot, Metcalfe. You don't believe in fairy stories.'

For a moment she wanted to deny it. Instead, she said, 'Neither, sir, do you.'

'No.' He repeated the touch of his lips to her finger and, without a word, turned and began to walk away.

What?

'Sir!' He did not seem to hear her. 'Where are you going?' Then, in desperation, 'Zahir!'

Without stopping, without turning, he said, 'Go home, Metcalfe. I'll walk back to the hotel.'

'But…'

He stopped. Looked up to a sky fogged with neon.

But? But what? What was she thinking?

As if in answer to her unspoken question, he turned and, as their eyes met, she knew 'what'.

She'd always known.

She'd been here before and the raw power of the heat-charged look that passed between them scared her witless.

She'd had the sense to take a step back and then, as if seized by a determination to destroy herself all over again, she'd undone it all with that 'but'.

And she had no excuse. She wasn't an eighteen-year-old with her head in the clouds and her brains in cold storage. At eighteen there was some excuse. At twenty-three, with her reputation rebuilt, responsibilities…

She was fooling herself.

This was desire at its most primitive. The atavistic urge that powered all of creation. Age, experience, counted for nothing. There was no immunity…

'But?' Zahir finally prompted, his voice as soft as thistledown.

Without thought she'd reached out to him. Her hand was still extended, as if imploring him to come back. Finish what he'd started.

Slowly, deliberately, she closed her hand, but somehow it stayed there and he took a step towards her.

Maybe the movement broke the spell. Maybe age did help, because she swung her arm wildly towards the far corner of the square. 'You're going the wrong way,' she said. 'You need Charles Street. Then, um, Queen Street. Then Curzon Street.'

'That's out of the taxi drivers' handbook, is it?'

'Yes. No…' Her eyes were still locked on to his. She could scarcely breathe. 'Queen Street is one-way. I'd…a taxi… would have to cut along Erfield Street.'

Zahir gently took her arm, opened the driver's door of the car and said, 'I'll see you in the morning, Diana. Ten o'clock.'

Zahir stood back as she climbed into the limo, fumbled to get the key in the ignition and, after what seemed like an age, drove away. Only then did he let loose the breath he seemed to have been holding for ever.

He'd only met the woman a few hours ago and yet it was as if he'd been waiting for her all his life. She was the one who made him laugh, made him dance. Made him want to sing.

Walking through the quiet streets, he should have been concentrating on the future, plans that had been a year in the making. Instead it was Diana Metcalfe who filled his head, heated him to the heart, made nightingales sing in the heart of London.

Her father was dozing in front of the television, not conspicuously waiting for his little girl to come home, but he never went to bed until he knew she was safely in. As a teenager it had driven her mad. It still did but, a mother herself, these days Diana understood the need to know that your family was safe before you could rest.

'Busy day?' he asked.

'Above average,' she said, managing a grin as she peeled off her jacket. 'An outbreak of food poisoning meant that I had the number one car and a sheikh.' About whom the least said the better. Her father could read her like a book. 'Did you manage okay?' she asked, by way of diversion. 'Freddy wasn't too much for you?'

'He was as good as gold. He's spark out, bless him.' He eased himself to his feet, limped into the kitchen, turning on the tap with his left hand, then holding the kettle beneath it. She wanted to say, Sit down…let me… but understood that his self-esteem was involved. Knew that the more he did, the better it was for his mobility. Her need, his determination, to look after Freddy for her had done more for his recovery from the stroke than all the months of phsyio. Had given him a reason to push himself to be mobile. 'What'll you have? Tea, chocolate?'

All she wanted was to get to her room, shut the door, be on her own so that she could unravel the emotional tangle she'd got herself in, get her head around it, but her father looked forward to hearing about her day. 'Chocolate, if you'll have some with me. Has Mum gone up?'

'Hours ago. She was rushed off her feet at the shop today, doing the flowers for some fancy society wedding. She looked whacked out.'

'She could do with a holiday,' Diana said, trying not to envy all those journalists and tour operators, being whisked away, first class on Sheikh Zahir's magic carpet. 'Maybe we could all go somewhere when school breaks up.'

'You should be going on holiday with people your own age,' he said, then looked away.

'I don't think Freddy would fit in with an eighteen-thirty package, do you?' she joked, pretending she hadn't noticed.

'We'd look after him. You need to get out more. Get a life.'

'Freddy is my life,' she said.

'Di—'

'How's the Test Match going?' she asked.

Once launched on the safer subject of cricket, her father's passion, all she had to do was say 'absolutely' in all the appropriate places while he gave her chapter and verse on the weaknesses in the England team, the poor eyesight of the umpires, the quality of the wicket, while she drank her chocolate. Then, having rinsed her mug, she dropped a kiss on his balding head.

'Tell Mum that I'll see to Freddy in the morning. I don't have to go in until nine. Don't stay up too late,' she chided, playing up to the pretence that he'd stayed up to watch something he wanted to see on the television, rather than because he was waiting for her to come home.

She looked in on Freddy, straightened the cover that had slipped from his shoulders, lightly touching his dark curls. Five years old and already a heartbreaker, just like the man who'd fathered him.

'Night, angel,' she murmured, picking up the snowstorm that sat on his bookshelf. The snowflakes stirred, but she didn't shake it, just returned it to its place. 'Sleep tight.'

Safe in her own room, she sat on the bed, opened the drawer of her night table and took out the little box in which she kept her treasures. At the bottom was a photograph taken at a party. Just a bunch of people turning as someone had called out 'smile'. It was mere chance that she'd been on the same picture as Pete O'Hanlon, that someone had given it to her.

All she had of Freddy's father.

The only reason she kept it was because, one day, Freddy would insist on knowing who his father was. By then, hopefully, memories, like the photograph, would have faded, people would have moved away and his name would have been forgotten. And Freddy would be valued for himself as a decent young man.

The only reason she looked at it now was because five years had, without her noticing it, dulled her sense of danger. Because she needed to remind herself how much damage falling in lust could do.

Eventually she closed the box, put it away. Hung up her uniform, laid out a clean shirt and underwear for the morning.

Brushed her teeth. Finally crawled into the same single bed that she'd slept in all her life. And discovered that she'd been working on the wrong memory because the moment she closed her eyes she was confronted with Sheikh Zahir's smile.

The one that barely showed on the surface, was no more than a warmth behind his eyes.

Felt his long fingers cradling her head, the touch of his breath on her cheek, his mouth…

Diana finally dropped off, but her sleep was disturbed by dreams in which she was driving a sparkly pink taxi around and around the inside a snow globe. She was constantly being hailed by Sheikh Zahir who, when she stopped, didn't get in the back but just looked at her and said, 'Kiss me, I'm a prince.'

Then, when she did, he turned into a frog.

She woke with a start, her heart pounding, her mouth dry, for a moment unsure where she was.

The low, insistent peeping of the alarm finally broke through the fug of sleep and, with a groan, she killed the sound, rolled over and got out of bed in one movement. It was still early and her eyes were heavy, but she didn't want to risk closing them and having that dream start up again.

Pulling on her dressing gown, she went across the landing to Freddy's room to be there, as promised, when he woke and give her mother an extra half an hour in bed. Make the most of the luxury of an unusually late start since she wasn't due to pick up Zahir from the hotel until ten o'clock.

Assuming, of course, that Jack was still laid low.

Say what she liked about him, Jack Lumley wouldn't malinger; he'd be back at work today if it was humanly possible. Or even if it wasn't. Inspecting his precious car for the slightest mark, the smallest bit of dust and heaven help her if he found any.

Let him look.

He'd never be able to tell his car had been out of the yard. Well, not unless he tried to sit in it. She'd had to pull the seat forward to accommodate her shorter legs and hadn't thought to put it back.

'Bad girl, Diana,' she said, grinning as she gave her wrist a light tap. 'Write out one hundred times, "I must always return the seat to its original position."'

'Mummy?'

Freddy blinked, then, wide awake in an instant, bounced out of bed, grabbing his 'good work' sticker and holding it up for her to see.

'Look!'

'Shh…' she said, putting her finger to her lips. 'It's early. Don't wake Grandma and Grandpa.'

'Look, Mummy!' he whispered, holding it right in front of her face.

'Terrific!' she whispered back, scooping him up and carrying him downstairs, treasuring this precious time when, for once, she could share breakfast with him, watch over him as he cleaned his teeth. Walk him to school so that her mother wouldn't have to go out of her way but could go straight to the bus stop.

Her dad was right, she thought, as all three of them muddled together in the hall, gathering their belongings, making sure that Freddy had everything he needed for the day, her mother was looking tired and, on an impulse, she gave her a hug.

'What's that for?' she demanded in her don't-be-daft voice.

'Nothing. Everything.' Then, sideswiped by the unexpected sting of tears, she turned quickly away, calling back to her father in the kitchen, 'I'll give you a call later, Dad, let you know what's happening.'

'Don't worry about us,' he said, coming to the door. 'I'll be waiting when Freddy comes out of school. Maybe we'll have a look at the river, eh? What do you say, son?'

'Can we?' Freddy's face lit up and, smiling at her dad, Diana reached for her little boy's hand.

Her mother coughed meaningfully, shaking her head. Then, 'You don't have to walk all the way to the gate. I leave him at the corner and he walks the rest of the way all by himself.'

'He does?' she squeaked. Then, doing her best to smile, 'You do?'

Freddy nodded.

'I watch him every step of the way,' her mother mouthed in silent reassurance.

'Well…' it was only a few steps from the corner to the school gate, but Diana still had to swallow hard '…that is grown up!'

Her little boy was growing up much too fast. Making giant leaps while she was too busy working to notice. To be a full-time mother.

But what choice did she have if she was going to make a life for him? She couldn't rely on her parents for ever. She'd put them through so much already. Could never quite get away from the fear that she'd caused her father's stroke.

'Don't forget that you've got parents' evening tonight,' her dad called after her.

'It's engraved in my brain,' she promised, turning to wave from the gate.

At the corner nearest to the school she managed to restrain herself from kissing Freddy, stuffing her hands into her pockets so that she wouldn't be tempted to do anything as embarrassing as wave. Watched him as he ran away from her and was swallowed up by the mass of children in the playground and waited to make sure that he was absorbed, accepted.

Why wouldn't he be?

Half the children in his class were living in one parent families. But at least most of them had a father—even if an absent one—somewhere.

She turned and, blinking furiously, walked quickly down the road to the Capitol Cars garage.

Zahir had not slept.

He and James had worked through most of the night, putting the finishing touches to details that had been a year in the planning.

It wasn't lack of sleep that blackened his early morning mood, however, but an email from Atiya, his youngest sister.

She'd written, full of excitement, about his forthcoming wedding, eager to let him know what she thought of each of the bridal prospects on their mother's 'shortlist', which was awaiting his return. Since Atiya knew them all and was evidently thrilled to the core at the prospect of him marrying one of her dearest friends, she had taken immense pleasure in describing each of them in detail so that he would have something other than their mother's opinion—what, after all, did mothers know?—on which to make his choice.

This one, apparently, had beautiful hair. That one a stunning figure. A third wasn't so pretty but had the loveliest smile and a truly sweet nature.

It had, he thought, all the charm of a cattle show, with him as the prize bull. It was, however, a timely reminder of who he was. What was expected of him.

Which did not include dancing in the street with his enchanting chauffeur.

CHAPTER FIVE

'DI…'

Sadie had been waiting for her and she crossed to the office, assuming that the summons heralded a return to normal and trying to be glad. Sheikh Zahir had no doubt regretted his impulse to kiss her, dance with her—fooling around with the 'help' was always a mistake—and conceded that James Pierce might have had a point. Given him the go-ahead to call Sadie and arrange for another driver.

Which, or so the small inner voice of reason assured her, was a very good thing. She was still fighting off the memory of that dream. It would save embarrassment all round.

She just wished her inner voice could sound more convincing. But then her inner voice hadn't felt the power of that final look, a connection that went soul deep…

'What's the plan, boss?' she asked with determined brightness. 'Back to normal is it? You should have phoned, I could have come in earlier.'

Sadie shook her head. 'I've got someone in to cover the minibus for the rest of the week. Jack is still *hors de combat* and, while he's promising he'll be in tomorrow, I can't see him being fit for anything but local jobs until next week. Are you going to be okay for another late one?'

Zahir hadn't pulled the plug?

The fact the brightness was no longer forced, but blindingly genuine, warned her that she was playing with fire. But it was so long since she'd been warm...

'How late? Freddy has a parents' evening at school this evening.'

'Well, let's see. Sheikh Zahir has to be back in London by six so, if you could handle that part of his day, I can find someone to cover the evening.'

'No problem, then.'

'Apparently not. I'll give you a call later to let you know who it is so that you keep Sheikh Zahir in the picture. And I'll write you in for the rest of this job.'

Diana swallowed. 'Thank you, Sadie. I appreciate your confidence.' Maybe, today, she'd live up to it.

Sadie, oblivious, smiled. 'You've earned it. Enjoy your day at the seaside.'

'The seaside?'

Sadie handed over the paperwork. 'Sheikh Zahir is visiting a boatyard and marina, apparently.'

'Really?' Obviously her idea of non-stop work and Sheikh Zahir's idea of it did not coincide. 'Well, great,' she said, taking the worksheet to check out where they were going, wishing it was Freddy she was taking for a day on the beach. Somehow she couldn't see James Pierce taking off his shoes, rolling up his trouser legs and going for a paddle.

Zahir, on the other hand...

She refused to go with that image. *No more of that, my girl, she told herself. Behave yourself. Just concentrate on all the extra hours it will mean.* The extra money. She might be able to manage something a bit special for her and Freddy in the half-term holiday. A short break at Disney-land Paris, perhaps, if she was lucky enough to grab a cheap last-minute deal.

Or maybe she'd be better advised putting the money in her savings account for his future. Except, of course that children didn't understand the concept of the 'future'. For them there was only *now*.

'Okay?' Sadie asked, when she didn't move.

'Fine. I was just wondering if you wanted me to bring you back a stick of rock,' she joked.

'I'll pass, thanks,' Sadie said with a grin. 'Besides, I doubt the kind of marina that a sheikh would patronize has much call for bright pink candy, do you?'

A timely reminder, should she need one, that he lived in a different world from the one she'd been born into. A reminder she'd do well to keep front and centre next time he looked at her. Smiled at her. Murmured something in that seductive voice.

Maybe she should invest in a pair of earplugs…

Sheikh Zahir was standing on the footpath talking to James Pierce when she pulled in to the front of the hotel three minutes before ten.

He was dressed casually in a cream linen jacket, softly pleated chinos, a dark brown band-collar shirt left open at the neck, with a slim leather document case hanging loosely from one hand. James Pierce, on the other hand, was giving no quarter to a day by the sea. He was dressed in a pinstripe suit with a sober silk tie—full city-slicker gear—with the laptop which never seemed to leave his side clamped firmly in his fist.

She groaned.

James Pierce had had it in for her from the moment he'd set eyes on her and would no doubt have some sarcastic remark all lined up to deliver on the subject of having been kept waiting; she was sure the fact that *they* were early would cut no ice with him.

He'd grumbled about being kept waiting last night; anyone would think she'd loitered, had stopped for a burger or something, instead of taking a straight there-and-back run from Mayfair.

But as Zahir caught sight of her—no smile of any kind—
he said something to the other man, then, as Top Hat opened
the door, stepped into the back of the car.

Alone.

James Pierce, having taken a moment to give her what
could only be described as a 'look'—what *was* his problem?—turned and walked back into the hotel.

Which meant that they were going to spend the entire day
alone together?

Be careful what you wish for…

'In your own time, Metcalfe,' Zahir said, when she didn't
immediately pull away.

'Isn't Mr Pierce coming with us?' she asked a touch
desperately.

'He can't spare the time. He has contracts, leases to sign.
A lawyer's work is never done.' Unable to help herself, she
checked the mirror. He was waiting for her, his look thoughtful. 'Disappointed, Metcalfe? Did you manage to break the
ice and make friends when you picked him up last night?'

'We didn't dance, if that's what you mean,' she said. So
much for keeping her distance. Being professional. 'I didn't
want to drive off and leave him if he'd just gone back inside
to collect something he'd forgotten,' she said in an attempt to
retrieve the situation.

'Forgotten?' Zahir marginally raised a single brow. 'Are
you suggesting that he's fallible?'

'Oh… No…'

Too late she realised that he was being ironic.

Oh, Lord…

She pulled out into Park Lane, glad of the turmoil of the
London traffic to keep her occupied, not that there were any
further distractions from the rear of the car.

Sheikh Zahir, having teased her once, presumably in repay-
ment for that 'dancing' remark, was apparently too absorbed

by the paperwork he'd brought with him to bother once they were on their way.

Which should have been a relief.

But it was like waiting for the other shoe to drop.

First her shoulder muscles began to tighten up, then her neck stiffened with the effort of keeping her mouth shut. Would music disturb him?

She glanced in the mirror, saw that he was deep in concentration. Had, apparently, forgotten she was there. An example she'd do well to follow.

Zahir stared at the papers in front of him, doing his best to concentrate on the figures, trying not to think about the woman in front of him, the nape of her neck exposed by hair swept up under her cap. Hair that even now was escaping in soft tendrils that brushed against her pale skin.

Trying not to think about how that hair, that skin had felt against his hand. The way his hand had nestled so neatly into her waist. How her fingers had felt against his lips.

His sister's email, annoying though it had been, had brought him firmly back to earth and he was resolute in his determination that this charming but, ultimately, foolish flirtation he'd begun without a thought for the consequences must go no further. Diana Metcalfe deserved better from him.

His family deserved better from him.

Today, he reminded himself, was all about the marina at Nadira Creek.

Lunch at the local yacht club with the CEO of the chandlery with whom he was negotiating a contract to run the dockside services for him. Then a tour of the Sweethaven Marina to take a look at the facilities offered at the top end of the business, which would also give him a chance to check out the latest in state-of-the-art sailing dinghies, diving equipment, windsurfers.

Last, but definitely not least, a visit to the boatyard to look at the yacht he'd commissioned more than a year ago and was now ready for his pre-delivery inspection.

And that was the only indulgence he would permit himself on this trip; the silk finish of polished mahogany and gleaming brass were a great deal safer than the touch of soft ivory skin. Warm lips.

Finalising the details of a contract was considerably less dangerous than teasing Diana Metcalfe in the hope of another glimpse of an errant dimple that appeared at the corner of her mouth when she was battling not to smile. And losing.

Safer all round than provoking her into forgetting to be polite, to just be herself. And then kissing her. Waltzing her along London streets…

He took out the folder detailing the management fees, working through the list of queries James had detailed, equally firm in his resolve not to catch her eye in the mirror.

Not to ask about her family. Why it was her father 'used' to sing to her mother. And, presumably, didn't now. Her life.

Ask her why, when she wasn't smiling, she sometimes looked a little…lost.

Diana checked the mirror as she approached a roundabout, joined the motorway. Sheikh Zahir was working, concentrating on the file he was holding, and yet she had the strongest feeling that, a split second before she'd glanced up, he'd been looking not at his papers, but at her, waiting for that moment when she'd checked the mirror, met his gaze.

Or maybe that was what she wanted to believe.

She was clearly going crazy.

It wasn't that she doubted his readiness to flirt; he'd already proved himself to be world class in the subject and she'd promised herself that today she wouldn't be drawn in, but keep her cool. Be a professional. Not because she knew James Pierce would rat on her to Sadie in a heartbeat if he suspected she'd stepped over some invisible, but definite, line in the sand. No matter how great the temptation. And she had been tempted; admitting to it made resistance easier.

Not because of her job, but because, to Sheikh Zahir, it would be no more than a diversion.

Probably.

No! Absolutely.

Utterly meaningless.

In which case, why would he think twice about snagging her attention? If it meant nothing, he'd do it. Wouldn't he?

Oh, get a grip, Di! Why on earth would a man with a stunningly beautiful princess hanging off his arm even look at you?

Good question. He had looked, looked again and then he'd touched, danced…

Maybe he couldn't help himself. If the newspapers were anything to go by, powerful men often couldn't. Help themselves. And power was, or so she'd heard, an aphrodisiac. Women probably threw themselves at him all the time. Maybe he considered her, as his female driver, to be fair game. A perk of the job.

A little squeak of distress escaped her and she caught a movement in the mirror as he looked up. Then, after a moment, looked away.

No. That was wrong.

Zahir wasn't like that.

He hadn't kissed her like that.

It hadn't been a grope. It had been the sweetest kiss. And if he'd expected more, he would never have left her last night, walked away.

Nevertheless, she took her sunglasses from the dashboard, flicked them open and put them on. A personal safety barrier against further eye-contact in the mirror, accidental or not.

A long, silent hour later, she pulled into the car park on the quay at Sweethaven, once a small fishing port but now the playground for well-heeled yachting types with all the money in the world to indulge their passion.

Tucked into folds of the Downs, where the river widened into an estuary before running into the sea, the small, picture-perfect town was well served with expensive shops and attractive restaurants.

The whole place positively shouted money; or was that the sound of ropes, or sheets, or whatever they were called, clanging against the masts of the flotilla of expensive yachts moored in the marina?

She opened the rear door while her passenger was still stuffing papers into his document case. Stepping out of the car, he handed it to her.

'Come with me, Metcalfe.'

What?

'Um…'

He glanced back. 'Lose the hat.'

Her hand flew, in a protective gesture, to her head.

'You don't like it?' she demanded, completely forgetting her determination to keep her lip buttoned. Or that she loathed the thing herself.

Drawing attention to herself was a mistake. He stopped, turned, taking a slow tour of her appearance, from sensible shoes, via trousers cut for comfort, a slightly fitted collarless jacket that was cut short above her hips until, finally, his gaze came to rest on that hat.

'I don't like anything you're wearing. Be grateful it's only the hat I want you to take off.'

For a moment she stood open-mouthed, but he'd already turned away and was walking towards a two-storey stone building with a sign that read 'Sweethaven Yacht Club'.

Who was that?

And what had he done with the Sheikh Zahir she'd danced with last night?

To think she'd been giving him the benefit of…

'Grateful!' She tossed the hat, along with her driving gloves, into the car. Then, on an impulse, she unbuttoned her jacket and added it to the pile and pulled out one of Capitol's burgundy sweatshirts that she'd stowed in case of emergencies—you wouldn't want to change a wheel in your best uniform jacket—and knotted it around her shoulders. Pulled a face at her reflection in the wing mirror. 'At least the man has taste.'

There was, she reminded herself, the beautiful princess as prima facie evidence of the fact. Which was maybe why, having removed her jacket, she clung to the safety barrier of the sunglasses. She pushed them firmly up her nose, locked the car and, taking a deep breath, tucked the folder under her arm and went after him.

Zahir, having reached the safe haven of the yacht club's entrance lobby, stopped to gather himself.

He could not believe he'd said that. Had no excuse, other than the build-up of tension, seeing Diana so close, knowing that she was out of reach.

When she'd done that not-quite-meeting-his-eyes thing, something inside him had snapped and, knowing that an invitation wouldn't bring her to him, he'd made it an order. And then had made a remark so blatantly personal that her shock had been palpable.

Maybe that was the answer, he thought, as he eased his shoulders. Maybe, if she thought he was some kind of sexual predator, she wouldn't have to fight quite so hard to contain that tormenting little smile…

'Zahir! I saw you arrive and was beginning to think you'd forgotten the way. Come on up…'

* * *

As Diana stepped inside the yacht club, everything went suddenly dark and, with the utmost reluctance, she pushed the glasses up into her hair and looked around.

A receptionist, regarding her with a smile, said, 'They're upstairs.'

'Oh, right. Thanks.'

Upstairs proved to be not offices but a restaurant and bar where Zahir and another man, of about the same age but slighter and with his face weathered by sun and sea, were standing.

They both turned as she approached. Zahir hesitated for no more than a heartbeat as he took in her appearance, before extending a hand to draw her into their conversation.

'Metcalfe, this is Jeff Michaels. He's going to buy us lunch.'

Lunch?

Zahir didn't wait for her to protest. Didn't give her time to consider whether she wanted to protest. That was probably a good thing, since he'd put her in a situation where it was impossible for her to tell him that this was *seriously* inappropriate. At least not without making them both look stupid.

Taking full advantage of her stunned silence—probably realising that it wouldn't last—he turned to his companion and said, 'Jeff, Diana Metcalfe is one of my UK team.'

'Delighted to meet you, Diana,' he said, offering his hand as if she were a *real* person. Reacting on automatic pilot, she took it, doing her best to respond to his welcoming smile. 'Can I get you something to drink?'

Um... Um... Um...

The confusion lingered, but thankfully the gibbering 'ums' remained locked up inside her head—'team' members did not 'um'—and, gathering herself, she said, 'Water, thanks. Still.'

Jeff nodded to the barman, glanced around at the busy bar and said, 'It'll be quieter on the terrace.' Before Zahir could answer, he turned to her, 'That's if you'll be warm enough, Diana?'

A little too warm if the truth were told, although it wasn't the ambient temperature that was heating her up but the fact that Zahir had hijacked her without so much as a by-your-leave.

What was he *thinking?*

Hadn't he learned a thing from his little moonlighting jaunt as a waiter? Food, more specifically feeding a woman, could lead a man into all kinds of temptation. Lead a woman, for that matter.

She tried not to look at him, but couldn't help herself. His face, however, offered no help, no clue to his thoughts. She'd seen him do that before, she realised, in the toy store, with a smile that was no more than a disguise. A mask to cover any hint of what he was feeling.

Then, and later when James Pierce had joined them, he'd given her a glimpse behind the mask, had drawn her into his private world with a silent invitation to become his fellow conspirator.

There was no smile hidden in the depths of his cool grey eyes now. Even the sensuous droop of his lower lip had been jacked up into a straight line.

Whatever he was thinking, he was making damn sure no one else knew. Including her. And tempting though it was to provoke some kind of a response she very much doubted he'd be amused if she excused herself on the grounds that today she'd had the forethought to provide herself with a packed lunch.

Played the thanks-but-no-thanks, see-you-later gambit.

Instead she gave Jeff one of her best smiles and said, 'I'll be perfectly warm enough, thank you.'

'This way, then.' He lifted an avuncular arm to usher her towards the terrace, then, obviously thinking better of it, let it drop, instead leading the way to a sheltered corner.

It was one of those perfect May days, the temperature in the mid-seventies, with just enough breeze at the coast to fill the sails of a flotilla of dinghies that were making a picture postcard scene of the estuary.

'Do you sail?' Jeff asked, following her gaze.

'No.' She sat down. Then, smiling up at him, 'Never had the opportunity.'

'Hopefully you will do soon," Jeff replied.

'As I said, Metcalfe is part of my UK team,' Zahir interposed smoothly. 'I'm in the process of setting up an office in London. If everything goes to plan, James will stay here and run it.'

'Expensive. I'd have thought it would be more cost effective to leave this end of things to specialist travel agents.'

'For the purely tourist end of the business, I agree.'

'You're expanding your business?'

'A business not expanding is a business in decline.'

'Right…'

The steward arrived with their drinks and the menu, and taking advantage of the distraction, Zahir looked across at her and their shared knowledge was like an electric spark leaping across a vacuum.

'It's just bar meals at lunchtime during the week, I'm afraid,' Jeff said, apologising to her rather than Zahir, then, apparently catching the intensity of the look that passed between them, fell silent.

'A sandwich is the most I ever eat in the middle of the day,' Diana said, filling the gap, when Zahir remained silent. 'And I don't always get that.' Then, when Jeff had gone through to the bar to place their order, she whispered urgently, 'What are you doing? Why am I here?'

For a moment she thought he wasn't going to answer, then, with a lift of his shoulders, he said, 'To create a level playing field.'

'What?'

'I find you distracting, Metcalfe. It's not your fault—you can't help how you look—but if I'm to be distracted, it's only fair that Jeff should be similarly handicapped. It seems to be working. He can't keep his eyes off you.'

She stared at him.

In her uniform, flat shoes, absolute minimum of make-up, she was about as distracting as lukewarm soup in the middle of winter. 'What on earth are you talking about?'

He blinked slowly and without warning a hot surge of colour rushed to her cheeks. 'Oh, no…'

'You distracted me when I should have been glad-handing journalists, although I have to say that the sheer effort of keeping you out of my head gave me a real edge over dinner last night. Those bankers didn't know what had hit them.'

'You did seem a little high last night. If you don't mind me saying so.'

'Billion dollar deals tend to have that effect. Make me want to sing, to dance…'

'Zahir!'

'You see. You say my name and I can't even decide what I want for lunch. Distracting.'

'If that's the case, then it would probably be a good thing if I left you to it and went for a walk,' she said, getting to her feet.

And he got himself another driver for tomorrow.

'Stay where you are, Diana.' Before she could open her mouth to protest, he added, 'Out of sight is not out of mind.'

'This is outrageous.' She glared at him. 'You expect me to sit here and "distract" the man, while you pull your tycoon act and take him to the cleaners?'

'Did I say that?'

'What else could you possibly mean?' she demanded. And she had the doubtful pleasure of seeing the impassive mask slip, feeling the heat from eyes that were—momentarily—anything but cool. 'You're quite mad, you know,' she said, subsiding into her chair, not in obedience to his command but because her legs refused to keep her upright. 'I'm not some *femme fatale.*'

'No?' Then, after a moment's thought, 'No.'

Dammit, he wasn't supposed to agree with her! And this

was definitely not the moment for him to smile. If that lip moved, sheikh or not, he was cats' meat…

Maybe he recognised the danger because he managed to restrain himself, confine himself to an apparently careless shrug.

'In that case, why are you making such a fuss?'

CHAPTER SIX

MAKING a fool of herself, more like.

Diana swallowed but her mouth was suddenly dry and she picked up her glass with a hand that was visibly shaking and took a mouthful of water.

She'd known, right from the beginning, that Sheikh Zahir wasn't going to be a conventional passenger. He might not have lived up to her Lawrence of Arabia fantasy, but it was obvious, from the moment that boy had cannoned into him, from that first meeting of eyes through the rear-view mirror, that he was going to be trouble.

For her.

And the kind of disturbance that even now was churning beneath her waistband confirmed her worst fears.

Inappropriate? This wasn't just inappropriate. This was plain stupid and Sadie would have an absolute fit if she had the slightest idea of just how unprofessionally she had behaved right from the very beginning.

Chatting to him as if he were someone she'd met in a bus queue. Dragging him off to The Toy Warehouse and giving him the down-and-dirty gossip on the frog and princess scandal. Sharing canapés with him on a riverside bench when he should have been working the media.

Sharing an earth-shattering, world-changing kiss with a man whose 'partner' was inside the gallery, taking the strain.

All mouth, no brains, that was her.

There was absolutely no way there could be a personal connection between them other than some brief sexual dalliance which would obviously be a meaningless fling for him—and she felt a moment of pity for the beautiful princess—while it could only be damaging to her, professionally and personally. Even supposing she was the kind of woman who 'flung' around with a man who was attached, no matter how loosely, to another woman.

Who 'flung' full stop.

One fling had got her into enough trouble to last a lifetime.

And if he had anything else in mind, well he was the dumb one. He was a sheikh. She was a chauffeur. He was so far out of her orbit that he might as well be on Mars and it didn't need the brains of Einstein to figure out how that equation would work out.

It wasn't even as if she was fancy-free, at liberty to indulge herself, take the risk, no matter how self-destructively. She had responsibilities. A five-year-old son she would always put first, not out of duty, but out of love.

Why, oh, why, couldn't her big chance have come on the day when the car had been booked to drive some grey, middle-aged executive whose only interest was the movement of the FTSE or the NASDAQ?

Someone who wouldn't even have noticed she existed.

'Tomorrow,' she began, determined to put a stop to this before one of them did something really stupid. Something that she, at least, would regret—and she already had enough of those to last her a lifetime. Before she forgot all of the above and began to believe what his eyes seemed to be saying. 'Tomorrow,' she repeated, with determination…

'Tomorrow I'm flying to Paris,' he said, cutting her short

before she could tell him that tomorrow he'd have another driver. If not Jack, someone else would have to take over from her, although what on earth she'd tell Sadie…

Somehow she didn't think, 'He looked at me and I came over all *inappropriate*…' would go down at all well. She'd be lucky to keep the school run. But she'd have to take that risk. Better to lose her job than fall back into a pit it had taken her months, years, to climb out of.

'Want to come?' he said, jerking her back to the here and now.

'To Paris. With you?'

'The alternative is being at James's beck and call.'

'Oh.'

What was that about being careful what you wished for? Although, if it meant she could keep this job for another day…

'Well, great!'

He wasn't fooled for a minute. 'He's not a soft touch like me, Diana. You'd probably be advised to bring a packed lunch,' he said. And then he smiled.

Not the mask smile. Not the meaningless one that had so annoyed her when he'd used it to reduce a careless shop assistant to slavery. But the one that spoke directly to her, that said, 'We are connected, you and I. Deny it all you want, but you know the truth.'

It took her good intentions, all her common sense and heated them to dust, blew them away, leaving her momentarily struggling for breath.

'I brought a packed lunch today,' she said. 'I was going to sit on the harbour wall and share it with the seagulls.'

'Were you? Well, the day is a long way from over. Maybe we could do that later.'

We…

'It won't be long,' Jeff said, rejoining them before she could say anything. Just as well. For the second time that day she was lost for words. That had to be a record… 'Do you want to clear up any final details on the contract while we're waiting?'

'I'm really quite happy with it,' Zahir replied, 'but, Metcalfe had a few queries.' He held out his hand for the folder she'd put on the table in front of her. She handed them over without a word and Zahir extracted a single sheet of paper from the file and offered it to the other man. 'If we can iron out these few details, keep her happy, you can have your office print up the final version and I'll sign it before I leave.'

Jeff glanced at the figures, then, thoughtfully, at her. She gripped her lower lip between her teeth to keep it tightly closed.

'There's no kidding you, is there?' he said with a wry grin in her direction. 'If I conceded the first three without an argument, will you consider splitting the difference on the management fee?'

Zahir rescued her, holding up a hand as if to silence her. 'Don't be hard on the man, Diana. That's fair.' Then, offering the hand to Jeff, 'We have a deal.'

If Diana had felt any concern about Zahir's intentions, Jeff's broad smile quickly reassured her.

'I'll fly out to Nadira next week to set things in motion, Zahir,' he said. Then, turning to her, 'Will I see you there, Diana?'

She'd just picked up her glass and taken a swallow of water, so Zahir answered for her.

'I'm hoping Diana will accept my invitation to familiarize herself with the resort in the very near future. If you're there at the same time we'll be glad to repay your hospitality.'

She choked and the water took the only available exit and shot out of her nose.

Gasping, shaking her head, completely unable to speak, she leapt to her feet and rushed off in the direction of the washroom.

Now what was he playing at?

Since she had no possible way of knowing, she concentrated on the practicalities of mopping the water from the front of her shirt while she regained her breath and her composure. Took her time about refastening the unravelling mess of her hair. Groped in her pocket for lipstick and came up empty. Remembered, too late, that she'd left it in her jacket pocket. Just as well; her lips had got her into enough trouble already without drawing unnecessary attention to them.

Finally, unable to put it off any longer, she returned to the terrace, where the two men were deep in a conversation involving boats.

Zahir looked up. 'Okay?'

'Fine. Thank you,' she said primly.

His only response was one of those quiet smiles that undid all the hard work of the last five minutes. At least with regard to breathing and composure.

It was all very well saying that he'd be in Paris tomorrow—and no, she couldn't possibly go with him—but she had the rest of today to get through before then.

And no escape.

The rest of lunch, however, proved uneventful since Zahir was more interested in what Jeff had to say than in winding her up. And, like an idiot, she actually found herself missing their dangerous exchanges.

Just how stupid could one woman get?

Afterwards, the two men set off to tour the marina and it was Jeff, not Zahir, who glanced back and said, 'Can we tempt you to join us, or are you more interested in the shops than boats?'

Freddy, Diana thought, would have been in his element amongst the boats. He loved going on river trips. And that was what they'd do this half-term. A jaunt up to Greenwich on the river to look at the Cutty Sark and the Maritime Museum. They could even take a ride on a narrow boat along the Regent's Canal to the Zoo.

She realised that they were waiting for her answer.

Or had she been waiting for Zahir to add his voice to the invitation? Encourage her to join them?

'The shops have it, every time,' she replied quickly, taking the wiser course and putting as much distance between them as possible.

The way things were going, he was bound to say something, give her one of those ironic looks that would leave her with an uncontrollable desire to push him into the harbour—and how would she explain *that* to Sadie?

'How long have I got?'

'How long do you need?' Zahir replied. Then, with a smile that suggested he knew exactly what was going on in her head, said, 'An hour should do it.'

She collected her wallet from the glove box, stuffed it into her trouser pocket and set off for the town centre. Although the possibility that she'd be able to afford anything in the small, exotic boutiques they'd passed on their way down to the quay was totally nil, she'd enjoy the window-shopping. She might be short of spare cash, but she could dream.

But Sweethaven, she discovered, had more to offer than just designer boutiques and when she saw a real old-fashioned bookshop she pushed open the door and went inside.

She browsed for something for her father. Found a paperback thriller that she knew he'd love. Then she spotted a circular stand containing the small children's books that she'd loved as a child and, as she spun it, looking for something that Freddy would enjoy, she found herself face to face with a familiar title in the fairy tale series.

She took it down, flipping through it, smiling at the remembered pictures, including the Prince, no longer a frog but respectably buttoned up to the neck in a fancy uniform as he stood beside the astonished princess.

On an impulse she picked it up, found another with every

kind of nautical knot for Freddy, before realising that time was running out and hurrying back to the quayside car park. Zahir and Jeff were already there.

'I'm sorry…' she began as Jeff shook hands with Zahir, raised a hand to her and returned to his office.

'No problem. We've only just got here. Did you find anything exciting?' Then, seeing the name on the paper carrier she was holding, 'Books?'

She'd been going to give *The Princess and the Frog* to him, just to make him laugh. Quite suddenly, it didn't seem such a bright idea. 'They're children's books,' she said.

'Oh? Whose children?'

Tell him…

Tell him and see that look? The speculative You've-got-a-kid? look. The one that says, Whoa! Easy…

While she stood there, frozen, he took the carrier from her, opened it and took out the thriller and held it up. 'This is what you give children to read?'

She snatched it from him. 'That's for my dad.'

He took another look in the bag and this time came up with the book of knots that she'd bought for Freddy. 'He's a sailor?'

'He was a taxi-driver. He had a stroke.'

That set him back. 'I'm sorry, Diana.'

'He's not an invalid.'

'But he can't drive?'

'No.'

He gave her a long measuring look, then took out the last book. And that made him smile. 'Oh, I get it. You wanted to check your version against the original.'

She shook her head. 'I was close enough, but when I saw it I thought of Ameerah,' she said, fingers crossed. 'Maybe she'd like it to go with her snow globe?'

'I'm sure she'd love it.'

'Good.' She reclaimed the bag, put the books away. 'I'll

wrap it for her,' she said, tucking it beneath her seat. 'You can give it to her on Saturday.'

'Why don't you give it to her yourself?'

'She doesn't know me,' she said abruptly.

'You can remedy that while we chug down the Regent's Canal.'

She wondered if he'd be as eager for her company if she suggested she bring her five-year-old son along for the ride. The one whose father had been a villain.

'I don't think so. Are you ready to go?'

He nodded but, as she backed out of the car to open the rear door for him, she discovered that he'd walked around and opened the front passenger door.

'If I sit in the back, Jeff, who's watching us from his office window right now, might just get the impression that you're no more than my chauffeur,' he said in response to her obvious confusion. 'You wouldn't want that, would you?'

'I don't actually give a damn what he thinks,' she replied. Definitely not a response out of the perfect chauffeur's handbook, but then he wasn't the perfect client. 'But you're the boss. If you want to sit in front, then sit in front.'

'Thank you for that. I was beginning to wonder for a moment. About being the boss.'

'Making me responsible for contract negotiation must have gone to my head,' she replied, before replacing her sunglasses and sliding in beside him. Bumping shoulders as he leaned towards her as he pulled down the seat belt, so that she jumped. Smiling at her as he slid it home with a click.

He was much too close. It was more than the physical effect of his wide shoulders, overflowing the seat beside her. His *presence* was invading her space, along with some subtle male scent that made him impossible to ignore and, despite her determinedly spirited, in-your-face response, her hand was shaking as she attempted to programme the SatNav with their next destination.

Five years and she hadn't once been tempted. Had never taken a second look at a man, no matter how gorgeous. Particularly if they were gorgeous.

Pete O'Hanlon had head-turning good looks. His only 'good' characteristic, but when you were eighteen and deep in lust you didn't see that.

Since then, she'd never felt even a twinge of that lose-your-head, forget lose-your-heart—desire that she'd read about. Had heard her girlfriends talk about. Hadn't understood it.

Not that she was taking any credit for that. Her life was complicated enough without making things even more difficult for herself. Motherhood, guilt had drained every scrap of emotion she'd had to spare. Add a full-time job and who had time?

And then…wham. Out of the blue there it was. The pumping heart, the racing pulse, something darker, more urgent, that was totally different, indescribably new, that she didn't even want to think about.

Making a pretence of double checking the address, she said, 'Do I get an explanation for what happened back there? The real reason you took me into your meeting with Jeff?'

He shook his head. 'It was—nothing.'

'Pretending that I was what? Your tame number-cruncher querying his figures? That was nothing?'

'Jeff was always going to agree to those changes—they were fair, believe me—but, since you were there I realised I could cut short the haggling.'

'Really?' The question was rhetorical. Ironic.

'Really. What man could resist flattering a pretty woman?'

'Remind me never to do business with you.'

'You wouldn't have any reason to regret it, Diana.'

Was that a proposition?

She glanced at him and then just as quickly turned away

as the tremor affecting her hand raced through the rest of her body so that she had to grip the steering wheel.

It sounded horribly like one.

'I've got nothing to offer you,' she managed, 'other than entertainment value and, just once, a short cut to a signature on the dotted line.'

'Diana—'

'I hope you both had a jolly good laugh when I snorted a mouthful of water down my nose.'

'It was an interesting reaction to my invitation to visit Nadira.'

Without meaning to, she looked at him. He was not laughing. Far from it.

'*That* was an invitation?' she asked disparagingly, as she tore her gaze away from him.

'You want a gold-edged card? Sheikh Zahir al-Khatib requests the pleasure…'

'I want absolutely nothing,' she said, furious with him. Furious with herself for letting him see that she cared. 'I just want to do the job I'm paid for.'

'It's no big deal, Diana,' he said carelessly. 'There'll be spare room on the media junket.'

'Oh, right. *Now* I'm tempted.'

How dared he! How damn well dared he invite her to his fancy resort for a week of sex in the sand—including her as a tax write-off along with the freebie-demanding journalists—and say it was 'no big deal'! That she would have no reason to regret it.

Too bad that the first man she had looked at since Freddy's father was not only out of her reach, but a twenty-four carat…sheikh. Her judgement where men were concerned was still, it seemed, just as rotten…

Zahir had actually been congratulating himself on his self-control as he'd climbed out of the car on their arrival at Sweethaven.

There had been a difficult moment right at the beginning of the journey when he could have easily lost it. He only had to look at Diana Metcalfe for his mind to take off without him. But he'd got a grip, had jerked it back into line, forcing himself to concentrate on what had to be done. Ignore the possibilities of what he deeply, seriously, wanted to do…

Had managed, just about, to keep his tongue between his teeth and his head down—mostly—for nearly two hours and since, like him, Diana had, after that dangerous first exchange, taken avoiding action and hidden her expressive eyes behind dark glasses, they'd travelled from the heart of London to the coast in a silence broken only by the occasional interjection of the navigation system offering direction.

It should have made things easier but, without the oddly intimate exchanges through the rear-view mirror that were driving this unexpected, unlooked for, *impossible* connection, he'd found himself noticing other things.

The shape of her ear—small and slightly pointed at the tip.

A fine gold chain around her neck that was only visible when she leaned forward slightly to check that the road was clear at a junction.

The smooth curve of her cheek as she glanced sideways to check her wing mirrors. He'd found himself forgetting the document he was holding as he'd been captivated by the slow unwinding of a strand of hair.

It was scarcely surprising that when, on their arrival at Sweethaven he'd been confronted by her standing stiffly, almost to attention, as he'd stepped out of the car—he'd lost it so completely that he'd found himself issuing not an invitation, but an order for her to join him.

Actually, on reflection, he hadn't got that bit wrong. The order part. An invitation would never have got her. An invitation offered her a choice which she would have had the good sense to decline.

She knew, they both knew, that there was, or at least should be, a barrier—a glass wall—between them. It had shattered, not when he'd kissed her, but with that ridiculous antique snow globe.

Diana, trapped in her role, was doing her best to repair the damage and he knew that nothing other than a direct order would have brought her into the yacht club. If he'd left it at that it might, just, have been okay, but he'd had to throw in that comment about her hat… And he refused to fool himself about the reason for it.

He'd wanted to see her hair again, the way it had been last night, when she'd stood by the river with the breeze tugging strands loose from her pins. Softly curled chestnut silk that had brushed against her neck, her cheek, his hand…

And it had been downhill all the way from there.

He'd stepped way beyond anything that could be considered acceptable behaviour when she'd challenged him and first his body, and then his mouth, had bypassed his brain.

He knew it would be a mistake to look at her now.

Could not stop himself.

She was staring straight ahead, the only movement the flicker of her eyes as she checked the mirror. If he'd been bright enough to sit in the back, he could have used that to catch her attention…

But then he'd have missed this profile. Missed her stubborn little chin, her mouth set firm, almost as if she were fighting to keep it shut. There was not a sign of that sweet dimple, just a flush to her cheeks that gave a whole new meaning to the old 'you look magnificent when you're angry' cliché.

The strange thing was, he couldn't remember ever having made a woman angry before. But then he'd never felt like this about any woman and maybe that was the point. To feel passionately, it had to matter. To her as well as to him.

Maybe that was why he was angry with himself. He didn't do this. Had never, in all his thirty years, lost his head over a woman, no matter how beautiful, elegant, clever. His detachment—and theirs—had been a safety net, an acknowledgement that no matter how enjoyable the relationship, it was superficial, fleeting. Because, even though he'd deferred the inevitable, putting it off for as long as possible, he'd always known that his future was, as his cousin had suggested, written.

That his choice of bride was not his alone, but part of a tradition that went back through the ages as a way of strengthening tribal bonds.

His head understood, accepted that kind of power-broking, but then he'd walked out of the airport into the sunlight of a May morning and, in an instant, or so it seemed now, he'd been possessed by a girl who had nothing to commend her but an hourglass figure, a dimple and a total inability to keep her mouth shut.

And it was that mouth, her complete lack of control over it, rather than her luscious figure, that had hooked his attention. Had somehow enchanted him.

Diana slowed, signalled, turned into the boatyard. Gravel crunched beneath the tyres for a moment and then she drew up in the lee of a boathouse and the silence returned.

She made no move to get out, open the door for him, but remained with her hands on the wheel, looking straight ahead. He unclipped his seatbelt, half turned towards her and when that didn't get her attention either, he said, 'I'm sorry.'

He found the rarely used words unexpectedly easy to say. Maybe because he meant them. He *was* sorry. Wished he could start the day over. Start from where they'd left off last night.

If it hadn't been for that damned email, reminding him that, while he'd escaped one future, there were some duties he could not escape…

Diana's breath caught on a little sigh, her lips softened, but still she didn't look at him, still held herself aloof, at a distance.

'If I promise that I will never embarrass you in that way

again, do you think you might just deign to come down off your high horse and talk to me?'

'High horse!' She swung round and glared at him. 'I'm not on any high horse!'

Indignant was better than silent. Indignant, her eyes flashed green. Indignant might so easily spill over into laughter. She laughed so easily. Made him want to laugh as no woman ever had…

'Eighteen hands at the very least,' he said, pushing it.

She shrugged, spread her hands in an 'and that means?' gesture.

He responded by raising a hand above his shoulder.

She swallowed. 'Good grief, we're talking carthorse, here.' Then, when he didn't respond with anything more than a twitch of his eyebrows, 'I might—*might*—just admit to a slightly overgrown Shetland pony.'

'One of those small, plump creatures with the uncontrollable manes?' he enquired, encouraged by the fleeting appearance of that dimple.

'They're the ones,' she admitted, doing her best to swallow down the smile that was trying very hard to break through. Then, having, against all the odds, succeeded, she added, 'Much more my style than some long-legged thoroughbred, wouldn't you say?'

'A perfect match,' he said.

For once she had no swift comeback and for the longest moment they just looked at each other, neither of them saying a word. But smiling was the furthest thing from either of their minds.

CHAPTER SEVEN

'DON'T you have an appointment to keep?'

It was Diana, not him, who finally broke the silence after what might have been an age, but was nowhere near long enough.

'Nothing involving money.' Zahir fought down the temptation to reach out, touch his fingers to her lips to silence her so that they could return to that moment of perfect understanding. Instead, he went for a wry smile. 'I'll rephrase that. It involves a great deal of money, but the negotiations were done and dusted months ago. I'm here to take possession of the finished article.'

'Which, since we're in a boatyard, I'm guessing would be a boat?' she said, looking around her at the vast boat-building sheds, the craft pulled out of the water and propped up in cradles awaiting work.

'Got it in one and you know how it is with a new toy. It's no fun unless you can show it off to someone.'

Her gaze returned to him. It was direct, straightforward. Honest. She might blush like a girl, but there was none of that irritating coyness about her. She was direct in her look, direct in every way. Even as she acknowledged the truth of his remark with the smallest tilt of her head, she said, 'Am I the best you can do?'

He sensed more than simple bafflement that he'd choose

to display his latest acquisition to his chauffeur. Suspected that her question was loaded, but he played along, turning to look in the back of the car.

'I can't see anyone else. Of course, if you would really prefer to stay here and feed the seagulls?'

Diana knew that feeding the seagulls was the safe option. The sensible option. But, for some reason, she wasn't doing sensible this week.

If she had been, she'd have politely accepted Zahir's apology and left it at that. Too late now, but then their relationship had gone far beyond politeness. Beyond the point at which she could pretend that she was just his chauffeur and use the car as her defence. The fact that he'd asked, rather than ordered only underlined that point.

He was learning.

Pity she couldn't do the same, she thought, as she opened the car door and stepped out, catching her breath as the breeze whipped at her hair.

At the marina, the sea, sheltered in the narrow estuary that the river had carved through the hills and corralled by wooden landing stages, had seemed deceptively tame.

Here the sea was a live thing, constantly on the move as it slapped against the concrete slipway, sucked at the shingle. Even the air tasted of salt.

She turned to Zahir, who was standing beside the car, waiting.

Tall, dark and so dangerous that he should have, *Warning! Close Contact With This Man Can Seriously Damage Your Peace of Mind!* stamped on his forehead.

The fact that he'd been able to tease her out of her strop the moment he'd put his mind to it was ample demonstration of the danger she was in. How would she ever be able to resist him if he really made an effort?

If he wanted more than a kiss…

She shook her head, recognising somewhere, deep inside

her where she refused to go, that his apology had been a rare thing. That he had been making a very special effort.

That resistance was imperative. And, taking a slow calming breath, she turned to face him.

'If you wanted to show off your new toy,' she asked, 'why didn't you bring the Princess with you?'

'Princess?'

He was good. He really looked as if he didn't know what, who, she was talking about.

'Tall,' she prompted, holding her hand several inches above her own pitiful height. 'Blonde.' She couldn't quite bring herself to say *beautiful*. 'Your partner, according to James Pierce?'

He leaned back, his brows drawn down in a puzzled frown. 'Do you mean Lucy?'

'I don't know. How many tall, blonde partners do you have?' she snapped, angry that he wouldn't just own up, tell her the truth. That while he was flirting with her, kissing her, dancing with her, he had a thoroughbred filly at home in the stable.

Angry with herself for allowing him to waltz away with her, when she knew…

'You were talking to her when I returned the tray. If that helps,' she prompted. 'She was wearing a pale grey…'

'I'm with you,' he said, getting the picture. 'But calling her my partner is stretching it a bit.'

'Surely you are or you aren't,' she said, hating him for not being honest with her. Hating herself for caring…

'It's not like that.'

'No? What is it like, Zahir?'

'What is it like?'

His long look left her in no doubt that she'd exposed herself, had revealed feelings that would have been better kept hidden and, damn it, she was really good at 'hidden'. She could keep a secret better than anyone she knew. She'd had years of practice…

'It doesn't matter,' she said, turning away, but he stopped her. All it took was a touch to her shoulder.

'It's like this, Diana.'

And she turned back. Forget the way he looked, the way he smiled so that she felt like the only person in the world. Who could resist that low, seductively accented voice as it wrapped itself around her, warming everything within her that was vital, female, bringing it to life?

Who could resist it, when she'd been dead inside for so long?

'Really—'

She made one more effort, but he raised a hand, demanding that she listen.

'Lucy—charming, beautiful Lucy—' she flinched at each word '—was the joint owner of one of those desert tour outfits. It was poorly managed, under-capitalised, going nowhere. And the man who ran it had been arrested for fraud, amongst other things.'

His mouth tightened as if just thinking about it made him angry and suddenly she was listening.

'My cousin, Hanif—Ameerah's father—knew that I was more interested in business than diplomacy and he encouraged me to step in, take it over, see if I could make something of it. I raised the capital—it didn't take much—but when I bought Lucy out I insisted she keep a small equity in the business.' He managed a wry smile. 'Just in case I was as good as I thought I was. She'd had a raw deal.'

'What a Galahad!'

'You don't understand.' He lifted a hand as if asking her to at least try. 'But then why should you?'

'I never will unless you tell me. Not that it's any of my business,' she added, realising, somewhat belatedly, that haranguing a client about business affairs was probably not an entirely wise move. Except that she'd stopped treating Zahir like a client from, well, the moment she'd picked up the shattered snow globe.

But the admission earned her another of those smiles—the real ones—so that was okay.

'Don't go all polite on me, Diana.'

Or maybe not.

'I'm listening,' she said.

He leaned back against the car, folded him arms, looked down, as if dredging deep for what he was about to tell her. 'The men in my family are diplomats. My grandfather before he became ruler. My father, uncles, cousins. I wanted something different. Like you, I had a dream.'

'Your own airline?'

'Not quite. It takes time to learn to dream on that scale. You have to start small, then, as your imagination grows, let the dreams grow until they are big enough to fill all the available space.' He glanced up at her. 'I got my chance because Lucy's life had fallen apart. I owed her. She uses her share of the profits to fund a charity she founded, which is why she turns out for the PR stuff, as she did last night, whenever Hanif can spare her.'

Hanif…

'Your cousin,' she said, finally working out where all this was going. 'Ameerah's father.'

'And Lucy's husband.'

Diana struggled to say something to cover her stupidity but for once words failed her and all she could manage was a stumbling, 'I…um…'

Oh…sheikh!

Zahir saw her difficulty. But then he'd seen everything. That was why he'd taken the long route to make his point when he could just as easily have said, *She's my partner, but she's also my cousin's wife.*

'That wasn't the kind of partnership you were talking about was it.' he asked very softly.

A hole in the ground, opening up to swallow her whole, would be welcome right now, she decided as, left with no place to hide, she shook her head.

'Whatever made you think—?'

'I saw her last night when I returned the tray,' she cut in quickly, before he reminded her exactly what she'd been thinking. 'You were together. You looked so close and when he saw me looking Mr Pierce told me that she was your partner. I thought…' She dismissed what she'd thought with an awkward, meaningless gesture.

'A simple misunderstanding.'

She didn't think so.

'*His partner*…' The way James Pierce had said it had been full of meaning. He'd meant her to believe…

No. That was ridiculous. Much more likely her imagination, working overtime, leaping to conclusions when she'd seen him standing so close to a beautiful woman just minutes after he'd kissed her.

Good grief, she must have it bad if she'd let her imagination run so *green*. She must really have it bad if she felt this good knowing that it wasn't true.

While she was still trying to find words that would not betray her as a complete idiot—a jealous idiot at that—he rescued her, making a gesture in the direction of boatyard.

'Actually, you're right, Lucy would have loved the chance to see the yacht. In fact she's calling in every favour I owe her in return for the right to give it a test run as a wedding anniversary gift to Hanif before it's chartered to the public.'

'You're going to charter it?' Diana asked, grabbing for the impersonal in an attempt to distract him from the fact that she'd just betrayed feelings that were just plain…*inappropriate*!

'I could not justify the expense for my own personal use. Even if I had the time. But today it is all mine.' And, with the slightest of bows, he offered her his hand. 'In the absence of Princess Lucy al-Khatib, Miss Metcalfe, will you do me the immense honour of allowing me to share this moment with you?'

He had never treated her as if she were just his chauffeur, but at this moment she recognised that he was treating her like a princess and she laid her hand against his.

He closed his hand over hers, tucked it beneath his arm and, heading for the boatyard office, said, 'My plan is to use the yacht as part of a wedding package. I'd value your opinion on that.'

'I don't think I'm your natural market, Zahir.'

He glanced at her. 'Are you telling me that you don't dream?'

'Not at all. It's just that my dreams are confined to pink taxis.' And a prince who turns into a frog. The only way this could turn out. But it was her Cinderella moment and she was going to make the most of it.

'There's nothing wrong with the pink taxi dream, but maybe I can broaden your horizons.'

'To what? A pink yacht?'

'Just wait until you see her,' he said, with a sudden smile that betrayed an oddly boyish enthusiasm. 'There's a very small island in Nadira Creek that is going to make a perfect wedding venue. I'm building a restaurant there, with a traditional wind tower to draw the air down over a basement pool to cool it naturally. A pavilion for romantic Westerners to make their vows.'

'It's just for tourists, then?'

'An Arab wedding traditionally takes place at the bride's home...' He shook his head. 'At Nadira, after the ceremony, the feasting, the yacht will be waiting to carry the honeymooners away, leaving the world behind...'

He left the rest to her already overcharged imagination.

'It sounds enchanting,' she said, concentrating very hard not to go there. 'And expensive.' Then, 'But very romantic.'

'It will be.'

'Which?'

'All three,' he assured her. And the boyish smile faded, leaving only a very adult warmth in his eyes.

The yacht certainly looked expensive. White, sleek, beautiful, and so much larger than she'd anticipated, that Diana almost succumbed to another '...*oh, sheikh...*' moment.

'You'd probably like to look around the accommodation, miss,' the boat builder suggested, 'while I show Sheikh Zahir the engines?'

Zahir hesitated, then, turning to follow the man below to inspect powerful engines that were, even now, sending a quiet hum through the yacht, he said, 'Go where you like, Diana. I'll catch up with you.'

She suspected that she knew at least as much about engines as Zahir. From the time she could reach inside the bonnet of his taxi, she'd been asking questions and her father had taught her all he knew, even as he'd taught her to drive on private roads, so that she'd passed her driving test only days after her seventeenth birthday.

But men were funny about stuff like that, so she did as she was told and wandered over the yacht, marvelling over the ingenuity of the fittings in the galley, sighing over the minimalist luxury of the accommodation. Coming to a halt when she opened the door to the main stateroom which, dominated by a huge bed, half hidden by rich silk drapes, was quite clearly the honeymoon suite. Zahir had certainly widened the horizons of her dreams she thought, as her imagination ran amok...

Definitely time for some fresh air, she decided, heading back to the deck. But the honeymoon image lingered and, as she stood in the prow, her dreams knew no bounds. A tropical sun dipping into the sea, the arm of a man who loved her around her waist, her head against his shoulder.

She shook her head to clear it.

Forget the yacht, the sunset. Only the man was important and she'd be wise to forget him too.

Everything she had, everything she could be, was down to her alone and on an impulse, she leaned forward, stretching out her arms like the heroine in the film *Titanic* and, in the absence of her own hero, telling herself that she could do anything, be anything, if only she had the courage…

Zahir dutifully stood over the glistening pistons as the engines were turned over because, as an owner taking possession, that was what was expected of him. Doing his duty when he'd far rather have stayed with Diana, wanting to see her face as he revealed his new toy to her. As he opened the door and she saw the stateroom. Certain that her reaction would tell him everything he wanted to know.

Perhaps it was as well he'd been distracted.

Better not to know…

When, finally, he could escape, he found her not below, exploring, but standing in the bow of the yacht, her arms outstretched like some figurehead… No… It was something else. A scene from a film.

She was dreaming after all and, smiling, he came up behind her, took hold of her waist and said, 'Do it properly. Step up on the rail.' Her response was to take a step back, drop her arms, but he urged her to go for it. Lifting her, he said, 'Reach for it, Diana. Reach for what you want most.'

'Zahir!'

His name was a wail of embarrassment, but he refused to listen.

'Trust me… I won't let you fall.'

Diana, feeling utterly foolish at being caught out play-acting this way, for a moment resisted, but his hands were strong, his support real, and suddenly she was there, leaning far out over the water, her eyes closed, arms stretched wide, reaching for her future as he leaned with her, his arms beneath hers, keeping her safe.

'I can feel the wind in my face,' she said, laughing, feeling like the girl she'd never been. And at her back she could feel Zahir's strength as he held her, the slight roughness of his chin against her neck, the warmth of his body quickening her to a womanhood she'd never known.

The thudding of her pulse at his closeness, an aching intimate heat, shocking in its urgency, was confirmation that life was to be seized and shaken and, for one mad moment, she came close to turning and pulling him over the edge with her, taking him with her as she plunged beneath the surface.

If they were both out of their depth they would be equal…

Except she was Cinderella and the minute they stepped off the yacht she would cease to be a princess.

'Are you sure this is a good idea?' she said shakily, backing away from the intensity of feelings that had almost overwhelmed her. Trying to keep this at a level she could handle.

She didn't do overwhelmed.

She didn't do dreams.

'It won't jinx the boat?' she persisted, when the only answer was his soft breath against her cheek.

The scene in the film had been beautiful, but the love affair, like the Titanic, had been doomed from the first reel of the movie and, in an attempt to claw herself back to reality, she opened her eyes to find that the view had changed. That they were far from the shore.

Confused, she looked down to see a lacy ripple of white where the bow broke the surface of the water.

She stared down at it for a moment, trying to work out what was happening, then, as the water moving away from her made her giddy, she pitched forward, crying out, certain she was about to fall.

But Zahir's hands were sure. He had her safe and, lifting her down, turned her so that she was facing him instead of the rush of water, drawing her close as she clung, shaking, to his shoulders, his arms around her as if he would never let her go while he murmured soft reassuring words against her hair, her temple.

She was still shaking, but not because she was afraid of falling. This wasn't fear, this was something darker, more urgent, and, as she looked up, she knew he was going to kiss her.

Not the way he'd kissed her before. This was not like that sweet, sensuous, barely there kiss.

He'd held her as he'd danced with her.

This was something else. This wasn't that light, floating touch as they'd slowly circled Berkeley Square. This was searingly close, a hungry, insistent need...

For the space of one, two, three heartbeats pounding in her ears, her head did its best to fight the seductive call to surrender, but by then her body had made a bid for independence and, overriding thought, reason, she was kissing him back.

No holds barred. No fooling. Minutes earlier she'd felt as if she were flying; this was the real thing.

Diana didn't want him to let her go. She wanted him to carry her down to that stateroom and put that incredible bed to the purpose for which it had been designed.

Maybe he would have.

Maybe, like her, he was beyond reason and in another moment they would have been beyond recall. Instead they were shocked back to reality by a sharp shower of cold water.

She jerked back, gasping for breath.

Zahir, damn him, laughed. 'Are you all right?' he asked, ignoring the water running down his face, instead wiping the spray from her cheeks with his thumbs.

'All right?' she demanded, her hair dripping down the back of her neck and trickling down inside her blouse. 'What kind of dumb question is that?'

'The "are you all right?" dumb question?' he offered.

'Fine!' she said. Beyond the fact that she'd temporarily lost her mind. That it had taken the equivalent of a bucket of cold water to bring her to her senses. 'I'm absolutely fine, if you overlook the fact that I appear to be at sea!'

'Oh, that…'

'Yes, that! Come and look at my new toy, you said. You didn't say anything about putting to sea!'

'Alan's idea,' he said. 'But running away to sea suddenly has a lot to commend it.'

She refused to answer that on the grounds that it might incriminate her.

'I'm sorry if you had a fright. Are you very wet?'

'Yes!' she said crossly. Being jerked down from that kind of high would make anyone cross. Then, more truthfully, 'No…'

'Sure? You don't want to stand around in wet clothes.'

How could she be sure of anything when she was standing this close to Zahir, her hands still clinging to his shoulders as if he were anchoring her to earth, his hands about her waist and everything in between…touching?

'Any excuse to get me out of this uniform, huh?'

Yes, well, it was the obvious next move after that mind-blowing kiss. Especially when she was clutching at his shoulders so hard that she was screwing up the linen of his jacket.

'You've got me,' he said.

And it was those three little words that brought her back to earth, to reality. He was the one thing she hadn't got. Not *him*. And she never would. Not for more than an hour or two.

That was too much like history repeating itself.

And slowly, very slowly, she loosened her fingers, doing her best to smooth the cloth over his shoulders. Except that linen didn't smooth. Once wrinkled, it stayed wrinkled.

A bit like her life…

'Sorry,' she mouthed silently, only to discover that Zahir was still holding her.

Zahir was holding this girl he'd only just met, who was nothing like any girl he'd ever dated, had ever dreamed of dating, and for some reason he just couldn't let go.

He just wanted to keep her this close, with her hands on his shoulders, his hands at her waist keeping her close. To sail away with her into the sunset…

Well, that was the fantasy that this yacht had been built for.

'You can let go now,' she said. 'I won't fall over.'

'Really? Are you absolutely certain that you've got your sea-legs? Suppose there's another big wave?'

'Good point,' she said, making a point of looking at her watch. 'We'd better turn around and go back if I'm going to get you to London by six.'

He didn't want to go anywhere. He wanted to stay here with Diana and, as she pulled away, he said, 'Forget London. Tell me about the yacht.'

Diana swallowed.

What she really thought was that a yacht costing millions was a very clear demonstration of just how far out of her depth her heart had swum. Heading out to sea, but on its own and sinking fast.

'Does it matter what I think?'

'Would you want to spend your honeymoon on board her?' he pressed.

'She's lovely,' she said, putting on a big smile hoping that he wouldn't notice that she'd avoided the question. Putting a safe distance between them as, trailing her fingers along the handrail, she walked along the deck. Away from him. Then, because she couldn't help it, glancing back. He was standing just where she'd left him, his arm still extended, as if to keep her close. 'Does she have a name?' she asked. Anything to stop herself from going back.

'Yes…' He shook his head as if trying to think. 'Yes. I'm calling her *Star Gatherer.*'

Star...

'You just made that up!' she declared without thinking and, as if she'd somehow released him, he joined her at the rail, leaning over it, looking down into the water.

'I can see why, after last night, you might think so,' he said.

'No...'

Too late to deny it. 'Yes, Diana. But in fact the name comes from the poem, Arab Love-Song.' And he turned and leaned back against the rail, with the smile of a man who had just had everything he knew confirmed.

'The Maiden of the Morn will soon/Through Heaven stray and sing,/Star gathering.'

'Oh. That's beautiful.' Then, staring down into the water rushing past the side of the yacht, anywhere, rather than at him, 'How will you get her home?' she asked, seeking a subject less...incendiary. 'To Ramal Hamrah? Will you take her there yourself?'

'I wish I had that kind of time to spare. Unfortunately, at the moment the sky has first call on my time.' Better. Safer, she thought, raising an eyebrow. 'You might recall that I have an airline to get off the ground.'

'A yacht, an airline? Tell me, Zahir, do you have a bit of a thing about transport?'

'I'm in the travel business.'

'Oh, right. Well, I suppose that would explain it.'

'Jeff's mustering a permanent crew for the yacht and they'll bring her home. It'll give them a chance to put her through her paces, get to know her quirks, on the way.' Then, 'If I offered you a trip to Ramal Hamrah in her would you be as quick to turn me down a second time?'

'That depends. Would I have to share her with a bunch of freeloading journalists?' Before he could answer, she said, 'No, I'm kidding. I don't have that kind of time either.'

But this time as she turned her wrist to check the time, he

took her hand, stopping her. 'We could always take her for a run across the Channel,' he said.

'The Channel? To *France*?' she squeaked.

His thumb was stroking the back of her fingers. 'We could have dinner in some little French café. I could take the train to Paris in the morning, while you return with the yacht.'

And the bit in between dinner and breakfast?

She couldn't breathe. It shouldn't be this hard to say no. If she just concentrated on that one word—morning. Remember that when morning came he'd be taking the fast train to Paris while her world would be in pieces.

Again.

And, on top of that, she wouldn't have a job.

'W-what about your dinner at the Mansion House?' she stammered. 'If I don't get you back to London by six, James Pierce will call Sadie Redford and get me fired. He really doesn't like me.'

'I like you, that's all that matters.'

'Zahir…'

He lifted her hand to his lips, kissed the tips of her fingers. So sure of her…

'No…'

Maybe it was the first time a woman had ever said 'no' to him, or maybe it was the undisguised anguish in her voice, but she now had his full attention.

'I'm sorry,' she said, 'but my evening is already spoken for.'

'Your only task this evening is to drive me to the Mansion House.'

She shook her head. 'Sadie has arranged for someone else to stand in for me.'

'I don't want someone else!' She shook her head. 'Are you telling me, Metcalfe, that you have a date?'

And that, Diana realised, was the answer. If he thought she was involved with someone, he'd stop this…whatever *this*

was. Save her from herself. Because, heaven help her, hard
as she was trying, she was finding it impossible…

'Is that so unbelievable?' she asked. 'A minute ago you
were inviting me to dinner in France.'

'I don't believe you.' Then, eyes narrowed, 'Tell me his name.'

'Freddy,' she said. How could she have been so lost in
desire that the whole world had suddenly been filled with
Zahir? Forgotten the child who was the centre of her world,
who, she'd protected from the consequences of her own stupidity since the moment he had been conceived? 'His name
is Freddy.'

Zahir felt his gut contract.

For a moment he hadn't believed her, had thought that she
was clutching at the face-saving excuse he'd offered, protecting him as much as herself from the fallout of such an ill-con-
sidered venture. But one look at her face warned him that he
was fooling himself.

She might have responded to his reckless kiss with all the
passion at her command. She had certainly displayed all the
signs of a woman betrayed when she'd thought he was involved
with Lucy, but, whoever this Freddy was, he brought a whole
new look to her face. A sweetness. A tenderness. Something
that he'd fooled himself he'd seen when she'd looked up at him
only moments before. When he'd had to force himself to say
something stupid like 'all right?' to stop himself from picking
her up and carrying her below, not as a choreographed move—
the opening sequence in a slow dance that would lead inevitably to that inviting bed in the stateroom—but as the
beginning of something rare, unexpected, precious.

His suggestion that they take 'French leave' had not, despite
all appearances to the contrary, been driven by a libido rack-
eting out of control, but because he wanted her with him.
Couldn't bear the thought of watching her drive away…

For a moment he didn't move, but watched as she stood,

one hand on the rail, her head slightly bowed, the sun lighting her hair like a rich halo around her face.

An illusion, he thought, turning abruptly and returning to the bridge.

'Time is short, Alan,' he snapped. 'I've seen enough. Let's get back to the yard so that I can sign the registration papers.'

CHAPTER EIGHT

SHEIKH ZAHIR did not invite Diana to join him while he signed the papers for his new yacht.

As she followed him ashore, he did not even look back as he dismissed her with an abrupt, 'I'll see you at the car, Diana. Be ready to leave in fifteen minutes.'

'Yes, sir,' she said, resisting the desire to say his name, feel it on her lips, reminding herself that was the way it was supposed to be.

Forget romance. The Cinderella fantasy was just that. A fantasy. She didn't believe in fairy tales and this wasn't the moment to lose her head. It was her job that mattered. This chance to move up the ladder. Get on. Get *somewhere*.

What she'd done back there had been right. For both of them. It hurt, but it would hurt far more afterwards when Zahir had returned to his real life and she was left with the pain.

The taxi was, probably always would be, just another fantasy, but becoming one of Capitol's senior drivers was within her grasp. Or it had been, until Sheikh Zahir had smiled at her and every bit of common sense had flown out of the window.

Before he'd kissed her. Before he'd danced with her, waltzing off with her heart…

Well, good luck to him. He could keep it as a souvenir of his trip to London. It wasn't as if she had any use for it.

What she needed was for the sheikh/chauffeur balance to be restored.

And it was.

Everything was back in balance.

So why did she feel so…bereft? So hollow? As if she'd just been offered the earth, the moon, the stars and had been too stupid, too scared to reach out and take them.

Because she hadn't been offered any of that.

What she'd been offered was an exotic, thrilling, world-well-lost one-night stand that she would never forget. But it would still just have been a one-night stand and without warning, tears filled her eyes, a lump rose in her throat and for a moment she couldn't move, but was bent double as the reality, the loss hit her.

She could never do that.

Never seize a moment. Take a chance. Grab at what life offered.

You made your mistakes and you lived with them.

'Your young lady doesn't look too hot, Zahir. If an hour sailing when the weather is this calm has that effect on her, it doesn't bode well for…'

Zahir stopped Alan with a look, then, unable to help himself, he turned to follow his gaze. Diana, arms around her waist and bent double, hadn't moved from the jetty, where he'd dismissed her, or walked away.

He muttered an oath beneath his breath but, before he could take more than a step, she straightened, swiping the palm of her hand over her cheek as she lifted her head in a gesture that echoed his own pull-yourself-together-and-get-over-it attempts to block out the pain as they'd sailed back to the boatyard.

Maybe her conscience was pricking her, he thought.

Last night, when he'd kissed her, danced with her, she

hadn't been giving her 'Freddy' a second thought and today she'd been a heartbeat from giving him everything.

But for a freak wave she would have.

And what did that make him?

Maybe he should be giving his own conscience a wake-up call, it occurred to him, because last night, when she'd returned his kiss, had sung to him as she'd melted into his arms, he hadn't been giving his own future as much as a first thought. He'd been too busy making a fool of himself over a girl he'd only just met to spare a second or even a third thought for the young women being lined up for him to pick out a suitable wife.

Whatever Diana had been doing, his actions had been far worse...

'Whatever it was, she's over it now,' Alan said, watching her walk swiftly down the jetty until she rounded the building and was out of sight.

'So it would seem.' Uncapping his pen, he began to sign a stack of documents. He would do well to follow her example.

Enough. Diana slumped behind the wheel, staring at the car phone. At eighteen years old, mired in a world of guilt as her mother had threatened, her father had looked at her as if he didn't know her, she'd sworn *never again*.

She'd got lazy. Complacent.

It was easy to hold off the attentions of boys, men, when there was no attraction, no temptation, desire. Pete O'Hanlon had seen her looking at him as if he were something in a sweetshop window and he'd used that. But she wasn't blaming him. She'd wanted him, had seized the moment without a thought for the morrow and she had to live with that.

Her solace, her joy, was Freddy and she'd been content. But it had taken just one look from Zahir's slate-grey eyes, one smile, to let her know what she was missing. Melt the ice-wall she'd built around her heart.

She caught her breath, shaking her head as if to clear away all that romantic nonsense.

Not her heart. Nothing that noble.

What Sheikh Zahir al-Khatib had done with a single look was jump-start a hunger, a need that was so far beyond her experience that she hadn't recognised the danger until it was too late.

Until she was experiencing feelings that were so strong that for a moment she had been in danger of repeating history…

No. This had to stop now. Now, before she wavered and did something really stupid and told him that Freddy was five years old. That her date was a classroom visit. Because, if she told him that, he'd know…

She reached out to hit the fast dial on the car phone to call Sadie, ask her to take her off this job—what excuse she'd make she didn't know, but she'd think of something. The phone rang before her finger made contact, making her jump nearly out of her skin, the caller ID warning her that Sadie had got in first. She was no doubt calling to update her on who would be driving Sheikh Zahir this evening so that she could pass on the good news.

She jabbed 'receive', but, before she could speak, Sadie said, 'Diana! At last! I've been calling you for the best part of an hour on this phone and your cellphone.'

'Have you?' She frowned, rubbing her hands over her pockets. No cellphone. 'I must have left it in my jacket…'

'I don't care where you left it! Where, in heaven's name, have you *been*?'

'Well…'

'No, don't bother to answer that. I can guess,' she said cuttingly.

What?

Diana straightened. 'Look, I'm sorry, but Sheikh Zahir…'

'Please! I don't want to know. I just want you to listen to me. You are not to come back to the yard. You will be met at the car park outside The King's Head in Little Markham by Michael Jenkins. He'll drive the Mercedes back from there. Sheikh Zahir's personal assistant has arranged for another car to be on hand to take him back to the hotel. You…'

'Whoa! Back up, Sadie. What on earth has happened?'

'You have to ask?'

Confused, miserable, she wasn't in the mood for games. 'Apparently I do,' she snapped back with uncharacteristic sharpness.

'You'd like me to read you the diary column from the midday edition of *The Courier*?'

'What?'

'Maybe it will jog your memory if I tell you that the headline is "The Sheikh and the Chauffeur"? Or do you want all the gory details of how Sheikh Zahir al-Khatib was seen gazing into the eyes of his pretty chauffeur as he waltzed her around Berkeley Square at midnight?'

'How on earth—?'

'For heaven's sake, everyone with a camera phone is an amateur paparazzo these days, Di! Even if the snapper didn't recognise Sheikh Zahir, a man dancing with his chauffeur made it a story. The fact that he looks lost to the world makes it the kind of story that *The Courier* was always going to run in its diary column. I don't imagine it took them more than two minutes to identify Sheikh Zahir. He's not exactly a stranger to the gossip pages.'

'He isn't?'

'He's a billionaire bachelor, Diana, what do you think?'

Think?

Who was thinking?

'Oh—'

'Don't say it!'

'I wasn't going to.' She swallowed. 'I was going to say that it's not the way it must look.'

Not *exactly*.

'I'm afraid the way it looks is all people are interested in.'

'No-o-o-o…'

Sadie just sighed.

'No. For what it's worth, I believe you, but it makes no difference. It's a good story and that's all the tabloids care about. What *does* matter is that we're under siege here.'

'Siege?'

'The hunters are out and you are the prey. Your name wasn't in the paper but it didn't take the sleaze-merchants long to find out which company is chauffeuring the Sheikh around London this week. I think we can safely assume that by now they have got not only your name but probably know the colour of the polish on your toenails.'

'I'm not wearing polish on…' She stopped. Sadie was speaking metaphorically. 'Sadie, I am *so* sorry. I promise you it was all perfectly…'

Innocent. She'd been going to say innocent. It wasn't true.

Innocent didn't feel the way she'd felt last night when he'd kissed her. When he'd held her. Had raised her hand to his lips. She remembered the way her skin had warmed to his touch. How her lips had wanted more of him. The sweet liquid meltdown in the pit of her belly as he'd waltzed her around the Square. Made her feel like a princess.

As for today…

She had compared her foolishness to her moment of madness with Pete O'Hanlon. He had never looked at her the way Zahir had looked at her. Had never made her feel the way that Zahir…

'Diana!'

She jumped as Sadie shouted her name. Realised that she had been talking to her, expected some kind of response.

'I'm sorry. I'm in shock.'

'Get a grip. You've got to keep your head. No doubt it'll just be a nine-minute wonder—'

'Less,' she said, determined to reassure Sadie.

It was already over.

'Let's hope so. I want you to take the rest of the week off. You've already got next week booked as leave for Freddy's half term holiday and Sheikh Zahir will have left the country by then. And yes, before you ask, you'll get paid. Your time will go on Sheikh Zahir's account as a disruption expense. I hope he thinks one dance was worth it.'

'No…' That wasn't fair. 'Sadie…'

But she was listening to the dialling tone. For a moment she sat there, numb with shock, then picked up her jacket and found her cellphone. She kept it switched off while she was driving, but the minute she thumbed it on she saw that she had more than a dozen voicemail messages.

Several from Sadie. A terse 'Call me' from her mother. A couple from her father, who'd been getting calls from neighbours, newspapers. Three from tabloid journalists offering her money for her story—how on earth had they got this number?

There were even two calls from gossip magazines offering sky's-the-limit deals for her 'Cinderella' story, with pictures of her and her family in their ordinary little terraced house in Putney.

They knew where she lived?

And finally one from an infamous Public Relations guru warning her to say nothing, sign nothing, until she'd talked to him.

It was like a verbal car wreck. Horrible, but so compelling that she couldn't hit the 'disconnect' switch, and Sadie's warning finally sank in.

These people wouldn't quit until they'd dredged up everything. How long would it be before someone was telling them that no one knew who Freddy's father was? Implying that she didn't know. That would really give them something to get their teeth into…

'If you've finished calling your boyfriend?' Zahir said, opening the rear door of the car. He'd removed his jacket and, as he tossed it into the back of the car the phone in her hand began to ring.

Startled, she gave a little shriek and dropped it at her feet, where it continued to ring.

'It's not…' she began, but her voice was shaking. Everything was shaking. 'I wasn't…' The voicemail cut in and the phone finally stopped ringing.

'Diana?' Zahir's soft query, no longer angry, just velvet concern, only made things worse. He opened the driver's door, folded himself up so that he was on her level. 'What on earth is the matter?' Unable to speak, she just hung on to the steering wheel, her forehead against her hands. 'Please… How can I help if you do not tell me?'

She shook her head, her throat choked with rage and misery. At her feet, the phone began to ring again.

Zahir reached in, picked it up and answered the call with an abrupt, 'Yes?' then listened for a moment before disconnecting the call without speaking again. Then he turned it off and placed it in his pocket.

'Who was it?'

'Someone from a magazine called *Hot Gossip*. The woman addressed me by name?' It was a question, one that required an answer, but all she could manage was a groan.

How useless was that? How pitiful? As if sitting here drowning in the unfairness of it all was going to help.

He had to know.

She had to tell him.

And, making an effort, she sat back, scrubbed at her cheeks with her hands and said, 'The office have been trying to get in touch with me ever since our nightingale two-step became public knowledge at midday.' She turned to face him, wanting to be sure that he understood. 'That was when *The Courier* hit the streets.' When he didn't immediately respond, 'I imagine Mr Pierce has been calling you too.'

'Yes,' he said, 'I imagine he has. But he can wait. I'm more concerned about you. What do you want me to do?'

'You?' She shook her head. 'There's nothing either of us can do except get on with life. It's all we can ever do. Get on with it. And to do that I have to get home.' Then, seeing his doubtful expression, 'Don't worry, it's all been sorted.' She began to explain the arrangements that Sadie and James had made but he brushed them aside.

'You can't go home, Diana. The paparazzi will have already staked out your house. It will be bedlam.'

She'd seen such things on the television news. Politicians caught with their pants down, being door-stepped by the media. It wouldn't be like that. This wasn't the kind of story that made the nine o'clock news, but she had no doubt it would be uncomfortable and her father was there on his own.

She glanced at her watch, checking the time. No, not on his own. He'd have been forced to confront them to fetch Freddy from school…

She groaned. 'Please, Zahir, get in. I have to get home right now!'

He didn't move. 'I'm so sorry, Diana.'

'Don't…' She shook her head. 'This is my fault. You were just happy. If I'd behaved like a professional…'

'Don't be selfish with the guilt, *ya habibati*,' he said, taking her hands, easing her to her feet, forcing her to look at him. 'There's always enough of that to go around.' Then, 'Call your family. Tell them that James will come and pick up your passport, an overnight bag. I can't stop this, but I can get you away until it's blown over…'

'What?'

What had he called her? A fool, an idiot, no doubt. Well,

he had every right and he hadn't done it unkindly, but almost tenderly. She shook her head. As if it mattered…

'You expect me to run away and leave my family, the people I love, to face this on their own?'

'If you're not there…'

'What? The journalists will just go away? They won't ring endlessly, harass my parents? The neighbours? Freddy…'

The horror of it hit her full force and, as her knees sagged, he released one hand to catch her, hold her close. And for a moment she leaned against him, clinging to him for support, for his strength, as the awfulness of it swept over her.

It wouldn't just be at the yard. It would be at her home, at school.

And how long would it be before someone was gossiping about Freddy? Saw the possibilities of making a little hard cash out of old photographs, speculating on just who his father might be?

She didn't care about herself. She had protected Freddy then. Had outfaced her mother's threats, her father's tears, had even told the Child Support Agency where they could stick their money. It would take more than a bunch of journalists to shake it out of her. But it would make her visible, make Freddy visible. Drag it all up again, the gossip. And he was getting older, his face was firming up; if people started to look again, what might they see?

No.

Who would ever believe that Pete O'Hanlon would have even looked at the last virgin in the sixth form? But it would still be a total nightmare for her parents.

Terrifying for a little boy.

Zahir was right. Her home, the place where she could hold out against the world, knowing that her parents would support her, whatever she did, whatever it cost them, was no longer a haven.

As she straightened, stood on her own two feet, she shivered. 'It doesn't matter about me, Zahir, but I can't leave my family to deal with this on their own. I have to get my parents and Freddy out of there too.'

Freddy.

There it was. Zahir had known. He'd heard this man's name on her lips, and seen her face as she'd spoken of him, but even while his head had understood what she was telling him, his heart had refused to believe it. Had clung to some forlorn hope…

It was his heart that had called her his beloved.

That she could never return his feelings, that he would never be her *habibi*, made no difference. She had made the nightingale sing for him, her smile had made the stars shine beneath his feet. She had given him a moment that he would carry with him always, but in doing so had brought this horror crashing about her. The least he could do in return was offer his protection to her and to all those she loved.

Even now, as she looked up at him, as he felt the flutter of her pulse against his palm, he could scarcely believe that she loved another man. Her eyes seemed to tell him that all she wanted was for him to hold her against his heart, enfold her in his arms. Keep her from harm.

'It is done,' he said. 'Call them and tell them to be ready.'

She had mockingly called him 'Galahad' and she was right to mock. Even now, when there were a dozen things he had to do to make this happen, he wanted nothing more than to hold her, promise her his world.

'Zahir…' His name on her lips was so sweet, but he did not look at her as he stepped back.

Did not dare look. What he was feeling meant nothing. He wasn't Galahad offering her a pure heart. There was no fairy tale, no romance here.

Worse, no honour.

All he'd had to offer Diana Metcalfe was one night in his bed and, in making that offer, he'd broken the cardinal rules on which he'd so prided himself. Never to become involved with anyone who might get hurt. There wasn't a thing he could do to prevent that now, other than give her sanctuary.

'Call your family while I talk to James and make the necessary arrangements so that we can leave before someone uses your cellphone to track us here.'

'Where are we going?'

Not we. Never we. He could not go with her…

'You and your family…' he could not bring himself to say her lover's name '…will be my guests at Nadira Creek for as long as you need a refuge. And I promise you that, while you are there, it will be off limits to journalists.'

Off limits to him.

Zahir retrieved his jacket from the rear of the car, dug out his own phone and, leaving Diana to call home, he rang James Pierce.

'Just listen,' he said, cutting him off before he could start. 'I want a private jet ready to leave Farnborough airfield early this evening.' He checked his watch. 'No later than seven o'clock. As soon as that's arranged, call Sadie Redford and tell her to send someone she trusts with her life to pick up a party of three and their luggage from Diana's home…'

He opened the car door.

'…I'm sorry, Freddy. Please, sweetie…' Diana paused with the endearment on her lips, looked up. Her eyes were full of tears but there was nothing he could do. No comfort he could offer her. No comfort for him…

'I need your address,' he said. She blinked, not quite with him. Never with him… 'For James.'

'Oh, right.' Then, 'Actually, it might be better if they leave the house by the back way through Aunt Alice's. Her garden backs on to ours. Ninety-two, Prince Albert Street.'

'Aunt Alice's,' he repeated. 'Will she be coming too?'

She almost smiled but the dimple didn't quite make it. 'No, Zahir. She's not a real aunt, just my mother's best friend.'

He nodded, walking away from the car as he gave James the details. 'Tell Sadie Redford the change in plans. Tell her… Tell her I'll bring the Mercedes back to London when I've dropped Diana at the airport. She can have someone pick it up at the hotel.'

'You're not going with her, then?'

There was something in James's tone that put an edge in his voice. He ignored it. 'Why would I do that when I'm a guest at the Mansion House tonight? Something you might mention to any journalist you encounter who expresses an interest in my immediate plans. But you'll have to cancel the Paris trip. I'm bringing forward the announcement of Ramal Hamrah Airways to tomorrow morning and I'll be going home straight after that.'

Ameerah would not forgive him for missing her party, but neither would Hanif and Lucy appreciate a Pied Piper trail of journalists invading their children's party.

At least he would make his mother happy. Hopefully give his father the grandson he desired. He owed them that.

CHAPTER NINE

It WAS a nightmare.

Zahir insisted on driving—and he was right, she was in no fit state to handle the big car—pushing the speed limit all the way to Farnborough. He'd been kind, gentle with her, but it didn't take a genius to see that he couldn't wait to rid himself of her.

Who could blame him?

The moment they arrived at the airfield—one favoured by the kind of men for whom the private jet was the standard form of transport and ironically a regular run for the limo drivers—he made his excuses.

'I have to go,' he said as, with one of the VIP hostesses standing by to whisk her away, he made a formal little bow. 'Your family will be with you very shortly.'

'You'd better get a move on,' she said, forcing herself to look at her watch, to look away from his beautiful face, even though she knew it would be the last time she'd see him. Doing her best to keep it light. 'It won't do to keep the Prime Minister waiting.' For heaven's sake, she barely knew the man. Why then, did it feel like the end of the world? 'But try not to get a speeding ticket or that'll be another black mark against my name.'

'I'll take care, but if I miss the dinner the press will leap to the conclusion that we are...' He faltered, a gesture filling the gap.

He was protecting her? Or was he protecting himself?

It didn't matter!

'You don't have to draw a picture, Zahir. Go. Now. I'll be fine.'

And with another bow he turned and walked away from her. It was odd. He was wearing a casual suit, and yet in her mind he was wearing robes...

'Would you like to freshen up while you're waiting, Miss Metcalfe?' The hostess, who had been standing at a discreet distance while Zahir had been with her, tactfully eased her into the sanctuary of a luxurious washroom where she offered a box of tissues.

'I'll come and fetch you when the rest of your party arrive.'

It was only then that she realised that tears were pouring down her face, dripping on to her shirt, soaking it.

Try as she might to forget, all she could think about was Zahir dismissing the dinner as unimportant when he was suggesting they sail across to France in his yacht. But for a freak wave they might even now be putting into some quaint Normandy harbour where she'd be waking in his arms to a French dawn, unaware of the furore...

She shook her head. It would, in the end, only have made things worse. She'd done the right thing. Even if it meant that Zahir thought she was...

Well, he must have a pretty low opinion of a woman who'd responded so fervently to the kisses of someone who was practically a stranger when she was involved with another man.

Had wanted him to do more than kiss her.

No wonder he'd dropped her and run.

She made an effort to stem the flow of tears she had no business shedding. Tidied herself up, directed the hand-drier at her shirt—as shirt days went, this was having a bad one—to dry herself off.

Putting on a front before her mother arrived.

Some hope.

She must have broken some kind of record with her packing, because Diana was still struggling to put on lipstick with a shaky hand when the hostess came for her.

Sadie's father, Daniel Redford, the man who owned Capitol Cars but now left the day-to-day business to his daughter, had brought her family to the airfield in the back of the old black London cab that he used as a town car. Clever of Sadie. Far less noticeable than one of the burgundy Capitol cars. And kind too, to call on her father to help out an employee who'd given her such a headache.

'I'm so grateful, Mr Redford…' Oh, damn, the tears were threatening again.

'It was no trouble. I enjoyed the cloak-and-dagger. We got away clean as a whistle,' he said. Such a sweet man. 'And don't worry about the yard,' he added, a reassuring hand to her elbow. 'The hacks are getting short shrift there. It'll be nothing but a nine-minute wonder, you'll see.'

Her mother, who'd apparently rushed home from work when the phone calls had started, was not sweet.

On the contrary, she was livid, and it was only Freddy's presence that kept her from speaking her mind. Her father, painfully, seemed unable to look at her. Even Freddy—normally the sweetest-natured of boys—had turned sulky because she'd missed the parents' evening at school.

So much for putting him first…

Maybe it was a good thing that Zahir hadn't stayed to witness the fact that not one member of her family was talking to her. The 'not again…' looks her mother was giving her. At least until they were ushered aboard the private jet, at which point she was too distracted by the kind of luxury that only the super-rich could afford to keep it up.

It was dark, the middle of the night, when they arrived at Nadira Creek. Even so, the air was soft, warm, scented with exotic blooms, and, as she looked up, the stars were like diamonds scattered over black velvet.

Zahir was right. It was awesome.

Like the villa that had been put at their disposal. What she'd seen of it was like something out of a dream. Not that she'd seen much. They were all too shattered by the swift turn of events, the rush, the tension.

But finally Freddy was tucked up and at last she was able to get out of her working clothes and take a shower in a bathroom that was about the size of her bedroom back home, using the kind of soaps that she'd only ever heard of.

Afterwards, wrapped in the softest towelling robe, she checked on her parents. They were already asleep, but, when she tried to follow suit, her mind wouldn't let go. All she could think about was Zahir. What he was doing. What he was thinking.

Had he been mobbed on arrival at the Mansion House? Probably not. With heads of state and cabinet ministers attending, security would be tight.

At the hotel?

Almost certainly. Not that he would say anything. He'd just have given the waiting photographers one of his show-stopping smiles. The kind that meant nothing.

But what was he feeling?

Anger. With himself, no doubt, for behaving like a fool. But with her too, for what he must feel had been her deceit.

She might not have lied about Freddy and if he'd asked her outright she would have told him the truth. But what she hadn't said had left him with a contradiction and he would not, could not, think well of her.

When the pale silver edge of dawn filtered through the lattice shutters of the balcony it came as a relief. She pushed one back and caught her first glimpse of Nadira Creek, shimmering, a pale and milky pink in the early morning light.

Shreds of mist clung to cliffs that rose on the far side of the water. Draped itself like silk chiffon amongst the date palms and what, unbelievably, looked like pomegranate trees in the gardens that sloped away from the terrace below her.

If yesterday had ended on a nightmare, today was beginning with something like a dream.

She quickly showered, dressed and, after looking in on Freddy, still dead to the world, she went downstairs to a huge sitting room where sofas, cushions and beautiful rugs were strewn across the dark polished floor.

But she didn't linger there.

Wide French windows stood open to an arcaded courtyard and she walked out into the misty dawn, drawn by the sound of water trickling down a narrow rill to steps that led down to a lily-covered pool. Beside it, a raised open-sided pavilion was almost hidden beneath a vast fig tree.

Like the house, it was furnished with luxuriously rich carpets and silk cushions, inviting her to curl up and sleep until the world forgot her. Before she gave in to the temptation, a phone resting on a low carved table, the only thing that was out of place in this Arabian Nights fantasy, burbled softly.

She looked around, but there was no one else in sight and, when it rang again, she picked it up. 'Hello?'

For a moment no one answered and, absolutely certain that she'd done the wrong thing, she was about to hang up when Zahir's voice said, 'Diana…'

Just her name, like a sigh, and her legs seemed to buckle beneath her so that somehow she was lying amongst the cushions, for all the world like some pampered houri waiting for her lord.

'Zahir…'

'It's early,' he said. 'You could not sleep?'

'The sun is telling me that it's early, but my body clock is telling me I should be at work,' she replied.

'So you're exploring?'

'Nothing so energetic. Just enjoying the view. It's beautiful, Zahir. Totally wasted on a bunch of journalists...'

She stopped. Not the wisest thing to have said, but when had she ever thought before she spoke?

'They have their uses,' he replied, with what sounded like a smile colouring his voice. 'But rest assured, no journalist will ever enjoy the view from where you are lying now.'

'Oh.'

Diana swallowed, blushing. What was it about the word 'lying' that was so...suggestive? And how did he know...?

She almost felt as if he could see her, touch her. As if he were there with her amongst the silken pillows, his hand cradling her hip, his mouth...

She cleared her throat. Struggled, determinedly, despite the unwillingness of the cushions to let her go, into a sitting position. Then, feeling slightly more in control, said, 'Do you want me to go and find someone for you? I haven't seen anyone, but the doors were open so I imagine someone is about.'

'No need. I just wanted to be sure that you'd arrived safely. That you're comfortable.'

'Comfortable is rather understating the case. I know your resort is supposed to be luxurious, but this is something else. Not at all what I'd expected.'

'Oh?' He sounded amused. 'What did you expect?'

'I don't know,' she said, looking up at the beautiful house built into the rock. The cool blue tiles of the arcaded courtyard, the wide wooden balcony with its fretwork shutters. Another floor above that. 'I somehow imagined a series of cottages set in a garden.'

Definitely not this Arabian Nights palace that looked as if it had been there for all time.

'Maybe I've seen too many travel programmes on the television.'

'Rest assured, Diana. Your imagination is in full working

order. The resort is on the other side of the creek. There is still work going on there, little privacy. I thought you'd be more comfortable in the house. Hamid, my steward, will take you across the creek in the boat, give you the tour whenever you wish. Does your father enjoy fishing?'

'I don't think he's ever tried,' she said. 'But he loves boats.'

'Which explains the book of nautical knots.'

'Oh, no, that was for…' Her hand flew to her mouth, stopping herself from saying the name. *Idiot!*

'I see.'

Did he? Had Freddy been mentioned in the newspapers? *'Single mother chauffeur dances with sheikh in the street…'* would appeal to a certain section of the press.

The silence stretched to breaking point until she could no longer bear it.

'Zahir…'

'Diana…'

They spoke at the same time, apparently both equally anxious to fill the void.

'What is it, Diana? Tell me…'

Tell him what?

That she wished he were here with her? That she'd wept when he'd left her? That there would always be an emptiness in her heart without him?

For heaven's sake, she'd only met him days ago.

But then, how long did it take to fall in love? She had no yardstick against which to judge her feelings. And even if it was love, so what?

He didn't believe in it. He'd told her…

'It was nothing,' she said. Nothing that she had any right to say. Nothing that made any sense. 'How was your Mansion House dinner?'

'Do you want a blow-by-blow account of what I ate? Or a

précis of the Prime Minister's state of the nation speech?' he asked. When she didn't answer, he said, 'No, I thought not.'

She glanced at her watch, calculated the time difference. 'Actually, shouldn't you be on your way to Paris?'

'Paris will have to wait. I've brought my schedule forward to take advantage of the unexpectedly high interest in my affairs. I'm announcing the new airline today.'

'Oh, well, good luck.'

'I think I can guarantee that every seat at the press conference will be taken.' Then, before she could think of a response, 'I have to go. Just ask Hamid for whatever you want, Diana. Do not be shy.'

About to say, Shy? You've got me confused with some other Diana... But, before she could speak, she was listening to the dialling tone.

'Mu-um!'

Freddy came slowly down the steps, rubbing his eyes, trailing his teddy behind him so that he bumped on every one. A sure sign that he needed a hug.

She replaced the receiver and swept him up in her arms and he clung to her, not too big, too grown-up for a cuddle today. She knew how he felt. She could do with one herself.

He recovered first.

But then her condition was terminal...

'Is that the sea?' he asked, perking up as he looked over her shoulder.

'It certainly is,' she said, gathering herself, making an effort at brightness.

'Is there a beach?' Now he wriggled, eager to get down and explore. 'Can we make a sandcastle? Does Grandpa know?' He hit the ground running, teddy abandoned at her feet. 'Grandpa! Grandpa!'

She picked it up, followed him, was just in time to see him

skid to a halt at the sight of Hamid, the white-robed steward who'd shown them to their rooms when they'd arrived.

'Good morning, *sitti*,' he said with a low bow. 'I hope you are comfortable?'

'We're very comfortable thank you, Hamid.'

'Sheikh Zahir wished me to assure you that his house is at your disposal. You are to make yourself completely at home. It is his wish that you enjoy your stay as his guest.'

His house? This was where Zahir lived? As in his actual home?

No wonder he'd sounded amused at her assumption that this was part of the holiday resort.

And he'd already spoken to Hamid. Had his servant put him through to the summer house? Well, of course he had. Why else would the phone have rung there?

Her hand went to her chest to calm the sudden wild beating.

It meant nothing. Nothing…

Hamid folded himself up so that he was on the same level as Freddy. 'What would the young sheikh like for his breakfast?'

Freddy shrank behind her skirt.

'His name is Freddy and the shyness won't last,' she assured the man. 'He usually has cereals. Maybe some juice?' She made it a question, unsure what was on offer.

He smiled at the boy. 'Maybe you would like to try a fig? Some yoghurt with honey? Or what about pancakes?'

'Pancakes?'

'I was with Sheikh Zahir in America. They eat pancakes for breakfast there, did you know?'

Freddy, eyes wide, shook his head.

He certainly knew how to win the heart of a small boy.

'And the *sitti*?' he said, rising. 'Pomegranate juice? New bread. Goats' cheese.'

Sitti? That was her?

'Why don't you surprise us, Hamid?' she said. 'Maybe tea?'

'Darjeeling? Earl Grey?'

'Darjeeling. Thank you,' she said, letting out a silent 'whew' as Hamid bowed and left them. *Goats' cheese for breakfast*? How the other half lived.

Then, laughing—something that after yesterday afternoon she'd thought she'd never do again—she said, 'Okay, young sheikh, I think we need to get you washed and dressed before breakfast.'

Zahir tossed the cellphone on the desk and dragged a hand over his unshaven face. It was six in the morning at Nadira, the best time of day, when the sun would be low, turning the rocks and sand pink. The creek deserted but for a few night fishermen returning with their catch.

And today Diana was walking in his garden, stepping where he'd walked, touching things that were precious to him. Lying where he had lain against the silk cushions in his summer house, surrounded by the scent of jasmine. But not with him. He could not go there while she was there. Could never see her again. Must never call her again.

He picked up the little book that lay on the desk in front of him. The book that Diana had thrust into his hand just before he'd fled the airfield, asking him to give it to Ameerah, and for a moment he held it against his lips, as if to transfer her touch to him.

He'd hated leaving her on her own, even though it would only have been for a little while. He'd wished to meet her parents, apologise as a man should, for having put them through such an ordeal. But to do that would have meant witnessing her face lighting up as this Freddy walked through the door. To offer his hand to a man who possessed what he most desired. And keep that desire from his own eyes.

He'd been a fool to ask Hamid to put him through to the

summer house, would not have done so if he hadn't been assured that she was on her own.

What could he possibly say to her when all the words that burned in his heart were forbidden to him? When all they could talk about was a formal dinner he'd attended? His press conference…

'You've got forty minutes, Zahir.' James looked at his untouched breakfast, the newspapers that lay unopened by his tray, and made no comment. He'd been pointedly not making any comment since he'd arrived back in London yesterday evening. 'I'll get you some fresh coffee.'

'Don't bother. Just see that this is gift-wrapped and delivered to Ameerah,' he said, handing James the book. 'It's from Diana,' he said, finding some consolation in being able to say her name. 'To go with the snow globe.'

'*The Princess and the Frog*?' James said, looking at the book, then at him. 'What on earth has that got to do with the Snow Queen?'

'The Snow Queen?'

Glacial, icily beautiful. He could see how the subject might appeal to a glass-blower but he was, he decided, glad that it had been broken. Its replacement might not have had any intrinsic value but it had warmth…

Or was that an illusion? Was it Diana, weaving her tale for him, who'd given the toy a touch of magic?

James was still awaiting an explanation and, with a shrug, he said, 'I'm afraid there was a slight accident at the airport. A small boy in a hurry. A concrete pavement. I had to find an instant replacement.' Then, 'Nothing nearly so precious.'

'You should have mentioned it. I'll get someone to sort out an insurance claim.'

'Let it go, James. Let it go. In fact, forget this too,' he said, dropping the book in the waste basket. 'We've more important things to do.'

* * *

It was late when he arrived in Ramal Hamrah, but Zahir had warned his mother to expect him. He wanted this over with and he'd changed on the plane, abandoning his suit and tie for traditional robes.

For a formal visit to his mother, *this* formal visit, only traditional robes would do. The gossamer-fine black and gold camel hair cloak. A *keffiyeh* held in place by a simple camel halter.

His mother was alone, standing in the centre of her drawing room—a princess granting an audience. He touched his forehead, his heart, bowed low.

'*Sitti*,' he said. My lady. Only then did he approach to kiss her.

She was slight and, as he straightened, he stood nearly a foot taller, but her slap as she struck his cheek with the flat of her hand had force enough to drive him back a step, ring his ears.

Futile, then, to hope that she hadn't seen the newspaper.

He bowed a second time, an acknowledgement that her anger was justified, her rebuke accepted without argument.

'I am here to inform you, *sitti,* that I am at your command, ready to meet with, take a bride from the young women you have chosen,' he said.

'You think it is that simple?' she enquired, her voice dripping ice. 'Yesterday I met with the Attiyah family. They have no male heir and mothers are lining up to make an alliance for their sons with Shula, their oldest daughter. You, my son, for reasons that I cannot begin to fathom, seem to be favoured above all, but this morning I received a note from the girl's mother, asking me to deny a rumour that you have installed your mistress at your house at Nadira.'

Well, that explained the slap. Embarrassing his mother was the sin.

'I will assure Kasim al-Attiyah, as I assure you,' he replied, 'that Miss Metcalfe is not my mistress. I have simply given her and her family temporary refuge…'

'Her father is not the one you have to convince. He is a

man and he knows that all men carry their brains between their legs.'

Having got that off her chest, her face softened and she laid the hand she'd struck him with against his cheek. 'Shula al-Attiyah is a modern woman, Zahir. She is well-educated, travelled, as are all the young women I've chosen for you to meet. I sought a true match for you, my son. Someone who understands your world. Who will be the kind of life partner you would choose for yourself.' She let her hand fall, turned away. 'But this is the twenty-first century and no Ramal Hamrah girl worth her salt is going to ally herself with a man who's photographed dancing in a London street with his—'

'Mother,' he warned.

'With a woman who, even now, is living in your house with her child. A boy the gossips in the souk are saying is your son!'

'What did you say?'

Zahir heard his mother's words clearly enough but they made no sense. He reran them over and over...

Boy...

Son...

'Is it true?' she demanded, while he was still trying to come to terms with what she'd said.

He shook his head. It couldn't be true...

And yet, almost like a movie running in his brain, he saw again the carrier with the books she'd bought. Saw himself opening it. Children's books, she'd said. *Children's* books. Plural. The fairy tale book had been for Ameerah. But the other one, the book of knots, that was the kind of gift you'd buy for a small boy...

She'd lied to him. No...

His gesture, pushing the thought away, was emphatic.

She had not lied.

He, in an offhand remark, had provided her with the excuse

and she'd grabbed at it, using it to keep him at a distance. And it would have worked but for the photograph in *The Courier*—

'You do not seem certain, my son.'

He was dragged back to the present, to the reality of what was rather than the might-have-been, by a suggestion of anxiety in his mother's voice, sensing that beneath her aristocratic posture was a genuine fear that, even in this most basic duty—to make a marriage that would bring honour to his family—he was about to fail her.

'You may rest assured that I met Miss Metcalfe for the first time this week,' he said, and his heart tore at the unmistakable sag in her aristocratic posture as the tension left her.

It was recovered in a moment and, with a gracious nod, she dismissed him. 'Very well. Call on me tomorrow at five and I will introduce you to Shula al-Attiyah.'

CHAPTER TEN

Zahir's first impulse on leaving his mother's house was to drive straight to Nadira to demand answers. But not dressed like this. Not wearing the robes in which he'd just made a commitment to marriage, an alliance that would bring honour to his family.

This was not the man who'd kissed, danced in the streets as if his life were his own.

By the time he'd showered, changed and was racing out across the desert, however, common sense began to assert itself.

It would be the early hours of the morning before he reached Nadira and he'd already caused Diana enough grief with his foolishness.

He slowed, pulled off the road and, wrapping himself in a heavy camel-hair cloak, began to walk.

He'd sworn he'd stay away from Diana, for once do his duty. It was his cousin, Hanif—a man for whom duty was as life itself—who had warned him that marriage was a lifelong commitment. Not something to be entered into lightly, but wholeheartedly.

And he was right. There must be no looking back over his shoulder. No lingering sense of unfinished business.

With the memory of Diana doubled up in silent agony on the quay seared into his mind, he had no doubt that there was unfinished business here.

Why had she lied to him?

He stopped. No. That was wrong. She had not lied. But neither had she contradicted him when he'd offered his own insulting interpretation. But what was he to think when one moment she was lost to the world in his arms, the next minute on edge, untouchable, desperate to get back to London?

He'd seen her pain, but had written it off as her own guilty conscience troubling her. Had turned away, so blinded by hurt, by a sense of betrayal, that he'd been unable to accept what, deep down, he'd known. That the betrayal was his.

His future was written. He could offer her nothing, whereas Diana…

Yesterday she could have made a fortune selling her 'story' to the press. She wouldn't even have had to sex things up. All she'd have had to do was tell it like it was and the entire world would have been enchanted.

As he was.

At first sight.

She hadn't even considered it. Not for a minute. From the moment she'd been told what had happened she'd thought only of her son. Her family. Of him. Apologising to him as if this was in some way her fault.

She had a son!

How old was he? Did he look like her? Or his absent father? That he was absent he did not doubt. She'd told him that she lived with her parents. Knew that she worked hard to provide for him…

He knew so little.

And yet so much. He knew that she was a loving mother. He's seen her face, tender as she'd spoken the boy's name. It was a look that had torn his heart out.

It was a look he'd seen tonight on his own mother's face as she'd lain her hand against his cheek.

Furious as she was, the unconditional love remained. All

she cared about was his happiness, a fact she'd demonstrated in searching for a bride who would please him, rather than the daughter-in-law she must have hoped for—an educated, travelled career woman, rather than a stay-at-home girl whose only thought would be to provide her with grandchildren.

He walked until pre-dawn turned the sky grey, coming to terms with what he must do. His parting from Diana had been abrupt, painful. It had not been done well and, before he could move on, embrace the life that awaited him, he had to thank her for what she'd done. Show her that he honoured her.

Zahir let himself into the quiet house just as dawn was turning from pink to gold and, for a moment, he stood in the tranquil courtyard and let the peace of the place surround him.

He had an apartment in the city, but he'd made no secret of the fact that this house belonged to his heart. That it was his home. His future. The place where he would, eventually—when he had time—bring his bride, make a family.

It was hardly surprising the gossips were having a field day, he thought as he crossed to the steps that led down to the pavilion.

Someone had beaten him to it. Diana…?

He paused at the foot of the veranda steps, listening to the soft sigh of her breath. Had she slept amongst the cushions, as he did on warm nights?

One step would bring him to her side. Her hair, tumbled over the silk, would be his to touch. Her cheek, her lips…

The thought made the heat sing in his blood.

'No…' The word was wrenched from him but, as he turned away, a tousled head appeared from amongst the cushions. Eyes the colour of a spring hedgerow met his.

Blinked.

Like Diana's. The same colour. The same shape, but not Diana's eyes. This was her child? Her son…

How could he doubt it?

The boy's hair was darker, but the curl matched hers. And his dimpled smile, like hers, went straight to his heart, capturing it in an instant as he sat up, yawned and said, 'Hello.' Then, 'Who are you?'

Zahir touched his hand to his heart, bowed formally. 'My name is Zahir bin Ali bin Khatib al-Khatib.' Then, when the boy giggled, he lowered himself to the veranda steps so that he was the same level as the child and said, 'And you, *ya habibi*? What is your name?'

'I'm Freddy.' Then, as if realising that this came up short, he said, 'I'm Frederick Trueman Metcalfe. I was named after Fiery Fred, the finest bowler who ever played cricket for Yorkshire and England.' The words came out all in a rush, as if it was something he'd heard many times but did not quite understand. He suddenly looked less certain. 'At least that's what my grandpa says.'

'It's a fine name. And are you going to follow in Mr Trueman's footsteps and play cricket for England?'

'No. I'm going to be a footballer.'

Zahir managed to hide a smile. 'We must all follow our own star, Freddy. Dream our own dreams.'

Live our own lives?

No! No...

Then, concerned, 'Are you alone?'

'I was looking for Mummy. She wasn't in her room when I woke up so I came here. She was here yesterday.'

They had both come here looking for her...

'Have you had breakfast?'

'Not yet.'

'Then maybe we should go and do something about that.'

'I had pancakes yesterday. Mummy had a fig.'

'Wouldn't you like to try one?' He indicated the tree above them. 'You could pick your own if you like.'

The boy needed no second bidding, but leapt to his feet. Then, 'I can't, it's too high!'

'No problem,' Zahir said, picking him up, but, as he hoisted him to his shoulder, they both turned as they heard Diana making her way up the steps from the beach. She was singing slightly breathless snatches of lyrics from a familiar song, filling in the missing words with the odd 'la-la' as she had when they'd danced.

'La-la, la-la… La-la, la-la…'

She appeared on the path below them, for a moment totally unaware that she had an audience. Then, as Freddy giggled, she looked up, saw them together and stopped in mid 'la'…

And his mouth dried.

She had been for an early morning dip and was wearing nothing but a simple one-piece bathing costume. Her creamy skin had dried on the walk up from the beach, but her hair was a mass of wet ringlets that dripped tiny rivulets of water on to her shoulders. Venus herself could not have been more beautiful, more enticing.

'Zahir…' She seemed as lost for words as he was. Then, recovering first, she said, 'I see you've met Freddy.'

'He's rather younger than I imagined…'

'I'm not young, I'm five!' the boy declared.

'But very big for five,' Zahir added quickly.

And Diana smiled.

Stood there in his garden, bare legs, bare shoulders, every curve of her body brought into the sharpest focus by the clinging fabric of her wet bathing suit, smiling that sweet, tender smile that would have tempted a saint. And he was no saint.

But then neither, it appeared, was she.

'I imagine he gets that from his father?' he prompted and her smile, along with the flush of exertion from the walk up from the beach, disappeared like water poured on sand.

'Freddy, I think we'd better go and find Grandma.' She extended her hand. 'Come on, she'll be wondering where we are.'

'I don't *think* so,' he said. Five years old and already resisting the tug of the apron strings.

'Freddy!'

'I *looked*. She's asleep.' The boy looked at him, a mute appeal for backup.

'Freddy and I were about to pick some figs. I'd invite you to join us but, much as I regret the fact, I'm afraid that with your colouring, you need to cover up before the sun gets any higher.'

Cover up…

Diana felt the heat flood into her cheeks as she realised just how little she was wearing. Just an old bathing suit that had been purchased for respectability rather than glamour. Something to wear when she took Freddy to mother and child swimming classes.

She hadn't even thought to take a towel with her, too locked into the idea of plunging into cold water to cool her overheated body.

Zahir was the last person she'd imagined meeting. Zahir looking at her as if she were Eve and it was the first morning…

'Um… Good plan…' she said, backing away in the direction of the house. 'You two g-go and make a start, while I…' she made a vague gesture to indicate her lack of covering, instantly regretting drawing further attention to the fact '…cover up.'

Then she turned and ran.

By the time she'd showered and gone through her entire wardrobe looking for something that would counteract the swimsuit look without looking as if she were hiding—cropped trousers, a long shirt with the sleeves rolled up—breakfast was well under way.

Zahir looked up, smiled, then continued talking to her father. Her mother passed her a cup of coffee without saying a word. Freddy looked up and said, 'Z'hir's taking Grandpa and me out on a boat. Do you want to come?'

She looked up, met Zahir's eyes and they were both remembering another day, another boat...

'My father keeps a small dhow here. For fishing. It's pretty basic.'

'Then I'll pass, thanks.'

'Do you want to talk about it?'

Diana and her mother were sitting on a rock above the beach, looking out over the water, watching the dhow set off down the creek.

'There's nothing to talk about,' she said, tossing a pebble into the water.

'I haven't seen you this...' she sought for the word. '...this *lost* since you were expecting Freddy.'

'That was different,' she said quickly. Then, when her mother just raised a brow, she shook her head. 'I can't explain it, but it's different, okay?'

'How different?'

But maybe not that different.

'It's easy to see how your sheikh might dazzle you,' her mother said. 'Sweep you off your feet. He's a very good-looking man. And charming too—'

'No.' Then, 'Well, yes. Obviously.'

The difference was that Pete O'Hanlon had dazzled her with his danger. Had tempted her for no other reason than because he could. Because it amused him to take something untouched and mark it as his own. He did not build things, cherish things or people. He destroyed them...

Zahir was nothing like that.

Her mother looked anxious.

'He didn't dazzle me.' At least not intentionally.

All it had taken was one look and she'd lost it. All that painfully learned control, forgotten in an instant, gone in a look.

Okay. That was the same.

But she wasn't an eighteen-year-old with her hormones on fire. She'd kept it together for Freddy. Just…

She turned to her mother. 'How can one look change everything?' she asked, needing someone older, wiser to tell her. 'How can I feel this way about someone I met a couple of days ago?'

He'd looked at her as if she were the first woman and she hadn't wanted to run and hide. She'd wanted to touch him. Had wanted him to touch her.

That was different.

She'd made him laugh.

He'd made her want to dance. Made her feel brand-new…

'I don't know,' her mother replied. 'How do you feel?'

'As if…' As if he had been made just for her. 'As if he's a perfect fit,' she said. 'As if it's…*right.*'

And that was different too.

She'd known from the moment he'd taken what he wanted that everything about Pete O'Hanlon was wrong. That she'd been an idiot. That the next day he wouldn't even remember her name…

'It's a mystery. They say it's just chemical attraction. Sexual attraction is nature's way of keeping the species going. Marriage is society's way of dealing with the consequences.' She smiled. 'Or it was.' She shook her head, sighed. 'It doesn't explain how I knew your father was the one the minute he looked at me, though.' Then, smiling, 'Or maybe it does. Maybe it was no more than lust and I just got lucky.'

'It's more than that. You love each other.'

'It takes a lot of love to hold a marriage together for twenty-five years. Not that falling-in-love kind of love, though. It's the love you work at, that evolves, changes to match everything that life throws at the pair of you. But luck helps.'

When Diana didn't respond, she said, 'Maybe this is your time to get lucky. Does Zahir feel the same way about you?'

'It doesn't matter what he feels.' Her voice was more emphatic than her feelings.

That he was feeling something she never doubted. That he desired her. That if she'd been a different kind of woman, one who didn't have to live well one hundred per cent of the time just to make up for the one time she hadn't, they might have had a brief, exciting fling.

But that was all it could ever be.

'In this world, Zahir's world, marriages are arranged. He will marry someone his family, his peers, deem a perfect match.'

Her mother frowned. 'He told you that?'

'We were discussing fairy tales. It came up…'

'There's no room for romance?'

'Respect lasts longer,' she said, managing a smile for her mother. Wanting to reassure her that this time she wasn't going to fall apart. 'We both agreed that fairy tales are for children.'

'And meanwhile he can dance in the street with any girl who catches his eye?'

'Nothing happened. Truly. If it hadn't been for that photograph…'

If it hadn't been for that photograph they'd be back in their own little worlds. She'd be back on the school minibus. He'd be doing whatever billionaire sheikhs did. 'A couple of kisses, that idiotic dance…'

'Sometimes that's all it takes,' her mother said, laying a hand gently over hers. 'A look, a kiss, for the magic to change everything. How many men have you kissed? I mean kissed wanting more?'

'Only one.'

'Freddy's father?'

Diana looked out across the water. Could see Zahir and her father laughing at something Freddy had said or done. It was the perfect image. A little boy with two strong men to keep him safe. Except that Zahir would be gone in an hour or two and, once they'd left this beautiful place, their worlds would not touch again.

'No,' she said. 'Not Freddy's father.'

'Diana…'

She turned her hand to clasp her mother's fingers. She'd never told. She'd protected Freddy. Had protected her family. Had protected everyone except herself.

It was a secret that had stood between her and her parents for nearly six years. When she'd put up that wall of silence, had refused to confide in them, had refused to cave into the threats of the Child Support Agency, telling them what to do with their money, something had been lost…

'Don't ask, Mum. If you knew, you'd look at him differently. You wouldn't be able to help yourself.'

Instead of pressing her, her mother just squeezed her hand. 'I'm proud of you, Diana. You're a strong woman and Freddy's a lucky boy…'

When the men returned, bearing their trophy fish, her mother took Freddy away to clean him up, her father went to take a nap, leaving her alone in the garden with Zahir.

'We have had no time to talk,' he said, 'and now I have to go.'

'Thank you for giving Freddy such a treat.'

'It was a pleasure. He's a lovely boy. But then he has a lovely mother. Walk with me to my car?'

She followed him up steps at the side of the house to a courtyard. It had been dark when they'd arrived, but now she could see that it commanded a view of the entire creek, and because she knew he was going to say something she didn't want to hear, she said, 'This is beautiful, Zahir. Has it always belonged to your family?'

'No. I came across the house when I was out sailing one weekend. A storm blew up and I took shelter in the creek. The place was uninhabited, falling to rack and ruin, but it was love at first sight and I bought it. Restored it.'

'You've done all this?'

'I made a start, did the early clearance, but life intruded. My family needed me. Then I got involved with the travel business. The truth of the matter is that these days I speak and it is done.'

'But the vision, the dream, is yours.'

'A man needs dreams to sustain him,' he said, turning abruptly away, opening the car door.

'We all need dreams.' Then, because the lie she had told hung between them and she wanted this over so that she could draw a line, begin to move on, she said, 'About Freddy…'

He stopped. 'You think that is why I came here today?' he said, not turning. 'To ask about your son?'

'Didn't you?' Then, when he didn't answer, 'I let you think he was my lover so that you would walk away.'

He straightened. 'Because you did not trust me.'

'No! Because I did not trust myself…'

As he swung round to face her, she faltered. 'Because once, when I was eighteen, I lost my head and hurt everyone who loved me…'

'Is being a single mother such a big deal these days?'

'No, but being a single mother and refusing to name the father is a very big deal.'

Zahir frowned. 'Why would you protect a man from his responsibilities?'

'I wasn't protecting him, I was protecting Freddy. I didn't want him tainted. Didn't want anyone to look at him and say, "Like father, like son…" Always be looking for the first sign that he was going the same way.'

He reached out, caught her elbow, and somehow she was leaning against him, his arm around her, not in an embrace, but as support.

'I was supposed to be the level-headed one in my year. The daughter every mother wanted...' She gulped. 'Maybe that was part of it. I was tired of being good. I just wanted to be like everyone else, part of the gang, but all those boys at school were so...ordinary.'

'And it took extra-ordinary to make you bad?' he said gently.

'Pete O'Hanlon was different. Five years older. And so gloriously, perfectly dangerous.'

The words, his name, had spilled out before she was even aware she was thinking them. More than she'd told her mother. More than she'd told anyone.

'He was the worst nightmare of every woman with an impressionable daughter. And boy, was I impressionable? He'd moved away, no one knew where he'd gone, what he was doing, but his cousin was in the same class at school as me and he came to her eighteenth birthday party. The air buzzed when he walked in. Every girl was suddenly taller, more alive. Every boy looked...dull.'

'But he chose you...'

He'd waited until she was leaving. Had caught up with her, offered her a lift home.

'There are more dangerous things than walking home alone in the dark,' Zahir said when, finally, she stopped. 'Where is he now?'

'The morning after I got everything I deserved,' she said. 'He and three other men held up a bank. The police were waiting. He tried to shoot his way out and was killed.' She shuddered. 'I may be wrong, but I don't believe that Sadie Redford would be so quick to invite Freddy over for a play-date with her little girl if she knew that.'

'The sins of the father?'

The only sound was the air humming as the heat intensified. The high pitched note of cicadas stridulating below them in the garden. The blood pulsing in her ears as she waited for him to say something, anything.

'You are his mother, Diana. Nothing else matters.'

'No.' Then, shaking her head, 'Why did you come, Zahir?'

'Because…' He lifted his hand to her cheek. 'Because I could not stop myself.' He did not smile as he added, 'It seems that I am not as strong as you.'

For a moment she thought he would kiss her, but he let his hand fall to his side.

'You should get out of the sun now.' Then, as he climbed into the car, 'I promised Freddy that I would take him sailing tomorrow. I'll be here at six.'

Zahir walked with Shula al-Attiyah in his mother's garden, while their mothers gossiped and kept an eye on them. She was, just as his mother had promised, intelligent, well travelled, lively. Perfect in every respect but one. She was not Diana Metcalfe.

He sailed with Freddy the following morning and afterwards he ate a sumptuous *mezza* served by Hamid in the shade of the terrace with Diana and her family. Then he walked with Diana in the garden as he had walked with Shula.

He could not have said what they talked about. Only that being with her was right. That leaving her felt like tearing himself in half.

In the afternoon he met Adina al-Thani. She was the girl recommended by his sister for the beauty of her hair. It was a smooth ebony curtain of silk that hung to her waist and it was indeed beautiful.

If it had been chestnut. If curls had corkscrewed every which way, it would have been perfect.

Later, he had dinner with his father, who had just returned from the Sudan. They talked about politics. About the new airline. They did not talk about his marriage. Or the visitors occupying his house at Nadira.

But when he was leaving his father said, 'I want you to know that I'm proud of you, my son. This country needs men like you. Men who can take the future and mould it to their own vision.'

And he wasn't sure if that made him feel better, or worse.

The next day he was forced to remain in the capital, deal with the mountain of paperwork that was coming in from London. Have lunch with Leila al-Kassami—the one who was not beautiful but had a lovely smile—and her mother.

She, of all of them, came closest to his heart's desire. Perhaps if the smile had been preceded by the fleeting appearance of a dimple, if she had caught her lip between her teeth to stop herself from saying the first thing that came into her head…

As they left, he saw his mother watching him with an expression close to desperation and knew that he was running out of time.

That evening he took Diana on a tour of his 'vision'. Showed her the cottages, the central building that would provide everything a visitor could dream of. The chandlery, the marina. The island where the restaurant was nearing completion. The pavilion where people seeking somewhere different to hold a wedding could make their vows.

She stood beside him beneath the domed canopy looking up at the tiny lapis and gold tiles that looked like the sky in that moment before it went black and said, 'It's beautiful, Zahir.' And then she looked at him. 'Like something out of a fairy tale.'

'Wait until you see the real thing…'

'Oh, but I have…'

'No. Tonight I'll drive you far beyond the reach of man-made light—only there is it possible to see the heavens as God made them.'

Once darkness fell, he'd take her into the desert and, maybe, beneath the infinity of the heavens, she would be able to understand, he would be able to understand why, despite the fact that she had somehow taken possession of his heart, tomorrow he would have to redeem his promise to his mother. Do his duty as a son.

'I will not be able to come here again during your visit,' he said. 'But I want to give you this gift.'

Diana heard the words. Heard more, perhaps, than he'd intended to say. Something that they had both agreed upon from the very first. That there were no fairy tales.

CHAPTER ELEVEN

ZAHIR was unusually silent on the trip out into the desert but, when he stopped the big four-wheel drive, he told Diana to close her eyes before he killed the engine. Turned off the lights.

'Keep them closed,' he warned, as he opened the door, letting in a blast of cold air. She heard him walk around the vehicle, then he opened the door beside her.

'Here, take my cloak, you'll need it,' he said, dumping something heavy in her lap, before lifting her clear of her seat.

'Zahir!' she protested. 'I'm not helpless. I can walk!'

'Not if your eyes are closed.' Then, 'You might want to hold on.'

Obediently, she wrapped one arm around his neck, clutching the cloak to her with the other, while he carried her surely and safely over ground that crunched beneath his feet. Cheating a little, lifting her lids a fraction so that she could watch his face, the way his breath condensed in little clouds in the faint light from the stars.

'Can I look now?' she asked when he set her on her feet.

'I'll tell you when,' he said, taking the cloak and wrapping it around her. Then, standing behind her, his hands on either side of her shoulders as if afraid she might fall, he said, 'Now!'

She would have gasped if she could have caught her breath. Instead, soundlessly, she reached out, first to the sky, then back for his hand. As if he knew exactly how she would react, he was there, waiting for her, taking her hand in his.

How long they'd been standing there when the cold finally penetrated her brain, she could not have said.

'You must be freezing,' she said and, half turning, she opened the cloak, inviting him to share the warmth. When he hesitated, she said, 'Come on, before I freeze too.'

He joined her, slipping his arm around her waist to bring them close enough to fit in together and they stood, wrapped up in its warmth, for the longest time, her head on his shoulder, looking at the heavens. Diana knew, just knew, that this would be the moment she would remember when she was dying.

'I never dreamed,' she said at last, 'that there were so many stars.'

'They say that if you took a handful of sand from a beach and each grain of sand was a star you can see—'

'—the rest of the beach would represent the stars that are out of sight. I read that somewhere, but when you see it, really see it, it's…incomprehensible.'

'In the face of such vastness it is impossible not to feel… humble.'

'Yes,' she said. Then, lifting her head, turning to look at him, 'But how great too! We're standing here, looking up into the unimaginable vastness of space, and our imagination isn't crushed by that; it soars!'

In the starlight she could see a frown pucker in the space between his eyes.

'All through history we've looked up there and made stories, strived to know the unknowable. We're less than grains of sand in the cosmic scheme of things, no more than the tiniest particles of dust, and yet we're huge. Giants.' She turned and stretched her arms up to the stars. 'We're the star-gatherers, Zahir! We can do anything, be anyone. Only our own fears hold us back…' And she'd spent too many years afraid to step out of the shadows. Afraid to grab the world by the throat. Seize the dream. 'Thank you. Thank you for showing me that…'

And then, because one dream was all she had, because they both knew that this was goodbye, she leaned into him, kissed him briefly on the lips, before saying, 'I need to go home.'

When Diana called James Pierce it was still dark at Nadira. By the time her mother was awake, she had packed.

'Where are you going?'

'Home.' Her mother looked doubtful. 'It's okay. According to Mr Pierce, some supermodel had a furniture-throwing fight with her boyfriend in a nightclub and they both got arrested. Our little story can't begin to compete with that.'

'Well, that's good, but do you have to rush back to London? You're on leave, anyway.'

'There are things I have to do, but you're all staying until Saturday. Mr Pierce is sorting flights for you. Hamid will have all the details.'

'And Zahir?'

'He's been more than generous with his time, but he's got a business to run. He won't have time to come out here again.'

'I'm sorry.'

'No.' She blinked away the sting of a tear. No tears… 'No regrets.' She hugged her. 'Give Freddy a hug from me. See you at the weekend.'

And two hours after that she was on her way to London, this time flying business class on a scheduled flight.

She suspected James Pierce would have put her in economy if he'd dared and actually she didn't blame him. She'd messed up his boss's big week. Had made extra work for him.

The only thing they'd both agreed on was that Zahir should not be told until she was home. She'd scarcely expected to find

James himself waiting to meet her, drive her home. A journey accomplished in almost total silence.

It was barely dark, just on nine, when he pulled up in front of Aunt Alice's. She didn't believe for a minute that anyone would be hanging around the house, but someone in the street would undoubtedly have taken the tabloid shilling to call in the moment she put in an appearance. She didn't blame them for that, but she wasn't prepared to make it easy for them either.

'Thank you, Mr Pierce. I'm very grateful—'

He dismissed her gratitude with a gesture. Then, 'I don't understand.' She waited. 'Why didn't you sell your story?'

'There is no story,' she said.

'When did that matter?'

She shook her head. 'I wouldn't do that to anyone, let alone someone I…' She stopped. 'Anyone.'

'No. I'm sorry, Miss Metcalfe. I saw how Zahir looked at you and feared exactly this, but I misjudged you. I thought you were—'

'A girl on the make?' She said it before he did.

'Under normal circumstances it wouldn't have mattered but Sheikh Zahir's family are in the middle of marriage negotiations on his behalf. It's a very bad moment to have some sordid story spread all over the media…'

'Arranged…' A small sound, as if all the breath had been driven from her, escaped Diana before she could stop it. 'Now?'

That was why he'd whisked her and her family to Nadira? Not concern for her, as she'd thought, but to keep her isolated? Out of the clutches of the press until the fuss had died down?

'It's the way they do things,' James said, mistaking her reaction for shock. Why would she be shocked? He'd told her how they did things…

But while she'd unburdened herself, had spilled out the

secret she hadn't even shared with her mother, he had kept this from her.

'If there's anything you need,' James continued, clearly anxious to be on his way. 'If you have any problems, please give me a call.' He handed her a card. 'I'll be staying in London for the foreseeable future.' He gave the smallest of shrugs and said, 'Zahir appointed me CEO of the airline before he left.'

She remembered. He'd mentioned it when they'd been at the yacht club. 'Congratulations.' Then, pulling herself together, trying to hang on to her sudden elation as she'd looked up at the stars, 'Maybe there is something. I'm going to need a bank loan to buy my first taxi. The last time I tried, I was shown the door.'

'You want to buy a taxi? Don't you have to pass tests to get a licence to drive a London cab?'

'I was nearly there once.' Then her dad had a stroke and her life had hit the skids for the second time and it had felt like punishment for her sins… 'I can do it again.'

'Oh, well, under the circumstances I'm sure Sheikh Zahir would be more than willing to—'

'No!' Then, 'No. That's not what I'm asking for. I don't want his money. Not even as a loan. What I want is for the bank manager to treat me with respect. Take me seriously.'

'I see. Well, in that case you're going to need a business plan and an accountant.' And wonder of wonders, he smiled. 'In fact you might try the Prince's Trust. They help young people set up in business. I'll make some enquiries.'

'No…'

She wasn't crawling back into her rut. She'd allowed herself to love someone and the world hadn't fallen apart. She'd seen the universe and she'd been inspired.

'Thank you, James, but I can do that.'

'I don't doubt it, Miss Metcalfe, but the number on the card is a direct line to my office. Give me a call if I can help.'

* * *

Zahir found his mother sitting in her garden. Kissed her cheek, took her hand.

'Are you well?' he asked, sitting beside her.

'By the will of Allah,' she said. 'And you, Zahir?'

'By the will of Allah,' he replied.

She smiled up at him. 'You look happy. I can see that you have made your decision.'

'I have. It was not easy but the woman who has won my heart has warmth, sweetness, honour. She has courage too. And family is everything to her.'

'Then it seems that I have found you a paragon!'

'No man could…' or would, he thought '…live with a paragon. Except my father,' he added swiftly. 'The women you chose were all equally charming and any one of them would make a perfect wife. For someone else.'

Her smile faded. 'Zahir…'

'When I was young, I had Hanif to speak for me, talk to my father, persuade him to let me take my own path, even though it was not the one chosen for me. Have I failed you, have I brought dishonour on my family?'

'My son…' She shook her head. Laid a hand over his.

'Now I am a man and I must speak for myself. I honour you and my father, as I have always honoured you. Will you not trust me in this greatest of all decisions to know my own heart?'

Alone in the house, Diana hadn't put the light on but had curled up in bed, hugging the cat for comfort.

She'd woken early—she'd just about adjusted to Ramal Hamrah time—and, because the alternative was lying there thinking about Zahir standing under that canopy with some perfect match his family had found for him, she got up and set about making a plan.

No. Not the canopy. He'd said that traditional weddings

took place in the bride's home. Well, obviously, he'd been thinking about it...

She concentrated on the list of things to do. First thing she'd call the Public Carriage Office and talk to someone about getting back on track with her 'appearances'—the tests of her knowledge of the quickest routes in London.

Then she'd go to the library and use the computer to follow up the stuff James Pierce had mentioned, check on the possibility of a start-up grant.

A princess.

She'd bet they'd found him a princess to marry.

Well, that was how it was in real life. Princes married princesses while Cinderella...got the frog.

She called Sadie.

'It's quiet here. No one at Capitol is prepared to talk and the media was reduced to printing a fuzzy school photograph of you.'

'Oh, terrific. One minute I'm hanging off the arm of a sheikh in the hat from hell, the next the world sees me in pigtails!'

'You looked cute.'

'I'm twenty-three. Cute is not a good look!' Then, 'I just hope that whoever sold it to them made them pay through the nose.'

She got a couple of startled looks from the neighbours as she walked down the street, but she just smiled and said, 'Gorgeous day!' and walked on. Called in at the bank to make an appointment. Visited the library.

She thought she was home clear when a journalist caught up with her in the supermarket.

'Nice tan, Diana. Been somewhere nice?'

'Do I know you?'

'Jack Harding. *The Courier.* Ramal Hamrah is very nice at this time of year, I believe.'

'And you would know that how?' she asked.

It was surreal but she refused to duck and run. She would

not hide. Instead, she carried on shopping, bought cheese, eggs, apples.

By the time she reached the checkout there were three of them.

'Will you be seeing the Sheikh again?'

'Can you pass me down that jar of tomato paste.' she replied.

'Are you going back to work?'

'Haven't you lot got a supermodel to harass?' she asked, losing patience.

'She's in rehab. And Cinderella is a much better story.'

'It's a fairy tale,' she replied. Then, 'Are you lot going to follow me home?'

'Will you make us a cup of tea and tell us your life story if we do?'

'No, but you could make yourself useful,' she said, pointing at her shopping. 'Carry that.' She didn't wait to see whether any of them picked up her bags, but just walked out.

She let them follow her up to the front door before she retrieved the carriers with a smile. 'Thank you.' Then, as she slipped the key into the lock, she glanced back. 'Will you be here tomorrow?'

'What's happening tomorrow?'

'Nothing. But the grass needs cutting and because of you lot Dad isn't here to do it.'

They laughed, but with the embarrassment of men who'd been caught out misbehaving.

'No? Well, sorry guys, but that's as exciting as it's going to get around here.' And with that she stepped inside, closed the door on them and leaned back against it, shaking like a leaf. So much for it all being over.

But she'd survived. And as soon as they realised there really was nothing in it for them, they'd drift away. A week from now no one would even remember that she'd danced with a sheikh in Berkeley Square.

Well, except for whoever made a little cash selling an old school photograph.

And her.

Her fairy tale prince might be unattainable, but he was unforgettable. And he had made the magic happen, had brought the world into focus, had reminded her that dreaming was allowed. That anyone could do it. That she could do anything...

Next year she'd have her own taxi. A pink, sparkly one that would turn heads, make people smile. And every day when she drove it around London, she'd thank him for hauling her out of the deep rut she had been digging for herself, had been hiding in.

She drew in a deep breath and walked through to the kitchen. Dumped her bags on the table.

The cat rubbed against her leg, then crossed to the door and, refusing to submit to the indignity of the cat flap when there was a human on hand to open the door, waited to be let out.

'You are such a princess,' Diana said, opening the door with a mock curtsey. And found herself staring at her fantasy.

The desert prince she had expected when she'd dashed to the City Airport. The whole white robes, gold-trimmed cloak, headdress thingy.

But it wasn't his robes that held her. She'd recognised what he was even in the most casual clothes. Now, as then, it was Zahir's dark eyes that drained the power of speech as she relived that moment when she'd first set eyes on him. But this time she recognised it for what it was.

The prelude to pain...

Ten minutes ago her life had seemed so simple. Her sights fixed on an attainable goal. Her heart safely back behind locked doors.

Now...

'Your Aunt Alice was kind enough to let me come through

her garden,' he said, answering the what-the-hell-are-you-doing-here? question she'd been unable to frame. He shrugged. Smiled. Just with his eyes.

Oh, no...

'Aunt Alice!' she exploded. 'Why did you bother coming in the back way if you're going to come dressed like Lawrence of...' she struggled to keep the expletive in check '...of Arabia?' She made a wild gesture that took in his clothes. 'And where did you park your camel?'

'I hate to disappoint you, Diana, but I came by cab.'

'Oh, great! The driver is probably calling in the story right now. I've only just got rid of three journalists who followed me home...'

And, grabbing his arm, she pulled him into the kitchen, shut the door and leaned back against it, hands pressed to her lips.

'It was not my intention to sneak in unobserved, but I only had Aunt Alice's address.' Then, taking her hands from her mouth, kissing each of them, he said, 'I suppose I could have walked along this street knocking on doors until I found you—'

'You might as well have done!'

Then, with a gesture of helplessness, she let it go. What mattered was not how but *why* he'd come.

'What are you doing here, Zahir?' she demanded. 'I've just about got my head around this and you've chosen to turn a nine-day wonder into a front page story...'

'I have nothing to hide and neither have you.' Then, 'Freddy asked me to give you this.' From somewhere in the folds of his robe he produced a small piece of rope. 'He wanted you to see the reef knot we made.'

Diana took it. It was warm and without thinking, she lifted it to her cheek.

Then, looking up at him, 'We?'

'The two of us.'

'But… You said you wouldn't be going back to Nadira this week.'

'Is that why you left?'

'No…' Then, because he deserved better than some feeble lie, 'Maybe. But it was more than that. You listened to my story and you…' She reached for the words. 'You set me free, Zahir. Showed me how insignificant we are, but how great too. I've spent years expecting nothing. Believing that I was worth nothing—'

'Believing that you were the frog?' He smiled. 'Don't you know that once you've been kissed by a prince all bets are off?'

'No. The true meaning of the fairy story is that we are all princesses. It's just that some of us lose the ability to see that. But you treated me like one. Gave me the courage to believe. To gather my own stars.'

There was a long peal on the doorbell. It hadn't taken long…

'Speaking of fairy stories, why did you come back, Zahir? Haven't you got something more important to do? Like arranging your marriage?'

Far from looking like a man caught out, he said, 'That's the beauty of a system like ours, Diana. Once I have made my decision, chosen my bride, I don't have to do a thing. Even as we speak, my mother is negotiating with my bride's family, drawing up the contract.'

'I can't believe you're saying that. It's…gruesome.'

'No, no… I promise you, the women will have a very happy time disposing of my assets. Squabbling over the exact size of the house my bride is to have in London—'

'A house?'

In London?

'A woman must have a house of her own. Suitably furnished, of course. An income to maintain it. A car.' He considered that. 'Make that two.'

'For heaven's sake!'

Tiny lines creased around his eyes in the prelude to a smile. 'Princesses are high maintenance.' There was another long peal on the doorbell, followed by an insistent knock. 'Do you want to get that?'

'No, thanks.'

He continued to look at her. 'Where was I?'

'High maintenance,' she managed. 'Two cars.'

'Oh, yes. Then, once all the practical stuff is out of the way, they get to the really good stuff. The jewels I will give her…'

She clutched her arms tightly around her waist, trying to hold herself together, and, as if to ease her pain, he laid his hand against her cheek, so that without meaning to she was looking up at him.

'My mother thinks I should give her diamonds, but I disagree. I think nothing would become her throat more than the soft lustre of pearls…'

'Please, Zahir! Don't do this to me.'

'What, *ya malekat galbi*? What, the owner of my heart, am I doing to you?'

'You know.' She moaned as, trapped, she had nowhere to run. No escape from his touch, from her body's urgent response to the darkening of his eyes, his scent…

'Tell me.'

'I can't be what you want me to be. Maybe an arranged marriage is different. Maybe with her house, income, jewels, your wife won't care whether you are faithful or not. But I do. I can't, I won't be your mistress!'

Even to her own ears, her cry had sounded desperate and he took her hand from her waist, lifting it to lay it over his heart, with the words, '*Ya rohi, ya hahati*. My soul, my life… I believe you.' And, as if to prove her a liar, her knees buckled and she fell into his waiting arms.

'Please,' she begged, her face pressed against his chest so that she could feel the steady, powerful beat of his heart. But what she was begging for, release or thrall, she no longer knew or cared.

He gathered her in and held her for a moment, his arms around her, his cheek resting against her head. And for a moment she felt as if she was in the safest place in the world and she cared. Cared more than anything. That gave her the strength to pull away.

For a moment he resisted, then he kissed the top of her head, eased her into the battered armchair which, since his stroke, her father used when her mother was busy in the kitchen—so that they could be together, talk, as she did the ironing, baked. It seemed to symbolise everything that was good and true and pure about their long marriage.

Everything that she was not…

As she made to move, get up, Zahir stopped her, knelt at her feet. 'Maybe just one diamond,' he said. And, opening his palm, he revealed an antique ring, a large emerald cut diamond supported by emeralds. 'A pledge, my promise, while your mother and mine enjoy themselves squabbling over where your house will be—in Mayfair or Belgravia—whether you should have diamonds or pearls, or both. Arranging our marriage.' He slipped the ring on to her finger. Kissed the backs of her fingers, kissed her palm. 'The beauty of a system like *yours*, twin of my soul, is that I do not have to wait until the contract is signed before I may see you. Talk with you. Be alone with you. Kiss you…'

His kiss was long, lingering, sweet…

The doorbell rang again. Someone hammered on the back door. Then the telephone started ringing.

Zahir drew back.

'That would be alone with a media circus…'

'Well, what on earth were you thinking? If you'd worn jeans, you might have got away with it.'

'When a man asks a woman to be his wife, jeans will not

do.' Then, 'Shall we make their day and go outside, pose for photographs? You can show them your ring, have your own Princess Diana moment.'

'I don't think so! Not until I've done my hair. Changed into something to match my prince.' She drew back, shook her head. 'How can I do this? I'm no princess.'

'Believe me, you're a natural, but if you are concerned about how we will live, your life, talk to Lucy. When she tells you her story, you'll understand that anything is possible.'

'Really?'

'Remember the stars.'

'And Freddy?'

'Freddy is your son and when we are married he will be mine, Diana. Ours,' he said, thumbing a tear from her cheek. 'Frederick Trueman Metcalfe bin Zahir al-Khatib. The first of our children.'

'I need to learn Arabic, Zahir. Will you teach me?'

They had stopped on their way from the airport to walk in the desert. A last moment alone before they were plunged into wedding celebrations. To look again at the stars.

He turned to her and she leaned into him for his warmth, for him to hold her. Wrapping his arms around her, he said, 'Where do you want to start?'

'*Sitti*,' she said. 'Hamid calls me *sitti*. What does it mean?'

'Lady.'

'*Lady*? Goodness.' Then, 'And Lord?'

'*Sidi*.'

'Tell me more, *sidi*,' she said, smiling up at him. 'What is *ya habibati*?'

'You have a good ear for the sound, my beloved. But a woman, if she called her husband "my beloved" would say *ya habibi*.'

'Tell me more, *sidi, ya habibi*.'

'To a child, to Freddy, I would say *ya rohi, ya hahati*. My soul, my life.'

She repeated the words. 'That's beautiful, but you might be better not telling him what it means.'

'He is beautiful. You are beautiful, *ya malekat galbi*. The owner of my heart. *Ahebbak, ya tao'am rohi*.' Then, after a slow, searing kiss that heated her body, melted her heart with his love, 'I love you, the twin of my soul.'

'*Ahebbak*, Zahir. I love you.' Then, as they walked on, 'I think I'm going to enjoy learning Arabic.'

He stopped. 'There is one more phrase I must teach you, *ya rohi. Amoot feeki*. There is no life without you, Diana.'

She took his hands, raised them to her lips. '*Amoot feeki*, Zahir. Is that right?'

He smiled. 'As good as it gets.' Then, 'It's nearly dawn. 'Come. I have something for you.'

'What? What more could I possibly want, dream of? A house in Belgravia, a BMW, more pearls than the ocean. Diamonds like the stars…'

'This is not something to be written down. This is a gift of the heart. My promise that I will always, before anything, do all I can to make your dreams come true.'

'Zahir… Every dream, every possible dream…'

'Shh… Wait…'

Dawn was turning the sky pink and blue as they reached Nadira and, as they drove in through the gates, the sun burst above the horizon to light up a pink, sparkly Metro taxi.

* * * * *

RESCUED BY
THE SHEIKH

BY
BARBARA McMAHON

Dear Reader,

I'm proud and happy to be an author whose stories have made it to the pages of Mills & Boon's books. This year is a minor milestone for me personally—my twenty-fifth year as a published author for Mills & Boon. What a joy it is to have my stories published in so many countries and languages, and then to hear from readers how much they liked them or how they touched their hearts.

Rescued by the Sheikh is my forty-fifth book with Mills & Boon. It's the story of two lonely people. One has not had much love in her life. A photographer by trade, Lisa is exploring the world when she signs on for an archaeological dig in the Arabian country of Moquansaid. When she falls for a dashing sheikh, she longs for what cannot be. Tuareg has known and lost love. His childhood sweetheart became his wife, only to tragically die a few years into their marriage. His heart shattered, and he knows he will never find love again. Only when a sudden sandstorm has Lisa rescued by the Sheikh, life changes for them both.

Mills & Boon® stories entertain and touch the heart. I hope this does that for you, dear reader!

All the best,

Barbara

Barbara McMahon was born and raised in the South United States, but settled in California after spending a year flying around the world for an international airline. After settling down to raise a family and work for a computer firm, she began writing when her children started school. Now, feeling fortunate in being able to realise a long-held dream of quitting her "day job" and writing full time, she and her husband have moved to the Sierra Nevada mountains of California, where she finds her desire to write is stronger than ever. With the beauty of the mountains visible from her windows, and the pace of life slower than the hectic San Francisco Bay Area where they previously resided, she finds more time than ever to think up stories and characters and share them with others through writing. Barbara loves to hear from readers. You can reach her at PO Box 977, Pioneer, CA 95666-0977, USA, and readers can also contact Barbara at her website: www.barbaramcmahon.com.

To Leslie McLaughlin—fellow genealogist and writer.
You are missed, dear friend.

CHAPTER ONE

LISA SULLINGER stopped the Jeep near the ancient structure and turned off the engine. The silence was complete. Only the ticking of the motor as it cooled could be heard. She had been in Moquansaid six weeks and loved the days she could spend exploring on her own. The desolate countryside spoke to her with whispers of secrets hundreds of years old. The raw umber color gave an ageless feel to a land that was as old as time. The sights she captured on film were unlike any photographs she'd taken in the United States. There was something special about this land and she cherished each moment, each image captured.

Now she gazed at the abandoned dwelling with fascination.

The terra-cotta structure was the only building as far as the eye could see. In the distance, mountains rose to the clear blue sky, their edges softened by restless winds. Several miles behind her was the archeological dig she was working on. Today was her free day and she was once again exploring.

Climbing out of the Jeep, she reached for her camera and bag. Her sturdy shoes protected her feet from the shifting sand. The jeans were hot, but she needed their protection. Her loose-fitting top was the only concession to the heat. Even after being exposed to the climate for weeks, she wasn't used to the constant high temperatures. Seattle had cooler weather—and lots more moisture in the air.

There was little vegetation growing. A few scrubby bushes struggled near the open doorway. Sparse clumps of grass grew in scattered disarray. She looked around, searching for a water source. She'd learned quickly nothing lived in this arid land without a constant water supply. There must be a well or seep or something or no one would have built a house and made a home here.

Outside stairs climbed to the flat roof. There was no glass on any window, the thick walls kept the interior in perpetual shade, and the open spaces gave ventilation. Lisa knew she'd find a dirt floor and little left to define the family who had once worked the land. The wooden door stood ajar. She peeped inside. The interior seemed dark after the dazzling afternoon sun. Gradually, her eyes grew used to the dim light. Drifts of sand filled the corners. There was no furniture. She walked through the three rooms that comprised the dwelling, trying to imagine the family that once lived here. How had they eked out a living? Nomads roamed the land, moving their sheep from place to place to let them graze on the limited grasses that grew. The oasis where the team was excavating was the only place for miles that had abundant water—it even had shade, with palm trees surrounding the site.

She went to each window taking her time to gaze out, wondering what it would have been like to live here a hundred years ago. Life would have been hard. But the beauty of the Arabian desert captured her heart. She had never been in a desert before and found every bit of it fascinating.

Snapping a few pictures, she felt dissatisfied. This didn't really capture the feeling she was searching for. Enchanted with the harsh setting of the land, the contrasts she unexpectedly discovered between barren sand and lush oasis, flat scrub and tall mountains, she wanted to portray this stark beauty with the intent of having another book published. She had enjoyed some small success with two books already. This one had to be extra special. Like the land she was visiting.

Going outside, Lisa climbed the stairs, gingerly testing each step to make sure it would hold her. She didn't want to fall through! Once on the roof, she kept to the edges, knowing they would be the strongest parts of the structure.

Looking around, she smiled her delight. From here the view was spectacular. She waited a moment before raising the camera to her eye. The illusion of coolness given by the mountains had her longing for shade and a cold drink. But she was on a mission—she only had one day each week when she could borrow one of the Jeeps, and they were scheduled to wrap up the dig before fall, so her time was limited.

She relished each opportunity to take photographs of the unusual and the beautiful. Too many people were ignorant about this area. If her photographs could highlight the people and places, it would help foster a bit more understanding between cultures. Plus, it would give untold numbers a chance to view places they'd never be able to visit.

Turning to face the south, she followed the changing landscape from hilly to flat, from scrub-covered to open sand.

She raised her camera and began to snap pictures.

Once satisfied she'd captured this scene to the best of her ability, she leaned against the parapet that surrounded the roof and gazed into the distance, her mind full of imaginative thoughts. She hoped she could do justice to the haunting beauty of this solitary place. Moquansaid had an ancient history. The dig she was working on as photographer was tied to one of the ancient trade routes. Had the caravans marched by this place as well? Had long-ago inhabitants watched, dreaming of the far-off lands they'd never see? She could almost hear the stomp of camels, the calls of their handlers.

Lisa turned one more time, not imagining the soft rumble of thunder she heard in the distance. Was a storm brewing? She scanned the sky, it was still clear and blue. A slight breeze from the west caressed her cheeks. She shivered involuntarily. She hated thunderstorms.

Glancing at her watch, she noted it was time to head back to the dig. Dinner would be served in a few hours and she was thirsty. She had the requisite three bottles of water in the Jeep, but wanted to make sure she never got down to the last one.

Descending the steep stairs was harder than going up. A gust of wind strong enough to knock her against the wall came from nowhere, startling her. She scrambled for a hold, losing her balance and slipping on the step. She fell almost halfway down. The hard edge of the stones bruised her legs and hands. But when she stopped falling, it was the throbbing in her ankle that worried her the most.

Slowly she sat up and checked her camera. A scrape

on the edge, but it looked intact beyond that. She'd hate to lose her camera—or what she had on this roll of film.

Using the wall for leverage, she tried to rise. Instant pain shot up her right leg. She sank down with a groan. The ankle that had been throbbing now burned with agony.

She rubbed it gently, feeling it swell even as she massaged.

Great, how was she to drive back to the camp if she couldn't use her right ankle? The Jeep was old and cranky—and a stick shift to boot. She needed both feet to drive the thing. Maybe it was a temporary knock that would ease if she just rested it for a little while.

The rumbling she'd heard earlier sounded louder. She looked up. The sky overhead remained cloudless despite the increase in the wind. It was blowing steadily now from the southwest. She bit her lip in apprehension. She disliked thunderstorms and certainly didn't want to be caught in one alone. At least being with others helped her maintain some control when the horrific memories threatened.

But with a cloudless sky, could that be thunder? Maybe it was the echo of a jet high in the sky.

She searched to the west, stunned to see what looked like a dark brown cloud sinking to the horizon. Two brief rainstorms had caught them unaware at the dig during the last couple of weeks. The rain poured furiously down for about ten minutes, yet before an hour had elapsed, all traces disappeared. The desert was a thirsty place.

Unless her ankle made a miraculous recovery in the next five seconds, she was going to be caught in the storm. Flashes of that night in the rain she'd lived through as a child danced in her mind.

The thunder sounded continually now. She inched closer to the building, remembering. Could she get inside and out of the rain in time? The roof had seemed solid, it had supported her weight when she'd been on it. If she stayed away from the open windows, she should at least keep dry.

Not like the night that had taken her mother's life. She'd been drenched for hours before rescue workers found them. Lisa inched closer to the house, trying to forget the trauma of her childhood, seeking shelter from the coming rain.

She scooted a bit more. Her hands were scraped and stung from trying to stop her fall. She could hardly rest her injured foot on the ground—it hurt under its own weight. Her camera and case were slung across her shoulder, both her hands were free. Maybe she could crawl. She did not want to get wet. She might not be able to shut out the sound of the storm, but she could avoid a repetition of the night that had changed her life.

The cloud was growing closer. She had to move.

Suddenly a man on a black horse appeared on the horizon. She watched in amazement as he rode the steed at top speed directly toward the building. In only seconds she recognized the traditional Arab robes and headpiece—the trailing end was wrapped across the man's face, leaving only his eyes visible.

The horse scarcely slowed when he reached the house. The man jumped off and caught a glimpse of Lisa.

He spoke in Arabic.

She shook her head, not knowing how to communicate. A glance over his shoulder had her eyes widening in dismay. The brown cloud was closer, blotting out the horizon to the southwest.

"English?" he said.

She looked at him. "Yes. What's that?" She looked back at the bank of clouds. It wasn't a thunderstorm after all. It didn't look like a tornado, but it appeared ominous.

"Come on," he said, motioning her to the doorway, already leading his horse there.

"I can't walk," she said, mesmerized by the clouds. "I've sprained my ankle." The noise was growing, like a freight train.

He muttered something, then came and stooped to pick her up, camera, case and all.

"There's no time," he said, almost running into the building, the horse right at his shoulder. "Sandstorm," he said, flinging a cloth over the horse's head and then wrapping himself and Lisa in his loose robe and sinking down against the wall.

She was nose to nose with a stranger, sitting across his lap, wrapped in the cotton material that smelled like sunshine.

Before she could protest, however, the wind began to howl. Stinging grit hit her arm and hands. She could feel the air pressure change. Her heart pounded. Fear tasted bitter in her mouth. It was different yet like the night she'd waited so long for help. No rain, but the noise was deafening.

"Ow," she said, pulling her hands in against her chest, between herself and the stranger. He wrapped his arms more tightly around her and lowered his head. He tugged the material over them better and leaned against the wall. Despite the thick walls of the house, the air was filled with sand. The cloth sheltered them, cocooned them.

Lisa could hear nothing beyond the rage of the

wind and the sound of sand hitting against the old structure. If she'd been caught outside in this, she wouldn't have survived.

Snuggling closer to her rescuer, she forgot about her ankle, her pictures, even her memories of the automobile accident. She couldn't imagine the havoc this wind would cause. Right now it was hard to breathe. Even wrapped in the cloth, sand seemed to permeate everywhere. She shifted slightly, her nose pressed against his neck. She could smell the male scent of him, mixed with the dry sand. The shrieking wind almost made her deaf. How was the poor horse faring?

Time seemed suspended. All normal senses were gone, only the pounding of her heart, the difficulty breathing and the relentless wind had any meaning. She could feel the strong arms holding her, was grateful for the protection the cotton cloth afforded. She wished the wind would stop. The surreal sound, the constant bombardment of sand was driving her crazy. Would it never cease? She could hardly breathe, couldn't think, could only exist and cling to the stranger.

And remember a dark night on a deserted road, the relentless rain, the cold and the loneliness. At least she was tightly held today. She wasn't alone.

Endless time later the wind began to grow quieter, or was her hearing going? She chanced opening her eyes, but could see nothing except the strong jaw of the man holding her. It was as dark as twilight. Would the sand bury the old house? Would they be lost and not found for a hundred years until another archeological dig chanced upon this place?

A few moments later he stirred and pulled away the cloth.

She gulped a breath of air, still full of the musty scent of sand. Dust danced in the returning sunshine.

"I think the worst is over," he said, looking out the window opening. More sand had drifted into the old structure. The horse stood patiently to one side, head lowered, back to the wall beside the window, the cloth the man had flung over his head still in place.

Lisa still sat in his lap, still burrowed against him. Slowly she sat up, feeling awkward. Looking up, she realized her face was scant inches away from his. Dark brown eyes gazed back. How did she thank a man who had probably saved her life?

She made to move, but the pain in her ankle shot through and she gasped, sitting back down hard on his legs.

"Omph," he said.

"Sorry. My ankle really hurts." She glanced around, searching for something to help her stand. The man gingerly moved her until she sat on the ground and with one smooth motion rose and went to his horse. He eased the cloth from the animal's head and brushed some of the sand off his long neck. The black color had turned dun with the coating of sand.

"Do you have those often?" Lisa asked, watching. It was still hard to breathe. Her nerves were settling now that the worst was over. Her heart still raced, however. What if she'd been alone? She would not have known what to do.

He turned and looked at her and she caught her breath. His dark eyes seemed fathomless. His skin was the color of teak, his features sharp and beautiful. She normally didn't think of men as beautiful, especially one with as much blatant masculinity as this one. But her mind couldn't come up with another word. Her fingers itched to lift the camera and capture him forever on film.

"Not often. But always with little warning. Aside from your ankle, are you all right?" he asked. He came over and stooped down, reaching out to brush his fingers lightly against the swollen skin above her shoe.

"Looks bad," he said.

Even his light touch hurt.

"I hope it's sprained and not broken. Is there any way I could get you to drive me to my camp? I'll never be able to manage on my own." She didn't know if it was appropriate to offer money or not. She didn't want to offend him.

"You're out here alone?" he asked in surprise. His dark eyes were steady as they held hers.

Lisa felt as if she were looking into a deep, dark mysterious pool. What secrets did this man hold? And why did she suddenly wish she could uncover them? Her usually practical nature took flight. She was consumed with curiosity about her rescuer. What stories could he tell of the desert?

"I'm with an archeological excavation just a few miles north of here."

"The Wadi Hirum dig," he said with disgust, glaring at her.

"You know it?" She couldn't ignore his changed attitude. Was there something wrong with the dig?

"I was with my uncle when he signed the paperwork authorizing it. He considered it a valuable piece of undiscovered history." He rose and went to the window, leaning on the sill, his attention no longer on Lisa.

"You don't approve, obviously," she said.

"No. I'm more interested in damming that pass to create a reservoir to help the current inhabitants than in learning about ancestors who are long dead."

"But history's important. It lets us know who we are. And the old caravan trails were lifelines for people who lived here and farther to the south centuries ago." She was not a historian herself, but taking photos of the artifacts the archeologists were discovering and listening to their hypotheses proved to be captivating. Couple that with her own imagination and she could almost see the men and women who had lived here generations ago— families who worked together to make the most of their time on earth. It wasn't even her country and she revered what they were learning. How could this man not?

"What's in the past is gone. I'm more concerned for the present." He returned and knelt on the sandy dirt. Gently lifting her leg, cradling her calf, he began to unlace her shoe.

"Shouldn't I leave it on?" she asked.

"I'll bind it with some material to contain the swelling. It would be best if we could get some ice on it."

"There's not much of that around here. I'll need a ride back to the camp. I can't drive with this," she said, watching his long fingers gently minister to her injury. She peeked at his face again. He was intent on the task at hand, which allowed her to study him for a moment. He had discarded the kaffiyeh and she was surprised to find his dark hair was cut in a western style, short and neatly trimmed. She was more used to the scruffy archeologists at the site who hadn't had a haircut in more than six weeks.

He took the material he'd used for his horse and ripped it into strips to firmly wrap her ankle.

It felt marginally better, though continued to ache.

Finished, he stood and reached over to pick her up.

Lisa flung her arm around his neck, once again so

close she could see the faint lines radiating from the corners of his eyes. How old was he, about thirty? He easily carried her out to the Jeep. She was impressed.

Sand was piled against one side of the open vehicle. The seat was covered and drifts ran up the tires. He set her down, waiting until she was balanced on her good foot. Lisa used the Jeep for support while he opened the driver's cutaway door. The key was still in the ignition. He tried it. The engine whined, but wouldn't start.

Going to the hood, he raised it. A moment later he slammed it shut.

"This car isn't going anywhere for a while," he said. "Sand is clogging everything. You'll need a mechanic to get it running again."

"It's not mine, it belongs to the team. Different people need it during the week," she said. She had to get it back to camp or they wouldn't trust her with it again. And she loved her forays into the desert.

"Then have one of them repair it," he said.

"What am I to do in the meantime? I can't stay here. I have no way to contact them. Can you take me there?" She looked at the horse. It looked large enough to carry both of them.

He looked to the north for a moment, then slowly shook his head.

"Too far. You'll have to come with me. I'm staying much closer."

Lisa stared at him a moment in wary uncertainty. She didn't know him at all. Wait—he'd said he was nephew to the sheikh who had authorized the Wadi Hirum excavation. Was that enough to guarantee her safety?

What choice did she have? Go with him or stay with a disabled Jeep, an injured ankle and three bottles of water. If she didn't show up at the dig by dinnertime, they'd get worried, but no one knew exactly where to look for her. Her independence may have backfired and caused her more trouble than she wanted.

"Go with you where?" she asked cautiously.

"I'm staying not too far from here. Once there, I'll call someone out to repair the Jeep. You won't be doing much walking or driving with that ankle," he said, already moving back toward the horse.

"Can you get word to my teammates so they don't worry about me?"

He nodded, never breaking stride.

In only a moment he led the horse over. Before Lisa could say she hadn't ridden in years, he tossed her up into the ornate saddle. A second later he swung up behind her, reaching around to gather the reins.

Lisa could scarcely breathe. His arms were strong and held her centered in the saddle. When the horse stepped forward, she grabbed one of the man's arms to steady herself. His muscles were hard beneath her fingers. He urged the horse forward and they headed due west.

It didn't take long for Lisa to grow comfortable enough to relax, but not enough she'd let herself lean back against the stranger. At least she didn't feel she would fall off at every step. The jarring gait, however, exacerbated the pain in her ankle. She was starting to feel other bruises as well. She gritted her teeth, hoping she could last until they reached wherever he was staying. She tried to remember the various sites marked on the map the senior archeologist had drawn for her when she explained what she wanted for her pictures. She didn't remember any settlement in this direction.

Before long, Lisa realized why. A couple of palm

trees rose in the distance. Anchored by them was a large tent the same color as the sand. As they came closer, she could see sand piled against one side. Obviously the tent had been well set up to survive the windstorm. There was no community, no house or electricity or phones.

"This is it?" she said dubiously. She had expected a small settlement or at least a home or something.

"I have a radio inside. We will contact someone shortly."

When they reached the tent, he easily slid down from the horse and reached up to lift her from the saddle.

It took a moment for her left leg to support her. She clutched the horse.

"I don't even know your name," she said, feeling decidedly uneasy by everything.

"I'm Tuareg al Shaldor, nephew to Sheikh Mohammad al Shaldor. Welcome to my home." He gave a slight bow.

"Oh, my goodness, that must mean you're a sheikh, too," she said faintly, as the realization sank in.

He inclined his head in acknowledgment as if it were of no consequence.

Lisa couldn't believe she was standing with a real sheikh. Granted, she'd been a member of the party welcomed by the older sheikh when their group had arrived in Moquansaid six weeks ago. But she had not spoken directly with the head of state. Their group had left for the dig the next day and she'd met very few people since who were not associated with the excavation.

She looked at the tent. It in no way resembled the canvas ones she'd seen while camping in the U.S.—or the ones they were using at the excavation. First, this one looked to be the size of the living room of her apartment.

It was tall enough to permit him to walk upright beneath the pitched roof. One side was weighed down with sand around the edge. How had it withstood the ravages of the wind? Glancing around, she noticed sand piled up against the trees. The storm had obviously not vented its full fury here.

"This can't be your home. Don't you live in the capital city?" she asked. Glancing around, the two of them were alone in the expanse. Where did he shop? Where was his food? What about a refrigerator?

"This is home when it suits me." Once again he lifted her as if she weighed little. No easy feat when she was also carrying more than twenty pounds of camera equipment.

If Lisa thought the outside of the tent was different, she was amazed by the interior. Instead of canvas or plastic sheets for flooring, there were actual carpets. Richly hued, they overlapped, completely covering the ground. It was dim without interior lights, but enough ambient light filtered in for her to clearly see the divan with scrolled wooden supports, the plump pillows of gold and purple and crimson offering inviting respite.

Brass and dark wood and rich colors filled her gaze wherever she looked. She yearned to capture every nuance on film. It was truly amazing. No wonder he found the amenities of home here. It was far more lavish than any home she'd ever been in.

"There's no ice, but I think if you elevate the foot, it will help," he said, lowering her onto the divan.

She turned her face, only inches from his. His voice was deep, with the hint of an accent she was not familiar with. His English was flawless. She spoke only a handful of Arabic words. And her pronunciation was probably atrocious. She nodded and said thank you in his language.

He glanced at her in surprise as he released her.

"I am honored you have learned our language."

"Not much. I can ask for water as well," she confessed, feeling foolish she had not made more of an effort to learn.

For a moment she thought she caught a gleam of amusement in his eyes. But he moved to the far end of the tent and swept a cloth off a small shortwave radio. In only moments he was speaking. She couldn't understand a word.

Hoping he was contacting the camp, she eased the camera case from around her neck and put it on the carpet. She raised the camera and looked through the viewfinder. She couldn't take photos of a private dwelling without permission and the light was poor, but what a coup for her book this would be. An authentic Arabian setting—out of The Tales from The Arabian Nights, no less.

Lowering the camera, she leaned back on the cushions, scrunching around a little to get comfortable. Before this mishap she'd considered herself lucky in getting the job at the dig. Granted, most of the photographs she took were for cataloging of artifacts—which didn't give her much leeway for artistic creativity—but she also took shots of the site as they uncovered new dwellings or other foundations. The major portion of her work could be handled sitting down and surely her ankle would heal soon enough that she could continue doing her job.

Tuareg switched off the radio and turned, resting one arm on the narrow table. "Your archeologists will be notified. Someone will be out to repair the Jeep tomorrow. And you can see a physician in the morning. For now, it grows late and the sandstorm was widespread. It would be too dangerous for us to travel to the city now. Rescue operations are underway. We'll stay the night here."

Lisa heard the words, but took a moment to fully comprehend what he'd said. "Stay here?" She glanced around at the single room. Lavishly furnished, sumptuous colors and textures. But no privacy. Where would she sleep? Where would he? "As in spend the night?"

Not that she was in any danger, she thought wryly a moment later. He barely looked at her, barely acknowledged she was present. And he obviously did not approve of the project for which she worked. What was she worried about?

"I assure you, you'll be perfectly safe," he said with a hint of sarcasm.

Lisa flushed. She wasn't the prettiest woman in the world, she knew that. But—

But what? Did she want him to feign undying passion, a lust that couldn't be assuaged by only looking, but needed touch and taste and feeling to settle?

Hardly. She was not the type of woman men became passionate about.

Though, for one moment, she wished she were!

CHAPTER TWO

"I ASSURE YOU I have plenty of provisions. There is unlimited water from the well. And we will be warm in the tent when the sun sets. You'll be fine until morning."

She nodded, knowing there was nothing she could do about the circumstances. Her entire leg ached now. Her palms stung and there was a growing discomfort on one hip. Without transportation or an idea of where she was in relation to the camp, she was truly stuck. Might as well make the most of it.

"Your furnishings are amazing. How did you get them out here?"

"Some came on camels," he said.

Lisa immediately envisioned a caravan like the ones of old—a long line of heavily laden animals trudging through the sand, stoically plodding to their destination, their backs covered with bundles and packages.

"The rest came in a truck," he said.

The image burst like a bubble.

"Would it be possible for me to take pictures?" she asked.

"No," he said unequivocally.

She set the camera down, disappointed. The spectacular nature of the interior would have been such a stunning part of a book about this area.

He watched her for a moment.

"Aren't you going to try to talk me out of my decision?" he asked.

She looked at him in surprise. "Would there be any point?"

"None." He rose and went to a dark wooden chest, its panels carved into intricate designs. Opening the left door, he reached in for a bottle of water. He offered it to her.

"Thank you." She opened it and sipped. She shifted again, trying to find a position that didn't hurt, but the mere pressure of her foot on the divan made it uncomfortable.

"Here, let me see," he said, coming back to the sofa.

He unwrapped the support bandages and the relief was instantaneous.

"I know it should probably be wrapped, but it feels better already," she said.

"It should be iced to slow the swelling, but I don't have any ice. I can draw some water from the well. It's cool. Maybe soaking it in that will help."

He left and in a moment returned with a large bucket almost full with water.

It was cool enough to startle Lisa when she put her foot into it. In only a moment her toes began to feel numb. She thought the water cold enough to help.

"Let it soak for a while. Tomorrow a doctor will examine it." He took a pillow and placed it beneath her leg, elevating it slightly so there was no weight on her foot. The ache began to fade almost immediately.

"I'm sure it's just a sprain," she said again, hoping it was true and that her recovery would be swift.

"And do you have a medical degree?" he asked.

"No, I'm merely hoping if I say it enough it'll be true."

She looked around, seeking inspiration for a new topic of conversation. "What do you do that you can live out here and not in the city?' she asked.

"I'm working on a project," he said. "Damming the Assori Gorge."

"That's not far from where the dig is," she said, recognizing the English name of the location.

"Which is why my project is on hold at the moment. I have had to postpone the next stage of construction to wait until the archeological excavation is completed. I am months behind the original schedule."

"A dam will destroy everything behind it."

"Which is why the excavation was permitted at this time and by an outside group. Haste is needed. We had no qualified individuals who could take on the project at this moment. Once you Americans have provided our cultural ministry with all the information found at the site, the construction will proceed."

"And change the face of the earth there forever. Don't you mind covering up a site of historical significance? What if others from your country wanted to stand where their forebearers stood or wanted to explore this land, which has remained unchanged for thousands of years?"

"What of the nomads who could benefit from a constant source of water? What of the children who wouldn't have to trample hundreds of miles each year and could instead be in school learning, exploring, discovering more than the history of a pass through the mountains that hasn't been used for centuries?" he countered.

Put like that, Lisa could understand the wish for the dam. A steady supply of water would change things—and for the better. But she couldn't help mourn the loss as well.

"Are you hungry?" he asked.

She nodded, surprised to realize it was early evening. She had hoped to be back at the dig by dinnertime.

"I haven't eaten since breakfast," she said.

"And that was probably toast and coffee," he murmured, going back to the chest and pulling out fruits and cheese.

"Actually, I had a big breakfast. I knew it would be a long time until dinner. I did snack midday." But she'd never expected dinner to be in a sumptuous tent on the edge of the desert.

He cut the fruit and sliced the cheese, placing them on china plates. He handed her one plate and a cloth napkin.

"Is there anything to wipe my hands with?"

"Of course." In only a moment she had a wet cloth and a small bowl of water. Once she'd finished, she picked up a slice of mango. The fruit's sweetness was a burst of flavor on her tongue. The juice almost more than she could keep in her mouth. Trying to eat without devouring the food was hard, it was so delicious. A slice of peach was next, then a piece of the cheese, sharp and tangy. The blend of flavors was amazing. She glanced at him. He stared at her as she ate.

"Am I dripping?" she asked, blotting her mouth with the napkin.

Tuareg shook his head and looked away. He'd been impolite. It was unlike him to be so interested in someone that he violated the manners his mother had instilled in him. He should be annoyed. His ride had been interrupted by the sandstorm and the tranquility of his life disturbed by the presence of the woman needing help. He could have left her, sent a message to the archeologists and had them retrieve her. But that had seemed too unkind.

Nura had often teased him about his arrogant ways. He'd never thought about it, only doing whatever he thought was right. Growing up as a relative of the rulers of their country had contributed to a certain amount of expectations for having things his way. He tried to temper that with compassion for others.

The thought of his wife brought the familiar pain to his heart. She'd been dead three years and he still missed her with an agony that wouldn't cease. They'd been soul mates from early childhood. He'd known from the time he was twelve that she would be his wife. She had looked at no other man, he at no other woman.

Though fate had separated them, it was only a matter of time until his own death would reunite them. The long years stretched out empty and lonely. He went through the motions of living, but nothing held any zest. Only his time in the desert brought solace. Now that had been disrupted.

He glanced back at his unwanted guest. There was no question she enjoyed the food he'd given her. He was surprised with the sensuousness with which she savored each bite. Surely she'd had fruit and cheese before. But from the way she was eating, he wasn't sure.

"What is this?" She held up a pinkish slice of fruit.

"Passion fruit," he said.

She studied it for a moment, then slipped it into her mouth, her lips closing over it in such a way that Tuareg felt it almost as a caress. Mesmerized, he watched her close her eyes as she slowly chewed. The expression of delight was impossible to miss. For a startling moment he wondered what else brought that look of sheer pleasure to her face. Making love?

Rising swiftly, he went to see to his horse. He had not made love to anyone but Nura and their last time had been years ago. It seemed like a shocking betrayal to even wonder about such a thing with another woman. Especially one he'd just met and who had no appeal to him. She looked very plain, with her brown hair cut to fall in a simple line. Her wide eyes wore no makeup, and her skin was dusted with a light trail of freckles. She was nothing like his elegant Nura.

The light of his life, Nura had been tall and slender and sophisticated. She had graced the embassies of a dozen countries. They had traveled extensively, always seeking the excitement she craved. London and Paris and Rome had been their homes. They'd visited the Far East and Australia, but she preferred the old grace of Western Europe to all else.

Even Moquansaid, he had to admit.

The horse was covered in sand. Tuareg found the bucket of tools, tipped it to empty the sand, and began to groom the horse. His stableman would have accompanied him on this trip had he asked. But he'd wanted the time alone.

El al Hamalaar stood patiently while he was groomed. The routine soothed and calmed the horse and helped Tuareg gain some equilibrium. He'd get Lisa Sullinger to a doctor in the morning, then transport her back to her dig. Life would resume its pace and the days would march on until he was old and frail.

He studied the sky. All signs of the sandstorm had vanished. He could send for a helicopter now, but it would be dark soon and he didn't feel the injury to her ankle was so great it couldn't wait another few hours.

Turning the horse loose in the small enclosure a little

later, Tuareg looked to the west. No clouds marred the sweep of color. Soon night would fall across the land and the sky would become alive with the light of stars.

The time he liked the best. A time to be shared.

Tuareg turned back to the tent. Perhaps not as unwilling a host as he thought he'd be. His guest knew nothing about him. For one evening he could be merely a man talking with a stranger—her ways would be different from his. Ships passing in the night. For the first time in years, he actually looked forward to the evening. There would be no sad memories tonight.

When he entered the tent, it was dark. He'd forgotten to turn on lights and of course his guest wouldn't know where to look for the lamps.

"Do you go to sleep with the sunset?" the voice came from the divan.

"My apologies. I forgot the lamps." He moved quickly to light the first one. The warm glow of the flame illuminated a small portion of the tent. In less than a minute, he'd lit four more. The colors of the tapestries and carpets warmed with the light.

"I'm tired, but even I do not sleep all the time it's dark," she said. The plate had been placed on the floor, the damp cloth on top. She had withdrawn her foot from the bucket, which enabled her to lay back on the divan. She looked settled among the cushions.

He took her plate and his and quickly washed them in the tub he used for such things. Sitting opposite her on one of the hassocks, he studied her. The lamplight added a sparkle to her eyes, made her skin look soft and satiny. He had felt her against him during the sandstorm, focusing on her safety while the wind whipped around them. For a moment he wished he could touch her skin again, just to see if it was as soft as it looked.

"So you are an archeologist?" he asked.

"No, a photographer. That's how I got to come on the trip. I'm a friend of a director of one of the corporate sponsors for the dig. When the regular photographer got sick, he proposed my name and here I am."

"And what do you photograph, the site itself?"

"That, each layer as it's uncovered and all the artifacts that are recovered. Even broken pottery is numbered, described and photographed. The catalog of the items found will be extensive. The photos will enable people to study each item, even if they never get to see them in real life."

He nodded.

"And I'm learning a great deal. The professor heading the project is an avid scholar of Arabic history. His descriptions paint a beautiful scene of the lives of people hundreds of years ago and the caravans that crisscrossed the land."

"With more romantic overtones than probably existed," Tuareg said.

"Meaning?"

"You make it sound like it was a magical life. It was hard. Men were gone for months at a time. There was no guarantee the caravans would not be set on by robbers or, worse, hit by sandstorms like today's. It was not a glamorous existence."

"It was, for its day. They were the travelers, they saw foreign lands and met different people. There are jobs today where men and women are gone from home for long periods of time. Many dangerous occupations. People still risk their lives to seek the unknown, to find adventure."

"Are you seeking adventure?"

She shrugged. "To a degree. This is very different from my life in the United States."

"Your family doesn't miss you with your being gone so long?"

"I have no family." The animation faded from her face. For a moment she looked resigned. "I have friends, but they are excited for my opportunity. No one misses me."

While Nura was gone, he still had family, from parents and grandparents and siblings to uncles and aunts and cousins galore. What would it be like to have no one connected to him by blood? To truly be alone in the world?

The pain of losing Nura multiplied by a hundredfold.

"I am sorry for your loss," he said formally.

"Thanks, but my mom died when I was six and my dad a couple of years later. It's so long ago I'm used to it."

"Who raised you?"

"I was raised in foster care, and was lucky to only have three different homes. Some kids are moved every couple of years. I even got to stay in the same high school all four years."

"Not adopted?"

She shook her head. "Too old."

"So now you live on your own. No husband or boyfriend?"

"Nope." She glanced at her camera. "I love photography and travel as much as I can to see the world." For a moment she hesitated, then said shyly, "I even had a couple of books published of my photographs."

"Excellent. I shall have to acquire copies so I can tell people I know the author." Family was important to Tuareg, even the accomplishments she shyly acknowledged couldn't make up for the lack of relatives.

She grinned. "I'm sure they'll all be duly impressed."

Tuareg felt an odd nudge in his chest. Her grin was infectious. He felt like smiling in return. Her gaze moved away from him and surveyed the tent.

"I was hoping to take a few photographs of your home. It's so unique. Think how it could enhance my book of Moquansaid."

"You are doing a book of Moquansaid?" he asked.

"That's why I was at the ruins. Professor Sanders told me of the site. He's been helpful in pointing out unique aspects of the countryside. Then, before we head for home later this summer, I want to take some photographs of the buildings in the capital city. The mosaics are quite beautiful. And I loved the fretwork that so defines Arabian architecture. Some of the places I saw as we rode through Soluddai were naturally framed by tall date palms. It's very exotic to someone from Seattle."

"Ah, that is where you live?"

"Yes. It's totally different from the desert. We have oodles of inches of rain each year. Here, there's hardly any."

"Oodles," he murmured. He had an excellent command of English. He'd attended school in England as a child. Yet he was unfamiliar with that word.

She smiled again. "In this case, it means lots and lots."

"I have heard the Pacific Northwest is quite wet. Too bad we couldn't exchange some sunshine for rain and equalize things."

She shifted slightly on the sofa and glanced around again.

"Do you need something?" Tuareg asked.

"Actually I was wondering where the bathroom was."

"For all I like to have the comforts of home here, it

is a tent. The facilities are several yards away and quite primitive." He rose. "I shall take you there. You will have privacy, but you wouldn't be able to get there on your own."

"I could hop," she said, swinging her legs over the edge of the divan. A grimace of pain showed Tuareg her ankle still pained her.

"And each hop would jar your injured ankle." He lifted her from the sofa and headed out.

The velvet darkness of night enveloped them as soon as they left the tent. The canvas sides glowed from the lamplight, casting faint illumination for a few feet into the desert. Beyond was inky blackness.

"Can you even see?" she asked, her arm around his neck.

She didn't weigh much, he thought as he walked in the sand. He knew the way blindfolded. It wasn't far.

"I know where I'm going. Wait a moment and your eyes will become accustomed to the light from the stars."

She looked up at that and sighed. "How perfect. I've noticed how beautiful the night sky is here. At home there's so much ambient light it's hard to see any but the brightest stars. This is wonderful. I've wondered if I could get my camera to capture the beauty."

He reached the small shelter that housed the portable toilet. It was only canvas on three sides, the fourth opened to the south. Taking several steps away to assure her privacy, Tuareg looked up at the sky.

She was right. It was a beautiful sight. He liked to ride in the dark on nights like this. His horse was surefooted and moved like the wind. Nura hadn't liked him going out to the desert. It was not the place for her. She much preferred clubs and elegant restaurants to solitude. He now had more solitude than he could ever wish.

"I'm finished," Lisa called. She hated to be dependent on Tuareg, but he was right. The short hops to the toilet had jarred her ankle and started it throbbing again. She'd never have made it all the way out from the tent.

He appeared out of the darkness and lifted her again. She had never been carried by a man before. It was quite romantic. It reminded her of the old movie *Gone With the Wind* where Rhett sweeps Scarlett up into his arms.

Of course, they'd been lovers. That made a difference. This man was merely moving her from one place to another in a way that kept her ankle from further injury. But for a moment as he strode across the ground, she closed her eyes and let her imagination soar. What if he were carrying her back to the tent for a night of love? What if after he placed her on the divan, he laid down beside her, holding her, caressing her, kissing her?

She popped her eyes open. That was totally out of the question. And she'd be crazy to even daydream about it.

Practicality came to the forefront. This man was a native of this country. She should be learning all she could about Moquansaid for her book. A chance like this wouldn't come again.

Once settled on the divan, she reached for her camera bag and rummaged around for the notebook she carried.

"Would you mind telling me a little about Moquansaid?" she asked. "I'd love some little-known tales to include in my book. If you wouldn't mind."

Tuareg turned the lamps low, then settled on some cushions on the floor near the wooden chest. He lay back. "What kind of stories?"

"Do you know anything about the ruins I was in today? Or about the caravans that traveled through the land centuries ago? Or tell me something about some of the notable buildings in Soluddai," she said, mentioning the capital city.

"The nomads have lived on the land since the beginning of recorded history. Perhaps before. We are a landlocked country, no access to the sea, so travel and commerce were limited to land routes."

Lisa listened attentively as Tuareg spoke. She loved his voice, deep and rich with just the hint of accent. She wished she could place it. Not that it mattered. She lay back, closing her eyes to better focus on the words. He painted a picture of a country little changed through the centuries, of a hardworking, family-oriented society that was little influenced by other countries until recent times. Gradually his voice grew dimmer and Lisa fell asleep.

The whump-whump of a helicopter woke Lisa. She sat up abruptly, dislodging a blanket that had been covering her. Glancing around, it took her a moment to remember where she was and why she was there. She didn't see her host. The sound of the aircraft grew louder. Was it landing right on top of the tent? She debated getting up and going to see, but when she moved to sit up, a sharp pain stabbed.

Slowly, she continued pushing herself up until she was sitting. The notebook she'd planned to use last night lay beside her. She placed it back in the camera case, made sure all her things were there and waited for the next step.

When the motors shut down, the silence seemed to echo. Then she heard men speaking in Arabic. A moment later Tuareg entered the tent. His robes flapped as he quickly covered the distance to the divan.

"Good, you are awake. Our transportation is here."

"Who could sleep? I thought it was landing right on top of me. How did you get a helicopter sent?"

"It is mine. I called for it last night." He leaned over to pick her up. "A quick stop at the restroom and then we head for civilization."

In less than ten minutes, Lisa was strapped into a window seat of the large helicopter. The gleaming white paint on the outside had golden Arabic script on the side. The roomy interior had seats for eight. She'd never flown in a helicopter before. She could see the entire interior. Tuareg sat in the pilot's seat. The man who had flown the aircraft to them sat in the copilot seat. Lisa watched, mesmerized as Tuareg started the engines and soon had them lifting straight up. She looked outside. A man stood beside the horse. Someone who had come to ride the horse back home maybe? Slowly the site grew smaller, the tent blending into the dusty sand until it faded from view. The camp passed behind them as the helicopter turned and headed north.

Lisa drew out her camera and began to snap pictures of the landscape below. She didn't have time to frame each shot or decide on the best way to capture the scenes, she just snapped picture after picture and hoped for a few good ones. This was fantastic. She hadn't thought about aerial shots before, but they could add another dimension to her project.

She wondered if she could arrange a helicopter flyover of the archeological site. That would certainly help preserve it for future generations after it had been beneath the water.

The noise in the helicopter was too loud for conversation. Lisa was just as glad. While she'd like to ask about what she was seeing, she was too busy making sure she got as many photographs as she could. When a roll of film ended, she would quickly insert a new one.

Tuareg glanced back once, then seemed to slow the machine down, dropping elevation slightly. She flashed him a bright smile and went back to snapping pictures.

She felt the change again when he began to slowly circle an estate. Putting the camera aside, Lisa gazed down at a large home, several satellite buildings and a paved driveway leading to a road that curved in front of the buildings some distance away and continued north and south. Other homes and buildings could be seen in the distance as she followed the line of the main road.

They were landing. Was this where her host lived?

A car was waiting at the landing pad and Tuareg gently placed Lisa inside. It took only moments to reach the circular driveway in front of the large villa.

The building was the familiar terra-cotta color of so many of the structures in Moquansaid. The keyhole doors and open windows with tile surrounding them encapsulated the spirit of Arabia she was growing to love. Flowers grew lavishly. The circular driveway enclosed a lush lawn. A lot of water was being spent on this garden, she thought.

No sooner was she inside than a distinguished gentleman rose from a chair in the foyer and hurried to greet Tuareg. They spoke quickly and then Tuareg carried her to a salon and set her on a chair.

"This is Dr. al Biminan, a noted physician from the capital city. He is here to look at your ankle. He speaks no English, so I will serve as translator."

The doctor examined her leg, ankle and foot, asking questions through Tuareg and nodding when she answered as he apparently expected. Soon he began to wrap the ankle in an ice bandage. He continued to talk to Tuareg.

"What's he saying?" Lisa asked when the translations seemed to stop.

"He's going to prescribe pain medication. You are to remain off the ankle for two days and see how it goes. His diagnosis is a sprain, not a fracture."

"Can I get back to the digs?"

"Soon. You will remain here for two days. Logistically it makes more sense. The doctor can then drive back at that time and reexamine you. If you were at the camp, how would he get to see you?"

"I can't stay here," Lisa protested.

"Of course you can," Tuareg said. "This is my private residence and if I invite you to stay as my guest, there is no problem."

CHAPTER THREE

LISA LAY BACK in the large tub, soaking up the bliss of the hot water. She was beginning to feel clean for the first time in two days. She had been assured her staying proved no hardship to Sheikh Tuareg al Shaldor. From the lavish displays of wealth in each room she'd seen, she knew it had to be true. The furnishings in the bedroom she'd been assigned were worth a small fortune. This bathroom was almost as large as her entire apartment. The tub was long and deep, and right now filled with hot water and a contented photographer. She raised her foot and looked at her swollen ankle. She'd removed the bandage to bathe, but would replace it when she was done.

Tuareg had arranged for a maid, Maliq, to stay nearby while she bathed in case she needed anything. But for now, she was alone and relishing every moment. In two days she'd head back to her job: the dry, sandy excavation that was proving more interesting than she'd originally expected. But the showers there were rationed. The camp was shared by so many that she was rarely alone except in her tent. This was utter luxury.

When she finished drying off, she hesitated, hating

to put back on the clothes she'd worn for the last two days, but having nothing else.

A knock sounded on the door.

"Yes?"

"Miss?" The maid opened the door and peeped in. "I have clothing for you," she said, pushing the door open. "I will have your own clothes washed and brought back later, but His Excellency sent these for you to wear until then." She held out a flowery dress in light blue and underwear still in the store wrapping. "Do you need help?"

"I can manage," Lisa said, wondering when the items had been purchased. Did he keep a small stock on hand for people who dropped in unexpectedly?

When she finished dressing and drying her hair, Lisa was tired. She'd been on her feet for several moments now and while she leaned most of her weight on her left foot, she needed to use her right for balance. It ached despite the painkillers.

She hobbled over to the door and opened it. The maid jumped up from a chair and smiled at her. "I have a wheelchair for you," she said, gesturing to her left. "I can push you. His Excellency is expecting to have an early lunch for you."

"Your English is good. Is it taught in schools here?" Lisa asked as she sank gratefully into the chair. As soon as she was settled, the maid began pushing her toward the door.

"Yes. I studied it in school. I traveled with His Excellency and his wife when they visited other countries. I liked that. My mother told me I would have better job opportunities if I could speak another language. I also speak French," Maliq said as they continued down the long hallway.

"I speak only English and a few words of Arabic," Lisa confessed, saying thank you to the young woman in her language.

"I can teach you more if you like," Maliq said.

"I would like, while I'm here." Lisa was intrigued with the idea. It would give her something to do. If she couldn't be exploring and taking pictures, what else could she do?

So Tuareg had a wife. Of course a man his age would be married. And Lisa suspected his wife would be as beautiful as he was handsome. Did they have children? For a moment she wished she had a special someone waiting for her as Tuareg had asked about. She had not met anyone to fall in love with. Would she ever? Or was wanderlust to be her companion through the years? Capturing sights and scenes and people through her lens and forever remaining on the outside watching, wishing.

When the maid pushed her onto a large patio, Lisa was enchanted all over again. The flagstone terrace was covered by a high trellis around which vines were entwined. The partial shade made it possible to be comfortable outside in the heat of the day. There was a fountain splashing merrily and a faint breeze. Flowers grew at the edges of the patio, bright red and sunny yellow, contrasting with their deep green leaves.

A round table was near the fountain, set for a meal.

She almost didn't recognize the man who rose when she came out. Tuareg had also cleaned up and was now dressed in casual western attire—khaki slacks and a polo shirt. The knit shirt delineated his muscular body. He was tall and physically fit. No wonder he could hoist her around so easily. She glanced around, but didn't see his wife. Was she away?

"Thank you, Maliq," he said to the young maid.
"Your services won't be required again until later."

She nodded her head and quietly slipped away.

"I know you must be hungry," he said, pushing the
chair up to the table. He locked it in place and took a
seat opposite.

"I am. But it was wonderful to have a bath. Thank
you for the clothes."

"They fit?"

"Perfectly."

"Then I am glad they were available."

A servant brought out a large tray with two plates and
two glasses with ice. He placed the dishes before each
of them and poured tea into the glasses.

A second servant brought out a tray with sandwiches
and fruit salad.

"I remember Americans like iced tea when the
weather is hot, is that not correct?" Tuareg said.

"I sure do. Thank you. This looks delicious." A flaky
croissant was filled with what looked like chicken salad.
There was fresh fruit and some sweet bread as well.
"Will your wife be joining us?"

Tuareg looked at her for a moment, then shook his
head. "Nura is dead. I am a widower."

"I'm sorry, I didn't know. The maid said she traveled
with you and your wife, I thought—" It was obvious she
thought the woman was alive.

"One adjusts," he replied, beginning to eat.

Lisa also began to eat, wishing she could think of
something to take the look of bleakness away from her
host's face.

She wasn't good with family situations. Living in
foster care for most of her life had left her constantly

on the outside looking in. She could empathize with others, but couldn't quite make the connection. Maybe it was why she was such a good photographer: she knew what to look for, she had been searching for special places all her life.

The meal was delicious. The chicken salad was light yet filling, made with celery and apple and walnuts. Fresh melons cut in small pieces complemented the salad. The drink was some kind of sweet tea, not quite like home, but delicious and refreshing.

Conversation lagged as they each seemed lost in thought. She risked another glance in his direction and was surprised to find him watching her.

A servant came out of the house and spoke quietly to Tuareg. He frowned, then rose, placing his napkin on the table.

"Excuse me a moment, it seems I have an unexpected guest." He walked around the table and followed the servant inside.

It seemed to be his day for unexpected guests. Lisa let out a small sigh. She felt awkward after mentioning his wife. She wished the maid had made it clear why all travel had been in the past. But even if she'd known, she'd be at a loss for words. What did a photographer have in common with a sheikh?

Lisa had almost finished eating when Tuareg and an older woman came out onto the patio.

"Mother, may I present Lisa Sullinger. Lisa, my mother, Yasmin al Shaldor."

Tuareg seated the older woman at the table. A servant hurried out and spoke in Arabic. His mother turned and shook her head, then turned back to Lisa.

"I did not expect to find Tuareg with company," she

said, her eyes studying Lisa. "I thought he was still in the desert, but I heard the helicopter earlier and took a chance he'd returned home."

"He very kindly rescued me when I hurt myself at a ruin," Lisa explained. Surely Tuareg had already done so.

"Indeed," Yasmin murmured, glancing at her son and back at Lisa. "How did that happen?"

Lisa explained while Tuareg sat back at his place, leaning back in the chair and watching the conversation without participating.

The servant returned with another glass and napkin. He poured tea into it for Tuareg's mother, then with a bow quickly left.

She smiled at Lisa. "You are eating earlier than I usually eat. I'm meeting a friend for lunch in a little while."

"We were in the desert this morning. This is our first meal," Tuareg explained.

"Since you have returned earlier than planned, perhaps you can now give thought to attending the party your uncle is giving for your cousin's birthday. Your guest would be invited as well," his mother said.

"Thank you," Lisa said quickly, noting the frown on Tuareg's face. "But I have to return to the dig."

"Dig?"

"She's with the archeologists at the Wadi Hirum," he said. "She'll be returning in a couple of days. The doctor who examined her ankle said to give it total rest for at least two days."

"I wouldn't intrude at a family party." Lisa knew better than to be the only outsider at a family gathering. Especially one in which the normal language was foreign to her.

He shrugged. "I'm sure my cousin would be delighted to have you attend. She likes large gatherings and the more interesting people there, the more she likes it. I was not planning to attend." He glanced at his mother and then looked back to Lisa. "If you would like to go, however, I would escort you. Perhaps you could take more pictures for your project."

Lisa smiled, wondering when the party was and how long she could stay away from the dig.

"Pictures for a project?" his mother asked.

Lisa explained.

"So if you do that when your time is free, do tell me how the investigation into the lives of those who lived at Wadi Hirum is progressing. Have any startling discoveries been made?" she asked Lisa.

"Not that I've heard. Though I'm not an archeologist, I'm fascinated by the artifacts they are uncovering— bowls, bits of glass and metal items. There have been a couple of pieces of art, statues that are small but beautifully carved from stone. And all of which are estimated to be several hundred years old."

Yasmin looked at her son. "And have you seen these artifacts?"

"No. I have not visited the excavation."

"Yet you are most anxious for them to finish so you can proceed with your project."

"Damming the river nearby," Lisa said with a frown. She knew, as did all on the dig, the terms of the permit. But none of them liked it. She wished there was something to be done to keep the land as it was. Or at least delay the flooding until all the secrets of Wadi Hirum had been discovered.

"You've heard of that?" Yasmin asked, clearly surprised.

"According to Professor Sanders, the only reason we are there is to rush through finding whatever we can before the deadline. Then the area will be flooded and lost forever. I hope we are able to get all the information of the earlier settlement before it's too late. The archeologists can't rush things too much for fear of destroying an important clue to the past. It seems a shame to stop on a certain date without completely exploring the entire area."

She looked at Tuareg, emboldened to ask. "It occurred to me as we were flying here that perhaps an aerial view would also be of value. Can I be taken back via your helicopter and given a chance to take some photos from the air?"

Tuareg nodded. "I'd be happy to also fly along the river so you can see what will happen when the pass is dammed. And how wide an area will benefit from the reservoir. Perhaps you'll change your mind about the project."

"Are you not in favor of the dam?" Yasmin asked.

"It seems a shame to eradicate all traces of the past," Lisa said.

"But the benefit to the present is what's important. The past should not be more important than the present," Tuareg's mother said, her eyes sad, her gaze on her son.

Lisa felt some unspoken communication was being exchanged between the two of them. Tuareg held his mother's gaze for a long moment, then looked at Lisa.

She felt herself grow warm with his regard. Taking a sip of the sweetened tea, she tried to keep her hand from shaking. She was affected by the man's nearness. Was she going to fall for the handsome sheikh just because he was the most exciting man she'd ever met?

Nonsense. She had more sense than that.

But she thought she might be tempted from the sheer masculine appeal the man had. She wished her friends could meet him.

The sooner she returned to work, the better. She should not be thinking such thoughts. Her place was at the excavation, not at an elegant villa belonging to a fabulously wealthy man. Talk about being out of her depths.

"Have you seen much of Moquansaid?" Yasmin asked.

"Only driving through from the capital on our way to the site when we arrived. Soluddai is a beautiful city. Then, of course, the countryside is amazing. How quickly it changes from the greenery in the city parks to the barren desert."

"We are a small country yet have moved into the twenty-first century with all speed," Yasmin said proudly. Her couturier clothes spoke of strong ties to Western Europe. Did she do her shopping in Paris?

Lisa wondered what it would be like to fly to Paris on a shopping spree. Fabulous, she bet.

"The avenues I saw in the capital city were lovely. I'm especially intrigued by the architecture of the buildings, the blend of modern high-rise glass and steel with ancient buildings of Arabic design. The melding of two different styles is fascinating."

"Lisa obviously has an artist's eye," Tuareg said. "She plans to write a book on what she finds in Moquansaid. Perhaps she can visit the city while she convalesces," Tuareg said easily.

"A book?" Yasmin said, looking at Lisa with new interest. "What kind of book?"

"A photographic one, mostly pictures with captions."

"She's published two such already. I've ordered them. You can see them when they arrive," Tuareg said.

"You've ordered copies?" Lisa was clearly surprised.

He nodded slowly. "I'm interested in seeing your work."

"Why?"

"Perhaps to grant you that request you made at the tent."

She blinked. He might let her photograph the interior of the tent? Would he also let her take pictures of this house? It was beautiful, inside and out. She wouldn't infringe on his hospitality, but she would be guaranteed publication if she could show aspects of Moquansaid that no one else had shown before.

Whoa, she was getting ahead of herself. He might not like what she'd done on the earlier books. He hadn't said yes yet.

"An interesting profession for a woman, a photographer. Do you take pictures of social events?" Yasmin asked.

Lisa shook her head. "I like capturing scenes that will have people thinking or remembering. One of my books was comprised of scenes of childhood. I traveled around the western United States taking pictures of carnivals and county fairs, swimming holes and tree houses, parks and playgrounds. Things from childhood to bring back fond memories for those who experienced them, or evoke a feeling of nostalgia for those who hadn't but feel that might have been a good part of childhood."

"Tree houses?" Yasmin asked.

Lisa nodded. "Perhaps not common over here?"

Yasmin looked at her son with puzzlement.

"A small platform usually in the lower branches of a sturdy tree where children play."

"How dangerous."

"No more so than other activities of childhood. What was the other book about?" he asked.

"Waterfalls."

"That's all?"

Lisa nodded, smiling. "It took me more than a year to get a collection of pictures of various falls. I tried for unusual vantage points. The top of Yosemite Falls, behind the water at Arabesque Falls, at sunset at Niagara Falls with the glow of the colors turning the water into a shimmering silk of reflections. Some are located in the midst of lush vegetation, others ephemerals in an otherwise barren landscape."

"So you travel extensively?" Yasmin asked. "As did my son."

Lisa looked at Tuareg. "But you no longer travel?"

"It was Nura's wish to travel. She enjoyed seeing new places, meeting new people."

Yasmin looked concerned as she watched her son speak. "You could go to those places again," she said gently.

"No." He pushed back his chair and rose. "If you will excuse me, I have some business to attend to."

"I'll stay and talk to Lisa until it's time to leave for my luncheon," Yasmin said.

Once Tuareg had left the patio, the servants quickly came and cleared the table, leaving only fresh tea and glasses for the women.

Yasmin checked her watch and then smiled at Lisa. "I can stay a little longer. Tell me how you came to be a part of the archeology team."

Lisa began telling her about the unexpected treat of traveling with the group. She made brief mention of each member and how they all worked together as a team. Her role was small, yet she felt it important. The topic moved on to the ruins she'd been photographing. Then to the sandstorm and the havoc a bad storm could cause. Fortunately they were not frequent, Yasmin said.

Before she left, Yasmin reissued the invitation to the birthday celebration for Tuareg's cousin. Lisa made a noncommittal answer and bid the woman goodbye. She'd enjoyed talking with her.

The quiet once Yasmin left was soothing. Lisa maneuvered her wheelchair around until she was looking over the garden. Tall shrubs gave a green backdrop for the blossoms that displayed every hue she could think of. The flowers were beautiful. She wished she'd brought her camera.

A short time later Maliq came to the door.

"Would you like to come inside? Rest? Or can I bring you something here?"

"Thank you. I think I would like to go lie down for a while." The next time she left her bedroom, she'd be sure to carry her camera.

To her surprise, Lisa slept more than an hour. She awoke refreshed and was soon chafing at the inactivity. She was used to doing, not sitting. She hopped over to the window and gazed out on the pretty setting. She'd love to walk around the estate. Testing her ankle gingerly, she quickly learned it had not miraculously healed while she rested.

Maliq entered a couple of moments later, several swimsuits over one arm.

"His Excellency wonders if you'd like to go swimming? He is taking a break and offered to take you with him." The awe in her voice let Lisa know the maid was impressed he would make such a request.

It sounded like heaven. The house was cool, but she'd love to immerse herself in a pool and enjoy the unexpected luxury. The excavation site was very dry and dusty. They'd all have loved a pool there.

In less than ten minutes the maid was pushing her into the foyer of the home, where Tuareg waited. Lisa had chosen a modest one-piece suit and wore a terry covering over it.

Tuareg had changed into shorts and a T-shirt. His long legs were tanned and the short sleeves of his shirt displayed his muscular arms to advantage.

"Thank you for inviting me. I love swimming, though I'm not sure how much I can do with this ankle, but I can at least enjoy the water," she said, trying to ignore the small thrill seeing him brought. He was her reluctant host, nothing more.

He spoke to Maliq in Arabic and took the handles of the wheelchair, pushing Lisa outside. He lifted her, chair and all, down the three shallow steps, then headed to the far side of the house. The walkway was comprised of fine gravel, not easy to push the chair on, but he seemed to have no difficulty.

"Did you finish your work?" she asked politely.

"Yes."

Rounding a bend, the path widened and changed to flagstone. The same stones that flanked the pool. It was an infinity edge pool, the far edge seeming to have no boundary, the water skimming over. Beyond was a distant view of the mountains.

There was a hot tub at one end. The main pool was Olympic size, with lanes clearly delineated.

"Wow," she said softly. Several tall palms shaded a portion of the flagstone. The coping, along with the pool itself, was in the full afternoon sunshine.

"You do swim?" he said, stopping the chair near the edge.

"Yes." Suddenly she felt shy about taking off her cover-up.

Tuareg had no such qualms. He quickly pulled his shirt off and soon kicked off his shorts.

Lisa stared. He was gorgeous. His shoulders were wide and bronzed. His muscles were sculptural. He glanced at her, raising an eyebrow.

She looked away and hoped the heat that rose in her face wasn't turning her skin as red as it felt. She took off the cover-up and, using the arms of the chair, stood shakily on one foot.

"I can carry you down the stairs," he said.

"No, I'm fine," she said. Before she could chicken out, she dove into the clear water. It was heaven. She struck out for the infinity wall, hearing the splash as Tuareg joined her in the water.

Kicking hurt her ankle, so she used her arms to propel her along. When she reached the wall, she clung, shaking the water out of her eyes and dipping her head back to get the hair from her face.

"Are you all right?"

"I shouldn't kick with my injured leg, but this feels wonderful," she said, smiling as she met his gaze. His hair was slicked back, his dark eyes fathomless. He turned and began to swim laps. Lisa watched for a few moments, then let her gaze move around the setting and to the distant views. It was so pretty her heart ached.

When she was sufficiently refreshed, she leisurely swam to the steps and hopped up to the coping. Sitting on the edge, she let the sun warm her while her feet dangled in the water. Idly, she watched Tuareg swimming. He must have made a dozen laps but showed no signs of slowing down.

She memorized the day. She had a journal at the camp, had been keeping one for years. With no family, she had only her friends to share her life with and her constant travel made real closeness difficult to achieve. Sara and Bailey were her two best friends. She kept the journal for herself—when she was old and unable to travel, she'd have a wonderful life to look back on.

The last two days would be most memorable. She didn't want to forget a thing before she could write the events down. What happened and how she felt about everything. Especially her awareness of the man swimming like the hounds of hell were after him.

Tuareg continued to push himself. The mindlessness of swimming helped him to forget. The exercise drove the demons away and let him sleep at night. Not for long, but enough.

Taking another deep breath, he turned, kicked off from the wall and headed back along the lane. He caught a glimpse of Lisa sitting on the edge of the pool.

He had a guest. Responsibilities. Slowing, he changed directions and swam over to her.

He held on to the side and shook the water from his face. "Ready to leave?" he asked.

"Not yet. This is lovely. Do you swim competitively?"

"No."

"You could. With endurance like that, and your speed, you'd probably win events."

He frowned and grabbed the wall with both hands, leveraging himself out to sit beside her. Water streamed from his body. The sun felt warm on his skin. Nura had not been one for swimming. She preferred to sit in a lounger and recline in the sun. If it grew too hot, she'd move to the shade. Her hair didn't like the water, she'd often said. He missed her.

"I assume you get a lot of use from this pool. Isn't the weather always warm?" Lisa asked.

"For the most part. We do get cooler temperatures during the winter months. But even then, it's warmer than most of the rest of the world."

"Seattle is cool more often than warm. I don't often swim in an outdoor pool. The local community center has a great indoor one. But, of course, no view except for the concrete walls. I wonder why they never painted a mural on it. That would give the place some ambiance." She gestured to the distant mountains. "Something like this would be terrific."

"Perhaps you should suggest it when you return home," he said.

"Have you been to Seattle?" she asked.

"No. I have visited San Francisco and Los Angeles on your West Coast."

"Come up sometime, it's a great place. Nothing prettier than a clear day with the sun shining on Mount Rainier. Happens at least a couple of times a year," she joked.

He nodded. "Perhaps."

Why had he said that? He had no interest in traveling. It had lost its appeal for him three years ago. He'd
gone with Nura to indulge her love for seeing new
places, meeting new people, partying at new clubs. But
it held no meaning for him without her. Yet he'd almost
agreed to visit Seattle.

He shifted and Lisa looked at him. Her eyes were
clear and direct; their gray color unusual. Sometimes
they were almost smoky-blue, other times steely-gray.
Could a person judge her mood by their color? Or was
it the color of her clothes that caused the changes?

"I want to thank you for your hospitality. I really appreciate it. However, I think I need to get back to the dig.
They're depending on me. I can still photograph the artifacts in the tent even if I'm seated. The work won't
wait, it's piling up," she said.

"The doctor said to stay off your foot for a couple of
days."

"I know, but the compound is small. I can easily get
one of the team to help me get around. Once on a stool,
I can sit all day."

"You can borrow the wheelchair if you like," he said.
It wouldn't be the best solution, the ground was undoubtedly rough. But it would keep her mobile while
protecting her foot. He could fly her to the camp and
check out the place before leaving her.

But why should he care? He scarcely knew her.

Yet for the first time in years he was interested in
something beside escaping to the desert. Her comments
about the site had him curious about the artifacts they
were uncovering. Was it a worthwhile excavation or
only a delaying tactic for his project?

"That would be a great help, thank you," she said.

He glanced at her. She was gazing over the infinity edge of the pool to the distance far beyond. She had made no effort to flirt with him. For some reason that annoyed him. Even before Nura died, women used to flirt and hope—for what he wasn't sure, some betrayal on his part to his wife? That would never happen. He had loved Nura since they were children. No one else could ever compare.

He was not interested in trying to find a new woman. He had his memories. They'd had several years together as man and wife. Those memories would have to carry him to the grave.

"We'll leave in the morning. I'll fly the helicopter so you can get those pictures you wanted from the air," he said, banishing his thoughts of Nura and concentrating on the present.

Her delighted smile startled him. What would it take to have her look that way more often? Obviously more than wealth and position—which he had in abundance. She was an interesting mix of naive enthusiasm and cautious constraint.

In a way, they were alike—neither was willing to risk much to connect with others. It didn't sound as if she had memories like he had. But why should that concern him?

He scowled and rose, heading for one of the chairs and the towels that were folded there. Snatching one up, he rubbed his hair, trailing the towel down the rest of his body to capture the last of the moisture. He took a folded one and walked back to offer it her.

"Towel?"

She smiled and reached for it, wringing out her hair once more before drying it with the towel.

Nura would never have let her hair become a tangled mess, but Lisa didn't even seem to notice. The sun caught glints of pure gold in the strands, changing it from mousy brown to gleaming chestnut. Nothing like the inky black of his wife's hair. But pretty.

Lisa lay on her bed and looked at a magazine after her swim. Tuareg had tea sent to her room, with sweet cakes and dates. She sat near the window when eating them, after first photographing the elegant china and sterling-silver tea set. She also took pictures of her room. While she might include the tea service, she knew she wouldn't publish the images of the room, but she wanted them for her personal album—to remember a fairy-tale day in a beautiful home that was so sad.

The sooner she got back to work, the better. Before she allowed herself to dream dreams that would never be. Or become enamored with a man still in love with his dead wife.

CHAPTER FOUR

LISA LEANED AGAINST the window and watched the earth skim by below her the next morning. Tuareg had agreed to take her back to the camp in his helicopter. He'd flown higher when they first started, now he'd lowered the craft and was moving slowly. She could see the ambling river below, gleaming in the sunlight. Trees and shrubs grew in profusion near the banks. As the land spread out, however, there was less and less vegetation. The gorge it wound through would be relatively easy to dam and the plains were sloped enough to provide a wide basin for the reservoir.

She looked at the dusty tents in the distance, their destination. Soon she'd be back with her fellow excavation team members and her time with the exotic sheikh would come to an end. She smiled sadly, already feeling the tug of regret. It had been an amazing couple of days. But she knew she was better back on her own, without the lavish displays of wealth, without the beauty of a home that would never be hers enticing her to stop for a while and enjoy.

And without the tug of awareness that sprang up each time she looked at Tuareg.

She thought of the Frost poem—miles to go before she slept. Always in the back of her mind was the hope of meeting that one special man in the world. The one who wanted the same things she did—family, a home, roots and ties. So far she'd been wary of the men she knew who professed to want one or the other. None seemed to offer what she yearned for. Better to remain alone than risk everything and lose. At least that was Lisa's philosophy.

She began to take pictures of the site, the faint trail of the caravans still visible on the earth.

"Can you see that?" she asked, excited about the discovery.

"What?" Tuareg had given her the copilot's seat and provided headphones so they could hear each other above the din of the rotors. But she had been silent most of their short journey. Now she pointed.

"That trail there, see it? It's where the caravans crossed hundreds of years ago. It looks a lot like the ruts of the wagons which crossed into Oregon and California in America's great western migration. The earth is packed down so hard after hundreds of wagons, it doesn't grow vegetation. This trail looks the same. Can you follow it?" She was excited. Would Professor Sanders be as excited? Maybe he'd already seen this, but for Lisa, it was a first. No wonder the archeologists became excited over a discovery. This was heady stuff.

Tuareg slowly turned the helicopter and began following the faint trail. From the air it was clearly delineated, no vegetation grew on the path, even though clumps of desert plants could be seen scattered on both sides of it.

They traveled for some miles with Lisa taking a picture every few moments.

She looked up and smiled at Tuareg. "I don't know if the head of the team knows how clearly this is visible from the air. We could probably follow it on the ground and see if there were other camps. Has it been mapped?"

"I have no idea," Tuareg said. "Had enough?"

She looked longingly at the trail that seemed to go on to the horizon and reluctantly nodded. "Thank you, this has been fabulous!"

"You have an odd idea of what is fabulous," he commented as he turned back toward the archeological site. Any other woman he knew would have angled to stay longer—attend that party his mother had talked about. But Lisa had a strong sense of duty and was returning to the hardships of an archeological dig rather than stay in his comfortable home.

Once landed, they were met by several of the members of the group. The shortest seemed to be the one in charge.

"There's Professor Sanders. I hope he's not mad at me for pulling him away from the work. He's really captivated by what they're finding," Lisa said, fumbling with her seat belt.

Tuareg reached over and swiftly unbuckled the cumbersome clasp. The back of his hand brushed against her ribs, causing her to catch her breath. Lisa swallowed hard, gathering her senses. She'd been touched before and a lot more intimately than a casual brush of the back of a hand. But this was almost like a shock of electricity. The sooner she got back to normal, the better!

Tuareg hadn't noticed anything out of the ordinary, she noted. Thank goodness. She took a deep breath and prepared to scramble out of the seat, always conscious of her injured ankle. It felt better today. Maybe a few more days and she would be able to use it normally.

He glanced at the men and women waiting before reaching out to lift Lisa from her seat. She flung her arm around his neck, her face close to his. If she leaned closer, just a little, she could kiss him.

She groaned at her errant thoughts.

"Are you in pain?" he asked.

She nodded, closing her eyes. If he didn't put her down right now she was likely to do something too stupid to even think about.

"Hold on, I'll have you out in a second," he said. From the way he held her, she knew he did not feel the attraction that seemed to draw every bit of her consciousness into focus on him.

The door slid open and Tuareg engaged the stairs. They unfolded and he carried her down to the ground.

"If someone would get the wheelchair from the back, I'll put Lisa in it," he said to the group.

One of the young men ran up the stairs and appeared seconds later with the folded chair.

"I'm Tuareg," he said, lowering Lisa into the wheelchair when it had been opened and placed on the ground.

"Thank you for bringing her back," the shorter man said, reaching out to shake hands. "I'm Professor Sanders, head of this expedition. We've missed her. Our thanks to His Excellency for sending her back to us."

Lisa opened her mouth to correct the professor, but Tuareg's hand squeezed her shoulder and she closed her lips. Glancing at him quizzically, she wondered what he was doing.

Leaning close he said softly in her ear, "Let them

think I'm the pilot, that's true, after all, and it'll save trouble and explanations."

She nodded. She hadn't thought about it, but she supposed if the team knew who he was, they'd be fawning all over him or trying to convince him of the worth of the dig, get him to delay the dam for a few years. She could see both sides of the issue and was glad she wasn't the one to make the decisions. She turned to Professor Sanders to tell him about the trail.

He was as excited as she and couldn't wait to see her photographs.

"Do you develop here?" Tuareg asked.

"When it's dark. I only have a tent, so have to wait for full darkness."

"And not on the night of a full moon," one of the others chirped in.

Professor Sanders enjoyed having a visitor and quickly made sure Tuareg turned Lisa over to the care of one of the junior members so he could accompany him on a tour of the excavation. The professor proudly related all they'd discovered.

Lisa watched as Tuareg walked away.

"Hot," Jamie Farris said. She was one of the graduate students on the dig. Her long hair was always confined to a braid and she wore the dusty brown clothes that mingled so well with the sandy dirt. So no one could tell if she needed a change of clothes, she often joked.

Lisa nodded in agreement. Tuareg was definitely hot.

"Need help?" Paul asked, going to the back of Lisa's wheelchair and starting to push her toward the tents.

"This ground is hard going," she commented as she bumped along.

"Once it gets rolling, it's okay. The Jeep was delivered yesterday afternoon. I think it's running better than before you took it out."

"We have a pile of things recovered over the last two days. I've cataloged them and left them in order for the photos," Jamie said. She glanced again over her shoulder where Tuareg and Professor Sanders were deep in conversation. "You think he'll stay for a bit?"

"I have no idea," Lisa replied, resisting temptation to do her fair share of staring. She hoped he'd come to tell her goodbye, but didn't count on it. He would be glad to have his unwanted guest taken care of.

Looking around, nothing in camp appeared to have changed.

"Didn't the sandstorm cause any damage?" she asked.

"Didn't even get a stirring of air," Paul said.

"Which would have helped. I swear it was a hundred and twenty here yesterday," Jamie said.

Lisa kept quiet about swimming in the cool pool, but wondered how the storm had formed and bypassed the excavation.

Paul wheeled her into the large tent where the artifacts were housed. There were boxes already packed, sealed and labeled. Others stood empty awaiting new discoveries. Lisa's photography gear was kept in her tent, in specially designed cases that withstood sand, dust and moisture. One set of all photographs was sent to the university each week, another set was packaged with each box as it was packed. A third set was put into binders with the catalog pages of each artifact. There were several binders already compiled.

"How long before you can walk again?" Jamie asked.

"If it's only a sprain, I should be able to hobble

around in another day or two," she replied, already growing impatient with sitting in a wheelchair.

At least she'd have the work to do to keep her mind off her injury.

"I'll come get you for lunch," Paul said with a cheery smile. He waved and took off. None of the archeologists liked being away from the dig for long. Jamie was right behind him.

Silence settled in the tent. Lisa glanced around with resignation. It was the same as she'd left it, except for the increased number of items needing to be photographed. She pushed on the wheels, relieved to find she could propel herself on the hard-packed dirt. Soon she had her camera and close-up lenses and was absorbed in her work. Thoughts of a luxury villa forgotten.

Tuareg listened attentively to Professor Sanders. He'd seen Lisa disappear into a large tent near the center of the compound. He hoped the tour would end up there. She had not even looked back.

She both puzzled and intrigued him. He felt jaded to the wiles of women. Flirting was an art form in the circles he and Nura had traveled in. Yet Lisa had displayed none of the lures he expected. Her gaze was frank and forthright, her smile almost contagious. Every time she was delighted in something, her entire face seemed to light up. He hoped she smiled at him again before he left.

Surprised at his train of thought, he concentrated on what Professor Sanders had to say. The man had a passion for the work and brought it alive for Tuareg.

"Tell me more about how you can determine the age," Tuareg said.

The professor was obviously thrilled to have someone new to talk to. All his team members, except possibly Lisa, knew almost as much as he did. A new audience was a treat.

By the time the sun was directly overhead, Tuareg had had enough. He appreciated the history of Moquansaid as well as the next man. But he was not someone to live in the past. The people who had inhabited Wadi Hirum had long died and become dust. Their ways were not his.

Once they had descended into the wide trenches, marked by strings and cards with numbers, the air had grown close. No air circulated belowground.

"So you can see why we were excited by that find. It proves beyond any doubt the people living here had contact with China." The professor held a small porcelain figure in his hand.

"You found that today?" Tuareg asked. The small figurine was of classical Chinese design.

"No, no, two days ago. But it is so amazing, I wanted to keep it safe until Lisa could photograph it."

"How do you know it wasn't dropped here long after the Wadi had been abandoned?" Tuareg asked.

The professor beamed, as if Tuareg were a prize student. "Because it was buried in one of the pots. The age of the pot, and the dirt surrounding it, match the rest of the area. Isn't it beautiful? Of course, we have samples of the dirt and the pot itself which have to be tested. I believe one of your universities will be able to do that within the next few weeks. But I'm sure I am right." Professor Sanders gazed lovingly at the statue. "An amazing find. Of course it has rejuvenated everyone, we hope to find similar treasures."

"What else have you unearthed?" Tuareg asked as he gazed ahead at a series of square holes, each carefully labeled.

"Come to the holding tent and I'll show you some recent items. And Lisa has photographs of everything neatly put in binders."

Tuareg refused to admit to himself that was the end result of his query. He wanted to see her again before he left. What better place than where she worked? He could remember her there.

He frowned. He didn't need to remember her. She was a stranger whom he rescued. She was better and now back to her life. They would never need to meet again.

Unless he took her to his cousin's birthday party as his mother had suggested.

The sun must be frying his brains.

Stepping into the large tent a few moments later, Tuareg felt the temperature change once again. It was still warm, but the blazing sun's heat was muted.

Lisa sat by a table; her camera was on a stand and trained on a small shallow dish. She looked up when they entered.

"I wondered if I'd see you before you left," she said. "I wanted to make sure to thank you for coming to my rescue."

"I'm sure I've been keeping him from returning, but it's so refreshing to show someone new what we're doing," the professor said. "I told him about your binders of images, would you mind showing him the things we've already discovered?"

"Not at all."

The professor invited Tuareg to join them for lunch in a short time and left him to Lisa.

Tuareg walked around the tent, looking at the artifacts still displayed and at the boxes packed and ready for shipment.

"Not quite up to your tent," she murmured, glancing around. The utilitarian setting was suitable for the work at hand, but she couldn't help comparing it to the tent Tuareg had in the desert.

"More practical," he murmured, looking at the pieces on the long table. The binders were stacked at one end. He picked up one and leafed through the pages. The color shots were perfect, from different sides, top and bottom.

"Doesn't seem very creative," he said.

"That part's not. But it pays the bills. The creative shots are in my tent. They are not part of the project."

He moved along the table and pulled out a folder. The pictures in this one showed the various members of the team at work. One or two showed them lounging in the late afternoon on flimsy aluminum folding chairs. Their faces reflected the exhaustion that comes at the end of a long day, yet happiness clearly showed through.

"And these?"

"For a memory book," she said, already adjusting the camera for a close-up of the shallow dish.

"Memory book?" he asked, closing it to watch her at work.

"I thought everyone would like a memento of the project. These people aren't all from the same university. Once the project is over, we'll all go our separate ways. So I thought a memory book of the time we spent here would be welcome."

"You're doing it for everyone?"

"Same photos, just multiple copies. Doesn't take long."

He looked at the pictures. They were good. It made him more impatient for the delivery of her books that he'd ordered.

"I don't see any of you," he commented when almost halfway through the stack.

"Can't take ones of myself," she said.

He watched her until she was finished with the plate.

"Give me the camera and I'll take some of you at the table."

She looked up in surprise. "You will?"

"Don't you think for a complete memory book all the members of the team need to be included?"

"I guess." She looked at the camera, then shrugged. "If you want to, why not?"

She fiddled with the settings and then handed the camera to Tuareg. "Just look through the eye piece, focus by turning the lens piece and then press here."

He stepped back, framing her with the table and artifacts. Taking several different angles, he snapped the shots.

"How long before you know if they turned out?" he asked.

"I'll probably develop several rolls of film tonight. I'm anxious to see the ones I got from the air. So I'll know then."

He glanced at his watch. "When is your lunchtime?"

"Around noon. If you have to leave before, they'd understand. Thank you for bringing me back. And for everything."

Tuareg didn't need to be thanked. He returned the camera and turned. "I will have the doctor come here tomorrow to check your ankle." He could easily send the man with his pilot. But Tuareg would rather fly the craft himself.

"It's fine. I won't walk on it for another day or two and by then it'll be all right."

"I'll bring him here to double-check. And to see the pictures," he said again. Did she not want him to visit?

Her smile once against made her eyes almost blue.

Tuareg nodded and left. He wondered if pleasure made her eyes blue. If so, it was an indication she would not be displeased to have him return. Interesting thought.

Lisa listened as the helicopter started and then rose into the air. The sound faded slowly. He was gone. But he'd be back.

As soon as she finished dinner tonight, she'd develop the rolls of film. From the ruin, to the garden and tea setting at Tuareg's home, to the trail the caravans had taken, she hoped every shot came out.

Gazing off into space, she wished she'd taken one of Tuareg. When he'd been taking her picture today, she'd almost asked for one of him. Not that she needed one to remind her of the sexy man. She had every moment in his company committed to memory. When she was old and gray, she'd be able to tell anyone who would listen about her adventures with a genuine Arabian sheikh.

The afternoon flew by with the work that had piled up in her absence. Lisa was tired after dinner, but anxious to see the pictures she'd taken. It was a dark night. She made sure her tent was tightly closed. She had black material within the tent to create a dark room to ensure the film wouldn't be fogged. Slowly, she worked in the darkness, sure of the different stages of the process. Soon she could turn on the red light, courtesy of their portable generator. When the photos began to show on the paper, she was pleased. The quality was excellent. The ruins were amazing. She hoped she could get back there before she left the country.

The ones at Tuareg's home were equally good. There were so many places there she would have loved to photograph. But only with his permission.

Even the ones he took of her were good. He'd framed her at the work table, with enough background that everyone on the team would remember how that tent had looked.

She put the ones of the caravan trail aside to show Professor Sanders in the morning. Maybe he'd want to expand the site. Or even find another one of interest to research once Wadi Hirum was covered by water.

It was late when she went to bed. The cot couldn't compare with the luxurious bed she'd had at Tuareg's home. Or even the divan in the tent. She still felt sore in places, stiff. Her ankle gently throbbed, a reminder she'd done too much.

But all of it faded as she lay awake long after she thought she'd sleep. If Tuareg came tomorrow, it may be the last time she'd see him. The thought made her sad. Yet she couldn't come up with a single reason to meet with him again.

In the morning, Lisa was pleased to realize her ankle no longer ached as much as it had. Now it only felt stiff when she rotated it, nothing like the sharp pain the day she'd injured it. It was definitely healing.

She remembered Tuareg's holding her. And the flashback memories from her childhood. She shivered slightly. She'd never forget the night her mother died. She'd been alone for hours, calling, afraid. She would have been totally freaked out if she'd been alone in the sandstorm. Tuareg had no idea how much his being there had meant.

When she heard the helicopter later that morning Lisa wheeled the chair to the tent entrance and peered out. The machine landed light as a thistle. Dr. al Biminan came down the steps, followed by Tuareg. Her heart caught, then beat rapidly. She snuck her camera up and took a photo with the telephoto lens she'd put on earlier. She had to work fast before anyone realized what she was doing.

By the time Tuareg turned toward her, she had the camera back in her lap, changing the lens before he came close enough to suspect she had taken his picture. This was strictly for her—not for distribution.

Tuareg ignored the members of the team who were gathered nearby, walking directly toward her tent. He wore dark slacks and a white shirt, opened at the throat. The sleeves had been rolled up his forearm. He looked as if he were taking a quick break from a business meeting. Did he only wear the robes when staying in the desert?

She pushed the chair outside and watched as he walked purposefully. She could feel the pull of attraction. If her heart weren't racing, she felt she could almost make herself believe he was no more important to her than any other man.

The doctor hurried beside him.

"Good morning," Lisa called as they drew near. The day seemed suddenly brighter.

"How is your ankle?" Tuareg asked.

"Much better, thank you. I've been taking the anti-inflammatory medicine. I stood on it for a few moments today and it scarcely hurt."

Dr. al Biminan smiled a greeting and spoke to her through Tuareg.

"The doctor hopes it is better. He brought a support boot for you to wear until it is completely healed." Without another word, Tuareg went round to the back of the wheelchair and turned it to enter the tent.

The doctor completed his examination quickly, then fitted the padded boot on her leg and foot with Velcro fasteners. It gave support yet allowed mobility. Gingerly, Lisa rose to stand on it. She felt no discomfort beyond a dull ache.

The doctor told her not to overdo it.

"When I need to, I can walk. Thank you. I'll continue to favor my other ankle until it's completely healed," she promised, inclining her head slightly in acknowledgment.

Tuareg said something to the doctor who smiled, nodded and then turned to leave the tent.

"Are you leaving already?" Lisa asked.

"The doctor wants to check out the dig. There is growing interest in some sectors as news of the discoveries are conveyed to the capital. He told me of his interest, so I thought a brief tour would be in order. What new treasures have been uncovered since I was here?"

"Nothing exciting. I've taken photos of the porcelain figurine, however. Professor Sanders said you'd seen it. Isn't it exquisite?" Lisa pulled a photo from the stack she was working on. She'd developed them among the others last night and was still writing the information on each artifact for the catalog.

"Very beautiful," he murmured, studying the figurine in the picture.

"My mother enjoyed meeting you," he said a moment later, laying down the photograph. He withdrew a small envelope from his pocket and held it out to Lisa.

Lisa opened it. The short note was in English,

inviting her to spend the weekend with Yasmin al Shaldor and reminding her of the party for her niece.

She looked up at Tuareg.

"She's inviting me to visit this weekend."

His eyes narrowed slightly. "Indeed?"

She held the note out to him.

He took it and quickly scanned it, then handed it back. His demeanor seemed to undergo a slight change. He seemed a bit more reserved. "If you accept, I can arrange to have the helicopter pick you up."

Lisa reread the note, surprised at the invitation yet puzzled by Tuareg's reaction. She'd enjoyed talking with Yasmin, but had considered it merely a polite interlude with a stranger. She had never expected to hear from Tuareg's mother again or receive an invitation to stay with her.

She eyed him for a moment, trying to figure out what had changed.

"I would love to go," she said. "Except—does she realize our attire is geared for the dig? I don't have any suitable clothes. I don't think I can attend your cousin's party."

"Do not concern yourself. My mother will understand. For her place, you have the dress you wore at the villa," he said, referring to the dress he'd provided.

"If that's enough," she said doubtfully. The dress his mother had worn the other day was definitely a couturier creation. Still, Yasmin had to know Lisa had come to work on an excavation and would not expect her to have a wide assortment of clothes.

She looked up into Tuareg's dark eyes. He was studying her closely. When she met his gaze, he looked away, picked up a small shard of pottery. "Part of a bowl?"

She nodded.

He replaced it carefully on the table.

"So you will go?" he asked.

"Yes. Please thank your mother for me. Will you be there?"

"No. When not at the desert, I stay at my villa. It is a short ride into the city. My mother has a place in a high-rise in the heart of Soluddai. Much more convenient for her when my father is traveling. They also have a home near mine."

"So we'll be at the apartment in the city?" she asked.

"Yes. The party will be close by. I need to return. I will send the helicopter for you on Friday at two. Will your duties permit you to leave by then?" Tuareg asked.

"I'll make sure I'm caught up by then," Lisa said. She was trying to gauge if he was displeased with her acceptance of his mother's invitation or not. Should she not have accepted?

He held out his hand for hers. Surprised, Lisa put hers in his.

"Come, see how you walk in that device. Once I know you'll be all right, we'll leave." He helped her to rise.

She walked around the tent, perfectly capable of managing on her own, yet her hand clung to Tuareg's. He seemed in no hurry to let her go.

"Have you been back to the desert?" she asked.

"Not yet. I will go again soon."

"It was so lovely. I hope to resume my explorations once I'm fit again," she said. "And if Professor Sanders will trust me with the Jeep."

"It is dangerous to go off alone," he said.

"You were living there alone."

"That's different, I'm familiar with the desert," he said.

"I'm learning. Now I know to take a thick cloth in case of sandstorm, make sure I have lots of water if I get stuck somewhere. And it wouldn't hurt to have a shortwave radio, but the camp only has a couple and I'm not high on the list to have one."

"The desert can be a ruthless place. Unforgiving."

"Yet you love it," she said softly.

He didn't reply, but sought the view from the open tent flap. It was as if the land called to him, grounded him.

"If you didn't go back to the desert, what have you been doing besides ferrying me around?" she asked, returning to the wheelchair.

He glanced at her. "This and that."

"Planning on the dam?"

"That is taken care of by engineers."

"And what did you study in university?"

"Mechanical engineering. I have had input on the dam."

"And on how to erect your tent so the sandstorm didn't blow it to the next country," she said. "What else do you do?"

"As in?"

"Do you have a job, go to work every day? Though I guess if you can take time off to fly people around in your helicopter, you don't have a regular nine-to-five job."

"I have offices in the central city. Most of my work is special projects for my uncle," Tuareg said. "And only recently. Before that, Nura loved to travel and we spent more time out of the country than here. You would have called us unofficial ambassadors for Moquansaid. At least that is what Nura often said. She loved Europe."

"Really? But this is such a cool place," Lisa said, surprised.

* * *

Tuareg stood in the opening of the tent, frowning slightly. It was an innocuous question. Yet it had him wondering not for the first time why Nura preferred to spend more time away from home than in it. She'd been given free rein in decorating the house he'd bought after they were married. Of course, she insisted she needed to travel to Paris and London to actually see the items she wanted—rich brocades and delicate lace, antique furnishings. But once the decoration had been completed, she had no desire to spend much time in the house.

Nor did she like the desert.

She preferred parties and shopping for new dresses and jewelry. Activities that kept her always on the move.

He looked at Lisa, her enthusiasm was genuine. She'd been fascinated by his tent, by the grounds at the villa, by the sights she'd seen from the air. Even about finding the tracks of the long-ago caravans. What was it about her that found the mundane intriguing? Was it the novelty? Or would she be just as enthusiastic in another ten years, fifty years?

He suspected the latter. She seemed to be someone who liked finding out how things worked, what caused events, about remnants of the past.

Tuareg wanted to leave. He'd done his duty, brought the doctor, given his mother's note. He'd thought it would be just a polite letter after meeting Lisa at his home. The invitation caught him by surprise.

He had thought today would be the last time he'd see her. Being around Lisa had him feeling emotions he'd thought long gone. Nura was dead. She had been his love since they were teenagers. He'd had three years to get over her death, but still felt her loss as strongly as that first day. No one could ever take her place.

So why did he think about brushing his fingers through Lisa's hair? He did not need to know if it was as silky soft as it looked. Why did he want to be with her when she went to the capital to photograph the old buildings? There were many others who could make sure she saw the best of the architecture. Why was he thinking of taking her back to his tent, sharing his special place with a stranger? That was his special haven. Even Nura had never gone there with him. Lisa was nothing like Nura.

The sooner he bid her farewell, the better.

"I'll send the helicopter on Friday," he said. Without another word, he headed for the craft. He needed to get away.

She was not beautiful as Nura had been with her height and sleek sophistication. Nura's dark hair had glowed in sunshine and candlelight. Lisa was not as tall, but more rounded. Her sunny disposition had him thinking more along the lines of…of…of a puppy than a sexy woman.

Not true. He didn't want to brush his fingers through a puppy's fur. Didn't want to see a puppy's reaction to the desert. Or listen to one talk excitedly about new experiences. Or try to determine exactly what made a puppy's eyes change color.

Dr. al Biminan saw him and hurried to join him. As Tuareg started the engines he glanced toward the large tent housing the artifacts. Lisa stood in the doorway. He couldn't see her clearly at the distance, but knew she was watching him. For an odd moment, he felt a lift in his heart.

CHAPTER FIVE

BY TWO O'CLOCK ON FRIDAY, Lisa was a nervous wreck. She had packed the nicest clothes she'd brought but she knew they would not be suitable for anything but the most casual visiting. Surely his mother realized that. Her note had said her husband was out of town and she'd love company for the weekend. Maybe she just wanted the novelty of learning more about Seattle and Lisa's work on the dig and they'd spend the time inside talking or sitting on a patio. Did the high-rise apartments in the city have terraces?

She heard the helicopter long before she saw it. She doubled-checked her tote. She had clothes, makeup and her journal. She'd caught up on her daily entries since she'd returned and knew she'd have lots of new experiences to capture. Her camera bag sat beside the tote. Unless invited to, she would not presume to photograph Yasmin's home. But if they went for a drive or something, she wanted to be prepared. She also packed a copy of the site's memory book, to share the excavation with her hostess.

Professor Sanders joined her to watch the white craft land. The golden lettering gleamed in the sunshine.

"You'll be back on Sunday, right?" he asked.

"Yes, professor. Shall I bring you back anything from civilization?" she asked. The man had a weakness for ice cream and lamented many evenings how he missed it.

"Only some ice cream, if you can," he replied, smiling at the absurdity. They had no way to keep food frozen.

The man who climbed down from the craft when it was stopped was unfamiliar to Lisa. She felt an immediate pang of disappointment that Tuareg hadn't come for her. He was undoubtedly too busy to ferry his mother's guest. Lisa lifted her things and headed toward the helicopter.

"Don't get used to city lights," the professor called after her.

Lisa shook her head. She was growing to love her work and became almost as excited as the archeologists when new finds surfaced. Maybe she'd try for another dig when they finished. Next summer she could be in the wilds of Mexico or the deep jungle of South America. She liked the quiet of the desert, the feeling of living closer to the earth, the discovery of lost people and how they lived.

But it was fun to take off for a day and soar above it all. How astonished ancient civilizations would be to see this helicopter.

"Hello. Lisa Sullinger?" the pilot asked, reaching for her tote.

"Yes. That's right."

"His Excellency gave instructions to fly you to his mother's home." He showed her to the stairs and stood aside as she climbed inside. She soon sat in one of the seats on the far side, next to a window.

The pilot went to the front. "His Excellency also said

you'd be interested in seeing some of the land from the air and to fly south for a short distance."

"Wonderful. The professor was quite excited about the shots I got last time," she said, already reaching for her camera. "I'm looking for trails where caravans moved generations ago."

The pilot quickly started the engines and soon had the helicopter rising above the camp and heading south. Lisa watched from the window, searching for the packed earth, her gaze skimming across the barren ground. She refused to acknowledge even to herself that she'd much rather Tuareg had come to get her. She focused on the task at hand, excited to find the faint wandering path a moment later. Caught up in taking pictures, she soon forgot her disappointment.

A half hour later, the pilot turned the craft toward the northwest and flew straight. Lisa settled back in her seat, gazing ahead as the capital city drew closer. From a mere smudge on the horizon until she could see the windows in the buildings, it drew closer and closer. The pilot flew to the limits of the city, then turned slightly, circumventing the space, talking constantly with ground control in Arabic. Finally, he turned left and moved to hover over a tall building. Slowly he settled on the roof. Two guards in uniform stood near the door to the stairs.

The high-rise building was near the heart of the downtown area of Soluddai. Other tall buildings surrounded the one they landed on. The engines were shut down and silence descended.

"One of the guards will escort you to Madame al Shaldor's apartment," he said, opening the door and extending the stairs.

"Thank you for a most enjoyable flight," she said,

gathering her things. She'd seen traces of the caravan tracks and caught a glimpse of the gorge where the dam would be built. The pilot took her tote and camera bag, handing them to one of the men who stood at the bottom of the stairs.

The elevator was quiet as it descended only a few levels before stopping and opening to a small hallway. There was only one door. Lisa realized Yasmin and her husband must occupy the entire floor. The uniformed guard knocked. A maid opened the door and ushered them inside. The man placed the tote and camera bag on the floor inside the door and left.

"Welcome. Madame is in the salon. Please." The maid led the way.

The apartment was huge. Lisa saw lovely inlaid tile and parquet floors as she quickly followed the maid. Soon they entered a sunny room with yellow silk walls and beautiful windows framing a view of the city.

Yasmin rose from her sofa and crossed to greet Lisa.

"I'm so delighted you accepted my invitation," she said. She smiled warmly at Lisa and gestured for her to sit on the sofa.

"I have called for tea. A delightful custom from the British. How is your ankle? Tuareg said the doctor pronounced it healing."

"It's so much better than the other day." Lisa showed off the dark blue boot she wore. "This enables me to walk with very little discomfort. I didn't appreciate mobility until I lost it."

The maid came in carrying a silver tray loaded with a heavy silver teapot, fine china cups and saucers and a delectable assortment of finger sandwiches and scones.

"It looks wonderful," Lisa said in appreciation.

"One of the pleasures of traveling, picking up customs from other locations and making them part of my own. I also like popcorn when watching a movie, which I started after a visit to America," Yasmin said with a smile.

Lisa laughed. "A very fine tradition."

"Tell me how you managed this week with your foot injured."

Lisa asked if she could have someone fetch her camera bag. Before long she was explaining how things worked at the excavation, sharing the photographs she'd brought and enjoying a delicious cream tea as if they were in the heart of London.

By the next evening Lisa felt as comfortable with Yasmin as she did with most people. The woman had been beyond gracious in making her feel welcomed. The food was to her liking and the discussion lively and delightful. Yasmin had traveled extensively, primarily to Europe, but she had also been to New York twice. Lisa loved hearing her talk about shopping in some of New York's exclusive boutiques.

Yasmin had prevailed on Lisa to attend the birthday party of her niece. When Lisa had protested that she had no proper clothes, Yasmin arranged a fast shopping trip. Lisa insisted on buying her own dress, much to Yasmin's dismay.

"I love buying clothes, for me, my daughters, nieces. Do let me," Yasmin had cajoled.

But Lisa had been adamant.

She was pleased with the deep rose color, the simple lines and the flattering fit of the gown she'd found. It had cost more, even with the exchange rate, than she would have spent at home. But she didn't want to disgrace herself with her hostess. She found some comfortable, low-heeled shoes to wear that did not hurt her ankle. She refused to wear the boot to a party. She planned to sit as much as possible.

Lisa had offered to take a small camera to photograph the birthday girl and provide a memento of the party as her gift. Yasmin was pleased with the suggestion. They agreed on a time to meet in the salon just prior to Tuareg's arrival. Her son would escort them to the event.

As the time drew near for Tuareg to pick them up, Lisa's nervousness rose. She was unsure if she should be attending. She didn't speak Arabic and doubted most of the people spoke English. Still, she'd mainly be on the sidelines and would enjoy seeing how the young woman's birthday was celebrated.

Yasmin looked almost as nervous as Lisa felt when Lisa joined her in the salon. Did she not like large gatherings?

"I do hope he comes," Yasmin murmured.

"Who?" Lisa asked.

"Tuareg. He hasn't been to any family gathering since Nura died. He said he'd escort us to this event, but I'm worried he'll cancel at the last moment."

"Was her death recent?" Lisa asked. She knew so little about the man and his past.

"Three years ago. Such a tragedy. They were a perfect couple. Both tall and slender. She had so much energy. Always on the go. She loved to throw parties and attend them. She would have made a big to-do about tonight's. There was never anyone else for either of them." Yasmin sighed slightly, looking sad.

"How did she die?" Lisa asked.

"Aneurysm. Totally unexpected. Suddenly she

screamed in pain, clutched her head and collapsed. Moments later she died. We were stunned. She was only thirty."

Older than Lisa was, but only by a year. "How tragic," she murmured. The woman should have had an entire life still ahead of her. "They had no children?" she asked. Much as she'd hate to be widowed, it would seem to make things easier if children were there to comfort her. Her father had told her she made it bearable after his wife died. Only—he'd died too soon himself. There'd been no one for Lisa after that.

"No children. Nura had too much fun traveling to settle down. I suppose eventually they would have had one or two. Now I will never have a grandchild from Tuareg. There is a picture of her on the table there. The children they would have had—beautiful."

Lisa rose and crossed to the table near the far corner. An enlarged snapshot showed a beautiful woman laughing into the camera, an attentive Tuareg beside her.

"He might marry again," Lisa said. Nura had been beautiful. Her dark looks dramatic, her eyes flashing fire and excitement. For a moment Lisa wished she could have met her, photographed her. Captured that beauty herself on film.

Yasmin shook her head sadly. "There could never be a woman who would capture his heart like Nura. I have other children and I hope they will all bless me with grandchildren. But not Tuareg."

Lisa frowned. The statement sounded melodramatic. The man she knew wasn't going to pine away the rest of his life. He was too virile and dynamic to grieve forever. One day he'd find someone as spectacular as this woman had been and fall in love all over again. She put the picture down just as the door opened and Tuareg stepped inside.

He caught the movement from his eye and turned, narrowing his gaze when he saw what Lisa had been staring at. She could read nothing from his expression.

"Tuareg, we were just wondering when we might see you." Yasmin rose. "We are ready. Lisa has offered to photograph the party and give the pictures to Jeppa as her gift."

"Then my cousin will be double lucky. I have one of Lisa's books as a gift," he said.

"You do?" she asked in surprise.

"The one with children and playgrounds," he replied.

She was touched he thought enough of her work to make such a gesture.

The limousine waiting for them was sumptuous. Lisa felt as if she were living a fairy-tale weekend. Would she end up without a slipper and have it all vanish in an instant?

In a short time they arrived at the home of Tuareg's uncle. As she walked up the wide sidewalk, Lisa wished she could begin taking pictures. The guests ran the gamut, from young and trendy to elderly and conservative. Laughter seemed the key for the night, no matter what age.

Inside she was treated to a beautiful setting. Lights glowed everywhere. The jewelry and shimmery fabrics of the ladies added to the sparkle. The men were handsome in their dark suits. It seemed everyone was in western attire. She was surprised at first. She had expected Arabian garb. It took several minutes for their small party to work their way across the entryway to greet Tuareg's cousin.

When they reached her, Jeppa did a double take when

she spotted Tuareg. Quickly she threw herself into his arms and hugged him, jabbering away a mile a minute. Lisa wished she understood what the girl was saying, but it was obvious she was happy to see Tuareg. Lisa drew her camera from her small purse and snapped a quick shot. A moment later Tuareg untangled himself from his cousin's embrace and switched to English as his cousin greeted her aunt.

"Jeppa, my mother's guest, Lisa Sullinger. My cousin Jeppa."

"Happy birthday, Jeppa," Lisa said. "I hope it's all right that I came."

"Of course. I'm happy to meet you." She laughed and hugged Tuareg's arm. "I'm so happy to have you here! A gift indeed for my birthday. Tante Yasmin," and then she switched back to Arabic.

"Come, I'll see you have something to drink. And introduce you to some other family members," Tuareg said a moment later, guiding Lisa away from his exuberant cousin.

It seemed as if Tuareg knew everyone there. He introduced Lisa to a couple standing near one of the tall windows, mentioning she worked at the Wadi Hirum excavations. It was a good icebreaker. Everyone seemed interested in learning about the dig. Another young man joined the group, then two elderly women—sisters, Lisa thought. From time to time, glances were exchanged between the people. Lisa tried to interpret what they meant, but she hadn't a clue. Was it awkward to have her at a gathering of family and long-term friends?

Tuareg made sure she was introduced to more guests. When she had a chance, she stepped back a little bit and lifted her small camera. "I do need to take photographs or I won't have any for Jeppa," she said. "I can manage myself if you wish to chat to friends." Her ankle was starting to bother her again. She'd have to find a chair and rest it.

"Tell me what you wish to take," Tuareg said.

"Would it be rude to just wander around and snap candid shots?" she asked.

"Not at all. Lead on."

"I'll be fine. You go talk to your friends." She looked around, people seemed to be staring at them.

He glanced briefly toward a group, then back to Lisa. "I've spoken to all I wish to."

"Oh." She was momentarily taken aback. But she wanted to give her hostess a memory book, so began to study the crowd, soon lost in framing shots and trying for different angles that would add interest to a picture.

When she had taken photos of a sufficient number of the guests, she worked her way toward Jeppa. The guest of honor should definitely be included.

She had just raised the camera when a man stepped in front of her and yanked it from her hands.

"Hey," she said.

Tuareg stepped closer and spoke quickly to the man. He hesitated a moment, then with a slight bow, returned the camera. His gaze never left Lisa, however.

She checked the camera, it was undamaged.

"A camera-phobe?" she murmured, glaring at him.

"No, simply making sure unwanted photographs aren't taken. I explained you were with me, and taking pictures with full knowledge of the family."

"Including Jeppa?" she asked, dismayed her surprise had been blown.

"No. If she notices, she'll think little about it. Continue."

Lisa smiled at the command. He did it without think-ing. "Yes, sir."

She took several good photographs of Jeppa, one of her dancing with her father, another of her laughing with friends. And one with Yasmin.

"Go stand by her and I'll get you both," she told Tuareg.

"Not this time," Tuareg said absently. He looked over the people dancing, the laughing crowd near the opened windows. He knew most of the people here, but had little to say to them. The mindless chatter seemed to ebb and flow like the sea. Nura would have loved it, greeting everyone, exchanging gossip and planning new parties. The appeal had lost its excitement for him long ago, though he'd continued to please her. Now that she was no longer with him, he'd just as soon spend time with his plans for changing a portion of the desert to a fertile irrigated plain.

"Then, perhaps we could sit over there. I hate to admit my foot is bothering me," Lisa said.

"You should have said something earlier," he said, taking her elbow in his palm and guiding her to one of the small alcoves. Empty chairs lined most of the area. The elderly sisters they'd talked with earlier were sitting near one edge. Tuareg deliberately chose the far side. He didn't want to get into conversations with friends.

Once Lisa sat down, he looked at her ankle.

"It aches, but I'll be fine. It was just the constant standing," she said, reaching down to rub it a little.

"Would you like to return home?" he asked.

She glanced at him. "So soon?"

He almost smiled. "I was ready to leave about two hours ago."

"What about your mother?"

"I'll find her and see if she wishes to leave now or have me send back the car."

"It seems a bit rude to leave so early."

"I've had enough. I suspect you have as well. With your ankle, you have a perfect excuse without offending anyone. Wait here, I won't be long."

He strode through the crowd, glad for the excuse to leave. Finding his mother, he made sure she had a ride home since she wished to stay longer. He went to his cousin, wishing her happy birthday once more and telling her they were leaving.

She smiled happily. "I'm glad you came. I enjoyed meeting your friend," she said with a look over toward Lisa.

He wondered what fantasies she was conjuring up. For a moment he almost set the record straight. But to give voice to it gave it more credence than warranted.

"I can't wait to get to know her better," Jeppa said. "I know it was hard, the first party without Nura. We all miss her," she continued. "I'm glad you've found someone else to spend time with."

"She is my mother's guest," Tuareg said tightly. Maybe he should set the record straight before Jeppa spread rumors to the contrary.

Jeppa laughed. "Of course, it would not be right to have her staying at your home with no chaperone. Your mother is doing it correctly."

Tuareg give his cousin a kiss on her cheek and turned to leave. Jeppa confirmed what he'd suspected when he first saw the note from his mother to Lisa. Was she matchmaking? His father was in Paris on business. Would he have interfered had he been home?

Tuareg crossed the room back to Lisa, ignoring the people who spoke to him. The sooner he got things cleared up, the better. Was Lisa in on the plans?

Lisa smiled at him when he reached her. Tuareg could see the strain around her eyes, however.

His confrontation would have to wait. She was not feeling well.

"Ready?" he asked.

"Yes, thank you. The longer I sit, the harder it will be to get up," she said, rising to her feet. She stood for a moment as if bracing herself, then stepped away from the chair.

He could see her limp as they moved slowly to the front doors.

"Shall I carry you?" he asked.

"Good grief, no. How embarrassing that would be."

Yet the perfect opportunity to link them together. Maybe this bout of matchmaking was only on his mother's part.

Or maybe he was imagining everything.

The limo deposited them at his mother's building a short time later. He rode up the elevator silently. He had a key, would let Lisa in and then leave.

"Are you enjoying your stay?" he asked as the elevator reached the floor.

"Very much. Your mother and I went shopping today. It was quite an experience. Then she kindly drove me around the city so I could get an idea of what I want to take pictures of before I leave at the end of the summer. I would have snapped some shots today, but didn't have my best camera. It's such a lovely city."

He stepped into the lobby and unlocked the door to

the apartment. Standing aside for Lisa, he followed her inside. She was limping more now than before. Lights were on in the entryway, but the rest of the apartment was dark. As if in agreement, they walked toward the salon.

"Oh, wow," Lisa said softly when they reached the archway. The wall of windows gave way to the lights sparkling in the capital city. The black of night was the perfect backdrop to the blaze of lights from office buildings, streetlights and homes.

"Don't turn on the lights," she said, moving across the wide room to stand by the windows. "This is spectacular." For a long moment she stared. Tuareg looked at the colorful scene.

"I wish I'd brought my other camera. The one I have wouldn't capture this view. It's so lovely."

Tuareg came to stand next to her. "You have lights in Seattle," he commented.

"Sure, and if I come into a room where I can see them unexpectedly, I'm just as taken. Isn't it pretty?"

She glanced at him when he didn't respond. He looked out the window but she wasn't sure he saw the lights as she did.

"Tuareg?"

He looked at her. "What?"

"I'm glad you rescued me from the sandstorm and introduced me to your mother."

"Fate."

"Maybe. Anyway, I had a nice time tonight. I didn't think I would."

"Why is that?"

"I don't speak the language and don't usually move in such circles."

He glanced at her then looked back out the window.

It was easier to remember she was merely his mother's guest when he wasn't looking at her.

Her eyes were dark and mysterious in the faint light from the cityscape. Her hair as dark as Nura's. For a moment, he wished they'd met in another life, another time.

"Such circles?"

"Mmm, sheikhs are Arabian royalty, right? I'm used to regular people."

"We are regular. You make it sound as if we're some exotic species," he said, now trying to see her better in the faint illumination.

Lisa shrugged. To her, Tuareg was exotic, but not because of his title, more because of his heritage. He was a handsome man, strong enough to lift her with little effort. Able to take care of himself and others. A worldly traveler, representing his country to other countries. And a caring man, trying to change the lives of nomads and offer a better way for them. Yet there was a solitude that seemed out of place. Not the self-sufficiency he evidenced, but the feeling he was apart from his friends and family.

Lisa continued to stare out the window, but instead of enjoying the lights, she was remembering being in Tuareg's arms, being held tightly while the wind raged around them. If she closed her eyes, she could still smell the male scent unique to him. Almost feel the steely strength of his arms, holding her securely against the ravages of nature. It had been a scary event, yet she had not felt afraid. He could make anyone feel safe.

Snapping her eyes open, she stepped away. A polite good-night and she would escape to her bedroom.

He reached out to stop her from moving away. Turning her slowly, he looked into her eyes, his dark and unreadable.

"I loved my wife very much," he said. "I'm not looking for another."

Lisa blinked. Where had that come from?

"Okay," she said.

"So if you think my mother is arranging things toward that end, rest assured it is not with my knowledge or permission."

"I never thought any such thing! You mean you think your mother would try matchmaking?"

"She's happy being married, she would like to see me happy again," he said simply.

"Well, she needs to understand you make yourself happy. And she's probably happy being married to your father. Not just being married." She pulled her arm away from his hand.

"Maybe we should say goodbye now and relieve your mind of any worries that I have designs," she said, stung by his suggestion. "I can hire a car or something to get back to the dig. I don't need anything further from you!"

"Perhaps designs is too strong? Maybe you just want to see what develops?"

"And why should anything develop?" she asked. "You kindly rescued me from a fall and the sandstorm. Now I'm better and we don't have any reason to see each other again. I shall thank your mother for her hospitality and return to camp. If she tries for any further contact, I'll plead too much work. That should protect you for any matchmaking endeavors."

He could tell Lisa was angry. He had meant to clear the air, not make her upset.

"My mother thinks she's helping me. She's worried that I haven't recovered from my wife's death."

"She knows you love your wife. But she said she doesn't expect you to marry again. I think you're imagining things."

"Even Jeppa thought that," he defended.

"I can't help what your cousin thinks. Thank you for bringing me back here. I need to get to bed and get off this ankle. Good night."

He studied her in the faint light from the window.

"I will always love Nura."

"There you are, then. No woman wants to come in second best—especially against a ghost who can do no wrong. Good night, Tuareg." She turned but once again he reached out to stop her flight.

The bright glare of light suddenly snapped on flooded the room. Lisa blinked at the brilliance and turned toward the door. One of Yasmin's maids stood on the threshold, looking startled. She said something in Arabic and bowed, backing away.

Tuareg called after her, crossing the room and speaking rapidly.

Lisa took a moment to get control of her emotions. How dare he suggest that she might have designs on him when it was his mother who had invited her. And she'd been careful at every encounter not to let her hopes rise. She knew he was so far from her realm that the most they'd ever be was cordial acquaintances. She was glad for the interruption.

She walked to the doorway, head held high.

Giving Tuareg and the maid a wide berth, she mumbled good night and fled down the hall to the room she was using. Tuareg called her name, but Lisa kept walking. Only when the door was safely shut behind her did she breathe again.

"Lisa?" He knocked on the door.

"Go away." She turned to face the door, half expecting him to barge in.

"I wanted to apologize if I was in error."

"Apology accepted. And you were. Good night."

"If you would let me explain."

"There's nothing to explain. Let's not make more of this than we already have." She waited, straining to hear any sound from the other side of the door. Endless moments ticked by. The silence grew. Sheikhs didn't fall for photographers from Seattle. Especially not rounded women with freckles across their noses, no family and not much sophistication. She knew that. She didn't need him telling her in so many words.

CHAPTER SIX

LISA GREETED HER HOSTESS the next morning with some reservation. She couldn't help wonder if Tuareg's assessment of his mother's offer of friendship had some merit. Why else would a woman a generation older befriend her? They had little in common, though Lisa had enjoyed her visit and found his mother charming and a delightful hostess.

Soon after Lisa was seated at the dining table, the maid entered carrying a tray of hot chocolate and hot coffee, which Yasmin then served, as well as fresh fruit and croissants. Lisa knew she could quickly get used to such luxury.

"I need to return to the dig earlier than expected," she said, hoping Yasmin wouldn't ask why.

"Oh dear, I thought we might go visit one of my dearest friends this afternoon."

"It would have been lovely, I'm sure, but the work at the site continues. We're up against a firm deadline and I need to do my fair share. Also, the sooner I can develop the pictures I took last night the sooner I can get the memory book to Jeppa."

Though how she was going to get the book to Jeppa

was unclear. Lisa would get her address and hope she could post it through the weekly pickup at the excavation.

"Stay until after lunch and I'll make sure someone takes you back if you must leave," Yasmin urged.

Lisa smiled and nodded, her heart beating faster when she thought about Yasmin calling Tuareg to arrange for the helicopter. It would take a couple of hours driving, but Lisa preferred that to being in Tuareg's debt for another trip. Or have him think it was a ploy to capture his attention.

He'd made it abundantly clear last night where his heart lay.

She nibbled on her croissant, wishing she had more of an appetite, but the thought of seeing Tuareg again had her on edge. Surely she could pretend nothing had happened and treat him casually as before. She had done nothing wrong. She wasn't matchmaking. And she didn't believe his mother was, either.

"How did you enjoy Jeppa's party?" Yasmin asked.

Glad for a safe topic, Lisa replied readily. Before long her concerns faded and she began to enjoy Yasmin's company again. The older woman was generous in sharing tidbits about the different relatives at the party. Lisa didn't remember half of the people she spoke of, but enjoyed the vignettes of each.

The time fled and before she knew it, Lisa heard the now familiar sound of the helicopter. She had her tote and camera bag by the front door. She was again wearing the jeans and long-sleeved shirt she'd arrived in, arms rolled up for coolness. And the support boot.

When Yasmin heard the knock at the door, she looked expectantly toward the entryway. Tuareg entered a moment later. His gaze went immediately to Lisa. She

smiled self-consciously and glanced away, her heart
pounding. Figured the one time she'd hoped he would
send his pilot, he had to come himself.

Goodbyes were quickly said. Two minutes later Lisa
stepped inside the helicopter. The man who had flown
her in on Friday sat in the pilot's seat. Lisa sat where
she had before. Tuareg sat in the copilot's seat, glancing
around to make sure she fastened her seat belt.

He'd scarcely said three words to her, she thought,
looking out the window, ignoring the pull of attraction
that had her yearning to gaze at him throughout the
flight. What would it be like to have his mother really
be trying to foster a relationship between them?

Would Tuareg take her on an actual date? Not a visit
to a family gathering, but to dinner, maybe dancing.
She'd love to be swept around a club to some soft
dreamy music, if she were held in Tuareg's arms.

The city gleamed in the afternoon sunshine, the white
of the buildings almost hurting her eyes. Slowly, the helicopter rose and she pressed against the window for a final
look when the craft turned and headed for the excavation
site. She sat only feet from the man who had accused her
of being part of a conspiracy to capture his heart.

Or, no, he had never put it quite like that, but that's
what Lisa would want if she ever fell in love. Complete
devotion from the man she loved. And Tuareg had made
it clear Nura had been the love of his life.

Her indignation to his accusations gave way as the
flight continued. She rotated her ankle, feeling it ache
again. Standing last night had not been the best thing to
do.

When they landed at the camp, Tuareg went down the
stairs first and turned to offer his hand to Lisa. She put

hers in his, feeling a jolt of awareness. Her glance flickered to his. His dark eyes watched her.

Licking suddenly dry lips, as she reached the ground, Lisa pulled her hand away. The pilot handed out her tote and camera case, which Tuareg snared. "I'll walk you to your tent," he said.

"I can manage," she said, holding out her hand for her bags. "I wouldn't want you to get the wrong impression."

He ignored her and gestured toward the center of the camp. "Go."

Suppressing a sigh, she gave in. It wasn't worth making an issue of it.

The others in the expedition were lounging around as it was Sunday afternoon. Several waved as Tuareg and Lisa passed, but no one rose to join them.

It was hot. No air stirred. The shade was limited to that made by tents and canopies. Tuareg stopped at her tent and handed her the bags. Glancing around, he leaned closer and spoke softly,

"I hope you have accepted my apology."

"Of course. It was simply a misunderstanding," she said. She couldn't help remembering how much more comfortable she'd been around him before, despite his being a sheikh. The party last night and his accusation after it had shown her what a fantasy world she'd been living in. She had better keep a good head on her shoulders.

But it was difficult with his face so close. By barely moving two inches, she could brush her lips against his jaw. Would he respond with a real kiss?

"Goodbye. Thank you for the ride." She jerked back and lifted the flap. Escape was uppermost in her mind. Head held high, Lisa held out her hands for her tote and camera case.

* * *

Tuareg knew he'd been dismissed. For a moment he was startled. It was an unusual experience for him. Nura would have called him spoiled and laughed at his surprise. He handed the case to Lisa and watched as she turned and entered the tent.

Would his wife have liked Lisa? The American woman was unlike most of the women he knew, who all seemed born with a sense of style and sophistication—like Nura.

Lisa, on the other hand, had a freshness that was appealing. And an enthusiasm that had him captivated. He'd been hasty last night in accusing her of a conspiracy with his mother with the end result of marriage. If he'd thought it through, he'd have realized his mother would want him to marry a nice woman from Moquansaid, not someone from halfway around the world.

And in all fairness to Lisa, she had never actually flirted with him, never given him any real reason to suspect she was in league to interest him in a relationship.

He turned and started back to the helicopter. He'd keep in touch with the site via the radio in future. Make sure Lisa needed no further medical attention.

Professor Sanders hurried across the compound, obviously eager to speak with Tuareg.

"Sheikh al Shaldor, I did not recognize you when you were here before. We are most delighted to have you visit again. Is there anything I can show you or explain about the project?" he said when he caught up with Tuareg.

Tuareg greeted the professor. "You gave me an excellent tour last time. You are accomplishing more than expected. My uncle is pleased."

"It's so fascinating. I'd be happy if you'd care to stay

longer and have firsthand experience at the next layer we are uncovering. We fear we will lose important data if we don't move rapidly. There is the risk of damaging new discoveries, but time is so short. Unless we can have it extended?" he asked hopefully.

"That is not my area," Tuareg said. The dig was already costing his dam project time and money. He would as soon have the archeologists leave tomorrow so the long awaited reservoir could begin filling.

"Perhaps you might speak to your uncle on our behalf?" the professor asked tentatively.

"No. I am anxious to have the excavation completed. I am involved in the building of the dam."

"Ah, I see. Perhaps if you'd stay and visit longer. See what we are discovering, learn more about the people who lived here you would see how beneficial the excavation is?"

Tuareg had reached the helicopter. He had no intention of changing his mind. Still, he'd learned more than once never to close doors completely.

He glanced over toward Lisa's tent. Did he have time to come again?

The fact he wanted to surprised him.

"Perhaps. I will contact you if I decide to visit again." He'd see if he forgot the pretty photographer in the next couple of days. If not, maybe he'd return for a visit.

"We would love to have you stay for a day or two. Our accommodations won't be what you're used to, but I think you'll find the work so fascinating, you'll be able to overlook the inconveniences," the professor said.

"I am used to," Tuareg paused for just a second, "camping out."

So the door remained cracked open. With a word of farewell, Tuareg climbed into the helicopter and they were off.

Lisa sat on her cot. He was gone. She was used to good-byes. The first had been the cruelest—the death of her mother only a few feet away from her on a rainy night in Seattle. Then her father's death a couple of years later. The homes she'd lived in were like a kaleidoscope in her mind. The Brewsters the best. The Mahoneys the worst. Goodbye to Jill when she moved to California. Goodbye to—

She pulled herself up sharply. She was not giving in to some pity party. For a few days she'd known a fasci-nating man who'd stirred her senses and taken care of her in a time of need. She reached for her best camera and headed for the large tent. Time to catch up on what she missed while gone.

Wednesday was a blustery day. The sky was cloudy but without any immediate threat of rain. The wind blew in gusts and every time a particularly strong one came, Lisa looked up in remembrance. She was uneasy, as always when storms threatened. The tent billowed and flapped in the wind. She had papers anchored beneath several heavy rocks, a bowl, two cups and a camera.

The air gusted again and the tent shook. She looked around, afraid it would pull up its lines and sail away.

"Interesting way to hold down the paper," Tuareg said from the opening.

Lisa jumped in surprise and turned to look at him, startled to see him. He wore the traditional robes of the desert, a turban covering his dark hair, its end hanging free to leave his face clear. Her heart skipped a beat. She stared.

"I didn't know you were coming. I didn't hear the helicopter," she said, reaching out for one of the cups to anchor the page she was writing.

"There are other methods of travel in the desert," Tuareg said.

"You rode over?" she guessed.

"Ham needed the exercise. And the weather is threatening. I did not wish to fly in it."

She glanced around at the flimsy tent and prayed it would hold against whatever weather came.

"I did not expect to see you again," she said.

"Professor Sanders invited me. He hopes to get me to lobby my uncle to change his deadline for the expedition."

"That would be wonderful—if you would. There is so much here that is still not recovered. Think of the knowledge that will be lost once the water floods the site."

"Do not start. You know my views, I'm unlikely to change them," he said, walking around the tent, looking at the various articles on the long tables.

Lisa felt a flare of anger that he so arrogantly dismissed their arguments. She would not deny his project held great value, but not everything could be measured in monetary terms. "Knowledge is valuable for its own sake."

A gust of wind caused Tuareg's robes to billow, fluttering. "The weather seems to be growing worse."

"Then why are you here? Shouldn't you be home where it's safe and dry?"

"A little rain never hurt anyone."

Lisa looked away, remembering.

"I will talk with the professor and see more of the site he's so proud of. Then, perhaps after lunch, you may wish to accompany me to a camp nearby of nomads grazing sheep who will have to move before the flood waters rise."

Lisa was torn. She knew it was better not to spend time with Tuareg, but the enticing thought of actually being asked to spend an afternoon with him was more than she could resist.

"A short ride in a Jeep. A quick visit and we return," he said, coaxingly.

Put that way, how could she refuse? Actually, put any way, she wouldn't refuse.

After lunch, Tuareg wrapped the end of his scarf around his lower face so only his eyes were visible. He had received permission from Professor Sanders to drive one of the Jeeps. Urging Lisa to bring a scarf to protect her face against the blowing grit, he chose a Jeep and they were off. He spoke little once they were underway. There was no road or even track, just endless dirt, scrub brush and clumps of grass.

They soon reached the banks of the shallow river and turned to follow the languid flow. The vegetation was not as sparse near the water as it was just a few hundred yards away.

"All this will be lost when the water backs up, won't it?" she asked at one point, taken by a pretty setting of trees beside the river. The leafy abundance stood in stark contrast to the barren plains on which the excavation was taking place. There were a few date palms near the seep that gave water to the Wadi Hirum. Nothing like these thick green trees. The limbs moved in the gusting wind. The water danced with small ruffled waves.

"It will take a number of years for the reservoir to

reach its full capacity. But this will be one of the first areas to be flooded," he said, studying the landscape.

"Just think, these trees have been growing for more than a hundred years. We may be the last people on earth to see them," Lisa said, feeling a little sad.

"You are a romantic. It is the nature of things to grow, live, die. New trees will grow with the irrigation the reservoir will provide. Crops will flourish where now nothing grows."

"Hmm."

"Do you think progress should not be made?" he asked.

"Of course not. I'd hate to be living like my ancestors. But it's still too bad we can't find other ways to move forward and yet leave the beauty of nature as we find it."

"Take a picture."

"Great idea," she said, already reaching for her camera. She may be one of the last people to see these trees here, but a photograph would capture them forever.

She snapped a few frames, then looked at Tuareg. "How about you go over there and stand by the trees to give perspective to their size."

He didn't move for a moment, then nodded and climbed down from the Jeep. The sunshine sparkled off the river, the shade looked cool and inviting. An Arab prince in full robes lent a mysticism to the scene. Lisa happily snapped several shots. Only she would know who was in the photographs. The way he wore his robes and the cloth across his face hid all traces of who he was, adding to the magical aspect.

"Enough," he said a moment later and strode back to her side.

"Thank you. I'll send you copies if you like."

"No need. There are none I share photos with."

Lisa reseated her hat, resting her camera on her lap. She refused to feel sorry for Tuareg in light of his statement. He had his parents and other family members. Friends, undoubtedly. She had no family, but had a few close friends to share things with.

Unlike him, she was not cutting herself off from life.

The thought surprised her. And it wasn't true. He was not cutting himself off from life. The man was involved in a long-term project to better his country. He obviously was on good terms with his mother and, she suspected, his father. And well loved by many if the greetings at the party were anything to go by.

Yet there was a solitary air about him.

"We'll be at the settlement soon," he said.

Lisa would be glad to arrive. The jouncing of the Jeep was uncomfortable. And twice her foot had hit the floor hard, aggravating her ankle. Every time the Jeep seemed to lean sharply to the right, she felt fear. The car her mother had been driving that fateful night had rolled to the right before coming to rest on its roof. The memory seemed to be burned into her. She would never forget.

She looked eagerly ahead to see the tents when they began to materialize. The nomads had dwellings that could be quickly taken down and moved to another site of forage for their animals. The sheep munched vegetation near the river, strung out along the banks for as far as Lisa could see.

Tuareg stopped near a tent on the edge of the cluster of dun-colored structures. Before she knew it, Lisa had been introduced and given a cup of cool water. The inhabitants were reserved but friendly, greeting her formally. Tuareg translated the welcomes.

Before long, however, she had the women smiling and the few children jumping up and down with excitement. Especially when she brought out some butterscotch candies.

"They don't often get treats like that," Tuareg said. "It was nice of you to think of them."

"Hard candy is the only thing that seems to travel well in this heat. I'd love some dark chocolate myself. And Professor Sanders would give half a month's pay for some ice cream. I'm happy the children like the candy."

After some discussion, not at all pleasing to the men of the group, Tuareg suggested they walk around so Lisa could see the current camp of the nomads. The children danced around them as they walked, shyly smiling at Lisa and holding out their hands for more candy.

A couple of the older men accompanied them, talking with Tuareg. "They are not happy about the dam," Tuareg said softly at one point.

"Would you be if it changed your way of life?" Lisa asked. "It appears not everyone is as excited about this project as you. Certainly the archeologists aren't. Now these shepherds."

He shook his head. "Maybe not. But this will improve things."

"Change is hard to deal with—no matter if it is good for you," she said, stopping to gesture with her camera to the men with them. Tuareg said something to them in Arabic and they nodded, wide smiles breaking out. At least they seemed agreeable to having their photographs taken.

The afternoon sped by. When Tuareg said they had

to leave to reach the camp before dark, Lisa was reluctant to go.

The wind had died sometime during their visit. Everything was still, as if waiting. The land was old and had waited for centuries—just for Tuareg and his project? Would she return some day to see the desert blooming?

"Thank you for bringing me here. It's been fun seeing the children. I'm not around kids much."

"You should be. You seem to relate to them in a special way—even without a common language."

"You were there to translate."

They reached the expedition camp before dark. Dinner had already been started in the mess tent and Tuareg and Lisa quickly went to wash before joining the others.

He took off the robes and slung them over one of the stools near the row of sinks. Beneath he was wearing western attire. Lisa washed her face and hands and tried to stop the sexual awareness that spiked every time she was near the man. He was so off-limits for her. Remember that, Lisa! she admonished herself.

Professor Sanders was sitting in the mess tent at one table with two of the students who were working on the camp. He waved at Tuareg when he entered. In only moments Tuareg had sat at the professor's table and the two of them were deep in discussion.

Lisa hesitated, then deliberately sat at a table with some of the graduate students. As soon as she finished eating, she rose and left for her tent. She wanted to develop the photographs she'd taken that afternoon.

Some time later, caught up in rediscovering the scenes of the afternoon in the photos, she heard Tuareg call her. Lisa loved her quiet time. Now she knew she'd gladly give it up for more time with Tuareg.

"I'm here. Wait a moment, I'm at a critical juncture and don't want to ruin anything," she called, hoping he wouldn't open the black cloth.

Five minutes later, she pushed aside the dark cloth and entered the central part of her small tent. Tuareg sat on her cot, leafing through the pages of the pictures of Jeppa's party.

"I was hoping you'd take that to her. I'm not sure how to mail them," she said.

"These are excellent pictures. You didn't just take a snapshot, you've captured the essence of each person," he said. "There are two books."

"The second is for your mother, as a thank you for her kindness in inviting me to stay with her."

She glanced at her watch. It was after eleven. "Aren't you leaving?"

"The professor asked me to stay another day. He wants to see you," he said, shifting slightly to get more comfortable on her cot.

"Okay. Did you wish to see the pictures from today? I've developed the film and made a set of prints."

"Yes." He rose, towering above Lisa. His head brushed the top of her tent. She pushed through the makeshift dark room curtains. When he followed, she could feel the warmth from his skin they stood so close. The space was ample for one, not two.

The red light bathed everything in an eerie color. The pictures looked gray in the light, but the colors would be vibrant, she knew. She waited as Tuareg studied the pictures, hoping he'd like them.

"They're good. You've captured the feel for the

setting. I like that one of the little girl. Are you planning these for your book of Moquansaid?"

"Yes. These would be in the desert section. I still want pictures of the capital city to show the contrast."

He turned, brushing against Lisa's shoulder. She almost jumped. Her heart rate sped up. For one second she wished he'd kiss her. She almost leaned toward him. Appalled at her thoughts, she stepped back, bumping the table with the chemicals. He would be horrified if he knew how her mind worked. It would give more credence to the idea of his mother's matchmaking.

"I think I'll go see what the professor wants me for," she said. "Thank you again for taking me today."

Tuareg had merely been kind to a visitor to his country. Nothing more should be read into anything he had done.

"You wanted to see me, professor?" Lisa asked when she entered the big work tent where the artifacts were housed.

"Ah, yes." He looked over her shoulder, then beckoned her closer. "Do you realize who exactly Tuareg is?"

"The man who rescued me from the sandstorm," she said.

"He's also a man of influence with the man who granted our excavation rights. I thought if Tuareg could stay a few days, really see how important our discoveries are, maybe he'd convince his uncle to let us remain."

"We're scheduled to leave at the end of August." Only nine weeks away.

"I know, but I can get an extension on my leave from the university. Most of us would be able to remain until the weather proved to be too inclement to work. Talk to Tuareg, convince him to use his influence with his uncle."

"I can't do that, even if I thought it would work. I don't have that kind of relationship with him. He's merely been kind to someone who he found during a sandstorm."

"Nonsense. You are a pretty girl, Lisa. I hardly need tell a woman how to use her wiles to get her way," the professor said.

Lisa laughed. "I think you've been buried in the past too long. Anyway, I'm hardly his type. I regret the deadline as much as anyone here. But I am not going to exert undue influence on Tuareg or any member of his family on our behalf. We knew when we arrived what the terms were."

"But if they could be changed!"

"Then it has to be done without my input."

She turned and walked back outside, almost crashing into Tuareg. It would be too much to hope he hadn't heard.

She smiled nervously, aware with every inch of her body just how close they stood. Stepping around him, she began walking away from the tent.

"The professor suggested you may wish to stay longer," she said. "To see how they are progressing on the dig. He—actually we all—very much wish we could stay beyond the original deadline."

"I heard."

"Oh."

He stopped her and swung her around to face him. It was dark in the compound, only faint light showing from the tents. She could hardly make out Tuareg's features.

"I would not change the deadline except to move it up. When the agreed time arrives, the professor and his team departs."

"I know." She sighed.

"Lisa, you are a woman of honor."

She blinked. What could she say to something like that. "Thank you."

He laughed softly. "You sound annoyed. Women prefer to be told they are beautiful. That they smell as sweet as the most fragrant flower. Their eyes rival the stars. Their lips are more delectable than the plumpest pomegranates."

She tilted her face and gazed up at the stars. They were sharp and clear in the desert night. If she didn't look at him, didn't listen closely to the mocking tones, she could almost pretend he were wooing her, caressing her with words. Painting a picture that would stay with her forever.

"It's so beautiful here. I love it," she said softly.

He leaned over and brushed his lips against hers.

She blinked and stepped back, startled.

He watched her carefully, then gently drew her away from the main path and into the shadows. Enfolding her into his arms, he pulled her close and kissed her again. This was no mere brush of lips but the powerful kiss of a determined man. After a second's hesitation, she returned the kiss, moving her mouth against his, opening for him when he teased. Heat seemed to spread from the soles of her feet to the top of her head. Breathing became difficult, but not needed. She had all she'd ever want in life with this kiss.

When he ended it, Lisa almost groaned in disappointment.

He took her hand. "Come, walk with me. We can look at the stars and feel the heartbeat of the desert."

He led the way, heading opposite to the dig site so at least she didn't have to worry about falling into any trenches. She wondered if he could see better in the dark than she could. The stars were bright, but there was no full moon to illuminate their way.

The silence grew as they left the soft murmur of voices behind. Soon only the soft sound of the breeze among the grass and caressing her skin could be heard.

"You have a strong affinity for the desert," she said.

"My people have lived on this land for centuries. It's a part of me. I could live my entire life here and not miss the city at all."

That confirmed what Lisa expected. While Tuareg was polished and sophisticated in the city surroundings she'd seen him in, he seemed much more connected to the untamed land of the desert.

Tuareg wanted to ask Lisa how she liked the desert. It did not call to all. The nomads who made it home, the people who had carved a country out of barren land— for them and their descendants a special bond had been forged. Never to be severed. But Lisa didn't come from such a background.

He stopped and, in a second, she stopped as well. They were alone. The sound of the night was elusive, there only for those who would listen.

Why had he kissed her? He'd dated once or twice since Nura's death. The events had been meaningless. He was better off spending time by himself or with family.

Yet something about this woman intrigued him. Had him temporarily neglecting duty to spend time with her.

Her lips had been as delectable as they'd looked. Her eyes fascinated him. She fascinated him.

He frowned, not liking the fact. He had no business thinking of another woman.

Yet Nura was gone. Had been for years. She was never coming back.

Tuareg wanted to capture the love he'd had for his wife. She'd been special. But time lent perspective. Nura had been his first love. His only love. He'd been faithful to her since they'd been children. She was special. But she had not been perfect.

He could remember the fights they'd had. Usually over something minor yet with all the passion each possessed. Days passed when she wouldn't speak to him. Maybe he'd not liked her as much as he normally did on those days. But he'd always loved her.

And on one point they had never agreed. She'd known he wanted children, but had refused until they'd had enough fun to last her a lifetime. He'd thought having children would also be fun. Seeing the ones today reminded him of the happy hours he and his parents had shared when he and his siblings had been younger.

He was drawn to Lisa Sullinger and didn't want to be. He'd rather live his life on his own terms. She would be returning to the United States at the end of the summer. Their worlds were too divergent to ever mix. He could give himself all the reasons in the world.

Yet there was something about her that fascinated him. She was always enthusiastic. Was that it? Or was it her delight in every aspect of life no matter how mundane? Or perhaps her optimism? Her way of seeing things with rose-colored glasses where most people would rail against fate? She had had a sad life losing her parents so young. Yet he'd never met a person with a sunnier outlook on life.

She reached out and touched his arm. He felt a tingle of awareness that had been missing from his life.

Frowning, he glanced at her, resisting. He didn't want any entanglements.

"I think we should go back now. It's getting late and you need to find out where you're bunking."

He lifted his eyes to the stars. Their brilliance rivaled any glittering lights man made. The desert spoke, cooling down after the heat of the day. He should leave. There was no reason to stay.

"The professor suggested I share his tent," Tuareg said. "Do you suppose it was to lobby for extension of the deadline?"

Lisa shook her head. "More likely it is the best one in camp and he's aware you are a sheikh. Be warned, it won't be like yours."

He turned and walked beside her back to the cluster of tents to the one the professor used. He'd leave in the morning. After he saw Lisa again.

CHAPTER SEVEN

LISA KEPT TO HERSELF the next morning. She couldn't believe Tuareg had kissed her or that she'd kissed him back. It had taken her forever to fall asleep last night. She'd relived that magical moment a hundred times. And fantasized a million different scenarios in which he'd kiss her again.

She left her tent a little later than usual. Breakfast was buffet style, so she could still get something to eat before beginning work. She was surprised to see the horse dozing in the makeshift corral. She thought Tuareg would have left at sunrise.

Rounding the corner by the mess tent, she came upon Tuareg and Professor Sanders standing in the shade. The professor held something in his hand and he and Tuareg were studying it.

Lisa stopped abruptly. Tuareg caught the movement and raised his gaze. She could read nothing from his eyes. Did he regret last night?

Professor Sanders turned and smiled. "Ah, Lisa. Just the person. Here's another porcelain statue, this of a small animal. Do you think it is a tiger? Maybe traded from the caravan, I was thinking." He held out the small object.

Automatically she raised her camera and took a picture.

Tuareg watched. "Maybe the professor wanted you to take it and look at it, not film it," he said.

She lowered the camera and looked at him.

"You seem to live life through the lens of a camera, rather than facing it head on," he commented.

Struck by the idea, Lisa hesitated a moment. She slung the camera strap over her shoulder and reached for the small statue. It was warm to the touch. Dirt clung to the crevices. She looked at it, but Tuareg's words echoed. Did he really think she didn't embrace life? Wasn't she here on this adventure instead of opting for a safe and boring routine in Seattle?

"Beautiful, isn't it?" the professor said, gazing at it.

"It is lovely," Lisa said. Her imagination sparked an image of a woman long ago who had been given this by a lover. How she must have treasured something so valuable and fragile—all the more so because of the giver.

She raised her eyes and met Tuareg's dark gaze. For a moment she could imagine he'd given her something as precious. If he ever did, she would treasure it and keep it with her wherever she went.

Gently she laid it back in the professor's hand. "No idea where it came from?" she asked. "I mean, from China or India? Would it have been a gift or a payment for something?"

"That we may never know. But this makes two fine statues, existing in an area of the world where porcelain was not common. Obviously brought by caravan. Don't you think they found these beautiful beyond anything they'd ever seen?"

"Judging from the stone carvings you've discovered, these were far finer than anything this group was capable of. Whoever owned them was probably considered the wealthiest member of the group," Tuareg said.

Lisa continued to the mess tent. She didn't like Tuareg's comment about her hiding behind her camera. Her friend Bailey said that sometimes. Lisa argued with her, but now another had said it. Could it be true?

She was slow to make friends, but that was because she feared making connections and then losing them. She'd become attached to her first foster mother after only a few weeks and had been heartbroken when she'd been moved from that home to another. She'd learned over the years to be careful where she bestowed her affections. It was safer to remain a bit aloof and not risk hurting her heart again.

But she didn't hide from life.

It was hot in the tent. She picked up her food and went outside to eat. The faint stirring of air kept it cooler than the enclosed tent. She found a spot in the shade from the overhang of the mess tent and sat down. Eating the croissant, she tried to imagine what the village they were excavating would have looked like five hundred years ago. The small trees were dependent on the subsurface water of the Wadi. Only during the rainy season was there plentiful water. The river was nearby.

The structures most likely would have been the color of the baked desert dirt. They would have been simple structures for shelter. Children would have played in front of the homes. Men would have tended the sheep or tried to grow something to eat. Women would have done the cooking. What had the house where the statues were found have been like?

She could imagine the men looking a lot like Tuareg, strong and fearless. Capable of dealing with the harshness of the land. He'd have fit in five hundred years ago as easily as he did today.

She heard footsteps and looked up. Tuareg walked toward her. He drew near and sank on the sand next to her. "I planned to leave first thing this morning, but your professor talked me into staying longer," he said.

He gazed around at the landscape. "A lonely place to live all those centuries ago, wouldn't you think?" he asked.

"They had family, friends. It was their way of life. They knew no other. I bet they were thrilled with the caravans that passed. Imagine what they dreamed of when speaking to the men leading camels laden with fantastic goods."

Tuareg laughed. Lisa blinked. It was the first time she'd heard him laugh.

"What's funny?"

"Your romanticized version. They were probably hardheaded tradesmen milking the caravans for as much booty as they could get away with. They most likely bargained for water in the dry season, sold grazing rights for grass for the camels."

"I like my version better," she murmured, feeling suddenly tongue-tied, unable to forget their kiss last night. Wishing with all her heart that he'd kiss her again.

"I'm leaving soon. I'll take one more look at the trench, then get Ham back home."

He rose and held out a hand to help her rise. She took it, letting go as soon as she was on her feet.

She swallowed hard and tried not to let the disappointment show. What had she expected, that he'd immediately say he wanted to stay, to spend time with her? Or sweep her into his arms and kiss her again?

He looked at her, his eyes dark and mysterious. She felt her heart flutter. His wife had been a lucky woman.

He reached out and rested his hands on her shoulders, drawing her closer. Kissing her a second later.

Lisa closed her eyes, the bright sunshine temporarily hidden as she savored the feel of his lips against hers, the teasing of his tongue, the fulfillment of his kiss. Sensuous yearning filled her. She wanted to be closer, to feel his body against hers, to have him sweep her away somewhere special just for the two of them.

She pulled back. It was broad daylight and they were at the side of the mess tent. Anyone could walk by. She wasn't sure what the kiss was about, was it merely farewell? Or something more.

"Lisa—"

"No, don't say anything. I think it's time to say goodbye. Thank you for all you've done for me. I appreciate it. But you yourself said this would go nowhere."

She turned and almost ran into the mess tent, dumping her plate and cup in the bin and catching her breath. She stood still, trying to hear Tuareg walk away.

"Do you need anything?" the student who had been designated dishwasher for this morning asked.

"No. Just, um, thinking." She turned and slowly went back to the large opening. Stepping outside she was relieved to see Tuareg gone. A moment later she heard the horse, but she kept her eyes down as she made her way to the work tent.

This archeological site would vanish before long, only her pictures would remain to show what once had been.

She might be destined to stay alone her whole life, but she could still leave something important behind.

Tuareg urged Ham away from the site and toward his tent. He hadn't meant to kiss Lisa again. He was not a

man to give misleading gestures. Any woman would be
justified to think he was interested by the attention he'd
paid over the last couple of days—especially kissing her.

And he was not. He'd had his one chance at love and
it had ended abruptly.

He needed to get back to his normal routine and not
let Lisa distract him. She had almost run from that kiss.
She was wiser than he.

Yet there were regrets. He'd enjoyed sharing the
desert with someone who seemed to like it as much as
he did. Nura never had. Tuareg waited expectantly. But
the searing pain didn't come. Just warmth and gentle
memories of the woman he'd loved. Was he healing?
Was the tearing grief from the early days finally easing?

He looked around the landscape he loved. There were
no memories of Nura here. She had never gone with him
when he'd sought the calming influence by staying a few
nights. Watching Lisa, he knew she felt totally differently
about the land. According to Professor Sanders, Lisa
often took off, as she had the day he met her, to explore,
liking the solitude and the unexpected sights she found.

Yesterday she'd delighted in photographing the empty
landscape as much as the children. Nothing as far as the
eye could see but the clumps of grasses that had prevailed
against the arid land and the few trees along the river, yet
she'd found these worthwhile to capture on film.

Lisa was totally different from any woman he knew.
She interested him with her openness and friendly de-
meanor. And enticed him with her smile and laughter.
His life had been devoid of laughter for a long time.

Was that reason enough to want a woman? Or was
there more? He'd like to take her away somewhere for
a few days, learn more about her life, her dreams. Hear

that laugher sparkle in the night. Awaken to her blue-gray eyes smiling into his.

Tuareg turned away from the image. It was impossible. But the longing didn't abate. Maybe he'd never love another, but he wanted Lisa.

And for the first time he didn't feel guilty about his desire. He was alive. Nura loved life, she would not have wanted him to shut himself away from the joys of living. She wrung every precious moment from her existence. Could he do less? To do so would dishonor what she valued.

Tuareg spurred his horse on and rode like the wind. He couldn't outrun the images in his mind, but he could try. He had only to reach the tent. Another day of solitude and he'd return to the capital city and plunge into the tasks that awaited. Work would bring forgetfulness.

After lunch, Professor Sanders asked that everyone join him in the work tent to pack the artifacts. What had been uncovered was being shipped to the state museum in Soluddai.

Lisa was assigned the task of keeping track of each item being packed in each crate and then pasting one copy of the inventory on the outside of each box.

"Tuareg arranged for this to be picked up and delivered this week. And for periodic pickups between now and the end of August," the professor said.

The camaraderie among the archeologists, both students and professors, was well established. Sometimes Lisa felt as if they talked in code. Once again she was on the outside looking in. Part of the group, yet not one with it.

As she worked, she wished Tuareg would come and

take her for a ride on his horse along the banks of the river. She shifted on the stool, thinking that she should wish her ankle miraculously healed so she could walk to the river by herself. Not that she could swim in that water, but it was always cooler in the shade of the old trees.

By the time dinner was ready, all the artifacts had been labeled and packed and the boxes were stacked near the tent. Tuareg had agreed to send transportation from Soluddai in the morning. Professor Sanders would accompany the cartons and turn them over to the minister of antiquities. One set of inventory lists and photographs would stay with the boxes, two copies would remain in camp for reference and one set was already packaged for mailing back to the university in Washington.

Lisa arose early the next morning. She heard unusual activity in the camp and after dressing went to the food tent. Several of the archeologists were eating, others had already been and gone.

"We're getting earlier starts now under professor's orders," one of the students said when Lisa asked why so much activity so early. "He wants every hour possible spent on the dig."

"When do the trucks arrive?" one of the women asked.

"After ten," someone called.

"Good, that'll give the professor a few hours of work before taking off for Soluddai," she said. "He'll spend every moment in the trench, I expect." With a friendly wave, she took her tray to the washing area and left.

Lisa got a cup of coffee and sat at one table with some fruit and cheese. She didn't have much to do until new items were unearthed. When she finished eating she'd go to the excavation to see where they were working today and if they needed photos of the site. If not, was her ankle up to driving a Jeep and taking another foray into the desert?

When she drew near the trench a short time later, she saw the flurry of activity. Everyone seemed to be at one end of the wide excavation.

Knowing something was up, Lisa quickened her pace.

"What's going on?" Lisa asked when she reached the group.

"We've found a burial site," one of the women said with excitement.

"Paul found it when he started a new direction," another said.

"Bones and some artifacts. More than one, it looks like," yet another said.

"This is amazing," someone else said in a hushed tone.

Lisa felt the excitement of the group. Would this be enough of a find to extend their deadline? She hoped so, but there was no telling how Tuareg's uncle would view this latest discovery. Tuareg wanted the dam to begin functioning this fall, to bring water to this area. A delay might mean another year before the reservoir would begin filling.

She peered over the edge, mesmerized by the careful work the archeologists were doing to uncover the bones.

When the two large trucks arrived promptly at ten, Lisa had returned to the work tent. Since almost all the artifacts were being shipped, she gave directions to the drivers on which few cartons remained. Where was the professor?

The trucks were almost loaded when Lisa saw him hurrying toward the compound.

"Lisa, thank goodness. There will have to be a

change in plans. I cannot leave the site in light of what we discovered this morning," he said when he reached her. "I'm needed here. We all are. I don't know if the sheikh will extend our deadline because of this discovery. In case he refuses, we need to get as much revealed as we can. I cannot afford time away from the site. You'll have to go in my stead."

"Me? I can't talk with the minister of antiquities. He's expecting an archeologist, not a photographer."

"You're a member of this team. You'll have to do it. Quickly, run and pack what you'll need. You have the notebooks and pictures. Write down any questions you cannot answer and I'll work on them upon your return. This discovery is too important to leave."

Lisa didn't hesitate. She wasn't needed here, but the professor was. She hastened to her tent to pack for two days in the capital city. In only a few moments she was back, bag and camera case in hand.

"Professor, who will take pictures of the discovery?" she asked.

"Oh, I hadn't thought about that. Maybe one of the students. Which camera should they use?"

It took almost a half hour for Lisa to instruct the student designated as temporary photographer. She left plenty of film with instructions not to attempt to develop the rolls, she would do so when she returned.

Finally, she climbed into the front of the lead truck and settled in. It was hot even with the windows open. She hoped the vehicle had air conditioning.

The professor gave her some last-minute instructions. "Tuareg was to meet me at the museum. Ask him to handle anything you can't," the professor said as the driver slammed shut his door and started the engine.

Lisa hadn't known Tuareg would be there. She had thought they'd said goodbye. Apparently not a final farewell.

The drive to the capital was uncomfortable. The large trucks lurched and bounced on the rough road. She hoped everything had been packed securely enough to survive intact. She briefly thought of taking pictures on the ride, but she never would have gotten a clear shot.

Thankfully, while still many miles from the city they reached paved roads and the ride became smoother.

Lisa was glad when the driver called to say they would reach the museum in only another half hour. Her anticipation at seeing Tuareg rose with each passing mile.

CHAPTER EIGHT

LISA HAD BEEN RESOLUTE in saying goodbye to Tuareg. Now it seemed as if the fates had stepped in to grant her a few more hours of his company. She watched eagerly as the driver navigated the city streets. She recognized the huge terra-cotta building when they turned onto the main avenue. Her heart thrilled at the sight.

When they reached the museum, there were several men in suits awaiting them out front. One had a clipboard and stepped up to the first truck that parked. He would remain to check off the boxes as the truck drivers unloaded them.

Tuareg was also waiting there. His expression of surprise let Lisa know he hadn't expected her. Was there disapproval in his face as well?

Introductions were made when she climbed down from the high cab of the truck.

"Where is Professor Sanders?" Tuareg asked.

Lisa stepped closer, her emotions mixed at seeing him again. This was strictly business. But she still felt her heart flutter the way it always did around him. "He was unable to attend. He sent me in his place."

The man next to Tuareg glanced at her and dismissed

her without a word. His attention turned to Tuareg. "We were expecting the professor. I wished to review the artifacts with him and go over his timetable for completion before the deadline imposed by His Excellency."

Tuareg glanced at Lisa. "Apparently you must deal with Miss Sullinger. She is the official representative of the expedition. I merely arranged transportation. Lisa, this is Mohammad bin Algariq, minister of antiquities."

The man drew a sharp breath. Lisa almost smiled at the expression of resignation on his face. Slowly he turned to study her.

"Very well. If you will come with me." He walked away without another word.

"Friendly, isn't he?" she murmured. With a glance at Tuareg, she dutifully followed the minister. Tuareg fell into step beside her. "I'll serve as translator," he murmured.

She nodded, then hurried to keep up with Mr. bin Algariq. It wouldn't do to become lost in the vast museum.

The next two hours were uncomfortable. Lisa knew the director disliked dealing with her, he made that abundantly clear. There were plenty of questions posed for which she did not know the answer. She carefully jotted them in a notebook. He grew more impatient with each unanswered query, but she only had the hastily given information from the professor and did her best to hold her own.

Once or twice Tuareg said something in Arabic to the man. It seemed to placate him for a few moments, but then his frustration rose again.

She was tired by the time the minister walked them back to the entrance.

A limo sat in the same spot where the trucks had been. Tuareg gently guided her toward the vehicle.

"You survived," he said.

"Barely. I'm not the lofty leader of the expedition, merely a flunky. I think the director was miffed someone of more importance wasn't sent."

"He'll get over it. I know he's delighted with the objects found at the dig," Tuareg said. The chauffeur had the back door opened and ushered them into the cool interior of the limo.

Settling back, Lisa felt rejuvenated just being in Tuareg's presence.

"Thank you for arranging for all the artifacts to be brought here before the end of the summer. He was impressed by the figurines, wasn't he? I know the professor will be pleased to have the invitation to stop by before departing."

She looked out the window. "Where are we going?" The professor hadn't even told her about the return trip. She was to remain in the capital for a couple of days on call for the museum in case other questions arose. Had he booked a room at a hotel nearby?

"We had a room at a hotel reserved for Professor Sanders. You, however, would be welcome to stay at my mother's apartment if you wish. Unfortunately, she flew to Paris a couple of days ago to join my father. But the staff remains. She would be most delighted to know you stayed there."

"I couldn't impose. The hotel will be fine."

"I think my mother's apartment would be better." His tone suggested arguing would be futile.

"Very well, then. Thank you." It would be nice to return to the lovely apartment.

"Perhaps you would join me for dinner," Tuareg said.

Another few hours together.

"I would very much enjoy that," she said. She looked out the window as the buildings swept by. She was too tired to think about photography now, but maybe in the morning she could take a walk and get some pictures. Not too far a walk though; her ankle was still not one hundred percent.

"Where would you like to go for dinner?" Tuareg asked.

She knew nothing about restaurants in Soluddai. And she really didn't feel like going someplace where everyone would be dressed up except her.

"You know what I'd love? An American hamburger with all the fixings." She looked at him wondering what his reaction might be. "Do you have places that sell food like that?"

"And what are the fixings?"

"French fries, onion rings and a bun piled high with lettuce, tomato and mustard and mayo."

He frowned. "Does all that taste good together?"

"Have you never had a hamburger with all the fixings?" she asked in mock dismay. "I thought you were a worldly traveler."

Slowly Tuareg shook his head, his eyes watching her.

Lisa laughed. "I'm teasing. If you find us a store, I'll buy everything and make you the best hamburger you'll ever have. That is if we can use your mother's kitchen."

"You'd cook it yourself?" he asked.

"Sure, why not? Wait, don't tell me you don't cook for yourself."

"Why would I when I employ several fine cooks?"

"Didn't your wife cook and you help out?"

"No," he replied. "Maybe she cooked as a girl but she had no need once we were married."

"Oh." She gave it a bit of thought, then shook away all doubts. She'd love to have a hamburger. And maybe show Tuareg the fun of cooking together.

"Then you can be my apprentice and we'll fix it together."

"That should prove interesting," he murmured.

Tuareg was amused by the enthusiasm Lisa showed for preparing a meal. She asked to be taken to a market that carried western food. His chauffeur found one on a street near the American and British embassies. Soon Tuareg and Lisa were walking up and down aisles of packaged food. Had he ever been in a supermarket before? He didn't think so.

Lisa pushed a cart and stopped now and then to place articles in it. Mustard came in yellow plastic bottles. Ketchup came in clear bottles showing the red sauce. Chopped pickles in another jar. Soon there were more items than he'd expect to need for a relatively simple meal. He knew what hamburgers were. He just wasn't sure they were the delicacy Lisa seemed to think they were.

Once they reached his mother's apartment, he directed the chauffeur to carry the sacks of supplies to the kitchen and inform the kitchen staff they were dismissed for the night. He almost shared the astonishment the man displayed.

"You'll have the bedroom you had before. Would you like to shower first?" he asked.

"Yes, thank you. I'll hurry. Shall we meet in the kitchen at six?"

Tuareg watched her walk away, wondering what he was in store for. Nura had never cooked anything as far as he knew. Nor did his mother or aunt. Was cooking an art left to only the working class?

He went to a second guest room to clean up—already anticipating the cooking adventure with Lisa.

Lisa ran the water hot and stood beneath it for a long time. When she finally had enough, she was delighted to find the dress she'd hung out had lost most of the travel wrinkles. She put it on, dried her hair and wandered back to the main rooms of the apartment.

She heard Tuareg and turned, her heart catching when she saw him.

"Time to cook?" he asked whimsically.

"Just about. I don't know where the kitchen is, though," she said.

He led the way.

The kitchen was a cook's dream. The gas stove had six burners and a grill. The stainless steel refrigerator was industrial size. The counters were granite, the butcher-block table in the center was huge. She quickly saw her dry ingredients on the counter neatly stacked. The rest was probably in the refrigerator.

"Okay, let's get started."

Lisa rummaged around for a moment, finding knives, bowls, pans and other items she wanted.

Taking the potatoes, she beckoned Tuareg.

"First we wash them to get the dirt off, then we'll cut them into thick strips for french fries."

She showed him how to do it. Once he was working, she pulled out the other items she wanted.

Lisa glanced over and bit back a smile. The setting was quite domestic. And probably something Tuareg never expected to do. She'd never thought much about it before, but if she ever married, she'd love to spend the end of the day together with her husband, preparing their evening meal. They'd talk about their day, make plans for the future.

"Is this something you do often?" he asked. A nice pile of sliced potatoes cut with precision was growing.

"Have friends over to cook dinner? Yes. Or I go to their places. We barbecue a lot in nice weather—which isn't often, I can tell you. Seattle has a rainy climate and is too cold in winter."

Lisa told him about her friends Bailey and Sara and how they experimented with a wide variety of cuisines when younger.

Once finished with his task, Tuareg brought over the potatoes and put them where Lisa indicated. He then went and settled on one of the high stools. He watched Lisa continue to bustle around. She thought about assigning him something else to do, but could do everything faster herself. She was glad he continued to stay with her, however.

He asked for more details on why the professor had not come. She told him about the burial site and the excitement it had caused.

When she fell silent, she glanced around, once again aware of how different their lives were. He'd never cooked, shopped for food or had a barbecue with friends. How strange that seemed to her. Did he think her lifestyle equally strange?

"You've grown pensive," he said.

"I was just thinking how different your life is from mine. I don't know a single person who has a cook, much less more than one. I guess it'd be fun to have meals prepared by someone else, except I do enjoy cooking."

"What else do you enjoy?" he asked.

She put the ground meat patties on a broiling pan and slid them into the oven. "Domestically I enjoy baking and working with the plants I have on my small patio. Bailey's watching them for me while I'm gone."

"You have an apartment, not a house?"

"I couldn't afford a house. My apartment is nothing like this one, however." Her one-bedroom place was small, with no view. But it was near the waterfront and she could walk to Pike Place Market in only a few minutes.

She drew out the pan and flipped the burgers.

"You said you have an apartment in the city?" she said.

"A pied-à-terre, really. I acquired it after Nura died. I don't stay in the city more than I need to for business."

"Because you prefer the desert."

"Exactly."

Tuareg bit into his hamburger some moments later with trepidation. The burgers were juicy and flavorful and he followed Lisa's example and piled the bun high with relish, tomato, lettuce and onion slices. She watched warily, hoping he'd think the meal worth the preparation.

"No wonder you were dreaming of something like this. It is delicious," he said.

She nodded, relieved he liked it. For a few moments she felt at home. Traveling was fun, but she longed for her own things, her friends. She felt lonely at the dig where all the archeologists had more in common with each other than with her.

When she reached for the iced water they were drinking she said, "I told you this was terrific food. We haven't had anything like this at the site. Not a bad trade-off for the special work being done there, but absence makes it all the more appealing when I do get it."

"As with the shower," he said.

"Right. Or the ice cream the professor misses. Anyway, I appreciate your letting me cook tonight."

When they finished eating, Lisa sipped her water and looked around the kitchen. "It won't take long to clean up," she said.

"Leave it. Someone will clean it in the morning."

She shook her head. "That's not right. We made the mess, we need to clean it."

"I pay people to do that."

Hopping off the stool, she reached for his plate. "I still want to clean the dishes."

She was stubborn. He could order her to leave everything as it was, but he had a feeling she'd just ignore him and do as she wished. Not many people ignored his orders.

A half hour later the last pan was dried. Lisa nodded in satisfaction as she looked around the immaculate room.

"I believe this is the longest I've ever been in a kitchen," Tuareg said. "Can we leave now?" He had enjoyed himself this evening. For a moment he wondered if every meal would be as much fun if Lisa were around or was this a one-off deal. Surely she'd appreciate others cooking for her on a daily basis.

She nodded, a happy smile lighting her face. He didn't understand the appeal of cleaning, but had been intrigued watching her change of expression. Her eyes were a silvery gray tonight. What did that mean?

"In my circle of friends, the kitchen is the heart of the home. Everyone gathers there if we are getting together for a meal. Good friends, that is. If it's a big party, then another room is more suitable."

"I believe we are more formal." He never knew Nura to go into the kitchen except to instruct the cook on what to prepare for a special meal. Her friends liked to gather in the salon, or meet at clubs where the entertainment was more exciting than a quiet evening at home.

Surprisingly, he no longer wished to go out to such places. He was more than content to spend a quiet evening with Lisa talking, learning more about her. Trying to guess how she would react to things was entertainment enough. Though that was probably unfair to her. Maybe they could go out later or tomorrow night. The professor had planned to stay two days, wasn't Lisa going to be here as long?

Tuareg escorted Lisa into the salon. She went to the window, gazing out over the lights that had come on throughout the city. He remembered the other night when she'd been so delighted with the lights. And the end result.

He wasn't making assumptions tonight.

"I never get tired of sights like this," she said.

"Perhaps you'd like to go out, see some of the city at night? There are some clubs that offer excellent entertainment."

She turned and tilted her head slightly as she gazed at him. "I'd rather drive around and see how everything sparkles at night. I'm not up to dancing or anything with my ankle."

"I'll call for the limo."

"And I'll get my camera."

He hesitated by the doorway. "No, tonight is for you to enjoy, not be working."

"It's not work. Think how great night photos would

look in my book." She was quiet a moment, then wrinkled her nose again. "You're right, it is work. Okay, no camera."

Fifteen minutes later they were sitting side by side in the limo. Tuareg closed the window between them and the driver after giving him instructions to drive around the different sections of the city.

Lisa looked eagerly out the window as they drove.

"Tell me about Soluddai. Is it Moquansaid's oldest city?"

"Oldest one continually occupied." Tuareg wasn't sure he wanted to be a tour guide, yet what had he expected when offering the drive? He suspected he had thought more about getting away from the apartment and the temptation it offered than the actual drive.

Now he sat even closer to her than he would have at the salon. He could smell her fragrance, almost feel the silky touch of her hair.

Lisa was nervous, and when nervous, she talked more than she should. Every time Tuareg paused, she asked another question. She was aware of him like she'd never been aware of another man. She could have listened to him all night long. His deep voice sounded like dark wine might sound. And was almost as intoxicating.

The warmth from his body seemed to fill the back of the car. She never knew how much longing to lean against another person would be hard to resist. The sweet torture was driving her crazy, but she wouldn't want to be another place on earth!

The lights at street level were so bright that some areas looked almost like day. She couldn't read the Arabic script that flashed and glowed in neon, but appreciated the variety of colors blending together in a rainbow of hues, each brighter than the last.

"Where are we now?" she asked as they drove along a busy thoroughfare.

"The primary tourist area. These restaurants and night-clubs cater to Europeans and are open far into the night."

Lisa glanced at him. "Is this where you used to come with your wife? You said she liked to entertain away from home."

"Sometimes."

Lisa noted he rarely talked about his wife. She guessed the hurt of her death was still too strong. She had heard often enough how devoted they'd been to each other.

It was late when they returned to the apartment. Tuareg escorted her to the front door and bid her good night there.

Lisa went straight to bed. Two hours later she awoke with a start. A storm had blown in. She hadn't noticed any signs on their drive, but then she'd been focused on the sights, not the clouds in the sky.

Lightning illuminated the sky. Thunder cracked immediately. She shivered, huddling beneath the covers. Rain poured down in rivulets on the windows. Lisa had left the curtains opened to enjoy the ambiance of the night lights. Now she could see the fury of the storm without impediment.

She swallowed hard, all thought of sleep gone. Once again she was a little girl caught in the smashed car calling for her mother.

Shivering despite the warmth of the bed, she gazed out the window, mesmerized by what she saw. She was dry and safe. Yet the old fear crowded her throat and her hands felt clammy. When she'd awoken with nightmares after her mother's death, her father had gathered her close, keeping her safe. After his death, there was no one.

Sometimes, she'd have given anything to have the comfort of another when she awoke remembering.

How long would the storm last? It seemed like forever. Yet a half hour later the worst had passed. She could still hear the faint rumble of thunder occasionally but the sky no longer lit up bright as day and the rain soon ceased.

She rose and put on another shirt over her nightshirt. Padding quietly to the kitchen, she prepared herself some warm milk. She needed something to calm her nerves if she was to get back to sleep. It was after four in the morning. She had not had enough sleep to remain awake. Yet her heart still pounded and the memories crowded in. She wished she knew Tuareg's phone number. She could have at least called him for someone to talk to.

The next morning, Maliq knocked on Lisa's door, pushing it open and entering carrying a tray of hot chocolate and warm croissants.

Lisa had slept past the time she'd planned to waken. She didn't recognize the maid at first, then was delighted to see a familiar face.

"I didn't know you worked here as well," she said.

"I do not. His Excellency had me brought here because I speak English and he said you'd be staying for a few days. It's my pleasure to be here. I have brought you breakfast," Maliq said. "His Excellency asks if you'd like to see some more of the city today."

"I'd love to. I've been wanting to take some pictures." Today she'd bring her camera.

Maliq set the tray on her lap. "I will let him know. The time given was ten. Plenty of time to get dressed after you eat." She bowed slightly and quietly left the room.

Lisa ate the buttery croissant and sipped the rich hot chocolate. Such luxury. A person could get very used to it.

Once she was full, she moved the tray and rose to dress. She checked her watch. It was almost ten. Being up several hours in the middle of the night played havoc with schedules.

Once dressed, she checked her camera case and was ready.

She headed for the salon. Tuareg was sitting on the sofa, portable phone at his ear. He noticed Lisa as soon as she stepped inside and rose. A moment later he tossed the phone onto a table and came to greet her.

"Camera at the ready?" he asked.

"I can't miss this opportunity. This book is important to me."

"So we're off. I thought after we finished our drive, we could have lunch at my home. It's a short drive from the city."

"Lovely." She'd like to see his place again. The gardens had been spectacular. This visit, she could actually walk around them.

When they reached the sidewalk, Lisa was surprised to find a small red sports car at the curb. The convertible top had been folded.

"Better to take pictures with," Tuareg said, ushering her into the front seat.

"Is this yours?"

"It is," he said, sliding behind the wheel.

"And do you drive very fast in it?"

"Most days. But not today. We'll go at a snail's pace so you can get your pictures."

She laughed, feeling carefree and happy. Another few stolen hours to enjoy with Tuareg.

Lisa leaned her head back, able to see everything without a roof. She brought out her camera and put it on her lap. She was ready.

Soluddai was a contrast of Arabic architecture and modern skyscrapers. Sometimes she felt as if she were in Los Angeles or Seattle. Others, in a time past. The ornate carvings and inlaid tiles gave a richness to the Arabic buildings that she captured with delight.

"I love the distinctive styles, so very different, yet blending together," she said, snapping a shot of a tall steel structure. "Sort of like the people I see on the sidewalks. Some are in traditional attire, others in clothes worn in Paris and Rome."

"Soluddai is a cosmopolitan city," he murmured, driving easily through the heavy traffic. "We blend old and new, East and West."

Lisa nodded. The longer she spent with Tuareg, the more the contrast in their own lives was apparent. He was used to cosmopolitan places like Soluddai. While she lived in a large city on America's west coast. She had a small, select group of friends. She had never been to London or Paris. Wasn't used to exotic sports cars. The gulf between them was never more pronounced.

For a moment she felt the gulf widen. It was impossible to stop, but she longed for some bridge that would enable the two of them to draw close. She knew he'd never forget his wife. She wouldn't fit in, she never had. But if they could only be friends—she'd be happy with that.

She could forget that the man she'd met in the desert

was Arabian royalty, used to servants and homes in three different countries. When it was the two of them, for short periods of time they could just be Tuareg and Lisa with no past or future.

"You've grown quiet," Tuareg said after a few moments.

"Thinking of how to outline the book," she lied. Suddenly the day didn't seem as bright as it had. Heartache lay around the corner. She wouldn't race to meet it, but it was inevitable. She'd fallen in love with a man so far out of her reach people would laugh if they learned the truth.

He turned into a large green park and stopped near the gates.

"Come, I'll show you one of the treasures of the park." Walking along a path lined with shrubs and small flowering plants, Lisa saw puddles from the previous night's rain. The day was beautiful, not a cloud in the sky.

"Did you hear last night's storm?" she asked.

"Yes. Did it waken you?"

"It did. I was glad not to be out in it."

"Here." They came out of the shrubs into a wide grassy area. In the center was a statue twice as large as life.

It depicted a camel and a man in Arab dress both done in gleaming white marble.

"It's beautiful," she said, pausing to take it in. The man was looking toward the mountains. The camel was heavily laden with packs, stoically plodding at the man's shoulder.

"What's it about?" she asked, snapping pictures.

"He represents Mohammad bin Ker-Al. Two centuries ago a band of soldiers was fighting to the north. They were cut off from their supply lines and death was expected. They fought bravely. Then on the darkest night, Mohammad made his way through with a single camel loaded with critical supplies, enabling the soldiers to live another day. By that time, reinforcements reached the battleground and the tide of the war turned. Mohammad was from Soluddai. The city honors him."

She could almost imagine the scene. The professor should see this and hear the tale.

She circled the statue still a few dozen yards away. She needed that distance to capture the full scene in her lens.

"Who carved it?" she asked.

Tuareg gave her the name of the artist and a bit of his history. "He died young. This was his most impressive work," he finished.

"It is impressive. I think I could make this the cover photograph of my book."

Tuareg had always had a secret fascination with Mohammad bin Saladar, the artist. He had other work in museums and one in front of a school. To be able to carve such creations from a solid block of stone amazed him. He wondered if the artist felt an affinity for the hero, both sharing the same name.

Even though the man had died before he'd turned thirty, he'd left a legacy generations revered.

Tuareg wondered what lasting legacy he'd leave. The dam, for one. It would not be looked upon quite like this sculpture, but it would make a difference for future generations.

He would have liked to have children. Nura had not been ready. Each time he suggested it, she'd countered with how young they were and how much she wanted to do before they had children.

Now they never would.

He still stood near the path. Lisa had moved to take

pictures from different angles. Did she ever think to marry and have children? Or was she bitten by wander-lust and too busy capturing images on film to create a real life for herself? From her interaction with the children at the nomad settlement, he could tell she liked them. He suspected she would make a good mother. For the first time in three years, Tuareg wondered if he could hope for a different future.

CHAPTER NINE

WHEN THEY RETURNED to the car, he suggested lunch. "We can see more of the city later, if you wish," he said.

"Fine with me."

Heading for the villa, he glanced at Lisa from time to time. She was so very unlike Nura. She didn't demand attention. Didn't have to have constant activity to be content. The drive was completed in almost total silence, yet he didn't feel any awkwardness.

She was relaxing to be with, as well as intriguing. An interesting combination. Were other women as easy to spend time with?

He'd called ahead and when they arrived lunch was ready to be served on the patio. They sat where they had before, only there was no wheelchair this time.

"It's so beautiful," she said.

The salad was crisp and cool. The rolls crusty and hot.

"Do you regret we didn't prepare the meal?" he asked as she took her first bite.

She grinned at him and shook her head. "I couldn't compete with this. It's so good."

They talked desultorily through lunch. When finished, Lisa asked if she could tour the villa. And would he permit photographs of the garden?

Tuareg hesitated. He valued his privacy. But a few photographs of a generic garden couldn't hurt.

"Film them without the house as a background," he said.

"Deal."

"Come, I'll show you through the house," he said, rising.

Lisa slung her camera over her shoulder and followed Tuareg. They went to the grand foyer and stopped. The marble floor was cool, the wallpaper a pale champagne color. An expensive chandelier hung from the ceiling. The home looked like a model for a fancy magazine.

"The chandelier came from France," Tuareg said. He led the way into the salon. Lisa followed, stopping at the door. She'd glanced in at this room when she stayed here before. It was decorated entirely in shades of yellow. Light yellow, deep yellow, everything looked similar. The only other colors were the deep tones of the wood of some of the furniture.

She was at a loss to find complimentary words. She didn't like it at all. She much preferred a more colorful setting.

"A bit formal," Tuareg said, looking around as if seeing it for the first time. "I rarely use the room."

"If you don't use it, why not change it to be how you'd like?" Lisa asked.

For a moment the question startled him. "Nura decorated it."

"In fact, the entire villa seems too large for one man. If you truly don't expect to marry again, why not sell it to a family which would fill it up. Don't you think the house deserves children laughing in the hallway, sneaking into the kitchen at night to get a snack? Or running around the garden. Can't you picture it? With maybe a dog barking as he ran with them and a cat curled up in the windowsill?"

He frowned. "I don't picture the house that way. I do not wish to sell it. It reminds me of my wife. Why would I wish to cut that memory away?"

"You'll always remember her, Tuareg," Lisa said gently. "You don't need things for that. Did she never change anything?"

"She was always changing things. This is the third rendition of this room. Once it was all done in pale greens. She would live with each decor for a while, then start over again."

He remembered how excited she'd get when she'd find materials or accessories to redo one of the rooms. He'd joked with her more than once that it was a good thing they had such a large house, it gave her enough rooms to play with. The thought brought an ache. But not the sharp pain he was used to.

For a moment, he also remembered arguing with her about her redecorating because of boredom. They were never home long enough to get tired of the rooms before she changed them. Nura had argued back that when it was perfect, she'd know it and not need to redo it again. Perfection had constantly eluded her, however.

"I didn't mean to make you angry," Lisa said.

He crossed to the window. The garden was in full bloom, the blossoms drooping heavily on their stems.

"I'm not angry." He turned, leaning against the sill. "I am satisfied with my life the way it is. My wife is dead. She won't ever be with me again. I know that. I've made a new life. It is different than the old, but suits me as it is. I do not wish to change the house."

"I never meant you should, only if you wanted it a bit different. I'd like to see some more rooms if you'll still show me."

They visited each room on the first floor. The dining room was huge, with chairs enough for twenty. Lisa tried to envision a dinner party that large. She preferred smaller gatherings where she could converse with all her guests.

He hesitated at a door off the foyer, then opened it and stepped aside.

The small sitting room was a jewel—with bright colors of crimson and navy and white. The furniture looked as if it had been designed for comfort, not looks. She stepped inside. So the salon was for elegance. Was this a family sitting room? A place where they had been informal, a place to relax together when no guests were present?

"This is so darling," she said. She itched to take some pictures. It was elegant yet warm—almost a friendly room.

She looked at Tuareg. He stared at the sofa, then looked reluctantly around the room.

"She loved this room most of all," he said softly.

"I can see why. The wide windows allow all the beauty of the garden to come in," Lisa said. She sensed a strong emotion in him and moved to the windows to give him some privacy.

"He still loves you," she mentally said to a long-gone Nura.

If he hadn't gotten over his wife in three years, it was unlikely he would this summer. And in any case, he'd never fall for someone like her.

Lisa felt empty. She wanted to return to the dig and forget the feelings Tuareg caused. Try to forget secret dreams and wishes that they could find a common ground.

It was time to face reality and get back to her life. The fairy-tale existence of Arabia wasn't for a practical photographer from Seattle.

Lisa was back at the dig before lunch the next day. She had not seen Tuareg that morning. The museum had sent a Jeep to drive her back. She didn't know if he planned to visit the apartment before she left, but only Maliq was there to wish her well.

After briefing the professor, she went straight to work. Everyone was still excited about the recent discovery. More bones had been found, as well as some small decorative items that looked like some kind of jewelry. The piece that caught Lisa's fancy was a small leaf made of a delicate translucent green.

"Is that jade?" Lisa asked in astonishment when she first saw it.

"We think so," the professor said proudly. "It needs to be authenticated. If so, this proves a connection with the silk road. Not only a north and south route, but now a connection to the Orient. It was with one of the bodies we uncovered."

"Wow." Even Lisa knew what importance that could add to the excavation. Would this mean they'd get their deadline extended?

"Too early to make a definitive claim, but we are fairly certain," the professor said.

She took pictures from several angles. The pale color showed up well against the dark background she used.

The rest of the day passed like any other for Lisa. But the buzz of excitement couldn't be hidden among the archeologists.

By the time dinner was served, Lisa felt more left out

than she usually did. She wasn't knowledgeable enough to discuss the implications of the recent find. She didn't have any close ties with members of the team. While they were all friendly enough, the new discovery was too exciting for them to indulge in idle chitchat. Sitting at one side of the group, she decided to take a walk after she finished eating.

She wandered to where the makeshift corral had been set up for Tuareg's horse. What fun it would be to mount up and ride beneath the growing moonlight. The landscape had a silvery aspect everywhere she looked—as if the world had changed to black and white. With the moon almost full, the stars weren't as bright, more like faint pinpricks of light on the black sky.

As far as she was concerned, this was the best time of day. The blazing heat had faded. The cool of dawn was hours away. She liked being outside at night.

Everywhere she looked reminded her of Tuareg. Was this how he felt at his home? Every sight a new reminder of his wife and what could never be? Most of Lisa's memories were her own, not shared with others. Sighing softly, she turned toward her tent. She'd bring her journal up to date and see about getting to bed early tonight.

She'd already developed the pictures she'd taken in Soluddai and gone through them several times, selecting the ones she wanted to include in her book. She loved the statue in the park the best.

And the one she'd caught of Tuareg as he leaned against his car waiting for her at one point during their day together.

The next morning Lisa was at the trench when one of the helpers ran over to her.

"There is a call for you in the main tent," he said breathlessly. "From Sheikh Tuareg al Shaldor."

Lisa almost ran to the tent, afraid he'd hang up if she didn't answer quickly.

"Hello?"

"Tuareg here. My uncle wishes to have a farewell dinner honoring the members of the excavation team the last Friday in August. Everything will be packed by then, correct?"

"I guess. I'd have to double-check a calendar." So much for the professor's hope that the deadline would be extended.

"Rooms will be obtained for everyone at the Luxor Hotel," he said.

Lisa knew it was the most expensive hotel in the capital city.

"How nice. Shouldn't you be talking to Professor Sanders about this?" she asked, puzzled by why Tuareg was calling her.

"Perhaps, but I wished to speak to you."

She sat on the stool nearby and smiled. "I'm glad to talk with you," she returned. Closing her eyes, she could picture him nearby.

"Have you been back to the desert?" she asked.

"I leave tomorrow for a few days. Ham will grow bored if not ridden occasionally. What have you been doing?"

"I developed all the photos I took in Soluddai. I'm uncertain now which ones to include for a book, however. I think I want something more. I love the picture of the statue. And some of the old architecture. For an American audience, I need more—something to capture the imagination."

"Such as?"

"I'm not sure. I hope I recognize it when I see it. We've had a most astonishing discovery here," she continued.

"Beyond the grave site?" he asked.

"They found a jade carving. To the professor it proves a connection with the silk road."

"Is he sure it is jade?"

"No, it needs to be authenticated. But like the porcelain statues, it lends strong credence to the possibility. It was discovered in the grave. Everyone here is quite excited."

"A find of major importance," Tuareg said thoughtfully.

"That's what they say. I've filmed it. It's quite delicate and lovely, very pale green with a translucence that looked ethereal."

"Are you equally thrilled?"

She laughed softly. "I'm not fully aware of all the ramifications. And finding such a treasure doesn't offer me the opportunity for increased fame as it does the professor. According to some of the students here, once it becomes known he's made such a major find, he'll be sought after for other digs. And it means more prestige at the university for him."

"But not for you?"

"I'm just the photographer. Thank you again for taking me to your villa the other day. I also have some terrific shots of the gardens. Maybe I'll do a book on gardens near and far one day. I could get in photos for Butchart Gardens in Vancouver, Kew Gardens in London and the Tuileries in France to add to the one with the statue of your hero."

"Ambitious indeed. When will you return to Soluddai?"

"Probably not until after we pack up for home," she said. For a moment she hoped he'd invite her to visit again.

"Will you be at the party your uncle is having?"

"Of course. We can also celebrate the resumption of work on the dam."

She sighed. He put such importance on the new construction—while her focus was on the past. "Then I'll hope to see you there."

"Lisa—"

"Yes?"

There was a pause, then Tuareg merely said, "Take care of yourself. I'll see you before you return to America."

Hanging up the phone she wished she could have found something scintillating to hold his interest. No matter how often she told herself there could be nothing between them, there was a small bud of hope deep within her that cried out for Tuareg.

Two days later three Jeeps arrived at the camp carrying men from the National Museum. Lisa heard them and went out of the tent to see who was visiting. In the lead Jeep was the minister of antiquities. Surprised to see more than a dozen men arrive unannounced, she went to greet the minister. At least she recognized him.

"Professor Sanders is here?" he asked when he'd acknowledged her greeting.

"At the trench. I can show you the way."

He barked out some instructions to the others. Two men went into the work tent, two came to walk with him, the others began unloading items from the vehicles.

Lisa glanced at them warily as they walked to the hole in the ground. "Is something wrong?" she asked.

"Nothing that concerns you," he snapped. In only moments they reached the steps that led to the lower level where the current excavation was taking place.

With the latest discovery spurring them on, the archeologists had renewed enthusiasm and embraced the longer days the professor had decreed. They were up and at the site by the time Lisa arose each morning.

Lunch breaks were staggered and dinner was late each night as they used as much daylight as possible.

"Professor Sanders?" she called.

He came around one of the corners. "Yes?" He didn't know the minister so Lisa made the introductions.

"I'm delighted you came to see the site," the professor said.

"We have come to do more than see it. As of today I am officially taking charge of the excavation. You and your team will pack your things and leave. We expect the site to be vacated by tomorrow afternoon," the minister said.

"What?" The professor was astonished. Work stopped as everyone turned to look at the tableau unfolding.

"We have until the end of the summer," Professor Sanders said.

"That has changed. I need you to show me what you've found since the shipment to the museum and then begin packing. My men will take over. The importance of the site has increased and we wish to be in charge."

"What happened to change things?" the professor asked.

"I believe a discovery of some importance has recently been made. A jade piece."

"We suspect it is jade. It needs to be authenticated."

"Which will change the entire history of the area. It is too important to leave to others. Our own historians will continue."

"But—"

"No more. Please, ask the members of your group to leave the site. We prefer you not mention any discoveries of this summer to anyone. We will release information to the world at the appropriate time."

Lisa watched, stunned. How had the minister heard about the jade?

Suddenly she felt sick. Had her sharing the discovery with Tuareg led to this? The look on the professor's face would stay with her a long time. He'd poured his heart and soul into this dig. They couldn't just snatch it away from him without any warning. Or take away his part in all the work this summer.

Turning, she hurried back to the work tent. She ignored the men now putting all the artifacts into cartons and went straight to the phone. She picked it up, then hesitated. She hadn't a clue how to contact Tuareg. But if anyone could stop the steamroller techniques of the minister, it would be him.

"Excuse me," she said, turning to the strangers. "Does anyone speak English?"

"I do," the younger man said.

"Could you please help me call someone?"

"Yes." He walked over. "Who do you wish to call?"

"Sheikh Tuareg al Shaldor."

The man blinked, then gingerly took the phone. He quickly connected with an operator and spoke rapidly. A few moments later he bowed slightly and handed Lisa the phone.

"Tuareg?" she said.

"I'm sorry, ma'am," a feminine voice answered. "His Excellency is not in the city at this time. Can someone else be of assistance?"

"Has he gone to the desert?"

"Who is this?"

"Lisa Sullinger. Is he in the desert?"

"I'm afraid the whereabouts of His Excellency are not for public knowledge. If I could take a message, I'll see he gets it when he returns."

"That'll be too late." Lisa hung up.

Dammit, there had to be some way to reach Tuareg. He would help, she knew it.

Could she find Tuareg's camp?

She had enlisted the professor's help one evening in reviewing local maps and deciding where other ruins might be located. She'd wanted to take more photographs—the last days of the Moquansaid plains—highlighting abandoned homes wherever she found them; picturing the oasis that would be underwater by this time next year.

She knew the location of the house where she'd fallen. Could she find Tuareg's camp from there? She had a vague memory of the way. Would it be enough?

She went to the large table holding maps and glanced through them until she found one that showed the old house. Studying it, she didn't see any other markings indicating a camp or settlement. But wouldn't he have set up the tent where there was nothing else? He wanted to be alone, not where others might stumble across the tent.

The professor entered the tent, glancing at the men working and then looked at Lisa.

"I'm afraid our expedition is over. I've asked for three days to pack up and arrange transportation. Not much time, but more than tomorrow's deadline."

"I tried to reach Tuareg, but he's not there. I think he's at his tent. If you'd let me borrow one of the Jeeps, I believe I can find him. He'd be able to stop this." She hated to admit her possible part in the Ministry of Antiquities learning about the jade. If she'd caused this situation, she better do all she could to get them out of it.

"Where is the tent located?"

"West of the old ruins where I fell. I can get there easily enough and then head west. I think I'll remember landmarks to help me," she said.

"You could get lost out there. It's too dangerous. We'll put in a call to His Excellency and see if we can come to some agreement."

Lisa watched as the professor went to place a call. Tapping her fingers on the table, she knew the moment his request had been denied by his expression.

Turning, she took the keys from the rack where they normally were kept and, stopping only long enough to get some bottles of water and some snack food, she climbed in the first Jeep and headed out.

This vehicle had GPS positioning and she hoped it would be enough to get her back if she couldn't find Tuareg.

She treated the desert with more respect after the sandstorm. But this was too important to delay.

By late morning she could make out the outline of several buildings and tall palms silhouetted against a clear blue sky. She'd found the old dwelling. She stopped briefly and got out to see if she could find tracks from Ham. But if they were there, they were covered over. The wind might not have been as strong as during the sandstorm, but it was consistent and would have easily erased all traces of the horse's passing.

She'd have to rely on her memory of that ride.

Having jotted the coordinates, she turned and began driving west.

By mid afternoon, Lisa was almost ready to return to camp. She was lost. The Jeep could easily cover twice the ground a horse would travel at a walk in the hours she'd been driving. She stopped the vehicle and, standing on the seat, she searched in a complete circle. Nothing.

Of course, she could be near the tent and have a hard time seeing it, it blended with the land. But she'd surely see trees denoting an oasis. There were none to be seen.

It was almost too hot to think.

It had been more than a week since Lisa had last seen Tuareg, but only a couple of days since they talked. Had he caused their expulsion?

Lisa was tired. She wished she could find some shade and lie down and take a nap. But she sat back in the driver's seat and started the Jeep again. Checking the gas gauge, she still had more than half a tank. Once she reached the halfway point, she'd have to return to camp.

Lisa turned north and drove for a half hour. Checking again, she saw nothing that looked familiar. Time was running out. If she didn't find Tuareg, they had three days to pack up and leave. She knew she couldn't cover the entire area. The distances were too great. But if she didn't find him today, she'd go out again tomorrow and the next day and search as far each day as she could.

Lisa stopped once more. The gas gauge registered half. She would drive back in a straighter line using the GPS device than she'd taken coming this far, but didn't want to risk being stuck in the desert.

Once more she scanned the horizon. Wait—there, to the north, those were palm trees. Was that where Tuareg camped?

She drove as fast as the Jeep would go over the rough

terrain. Almost bouncing out of the Jeep at one point, she slowed. Now that she thought she was almost there, she could hardly wait.

Soon she saw the trees, then the tent's roof. As soon as she reached the tent, she stopped the engine and jumped out.

"Tuareg?" she called. She raced to the opening, stepping inside. It was Tuareg's tent, she recognized every fantastic piece inside. But it was empty.

Was he riding Ham?

She could scarcely breathe. Was he coming back? Or had he left to return to the city? She ran outside and around to the corral where the horse stayed. There was fresh water and hay stacked outside the rails. He was coming back, she thought. She hoped.

Walking slowly back to the Jeep, she climbed in and reached for a bottle of water. It was tepid, but wet. Sipping, she kept watch. He had to be returning.

CHAPTER TEN

TUAREG RETURNED TO his tent near dusk. He and Ham had ridden a long distance, but the horse was still full of energy. It was Tuareg who was tired.

As he crested a knoll, he saw a Jeep at the tent. Too far away to see who was sitting in it, he became wary. Few people knew where he erected the tent. Was there an emergency?

"Tuareg!" Lisa called when he was still some distance away. She climbed out of the Jeep and started running toward him.

He urged Ham to a faster gait and in only a short time pulled in beside her, dismounting.

"What are you doing here?" he asked, surprised to see her. Surprised at the feelings seeing her brought. He wanted to pull her into his arms and make sure she was safe. Her face was red with sunburn. Glancing beyond her, he saw the Jeep. Had she come all this way alone? It was dangerous in the desert for someone who didn't know it well.

"Tuareg, something terrible has happened and I need you to make it right," she said, clinging to his arm. "Please."

"What's wrong?"

"Your minister of antiquities arrived at camp this morning and ordered us to leave."

He began walking toward the tent, holding the reins, Ham following.

"I know," he said.

"You know?" She stopped and stared at him. "Did you send him?"

"No, my uncle sent him. But I told him about the jade discovery. The porcelain figurines caused a lot of interest when they were unpacked. With the latest find, the site takes on new meaning."

"Professor Sanders was heartbroken when ordered to leave. He's put a lot into this excavation. He can't just be sent away. He deserved credit for the discoveries."

Tuareg kept silent. The ins and outs of the situation didn't greatly concern him. His uncle had made the order.

"Tuareg, please help us."

"It's not my responsibility to change my uncle's orders," he said. They reached the rails where he kept Ham. He unsaddled the horse and turned him loose in the enclosure. There was plenty of water. Tuareg forked some hay in and turned.

He almost bumped into Lisa. He drew a deep breath. He hadn't wanted to see her again. He didn't like the feelings that were building whenever she was around.

He'd never thought to get involved with another woman. He didn't want to be. There was too much risk of another death. Another crushing heartbreak that would alter life forever.

He knew it was cowardice, but he couldn't bring himself to open up to the desolation such a loss brought.

No one understood. His mother urged him to get

out and meet other women. As if Nura had been one of several and all he had to do was go pick a new model.

Lisa put her hand on her arm, looking up at him. "I'm asking you to help us. Help Professor Sanders. I need you to make it come right. I'm the one who told you about the jade. That's what it's all about, isn't it? If I'd kept quiet, none of this would have happened."

"The porcelain pieces sparked their interest. Those set the thing in motion. Discovery of jade only hastened the end."

"So you won't help me?"

He started to say no, then reconsidered.

"I'll make no promises, but I'll contact my uncle."

"Oh, thank you, Tuareg," Lisa said, throwing her arms around his neck and pulling his face down for a kiss.

He responded with alacrity, gathering her in his arms and turning the thank you peck into a full-blown kiss. The heat of the sun could not rival the heat that exploded within the embrace. She clung and he drew her closer, wishing never to let go. If he let himself think of the danger she'd faced, alone in the desert, it would chill his blood. He wanted her always laughing with eyes sparkling.

Slowly, they pulled apart. She was breathing hard. He was, too. She looked so full of hope his heart twisted. For one blinding moment, he wished she'd want him with the same passion she displayed for saving Professor Sanders's position.

"I told you no guarantees," he said, before she came to expect the impossible.

"I know. But at least you'll try. Thank you."

He strode into the tent and went to the radio. Lisa followed and sat on the divan, watching as if he could do no wrong. He'd been the one to tell his uncle about the jade and the hypothesis of the connection to the silk road. His uncle had immediately set in motion the rescinding of the permit for the archeologists.

Tuareg could feel the suppressed expectation shimmering from her as she steadily watched him. The result of his conversation with his uncle was not going to be the one she hoped for.

"I understand," he told the older man. The events set in motion would not be halted. The archeological team would have to leave.

He turned away, not wanting to see the disappointment on her face. Soon enough he'd have to confront that.

"I will personally go to the camp and make sure things go as you wish," he told his uncle.

He hung up.

"Well?" she asked.

Slowly he turned. He shrugged out of his robes and went to the cooler to get a cold drink. "Do you want something to drink?" he asked.

"He said no, didn't he," she said, drooping with disappointment.

"He said no," Tuareg confirmed. He hated to see her so unhappy. She looked so defeated sitting there.

"You have the pictures you took. The notebooks," he said.

She shook her head. "They took all my pictures as well. I hope to get the ones back that aren't of the site, but even that's not certain." She went outside. He heard her cross the ground and then the sound of the Jeep.

Was she leaving? Quickly he followed, reaching the flap as the engine started.

"It'll be dark soon," he said, hurrying toward the Jeep.

"I have headlights," she said, backing around.

"Wait and I'll go with you."

"What for?" she said. "We'll pack and be gone in three days. We don't need you there."

"You came to me for help."

"Which you didn't deliver."

"Lisa, it's not my decision."

"Maybe not, but it's my fault you learned about the jade. What an idiot I've been. The professor will probably hate me for telling you." She glared at him. "And you for telling others."

He reached the Jeep and held on to the edge. "Let me go with you. I can try to get your photographs back."

She didn't respond immediately.

"I need to take care of a few things. I can be ready to leave in ten minutes."

Before she could reply, he reached across and turned off the engine, pulling out the key.

She glared at him. "Looks like I have no choice."

"Ten minutes."

Tuareg went to the tent and gathered what he'd need to stay a few days at the camp. He contacted one of his employees to instruct him to come care for Ham. He was ready in less than the ten minutes promised. He couldn't change his uncle's decree, but he could mitigate the situation. And make sure Lisa got her pictures back—all of them.

When he reached the Jeep, Lisa hadn't moved.

"I'll drive," he said.

She shrugged and slid over to the passenger side.

Tuareg glanced at the GPS indicator. "Is that set for the camp?"

She nodded.

"Lisa," he said in exasperation, "not talking to me won't change a thing."

"Yes, it is set to the camp."

"I'm surprised you found me," Tuareg said, starting the engine.

"It wasn't easy. You'll see we're right at halfway on gas. If I hadn't seen the palm trees on my last survey of the horizon, I would have headed back and tried again tomorrow."

Tuareg glanced at her as the Jeep bounced over the uneven ground. "If something had gone wrong, you could have been in serious trouble going off like that. What if you had not found me and gotten a flat tire or something?"

"I didn't," she said.

"I know. But the desert is a dangerous place."

She sighed softly and looked around her. "Maybe, but I think it is also a place of beauty. Being here has shown me a whole different way of life. I may consider moving from Seattle when I return home."

"To?"

"Arizona, New Mexico—one of the desert states." She'd toyed with the idea for a while now. She loved the clear sunshine, the way rocks and land changed color with the sun's travels. She'd miss Bailey and Sara and her other friends if she moved, but she would always have their friendship and she'd make more friends wherever she settled.

The thought of a flat-roofed home with terra-cotta walls blending with the landscape held great appeal. She'd love to see the shimmering colors of the desert come alive each day.

"Not everyone likes the desert. Or they grow tired of it after a time," Tuareg said.

"Hmm," she said, drinking from one of the bottles of water she'd brought along. "Do you?"

He shook his head. "I was born here, of a line of people who have lived in Moquansaid forever. It's a part of me."

"Yet your villa is lush with vegetation, flowers and flowing water."

"I like an occasional oasis in the desert, don't you?"

She nodded. "That's part of the unexpected appeal of the place, the contrasts. I think I could have lived in Wadi Hirum. Only I would have built my house closer to the river."

"Maybe the river flowed closer to the settlement five hundred years ago," he said.

"There's a thought," she said.

As they bounced along, Lisa wished she didn't feel like a traitor to the professor. Once or twice the Jeep swerved around a clump of grass, feeling as if it might continue in a rollover. She gasped and clutched the edge of the Jeep.

"I won't wreck the car," Tuareg said.

"My mother didn't think she'd wreck the car, but accidents happen," Lisa said, feeling her heart pounding. She liked dry, straight roads.

"Is that how she died, in a car crash?"

"Yes."

He glanced at her. "How old were you?"

"Six. I was with her."

He looked startled at that. Lisa wondered why she'd told him. She hadn't spoken of that night in a long time.

"Were you hurt?"

"No, but I was pinned in the car, my foot was caught.

It was pouring rain. Cold. Dark. I kept calling for my mother, but she never answered." Lisa couldn't help shivering in memory. That horror would never completely fade.

"What happened?"

His calm tone helped her get past the emotional flashback and respond in an equally calm tone.

"After what seemed like forever, another car came along and stopped. Then it was a trip to the hospital for me and my father came for me. A couple of bones in my foot were broken. The same foot injured during the sandstorm."

"You never get over something like that."

"No." They drove in silence for a while.

"Were you with your wife when she died?" she asked. His mother had said she'd had an aneurysm.

"It was a family gathering. We were at the table eating when she screamed in pain. Everyone looked instantly, but before I could react, she fell back, slid off her chair to the floor. By the time I got to her, she was dead."

"I'm sorry for your loss."

"And for yours."

Lisa would have thought the common loss of loved ones might bring them closer together, but Tuareg seemed to withdraw within himself after telling her about his wife's death.

It was late by the time the lights from camp were seen. When they arrived, Professor Sanders came out of the work tent.

"We were growing worried about you, Lisa. Your Excellency, is there anything you can do for us?" he asked Tuareg.

"I cannot change the ministry being in charge now. But Lisa told me about the order to keep the discoveries quiet. You pushed for the excavation, you have found the items of major interest. You will get credit for that. And I need to talk to the man. He has no rights to Lisa's photographs."

"I'm not so interested in credit as in what else might be discovered. These artifacts will alter the way we view history in this part of the world," Professor Sanders said.

Tuareg climbed out of the Jeep and went to the work tent. Lisa watched him disappear inside then looked at the professor. "I'm sorry, I really thought he could make it right."

"There are lots of disappointments in life. But we all move on. I'm glad you got back safely." He turned and walked slowly toward his private tent.

Lisa went to the mess tent to get something to eat. Checking the shower schedule, she saw it was free and quickly signed her name to the board. Everyone else was talking in small groups and generally complaining about things. She'd never have a better time for a quick wash.

The shower was nothing like a real one. The water was gathered in large tanks suspended from a high platform. During the day the sun heated it. By early evening it was warm enough to enjoy.

She gathered her towel and some clean shorts and a shirt and headed for the shower stall some distance away from the camp. The wooden platform where bathers stood had wide slats which allowed the water to drain away in the desert. Several plants had blossomed with the unexpected treat of water over the last few weeks.

The shower was enclosed on all sides by canvas panels. Lisa sometimes wished they'd have one facing away from camp be clear plastic so she'd have a view while she bathed.

As she crossed the compound, Tuareg joined her.

"Your pictures are being segregated and will be returned to you in the morning. I also insisted on the negatives. You are allowed to take one copy of each of the notebooks. If you choose to give them to the professor, that's your privilege."

"Oh, Tuareg, thank you. So he will have a complete set of all that was discovered here this summer?"

He nodded. "Were you going for a walk?" he asked.

"I'm headed to take a shower."

"And it's that way?"

"It's not plumbed, just gravity fed. And a bit away to assure privacy."

"Then I'll walk with you."

When the canvas structure came into view, Lisa wondered if he planned to wait while she showered.

She glanced at Tuareg. As ever, he was watching her. The light was fading, but she thought she saw a glimmer of amusement.

When they reached the shower, he studied it for a moment, then glanced around. "No bench?"

"What for?"

"For people to wait."

"We sign up for times, no waiting."

"I'll wait for you."

The thought of disrobing and showering with only a piece of canvas between them had Lisa growing warm all over. It seemed very intimate.

She walked to the opening. There were hooks on the

wooden frame for clothing and towels. She hung her
clean clothes and the towel. Taking her soap and
shampoo from her small bag, she placed them where she
could reach them. She peered around. There was no
one in sight. Still she hesitated to disrobe. But the
minutes were ticking by and her time slot could be
shortened if someone else came.

Before she could change her mind, she swiftly took
off her clothes and stepped beneath the high shower head.
Pulling the cord, she tied it in place as the warm water
caressed her skin. She turned it off to lather her hair.

"Finished already?" His voice came from just on the
other side of the canvas. Lisa jumped.

"No, we don't waste water. I'm soaping up."

"Ahh."

She shivered. "You're making me nervous," she exclaimed.

"Why is that?"

She bit her lip, pulling the cord and letting the
water wash over her. "I'm not used to…to company
while I bathe."

She heard him laugh softly. Her lips turned up involuntarily.

"An interesting tidbit to file away," he said.

"Go take a walk," she said.

"I won't go far," he replied.

She strained to hear, but couldn't tell if he walked
away or not.

Speeding through her wash, she soon wrapped her
towel around her and dried off. The clean clothes felt
wonderful. She combed through her hair, but left it to
dry in the arid air. It would be by the time she reached
her tent.

Gathering her things, she stepped around the enclosure. There was no one nearby, so he had walked away.

She headed for the compound. When she drew close to her tent, she looked for Tuareg. There was no sign of him.

Tuareg stayed in the shadows watching to make sure Lisa returned safely to her tent. What was he going to do about Lisa? Instead of another month before she would leave, his uncle had moved up their timetable. She could be gone as early as the day after tomorrow.

He knew that each night as he tried to sleep, the thought of Lisa would surface. He could picture her joy in taking pictures. Her enthusiasm in preserving for the present places of the past. He could imagine her carefully framing each picture to give it the best showing, the care she'd take on her book.

It was like her to think of making a book of the plain as it was today and would never again be. He'd be interested in seeing such a book.

He wrestled with the longing to go to her, hear her laughter, be enchanted by her grin.

But could he let Nura go and fall in love with someone else? It always came back to that.

He'd been afraid today when he thought of Lisa going off on her own and traveling where there was no help to be found. If she'd had a flat tire or blown an engine part, she could have been totally stranded. How long would a search team have taken to find her?

Would he ever have learned of her death? The thought appalled him. Was it already too late to turn away?

CHAPTER ELEVEN

TIME DID NOT STAND STILL. Two days remained before Lisa had to leave. Then Tuareg would say goodbye to Lisa Sullinger. She'd return to Seattle, he'd return to his empty villa.

"When is the best time to visit Seattle?" he asked.

"What?" she said. She was sitting on her cot looking at the photographs, trying to ascertain if the minister had returned all she'd taken. Tuareg sat near the table watching her.

"What season is your best in Seattle?" he repeated.

"Summer, I guess. Though it rains a lot. Still, it's gorgeous when it's dry. You planning to visit?"

"Maybe."

"I have to tell you if you wait until next summer, I may be gone."

That startled him. "Gone where?"

"I don't know, but I've really enjoyed my summer here and thought I'd apply again for one of the expeditions. Jamie said they might be able to get one going near Damascus. Or maybe I'll sign on for one in Mexico. Imagine, hot and humid. I'd probably hate the weather but be as fascinated by the discoveries as I was here."

She had another life. One that didn't include him. She wouldn't be sitting in her apartment awaiting his visit. Tuareg rose and paced the small interior.

"What are you doing?" she said looking up at him.

"Nothing." He stopped.

"I'm almost done."

What would things be like when she was gone?

He wasn't sure he wanted to even speculate. Maybe he should seriously consider visiting Seattle before next summer.

"What do you think?" she asked, holding up a picture of the statue in the park.

He forced himself to study the photographs when everything inside him suddenly wanted to ask her to stay.

Lisa sat on a box and watched as the tents were struck. Her personal items had been boxed up yesterday. She'd packaged most of her pictures to be shipped home from Soluddai, but was carrying all the negatives. One or the other was bound to reach Seattle.

Jaime and Paul had left with half the crew to facilitate the loading of the equipment at the shipping terminal in Soluddai. Professor Sanders and the rest were scampering around, making sure everything was taken care of. Her work was finished. She'd shot a couple of last-minute pictures for the memory books, double-checked on everyone's address and now had nothing to do but sit and watch.

Tuareg had left with the truck carrying their equipment. He'd offered to return to fly her to Soluddai, but she'd declined. She wanted this time with her summer companions. After the flight in two days, she wouldn't see most of them again. The professor, maybe. She'd already spoken to him about another expedition.

She watched, trying to keep her mind a blank. She was staying at Yasmin's apartment tomorrow night after the reception. Then early the next morning they'd all board a plane, head for Rome and then home. She would not think about it. She'd take each moment as it came and not dwell on the goodbyes that were inevitable.

Lisa was used to goodbyes, but she never liked them. Yet she knew better than most that relationships were fleeting.

The sun was hot. She blinked back tears. This time next year, water would cover the earth where she sat. The trees that had given them shade would be rotting. The traces of the people who had one time lived here would be gone forever. And the man she'd fallen in love with would ride his horse on the desert—alone. It was all sad.

But nothing was as sad as leaving Tuareg behind. She wished she were brave enough to tell him how she felt. Would knowing someone else loved him have him change his mind about taking a chance? She didn't think so. If she did, she'd risk it.

The reception was lavish. The grand hall of the museum had been thrown open to patrons of the museum, special guests and the members of Professor Sanders's archeological expedition. Lisa wore the same dress she'd bought for Jeppa's party. She saw the young woman shortly after arriving. Jeppa had greeted her with a friendly wave and later came to speak with her.

Yasmin had picked Lisa up at the hotel that morning and they'd spent the day in her flat. Lisa had met Tuareg's father and been charmed by him. She could see a lot of him in his son. Yasmin had not said if Tuareg still planned to attend the festivities or not.

Lisa glanced around the crowded room. There were several tall men with dark hair, but none were Tuareg. Each time she saw one, her heart skipped a beat. Disappointment followed when she didn't recognize the man.

Despite essentially being booted out of the country, Professor Sanders was the man of the hour. Even the minister was smiling. Lisa raised her camera to capture the moment. The final set of photos for the memory books, unless she took one tomorrow as they boarded the plane.

"And who takes your pictures for the memory book?" a dear familiar voice asked.

She turned, her heart leaping in gladness. "You do," she replied, handing him her camera.

Tuareg took several shots, one with her and the minister, who once again beamed his pleasure at the results of the excavation so far.

Lisa made a wry face when they moved away. "What a change from my bringing the first set of boxes," she murmured as Tuareg walked with her. She wished they could escape to quieter locations in the museum, spend these last hours together, just the two of them, instead of being with a group of two hundred.

"He is in very good favor with my uncle and it shows. Do you wish something to drink?"

"Yes, please." She should be angry at Tuareg for hastening their departure. For not finding in her what she found in him. But the fleeting moments were too precious. She'd hold on and let anger build tomorrow.

He summoned a circulating waiter and they both took glasses.

"To a bright future, Lisa Sullinger. May your book

bring you fame and fortune." He touched the rim of his glass to hers.

"Thank you," she said, looking away lest he see the gathering tears.

She wasn't sure she could do this—pretend she was having a good time when her heart was breaking. How much longer until the event ended? Could she pretend her ankle hurt and she needed to leave early?

"There you are, Lisa. Come with me. I have a friend I want you to meet," Jeppa said a moment later. "He's going to graduate school at Berkeley, but that's not that far from Seattle, is it? He could fly to visit you. He's a lot of fun." She linked arms with Lisa and escorted her away from Tuareg.

Lisa glanced over her shoulder and shrugged. Maybe it was best to stay busy. Keep the sad thoughts at bay.

"Lisa, this is Hamid. Hamid, Lisa is a famous photographer, I have one of her books." Jeppa made the introductions and encouraged them to exchange contact information.

Lisa smiled politely. Hamid looked to be about her age and was going for a specialty in medicine. He asked for Lisa's address and told her that once he was settled, he'd call her. When he saw another friend, she was left alone. Searching for Tuareg, Lisa couldn't see him. Had he left already? How much longer would the reception last?

The next morning, leaving her room was difficult because of the tears that ran down her face. She would mop her eyes, begin to leave, think of the final departure and the reality of saying goodbye would strike and she'd start crying again.

"For heaven's sake, get a grip," she admonished

herself, trying to stem the flow of tears. She could write to Yasmin. Learn about Tuareg from her letters.

It was infatuation. She'd get over him as soon as she became involved in other activities at home.

She had Hamid's visit to look forward to.

Tears started again. She bit her lip, took a breath and went to the bathroom to splash cold water on her face.

"Do not start again," she told her reflection.

It was not only Tuareg, though he was the one she'd miss the most. The thought of bidding everyone good-bye tore at her heart. She hated farewells. She'd spent her entire life leaving or being left. When did she get to stay? When did she get to be part of a family that would never go away or send her away?

"Maybe never. Suck it up and get this show on the road," she said. Taking another deep breath, she went back to the bedroom, gathered her camera and carry-on bag and left the suitcase for the maid to take to the car.

She thanked her hostess without more tears, though they were perilously close.

The drive to the airport was in the luxury of a limo. She watched the buildings of the city speed by. She had not spent her last days taking photos as she had originally planned. Maybe some day she'd come back and take more in the city then. If she ever came back to see the reservoir.

Once at the airport, she quickly found her friends. They checked bags, went through security and waited at the gate. The large jet would board soon.

Everyone was somber, sulky almost. No one talked. The flight was called and they queued up to board.

Lisa looked around one last time. She had hoped—her heart stopped, began to pound.

Tuareg was striding toward her. He'd come after all

to bid her goodbye. Last night he'd disappeared before she'd had a chance to tell him goodbye. She was so thankful he'd come today.

She darted out of line.

"Lisa?" Professor Sanders called in bewilderment.

"I'll be right there," she called back, heading for Tuareg.

"You came," she said when they met.

"I couldn't let you leave without saying goodbye."

"Thanks for everything." She couldn't say anything more. Her throat was closing. To her horror, her eyes filled with tears. They spilled down her cheek. She wanted to invite him to Seattle, to ask him to proof her book before the final submission, to tell him she loved him. Only the tears spilled faster than she could think. She caught back a sob.

"Ah, Lisa, don't cry. You break my heart."

She shook her head. His heart had broken when Nura died. And she guessed it would never heal again.

He pulled her gently into his embrace, holding her while the tears flowed. She felt safe. As she had when her father had held her so long ago. As she had during the sandstorm in a stranger's embrace. She would always feel safe in Tuareg's arms.

"Don't go," he said softly.

"What?" she asked, resting her forehead against his shoulder, breathing in the scent she remembered from that first day at the ruin when he had sheltered her from the storm's fury.

"Stay. With me. Don't go."

She hadn't heard him right. She had always had an abundant imagination. Now she was imagining what she wanted most to hear.

Slowly she pulled back until she could see his eyes,

dark and sad, they tugged at her heart. Passengers passed, one bumped her slightly, but she didn't notice. Another boarding call was made in three languages. Her time was limited. But she couldn't move an inch.

"Marry me, Lisa. Stay here in Moquansaid. Publish your book, find new subjects, only don't leave. I'll get you on a dig with local scholars. You can photograph the inside of every building anyone in my family owns. Take photos of every structure in the city."

She put her fingertips over his mouth. "Tuareg, are you crazy?"

"Only if I let you go. I realized that last night. When Jeppa introduced you to Hamid, I was struck by the thought of you with someone else. I couldn't bear that. I loved Nura. You know that. But I love you—differently, passionately, forever. You said once I could find another love. Not someone to replace her, but to succeed her. You are that someone. I fought against it. My mother and Jeppa suspected my feelings long before I did. I felt I was disloyal to Nura if I found another woman. But Nura was a generous woman. She loved me and wanted my happiness no matter what. She would be upset if she'd known how I cut myself off from new experiences for mourning her."

"I'm nothing like her," Lisa said.

"I don't want you to be. Your eyes change color. Now they are silvery and sad. Sometimes they are smoky blue. Other times gray. I'm always trying to figure out what makes them change. I could spend a lifetime figuring that out."

"Really?" She began to smile.

"They are growing blue," he said. "And your grin is infectious. I could watch your delight in things all day long. When you greeted me a few weeks ago at the camp, I knew I wanted you to show that same happiness when I returned home each day. To see you each morning, love you all night long, learn to cook together. Lisa, you have already enriched my life, I cannot imagine living the rest of it without you. Say you'll marry me. If you don't like Moquansaid, we can find a place we both like."

"I do like Moquansaid. I love the desert. And I'd love to marry you! Would we live in your tent?"

He laughed, picked her up and spun her around. Passengers stopped and stared. The man at the ticket counter called out something.

Tuareg replied in Arabic.

"What?" Lisa asked, looking over her shoulder. They were closing the door to the ramp leading to her plane. "My plane, I'm going to miss the plane."

"So? You've said you'll marry me. We'll fly to Seattle in a few days, pack up your things and ship them back here. Let that plane go. There are others."

She looked at him. "Are you sure?"

"That I love you? Yes. That you mean as much to me as Nura, that and more. She and I were children together. We knew each other so well. I loved her, but it was a love that had grown complaisant. With you everything is new and different. You fascinate me. You delight me. You make me so crazy with desire I'm a saint to resist sweeping you away and making love to you for a week. Say we can marry soon."

Lisa laughed. Tears dried on her cheeks. Her heart swelled with enchantment. "I have no family, only a few friends who could probably fly out here with a few days' notice, so there's no reason to wait—and every reason to hurry."

"Oh, and why is that?" he asked.

"I want our honeymoon at the tent—and we have to get there before the water rises. Oh, Tuareg, I love you so much!"

He pulled her tightly into his arms and kissed her.

EPILOGUE

LISA STOOD ON THE SHORE and gazed over the wide expanse of water. The sun was shining, as it usually did. There was a light breeze, enough to ruffle the surface of the reservoir. She couldn't see the other side. Despite her reservations, her thoughts of the ruins now flooded, the setting was beautiful.

She raised her camera and took a picture. Soon new plants and trees would grow, watered by the reservoir. She turned and spoke haltingly to the woman she'd come to visit. One of the nomads from her visit last summer. Her Arabic was still imperfect, but she practiced daily, speaking with all her new family, enduring their laughter and gentle smiles when she got something wrong.

She didn't care. She relished them all and they seemed to love her. She'd found her place in the world and loved every aspect of it.

"How do you like all the water?" she asked.

The woman looked at the neat rows that had been planted, green shoots already showing. "It is different. But it will be good. The men have the hardest time. They like to roam. Now we are staying."

Lisa took a picture of the neat parallel row of homes. The terra-cotta color as appealing to her today as when she first arrived. She lowered her camera and reached into her tote, pulling out a photograph of the woman and her children she'd taken on that first visit. She'd had it framed. She handed it to the woman, smiling at the expression of wonder on her face.

"It will be in a book that will be published next year," Lisa said. She was delighted with the way the book had come together. She and Tuareg had worked side by side in selecting the photographs. He'd put her in touch with a professor at the university in Soluddai who had added facts for each caption. The publisher of her previous books had been thrilled with the new work, claiming it would sell not only to the general population, but to universities as a study of what could be done before change took place. Lisa was delighted and already had an idea for another project.

"Thank you." The woman bowed, then smiled. "I wish you happiness," she said, gesturing to Lisa's stomach.

She was a month away from giving birth to their first baby. She grinned. "I have happiness, but thank you. It will only grow with this baby."

"What will grow?" Tuareg asked, coming to stand near her, surveying the rows of crops. She still thrilled every time she saw him. It was hard to believe they'd been married almost a year.

"Happiness," she said simply, knowing they would have an abundance of it for all their lives.

THE DESERT
PRINCE'S PROPOSAL

BY
NICOLA MARSH

Dear Reader,

Have you ever dreamed of being swept away to an exotic location? To a far distant land with sweeping desert sands, a lush oasis, an opulent palace? And, of course, such a magical place would have a prince ruling it—a striking, sexy, powerful prince, used to getting his own way.

If this fantasy sounds intriguing to you, imagine the fun I had creating Adhara and its ruler, Prince Samman al Wali.

As we all know, every strong alpha male needs a heroine to match him in every way, and Bria Green more than fits the bill.

She's independent, confident, and focussed on making it to the top of her career. That is until she meets the mysterious Sam, unaware that her trip to Adhara will change her life in ways she never thought possible…

I had a wonderful time writing this story. From the hip vibe of Melbourne to cosmopolitan Dubai, from a private desert oasis to a French-inspired palace, I let my imagination run wild.

I hope you get swept away to Adhara too!

Best wishes,

Nicola

Nicola Marsh has always had a passion for writing and reading. As a youngster, she devoured books when she should have been sleeping, and later kept a diary whose content could be an epic in itself! These days, when she's not enjoying life with her husband and sons in her home city of Melbourne, she's at her computer, creating the romances she loves in her dream job. Visit Nicola's website at www.nicolamarsh.com for the latest news of her books.

For my very special Nan, who takes great pride in every book I write (and who introduced me to the wonderful world of Mills & Boon all those years ago!).